D1175747

Getting Off Clean

Getting Off Clean

❖

TIMOTHY MURPHY

PROPERTY OF
Kankakee Public Library

ST. MARTIN'S PRESS ❧ NEW YORK

GETTING OFF CLEAN. Copyright © 1997 by Timothy Murphy. All rights reserved. Printed in the United States of America. No part of this book may be used or re-produced in any manner whatsoever without written permission except in the case of brief quotations embodied in critical articles or reviews. For information, address St. Martin's Press, 175 Fifth Avenue, New York, N.Y. 10010.

Library of Congress Cataloging-in-Publication Data

Murphy, Timothy
    Getting off clean : a novel / Timothy Murphy.—1st ed.
      p.   cm.
    ISBN 0-312-15132-2
    I. Title.
  PS3563.U76196G4   1997
  813′.54—dc20   96-31840
                                      CIP

First Edition: March 1997

10 9 8 7 6 5 4 3 2

To my mother and father, without whom—

Acknowledgments

Much gratitude to Neil Olson and Keith Kahla, as well as to the trusty Mikel Wadewitz. Thanks to many good friends, including Dan "Kitty" Casto, Benjamin Feldman, Raphael Gancayco, Jeffrey Golick, James Hannaham, Melissa Levis, Gillian Maimon, Maggie Malina, Sarah Saffian, Kate Steinberg, Maria Striar, and Akhil Unni. And special thanks to my brother, Daniel Murphy, for his love, support, and good humor.

It is my impression that the young cannot fool anybody,
except those people who wish to be fooled.

—James Baldwin,
Just Above My Head

September 1986

As soon as he walks in, it's uncanny, I know we're both guilty. It's quiet in the sub shop except for the sound of the hit radio station, and it's quiet in the parking lot outside, nearing ten o'clock now. Nearly time for me to close the place and head home. But when he walks in, I'm hearing another sound in my head. Is it pretentious to say that it sounds like the violins in a piece of modern music, something sweet and pointed with meaning, but odd as well, like it makes the back of your neck warm because it doesn't belong? Because it sounds wrong—doesn't fit, doesn't click—but you like it anyway?

He is black and looks rich. He doesn't live in town; I've never seen him before. I know he must be one of the kids who go to St. Banner, the private school about five miles outcountry, because he's preppy like them, and already he's given me that look that says, "I see you, but I don't *see* you." It's peculiar; he's preppy like them, only more so, like he's a parody of it all, and it's hard to tell whether he knows it or not. He's wearing madras shorts, a white button-down shirt, and tassel loafers, without socks, that look like he shines them every morning. There's a fat gold watch on a black strap, and it leaps out at me like his glasses, little horn-rimmed glasses on a smallish nose. Behind them, his eyes are adjusting to the air-conditioning, and he's got a haircut so clean it almost forms right angles over his temples.

Now he's in the doorway, standing ramrod straight and holding a rolled-up magazine like a musket in both hands, and the impression he gives me is of the one black guy in an upscale clothes catalog, surrounded by white guys, and trying to look like the matter has never crossed his mind. I'm behind the counter across the room, wrapping up sliced pepperoni, watching him and feeling instantly self-conscious for us both.

He's just standing there, his brow deeply furrowed, as though he's contemplating some great question of life. Then he strides up to the counter, his loafers clacking against the floor. I keep my eyes on the pepperoni, pretending I'm not especially interested.

"Sir," he says, very clearly and formally, like I'm the first person in the wilderness he's come upon in days and he's calling to me from an opposite riverbank. His voice is deep and cultivated. He almost sounds a little bit like a TV news broadcaster, or a Shakespearean actor.

Finally, I look up, hoping to seem as bored as possible. "Hey," I say. "Can I get something for you?" I ask, aiming to sound distracted and to hit the *r* in "for" and thereby conceal my Massachusetts accent, which I've been trying studiously to lose all summer. It isn't easy to do both at once.

He lets out a long, exaggerated sigh and looks heavenward. Then he puts his magazine on the countertop and folds his hands very neatly on top of it. I glance at the magazine. It's *The New Yorker,* which I'm pretty sure I've seen before, probably at a bookstore in Boston, where I go quite frequently when I have the time.

Then his eyes settle on me and he leans in to ask, in what seems to be a very searching, intimate way, "Do you make a focaccia bread pizza?"

He says this fancy word, *focaccia,* very slowly and precisely, as though he's sure I've never heard it before. Unfortunately, he's right, and I'm so flustered that before I can say something like *I'm sorry, we're out for the day,* I say, like a complete provincial, "What might that be?"

He gives me a weary, benign smile and says in a deliberate, patient voice, "It's an Italian bread. It's very chewy, very dense. The Italians use it chiefly to make dinner breads, but you'll also find that some of the better American pizzerias make a very fine pizza with focaccia dough." Each one of these Italian words he's careful to enunciate for my benefit, breaking them down into their syllabic parts and lightly rolling the *r*'s.

Obviously, he wanted to make me feel like a dumb townie, and he's succeeded. All I can hope for is to make him feel crummy for his snottiness, so I say, "Well, I'm afraid this isn't one of the better American pizzerias. It's just B.J.'s Sub Shop in West Mendhem, Massachusetts." I try to say this in a way that makes it clear I hold West Mendhem in as much contempt as he does.

He casts his eyes down to the magazine and smooths the cover with his long, spidery-looking hands. "I'm sorry. I guess I should have expected as much."

His eyes are still downcast and I can't tell if he's faking contrite or if he really means it. He looks up, meekly. "Do you have any sun-dried tomatoes?"

"No," I say, firmly this time. Then, triumphant, "They're out of season."

He looks up at me again, now with one brow arched wildly above his eye. Then, much to my surprise, he laughs right at me, a short report, deep and harsh. He looks down at his magazine, obsessively smoothing the cover, and goes on laughing. It's more contained now, like what was going to be an assault on me he's turned into a private joke for him alone to savor.

I'm feeling quite bereft and uneasy now, having absolutely no idea what he finds so funny. "Are you quite all right?" I ask, loudly enough to top his laughter.

He makes a show out of pulling himself together, wiping his eyes and clearing his throat. Then, folded hands propped back up on the countertop, he gives me the same old earnest look he did the first time, the trace of a smile still on his face. "Yes. Please forgive me. I'm quite all right," he says, then, just under his breath, mimicking me, " 'Out of season.' " A moment later, he's looking at me earnestly again, as though he didn't say a thing, as though I didn't hear a word he said.

"Is there something else I can get you?" I ask, adopting the same patient, snotty smile he gave me. "I've got to be closing up soon and getting back to my fourteen younger siblings up in the hills."

He looks at me, his face full of mock concern. "Fourteen siblings? Good God. How do you manage?"

"I feed them all from the same trough. It hasn't been easy since both my parents drowned in the tub when they were making moonshine."

He laughs now, and because it's the same laugh as before, I don't know if it's mean or phony or genuine. "I see," he says, slowly, pulling his chin. "I see." Then, suddenly businesslike, "Would you get me a slice of plain pizza, just warm, please, not scalding hot. And a Diet Coke with *very little ice.* Thank you."

And with that, he retrieves his magazine, sits cross-legged at a table across the room, and deposits his head inside the pages, immediately engrossed in a riveting story. I notice how his loafers barely hang from his feet; at an angle, they reveal the white bottoms of his feet like half-moons.

I put his pizza slice in the oven and go back to wrapping the medallions of pepperoni. He's distracted me; I'm forgetting that I've got a lot to think through tonight. Even in the summer, I lead a very full life and my mind is usually preoccupied, as it is tonight. As it was tonight, I mean. Because now I'm putting his pizza under foil, on a paper plate, then I'm getting him a Diet Coke from the dispenser with *very little ice,* and now, frankly, I'm wondering if I should call him up or walk it over to where he's sitting, looking positively transfixed by *The New Yorker.* Because even though it's five minutes to ten and I should be officially closing right about now, I'm thinking about the tedium of driving home in my mother's beige hatchback with the strawberry air freshener and the little *St. Christopher Pray for Us* medallion hanging from the knob on the glove compartment. It's the tedium of driving home in the dark in humid weather along the same route I've taken every night this summer, past the Cumberland Farms and the video stores and little white cape houses. Then coming home to a humid house with the dull buzz of my father's Red Sox game coming from the television in the den, the screaming match between my mother and Brenda when Brenda comes in drunk around midnight, and the dull buzz of Joani struggling with a Dr. Seuss book, and me upset as usual that Joani's twelve and she's still learning to read.

I glance over at him reading, and I think that an authentic member of the St. Banner's intelligentsia has walked into the sub shop where I work, in the intellectually barren town of West Mendhem, Massachusetts—and what am I? I wrote a twenty-page term paper on fatalism versus determinism in the plays of Eugene O'Neill this past spring that Mrs. Bissett said was the best piece of writing she had seen in twenty-one years of teaching. I just saw an Eric Rohmer film in Cambridge with my best friend, Phoebe Signorelli, last week. And I have an application to Yale University waiting to be filled out at home, and a sweatshirt to match.

"Here's your pizza," I say, putting it down in front of him with the Diet Coke.

He looks up briefly, seeming startled. "Oh," he says. "Thanks so much." He moves the pizza away from him slightly on the table and goes back to his magazine.

I pull out a rag and wipe down the next table. "You can pay for it up there when you're done," I say.

"Okay, thanks." Not looking up.

I keep wiping. "How's the Coke?" I ask.

He swats the magazine into his lap with much flapping. "I'm *sorry?*" he says, looking at me now, his deep voice rising flutily in irritation on *sorry*. Now I know I've spoken out of turn to one of the St. Banner elite, and I feel frightened and emboldened.

"Your Diet Coke," I say. "How's the ice?"

He peers over the top of his glasses and glances into the paper cup. "That looks just about perfect," he says, and regathers his magazine.

I decamp behind the counter. He eats his pizza—in mincing, tentative bites, I notice—and I go about my business. If he wanted to, he could see me right now stooped, straddling a huge white bucket, pouring steel tureens of tomato sauce back into their container for overnight refrigeration. I start to feel stupid, start to ask myself what I was thinking when I approached him.

7

"Hello back there?" I hear his voice from over the counter. Surfacing, I realize I've spilled tomato sauce on my T-shirt.

"Uh-huh?" I ask, wiping off my shirtfront with a rag.

"Do you sell smokes in here?"

"Excuse me?"

"Smokes. You know, puff puff puff? *Cigarettes?*" He mimes someone inhaling furiously on a cigarette.

"Oh. No, we don't." I should have known he smoked. They all do up at that school, just like the Algonquins, who were a sophisticated group of literary friends in the early half of the twentieth century, by the way. I'm fond of them.

"Well, is there anywhere around here within walking distance where I could get some at this hour of the night?"

"There's Cumberland Farms about two miles away. Do you have a car?"

He laughs shortly. "No, I don't have a car. I walked here. I'm a foot traveler." He lifts one leg stiffly in the air, holding a loafer aloft.

"Oh." I smile a little, stiffly as well, as the remark seems to call for brittle sour humor. "Do you go to S.B.A.?" I ask him.

"Do you mean do I go to Mendhem?" he says, faintly disdainful.

I forgot that little difference—that the local people, the townies, call St. Banner Academy by its initials, S.B.A., short and serviceable as a landmark when they're giving directions to the Topsfield Fair or the roadside summer corn stands outcountry. Everyone at St. Banner calls it Mendhem, as though the name of an entire town only existed to indicate the ninety-eight-year-old school that sits on one hundred acres of prime wooded real estate at the foot of Lake Chickering, as though in the world of exclusive boarding schools West Mendhem constitutes no more or less than the home of St. Banner Academy. Frankly, I don't know if it does constitute more than that—other than a thorn in my side.

"That's right, I forget you guys call it that."

"Well, now you won't," he says briskly, then, with a big heave of duress, "*Yes,* I go to Mendhem. Or at least I will, as of next week when studies *commence.*"

For all his obvious boredom, he's at least given me a straight answer.

8

"Why are you back so early?" I ask, refilling the napkin holder and trying to match his idly conversational pitch.

"I had to come early for Minority Acclimation Week," he says in a disgusted singsong. "It's me, a scholarship girl from the Bronx, and about nineteen Orientals who are all ready to just go-go-go!" This is followed by the frantic mimicry of someone running wildly in place, eyes wide, tongue wagging.

I'm taken aback by this outburst, and laugh weakly, which he mimics as well before collapsing back into dourness. "Are you a freshman?" I ask.

"I should be a freshman—in college." He says the word *college* like it's a curse, but I notice he's at least relegated the magazine to a chair. "But I'm starting as a senior because this is my third stab at the great boarding school experiment."

"Oh," I say, careful to hedge my curiosity. He's starting to give me the inside story on boarding school life, something hidden to me on the opposite side of private woods and high stone walls. "Why's that?"

"Because I was kicked out of the first two. Haven't you ever read *The Catcher in the Rye?* Don't they make you read that in your school so you'll learn all about postwar adolescent anomie?"

"I did read that." I bristle. "When I was thirteen. On my own time."

He throws back his head, then, in a long, insufferable drawl, "Pre-*coc*ious you!"

"Precocious," I say aloud, appreciatively, before I can stop myself. I can't help it. It's a good word. I finally looked it up a few months ago after seeing it half a dozen times and scrawling it down under "Words Undefined" in my notebook. That, along with *prolific*, another new favorite of mine. But now that I've said it, I'm embarrassed.

"Yes! You!" He nods emphatically. "Precocious!"

"I like to think," I say feebly. Then, to keep him on the line, "What were you kicked out for?"

"For civil disobedience."

"For what?"

"For smoking at the first one. Then, at Exeter, for flunking."

"You flunked?"

"Only for lack of effort," he says blandly, as though he doesn't really care whether or not I know why he flunked. "I knew it was coming. They had been warning me for four months. Then they called me into the advisory room with all the gorgeous oak and they told me not to come back after the winter break. They said that they had cut me more breaks than anyone ever before. Because they didn't want to lose me. But that I had pushed them to it, *perversely and defiantly*, even in the face of their concern. So I packed my trunks and I took a slow train to Virginia."

As he tells me all this, offering slow, deliberate segments of information, he stares blankly out the window of the sub shop onto the barren parking lot. He's silent when he finishes, reaching for his magazine, rolling it up and holding it to his lips like a chalice. It feels like someone's big moment in a play, the moment they reveal all, the moment they lose themselves in memory and all you can hear is the buzz of the spotlight that bathes them, alone.

"It sounds dramatic," I say.

He snorts, and turns to me. "It's tawdry and cheap. But *moi*"—here he clutches the magazine and speaks into it intimately, like a microphone—*"moi, je ne regrette rien."*

"Me, I regret nothing," I say—like I'm taking an oral exam in the language lab.

"Ah," he says in a mock-deep voice, deeper than his regular voice. "You know your Piaf."

"I take French," I say.

"Have you been?" he asks.

"No," I say. "Not yet. Maybe next summer." I hope he doesn't probe further. Besides Montreal, and Disney World when I was ten, I haven't been anywhere.

He doesn't probe. "I have. My French teacher at Exeter told me they'd love me there," he says, entirely to himself.

"Did they?" I ask absurdly.

"I went before he told me. I suppose they did. But I don't remember. I was too young."

Why do I see him at eight or nine, in the same glasses and loafers, only in boy's sizes, prowling skeptically around the Louvre, or under the Eiffel Tower, accompanied by—whom? His mother? His father, a diplomat? Family friends who've taken him along? A nanny? Frankly, I can't picture him with anyone.

Then suddenly he's lost to me, sitting there, nudging the pages of the magazine into tiny dog-ears. I've been leaning behind the counter, hiding my body in shorts and Converse high-tops, carrying on this conversation. It's ten past ten and I haven't even mopped the floor. If my boss were to drive by and see the shop all lit up, I'd catch hell. He's pushed his pizza and drink aside and I've got to ask him to leave somehow, but now he's dog-earing those pages like a crazy man, like it's his consuming project. He's a million miles away again, and I'm anxious with the silence, but there's something underneath my anxiety that's making me want to sit down. It's an activity in my stomach that I swear I've had before, but for my life I can't remember when.

"I've got to close up," I say.

He looks up, alarmed. "But what about you?" he says.

"What about me?"

"Aren't you going to tell me your story?" He brings his cup and plate to the counter and hands them to me.

"What story?" I say, taking care of his trash.

"Aren't you going to tell me your hard-luck blue-collar story—stuck in a dead-end town, and dying inside?"

He's got that deadly earnest tone in his voice again. "I don't have any story."

He laughs curtly. "Oh, *please*. You must! Are you B.J.?"

"No. That's my boss's father. He started the shop in 1966. But he's got prostate cancer now."

"I see. Then who are you?"

"I'm Eric," I say. "Fitzpatrick. Who are you?" It seems only my privilege to ask in turn.

He's looking at me sternly on a sharp intake of breath. Now it's like any time he spent ignoring me he's put completely behind him and he's looking at me like I'm an object of study, a stuffed thing. It's hard to stare back; I try a wry smile but he doesn't respond. So I just raise my eyebrows in alignment with his and wait. His face is hairless and matte brown, critical and severe, and I can't seem to pull my eyes away from its cruel, unyielding cast. He puts his elbows up on the counter again and folds his hands.

11

"It's Brooks," he says, careful and hushed. "It's Brooks Jefferson Tremont."

"Oh," I say, hushed as well. For a moment, neither of us says anything. I feel as though he's just shared with me some monumental secret—but why? I'm thinking. It's only his name. We're face to face across the counter. The announcer on the hit radio station says it's a quarter past ten.

He looks down, looks up again. "Do you live around here?" he asks, still hushed. This feels like a prison visiting scene on TV, when they're talking on phones through glass, low, because they're planning an escape. Now I'm hearing everything. The buzz and tremble of the air-conditioning, the weather report on the radio, the hum of the refrigerator.

"I live a few miles away," I say.

"Uh-huh. You're in high school?" He keeps looking down at his hands, and up again, a funny kind of prayerful motion.

"Yeah. I'm a senior this year."

"You gonna go away after that?" He's slipping into some kind of slang, real quiet and a little slurred.

"Yeah. I hope so. I really hope so."

He laughs a little, not cruelly though. "Oh, yeah? Where you gonna go?"

I'm starting to feel a little drowsy, but pleasantly, as though I could go on answering questions like this all night, and without thinking much of it, I put my own hands on the counter, folded, across from his. "Oh, I don't know. Maybe Harvard. Maybe Yale."

He smiles again. "You're real ambitious, aren't you?"

I smile back now. "I don't know. I guess so. I just wanna get out of here, that's all."

"Are you a homosexual?"

It's like, if my stomach has been ready to turn over—and it has been—it finally does, sickeningly, and I'm trembling. He's half-looking at me, and I know he can see my eyes dilate and my face go chalk white.

"I'm in high school," I say. "I'm seventeen."

"I'm eighteen," he says.

"So?" I say. "I'm seventeen."

"Well?"

"Well *what?*" I say, but it catches on the lump in my throat.

"Well, *are* you?" He's still half-looking at me, and for the first time I see that his folded hands are shaking, too, his knuckles like white marbles underneath his skin.

"Well, no, I'm not."

"Oh. Well, neither am I."

"Good for you." I'm nervous as hell now.

"Isn't it, though?" he says smartly.

We're silent, smirking dumbly at each other. "I've got to close up here," I say, picking up my rag.

He puts his magazine under his arm. "I'm going to buy some smokes."

"Great."

"Here." He reaches into the pocket of his shorts and throws a crumpled five-dollar bill on the counter. "I forgot to pay. *Ciao,*" he says emphatically, and before I can make change, he's gone, the bell on the door sounding dully in the shop. I can see him walking, fast, across the parking lot, his hands in his pockets, elbows out, heading in the opposite direction from Cumberland Farms.

Faster, more precisely than I've ever done before, I sweep, mop, wrap, wipe down, and close up the shop, but it's still eleven o'clock when I finish. The heat jars me in the empty parking lot, darker now for want of the light thrown all night from the sub shop. The turnover of the engine in my mother's hatchback is loud enough to wake the dead, and in a moment I'm navigating the same streets on my way home, the funereal familiar shadows of roofs and trees. I can't get the question out of my head; it keeps playing itself back to me in his exact pitch and cadence until it's like a record snagging on the same phrase. And me, stupidly, *I'm seventeen. I'm seventeen, I'm seventeen,* as though that had anything to do with it. And his face, every minute posture of his face more deliberate than I've ever seen in a face before—every tic, like someone able to manipulate his own mask.

I'm pulling into the driveway now, necessarily stuffing tonight away in the back of my mind, somewhere hopefully too remote to retrieve.

From the den, like a slide show, come alternating shades of blue from my father's baseball game, and more lights on upstairs. Well, here I am. It is now nearly Labor Day, 1986, in the town of West Mendhem, Massachusetts, and I am seventeen, a hard worker, full of plans and discipline and purpose.

One

❖

West Mendhem is one of those old Massachusetts towns—north of
Boston, just below New Hampshire—whose name corresponds to a
place in England from which religious people fled, hating England,
missing England so badly they named their settlements after the very
places they came from. When you drive into West Mendhem over any
one of its six borders, you pass the same municipality sign you'll pass
on your way into any Massachusetts town, announcing West Mendhem,
incorporated sixteen-something-something, framed around a seal of
Indians canoeing on the great lake upon which sit St. Banner and some
very fine old country estates. There's a study of West Mendhem in a
book of anthropology I read once in a history class, delineating the pat-
terns by which young men in old West Mendhem left their family home-
steads to settle their own at a much later age than the young men in most
New England towns. Young men here didn't leave their homes until the
unseemly age of twenty-one instead of the median eighteen, because
West Mendhem was primarily a farming community, a turkey-raising
community, and progeny were tied economically to the money-raising
concerns of the parents.

Not a great deal has changed; there are dozens of young men who
graduated from West Mendhem High School ten years ago and you can

see them around town operating the DPW trucks that vacuum leaves in the fall and blow snow in the winter. Maybe you can see them in their parents' homes, ranches, and garrisons, getting stoned in the bedrooms where they grew up, listening to hard rock on WAAF, their wallpaper still the train or football-pennant pattern they chose when they were ten. You can see the girls as teachers in the elementary schools where they went to school themselves, or maybe filing cards at the library, running the concessions table at football games, or, like my sister Brenda, behind the counters of shops downtown. At night, you can see them all at the Hayloft, in work boots and Fair Isle sweaters and Irish claddagh rings, drinking Coors, listening to Steve Miller, anticipating their two weeks of vacation in a cottage on Lake Winnipesaukee in New Hampshire, screaming and bellowing, "Get outta heah! You fuckin' queeah, you're a wicked liah!" In a few years, you can see them marrying each other and starting all over again.

There are three ancient burying grounds in West Mendhem, one behind the old North Church, designated by the state an official historic preservation site, contained by an old stone wall with a plaque dating the spot to 1666. The other two lie in neglect in the fields between the old houses on Scholarship Road, headstones lodged semirecumbent in decay, obscured by weeds and the warping of the ground. From the dates I witnessed when picking through them, I knew they were just as old as the official site, and there may be dozens more like them in town, but those I haven't found.

When I was a freshman in high school, our history class took a field trip to the official site to coincide with our study segment on colonial America. A woman from the historical society gave the tour, a rich woman with a clear, deliberate voice who owned a horse farm on the border of West Mendhem and Boxford. She herded us away from the separate places where we were creating stencils of the headstones with pencils and tracing paper and directed our attention to a tiny headstone isolated on a little rise in the ground. "Here lies the body of Charity Bradstreet, daughter of Samuel Bradstreet and his confort, Mary, b. 1684 d. 1686." There was also a biblical quote about children that escapes me, and above the script, the rendering of a tiny skull, the cavity of the mouth carved into a frightened, perfect O, and the skull was framed by the delicate wings of angels. The woman from the historical society squatted down sturdily in her horsey-smelling overalls by the headstone, pointed to the little winged skull with her pinky, and said, "Now, my question to you kids, with your video games and MTV and fancy New Balance shoes, is, 'How did West Mendhem progress from this incident of a little dead two-year-old girl to all the technology and modernity that's around us today?' " Nobody, including me, had an answer. "Maybe that's an essay question your teacher wants to assign you." Our teacher, in the back of the group, laughed and shrugged.

But later that night at home, I couldn't stop noticing the modernity—the microwave oven, the VCR and the cable hookup, Brenda's stereo, Joani's digital watch (because she has a hard time with a traditional face watch), my father's electronic adding machine, my mother's shiny manmade-fiber sweatsuit. I looked around my own room—books, bed, magazines, duffel bag, tapes, and a small cassette recorder that sat atop my night table. I was largely exempt from modernity, I thought. But it was November, cold that night, and the heat had come on. I thought about the yards of coils and wires and pipes underneath the house and below the streets that brought us heat and water, light and ringing phones. And I still couldn't trust the resiliency of the line of progress that brought us from then to now. It seemed like at the center of West Mendhem there was still a barren cavity where Charity Bradstreet lay, and for all the high fidelity of beeps and clicks and buzzes I could hear the moaning sound of wind inside this perfect O, a few leagues below everything else.

When I wake up the next morning, Joani is pulling at my sheets and chanting, "Wake up Erky, Wake up, Erky." She's nearly twelve now, but as recently as two years ago, she couldn't say my name properly and called me Erky. Then one day my mother found Joani sitting in her room, pasting a picture of me onto construction paper to make me a Valentine's Day card, saying over and over again to herself, "E-ric, E-ric, E-ric." That night at dinner, my mother said, "What do you call your brother, Joani?" And Joani looked up and said, "Erky Fizzpatrick," just like she always had. She's been calling me that ever since.

I look at my radio clock and crash back down into the pillow. "Joani baby, it's eight-thirty."

"I can't sleep in the other room. Grandma's snoring. Lemme lie down with you."

I know Joani isn't lying, because I've heard our grandmother snoring and she sounds like the apocalypse. I look up at her. She's got short, easy-care hair that's mussed up from bedhead and she's wearing her favorite Strawberry Shortcake nightgown, which is covered with pills. If you just glanced at Joani fast, you might not put it together that she has Down's syndrome; you might just think she had two wandering eyes and a chubby face. You probably wouldn't put it together that she's that different at all, until you talked to her a little bit. When we were both younger, I was more aware of how different she looked, especially because other kids would gladly bring it to my attention. But after all these years, I've settled into her face; I can see how she looks like my mother and I can see how she looks like my father. It's only when I see some other kid with Down's that I'm startled a little bit.

I sit up in bed and put my T-shirt back on; it was muggy last night and we only have little window fans, because my father thinks air-conditioning is a waste of money and putting up with humid weather builds character. He thinks any kind of "putting up with" builds character.

"You can sleep with me if you let me go back to sleep," I say.

"Okay. I'll let you sleep. Go back to sleep."

She climbs in under the sheets and I give her one of my pillows, grudgingly, because I like to sleep on two. I turn around and try to go back to sleep, but pretty soon she starts in with her sighing—long, theatrical sighs, mimicking my mother, which means she wants to talk. At first I ignore her because I really want to sleep, but then I start to feel guilty, as usual, then I start to feel angry with her for making me feel guilty. Then finally I feel guilty for feeling angry with her. It's not her fault that she likes me the best.

"What'd you do last night?" I ask her, half my words muffled by the pillow.

She stops mid-sigh. "Eddie came over last night." Eddie is her best friend from special ed at school. They're in the same Aptitude Group, which as far as I can tell means they've both mastered the alphabet but are still grappling with *Green Eggs and Ham*.

"Oh, yeah?" I ask. "What'd you do with Eddie?"

"We played Atari. We played Pac-Man and then we played Ms. Pac-Man. I won the whole times."

"You won the whole time," I say automatically.

"I won the whole time," Joani says. We do this constantly. I correct her, she repeats back, and we go on. I'm the only one in the family who picks up on all her speaking errors, even the small ones, so I feel like it's my responsibility to set her straight.

I flip my head over and face her. She's picking pills off her nightgown and flicking them in the air.

"Why you doin' that, Joani?" I say.

She stops, blushing, and clamps her hands on top of her head. "I dunno."

I lean over and try to smooth down her hair. I like it; it's fine, like a baby's. She closes her eyes and sighs, smiling. "Are you and Eddie in love?" I ask.

She flops over and hides her face in the pillow, laughing. "Erky, shut up!"

"Are you? You can tell me, Joani."

"He loves me," she says into the pillow. "I don't love him."

"Why not?"

"Because he's weird. He sucks his fingers and he's always singing the *Happy Days* song."

"So what's wrong with that? He's eccentric."

"What's that?" She's serious now.

"Eccentric. It means somebody who has unusual habits. Like how Grandma used to wear wigs all the time. Or how Ma can't sit in the back of the car without getting sick. Or how you pick at the little balls on your clothes."

"I don't do that all the time!"

"Yeah, but you do it sometimes, so it makes you eccentric. It makes you an individual. That's okay."

"Ex . . . trick . . . extrick . . . extra. What is it?"

"Eks-sen-trick," I say slowly, breaking apart the syllables.

"Eks-sen-trick," she says back to me, singsong.

"That's it. That's what you are. That's what Eddie is. So now you guys can be in love."

She laughs, dropping her elbow and smashing her face back into the pillow. Her little chubby white hand is clenched around the sheet. To see those hands for the first time, when they brought her home when I was six, was a sight. They sat down me and Brenda, who was nine, and told us we had a sister. Nothing was wrong with her, they said, but she was different. She was going to progress slower and we had to look out for her and be nicer to her than we were to each other.

"Do I have to take her everywhere?" Brenda barked. She was big for her age, broad-shouldered, and preoccupied with her first year of judo classes at the YWCA.

"You don't have to take her anywhere right now," our mother said. "But in a few years it might be nice if you got over yourself and showed her a little support."

Brenda scowled. "Am I gonna have to beat up people that give her crap?"

"Watch that kind of talk," my mother said, perched on the edge of the couch, her arms crossed combatively across her chest. Back just two days from the hospital, she looked ashen and exhausted. She would be away from her job as nurse at the Prospect House Nursing Home for three months, and the thought of long days alone with a third child—a problem child—was already making her edgy. Then, "No one's gonna give her crap."

"You just said *crap* yourself!" Brenda screamed, outraged.

"Shut up," my mother said wearily. Meanwhile, I was trying to formulate a question, wondering if I might spare my parents by looking it up in the World Books, which they had ordered more for me than for anyone else. As we sat, I could see them on the mantel, gleaming in fake gilt and wipe-clean leatherette, all twenty volumes flanked by twin casts of *The Thinker*. Under what would I look? "C" for children, "B" for babies? Did the little baby have a disease? What was it called? Would she live?

My mother leaned over and brushed crumbs aggressively off my T-shirt. "Whaddya wanna ask, Eric? Just go ahead and ask it."

"What is it called?"

"What is she called? We told you. Joan Erin Fitzpatrick. But we're gonna call her Joani."

"I mean, what's her thing called?"

"It's called Down's syndrome. She's got a moderate form. It's not the most severe." The name conjured for me the image of submerging, of my alien new baby sister, undiapered, attached to nothing, falling deeper and deeper in water or in black space, somehow losing brainpower as she fell.

Brenda looked terrified. "Is she a 'tard?"

"Brenda, don't you dare let me hear that word again in this house. You don't say it *anywhere!*" my mother said in her sharp I'm-disgusted-with-you tone. Brenda blushed, contrite. "She's *mentally retarded,*" my mother went on, articulating the phrase at Brenda in further rebuke. *"Mildly."*

"Why did God make her like that?" I asked. I was thick in Sunday mass, CCD classes, and my grandmother's constant Jesus-and-the-saints stories at the time; it wouldn't have occurred to me that Joani's condition was attributable to anything other than God's pointed choice.

My mother hugged me, brisk, businesslike. "Honey, he did it to see how good and how strong we could all be. Isn't that right, Art?"

My father had been standing by the living room window throughout this conference, silent, minutely examining something, maybe the state of the front lawn, which he had neglected in the past two weeks. It had been his first day back to work in a week; he was still in work armor, combed, buttoned, and polished, but around his leaking eyes and chapped mouth he looked permanently bugged.

"Hunh, Terry?" I saw his head follow the arc of the neighbor's Airedale cutting across the front yard; I saw the single loose lick of hair bob on top of his head when the dog barked outside. It was September.

"Isn't Joani a special chance for all of us to show God how good we can be to her and to each other? That's what I just told Eric."

My father turned, glistening around the eyes. If you didn't know him, you would have thought he had been crying, but he wasn't; it was only his usual leakiness. He bongoed his stomach and smiled brightly at us.

"Isn't that right, Arthur?" my mother said in the same voice.

" 'Bout what, honey?"

"About Joani. What I just said about her."

My father made one of his trademark creaking sounds before he answered, comic and exaggerated. "Your mother's always right, Eric." He stuck his thumbs in his belt loops and stretched his back.

"I hate it when you say that," my mother said, at the same time that

Brenda squawked, "No, she's not!" I think I laughed then. It was a familiar exchange, and for a moment I was glad that the four of us were in here and the special new challenge with the little white hands like uncooked biscuits was asleep down the hall. There was plenty of time to service God and contend with her later.

I'm tickling Joani now and she's laughing harder when we both hear a protracted moan from her room, where Grandma is sleeping on the second twin bed. She's seventy-six; a week ago, Auntie Irene stopped by her apartment to drop off fresh eggplant from the farm stand and found her lying on her bed, saying her rosary and breathing like she had an amplifier in her throat. On the way to the hospital in the ambulance, my grandmother asked Auntie Irene where she had put the eggplant.

"Calm down, Ma. You're sick," Auntie Irene said, rearranging my grandmother's rosary in her hands. "I left the eggplant on the table."

"It's not gonna keep."

"Ma, it's fresh. It'll keep."

"You should have put it in the crisper. It's not gonna keep in this muggy weather."

"I'm not thinking about the eggplant right now, Ma!"

"You're not, but I am. You never think about nothin'."

They said my grandmother had had a minor stroke. We all visited her on Saturday; at one point there were twenty of us in a pack outside her hospital room, waiting to visit in shifts of three at a time. A few days later Dr. Mullane let her out with a new round of pills.

"Stay off your feet, Doris. Your children and your grandchildren can cook for themselves for a few weeks."

"Your mother raised a good son, Joey," my grandmother said as my mother and aunts packed her up.

Later, Dr. Mullane took my mother and her sisters aside and told them it was dangerous for my grandmother to go on living alone; what if this had happened in the middle of the night and she couldn't get to the phone? He told them they should start thinking about alternative living arrangements. "Terry and I work at the two best nursing homes in the area and I *still* wouldn't put my mother in one of those jail cells," announced Auntie Irene.

So now, while everyone figures out what to do with her, my grandmother is staying with us—sneaking into the kitchen in the afternoon when nobody's home and cooking our dinners, amusing my father and me, worrying my mother, driving Brenda crazy, and scaring Joani awake with her snoring and moaning, like she's moaning right now. I think I hear her moan after our grandfather, who died before I was born—"Oh, Georgie, oh, oh, oh!"—but I may be wrong.

Joani looks dismayed. "What's she yelling about?" she asks me.

"She's just talking in her sleep. Everybody does that. Especially old people."

"Who's she talking to?"

"She's talking to the people in her dreams, like Grandpa and all her old friends. Don't you have people you know in your dreams?"

"I don't have any dreams," she says.

"Everyone does. You have to, or you go crazy."

"I don't have any," she says flatly.

"Oh. Well, I see." But I can't contest further, because I, too, usually remember only whether my dreams please me or trouble me, but never what happens or to whom, by whom. All tone, no content, which is maddening.

"I'm gonna go wake her up," Joani says abruptly, clambering out of the bed. I check my digital radio clock; it's nine o'clock now.

"Hold on. I'm coming," I say, sitting up and pulling on my shorts while Joani waits by the door, giving me a skeptical look I can't place.

The bedroom is about ten times hotter than the rest of the house, and still dark from the drawn shades. Grandma's lying in bed on her back, her short and stout frame obvious under the sheet, the same string of blue glass rosary beads she's had since she was a girl clicking faintly in her hands.

"What are you doin', Grandma?" Joani says in a whisper.

"I'm sayin' my morning prayers," she says in her loud, half-deaf voice. "I'm prayin' that I live to see your children, and your children's children."

"You've got a lot of years ahead of you, Grandma," I say, knee-jerk, and sit down on the floor by the bed. Joani belly-flops into the bed next to our grandmother. The two of them have always been buddies; our grandmother doesn't treat Joani any differently, but I'm pretty sure that's because she hasn't caught on that there's anything different about her. She thinks all her grandchildren are brilliant, which is flattering but highly debatable if you knew all my cousins.

"How you feeling today, Grandma?" Joani asks, curling up next to her.

"I feel good today. God's putting me back to normal. I'm gonna get up and cook for the big barbecue today."

"I think Ma's cooking everything, Grandma, and Brenda's helping. You should try to rest," I say.

She snorts broadly. "Brenda can't cook. She could cook good if she set her mind to it, but she doesn't. How can she learn to cook when she's always outta the house? I ask her if she wants me to show her and she tells me she's got other plans. Good for her, Miss Busy Bee."

"Brenda doesn't have time to cook, Grandma," I say. "She works fifty hours a week at the card shop. She's a career woman." I love saying this to my grandmother about Brenda. It drives her crazy.

"So what!" she says, spitting the words into Joani's face. Joani winces. "I was a career woman, too. When your grandfather died I worked in the intimate apparel department at Cohen's for twelve years. I was the best saleslady they had. All the Jewish ladies came in and said, 'I want Doris Ianelli, that Italian. She's the best saleslady in the store.' Now all they got in that place is cheap junk. Ever since the P.R.'s moved in."

"P.R.'s" is my grandmother's code for Puerto Ricans, who according to her are the primary reason why Leicester, the old city next door, "got bad" and why, after sixty-nine years there, she had to "get out," just like all the other "good ones." When she gets on the subject of the P.R.'s, I usually try to steer the conversation away, especially if Joani is around.

"Maybe if Brenda and Frankie get married, she'll learn to cook," I say offhandedly.

"I pray to God every night," she says.

"So do I," says Joani, out of nowhere. I look up at her, but she's pulled the sheet up over her head. I wonder if this is true. Brenda doesn't go to church anymore, and I pretend to, but I really sneak along a book and go sit inside Dunkin' Donuts for an hour. Joani still goes with our parents or with Grandma when she's visiting, but it never occurred to me that she might take it any more seriously than we do. I picture her lying in her little twin bed, praying, and for some reason the idea depresses the hell out of me. Then suddenly it's one of the contemptuous thoughts about my family I feel guilty for having, and I squash it up in my mind and throw it away.

"Good. You should," my grandmother says firmly, then, "Do you say the prayer I taught you to say before you made your First Communion?"

Joani doesn't answer. Instead, she sticks her head out from under the sheet and asks my grandmother, "Will you tell me the pressha cooka story?"

"You wanna hear the pressha cooka story, honey?"

"Yeah," Joani says.

The pressure cooker story is a story Grandma has told us about a hundred times. It's about how once her pressure cooker, filled with a boiled dinner, exploded, and when she walked into the kitchen, meat and vegetables were dripping from the ceiling and walls. She can't remember exactly when the incident took place, but I've dated it to about 1963, just after the Kennedy assassination. I have no reason to believe it never happened, because not once have the details of the story changed in the telling; my grandmother even remembers the exact contents of the pressure cooker and how long it took her to scour down the kitchen before the company arrived: fifty-three minutes flat. Apparently she foresaw that this would one day be a great story of will and perseverance, so she timed it. Joani finds this story hysterical and even likes to tell it along with my grandmother.

"For our twenty-fifth anniversary, your grandfather gave me—" Grandma begins, ceding to Joani.

"A pressha cooka!" Joani screams, exploding in laughter.

"Uh-huh. A pressha cooka. I was the first one in the Sodality to get one, and Mary Trotta comes up to me and says—"

And says, "Doris Ianelli, are you gettin' snobby with us, goin' an' gettin' a pressha cooka?" I say to myself, slipping out the door. I go into my room to pull up the shades and notice the T-shirt I was wearing last night, pizza-sauce stains blotted to pink across the chest. Now the night comes back to me with a little quickening of the heart; the exact transactions of that strange conversation have already blurred, swirling into the vortex of the final exchange, and I'm appalled at the clarity with which my own strained cadence comes back to me: *I'm seventeen.* In the bright light of my bedroom, in the familiar light of my own house, with my grandmother's ancient voice rasping from the other room, the whole memory seems unreal now and eerily exotic: a rich black guy with that Public Radio voice, dropping phrases in French and Italian in the middle of a sub shop, those glowing loafers and attenuated hands. And something unseemly at the center of it, one incongruity to outstrip all other incongruities. It has nothing to do with me, I think, certainly nothing to do with this house, this family, and nothing to do with the light of day.

Coming down the stairs, I hear them fighting.

First my mother: "How goddamned dumb can you be? Didn't you listen to the doctor? Aren't you up with the times?"

Then Brenda: "Don't you call me fuckin' dumb!"

"You use that kind of language around this house, young lady, and you can get the hell out and get your own place with your prison guard. See if I care."

"You would! You would care! That's just it! You try to come off to me like you're Miss Oh-I-Don't-Care-About-What-People-Think, but you're so brainwashed by the Catholic church, it'd drive you crazy."

"You're gonna hate yourself when you're putting me in the ground in a few weeks, you little brat."

"Good morning?" I say tentatively when I walk into the kitchen, and they both stop screaming.

"Good morning, honey," my mother says mechanically, her back to me, still in a nightgown, tossing a huge salad in a bowl.

"Hi, Eric," Brenda mumbles into her coffee cup. She looks ghastly this morning, bereft of her usual moussed-up hair and foundation-mascara-blusher-et-cetera face. She's wearing the same oversized West Mendhem High Krimson Warriors football sweatshirt she inherited from Frank three years ago when they graduated, so it's impossible to see if she's starting to get big. Her legs are in tight acid-washed jeans up on one of the kitchen chairs, and I can see the bottoms of her feet are dirty from walking around the house barefoot. Her usual soft pack of Newport Menthol 100s is on the kitchen table, but she's not smoking one at the moment, which is rare. On some level, Brenda respects me because I do well in school and she never did, and because I know a lot of big words. (In fact, she was the one who gave me my hated junior high school nickname, The Walking Dictionary.) But on a more common level, she pretends to care as little about my opinion of her as she does about the rest of the world's, and that seems to be the mood she's in this morning.

"What time did you get in last night?" she asks me, indifferently. "I saw your light on when I got in."

"I got in around eleven," I say, pouring a cup of coffee at the counter and resisting a paranoid instinct to glance around and assess the look on her face. "I was up reading."

"Did you go out with Phoebe or Charlie after work last night?" my mother asks, back still to us.

"No. I had to stay late closing up the shop. Phoebe went to a concert at Great Woods and Charlie's just getting back from drum camp today. They might come by later."

"That's nice," my mother says placidly, even though I know she's adopting this placid tone just to annoy Brenda. "You know you don't need to come right back with the car after work, Eric, as long as you call to let us know you'll be late. You know that we trust you."

Brenda slams her fist down on the kitchen table and whips her head toward my mother's back. "Oh my *God!* I know you say those things to Eric just to piss me off!"

Big, theatrical, Why-do-I-deserve-this? sigh from my mother. "I say *what* kinds of things, Brenda?"

Brenda clutches the edge of the kitchen table and screams, her bloodshot eyes about to burst out of her head. In the den, I hear the steady rhythm of my father turning the pages of the newspaper over the drone of the baseball game. The louder the house gets, the calmer he becomes, and I've long since stopped waiting for the day when he explodes.

"Those kinds of things, *Teresa,"* she says, calling my mother by her full name, which my mother hates. "When you say something nice to Eric, but you're really taking a stab at *me."*

Finally, my mother wheels around, brandishing her huge wooden salad fork at Brenda. "Do you know what you are?" she says to Brenda. "You're a paranoid schizophrenic. That's the only conclusion I can draw. You think the whole world is out to get you, but *you* bring it on yourself!"

"If I'm a paranoid schizophraniac," Brenda mispronounces, "it's your fault. You're the one that always made me feel like a freak."

My mother laughs sharply and rolls her eyes, hand on hip. "Oh, really?"

"Yes, *really.*"

"How?"

"Oh my God! How can you ask how? Through my whole friggin' life! What about when I picked out that First Communion dress with Auntie Irene and you told me I looked like a marshmallow in it?"

I laugh now, snorting up some coffee. I can't help it. I've seen Brenda's First Communion pictures: she's an overweight seven-year-old in a frothy white crinolined confection that fits her like a powdered zeppole, a ring of crushed daisies falling off her head as she scowls at the camera in front of St. Agnes's church.

"Oh, fuck you, Eric!" she spits at me. "I've seen your First Communion picture, and you look like a little skinny wussy-boy!" I laugh again. She's right; there I am, in a polyester navy blazer and polyester chinos that ride halfway up my arms and legs, hair plastered to my head in a side part and over my ears, smiling dewily like an oversuckled mama's boy.

"Come off it, Brenda," my mother says. "I never said you looked like a marshmallow. I said you looked like a pretty little cream puff."

"No you didn't! I remember you saying, right in front of Grandma and Auntie Irene, 'Doesn't she look like a marshmallow? Couldn't you just gobble her—gobble her up?' " Brenda's voice breaks here, and I recoil. I've heard that break before, and it usually means she's going to cry, which is always a tough thing to witness in a hard-ass like my sister.

Now my mother is ashamed. "Honey, I never said that," she says flatly, turning back to the salad. "But you remember what you want."

But it's too late. Brenda tears her hands through her hair and emits a long prefatory creaking sound before she erupts into full-blown sobs. "And now I'm gonna start looking like a marshmallow all over again!"

"Oh, for God's sake." My mother sighs, throwing down the salad fork and awkwardly scooping Brenda out of her chair and into her arms. "Honey, you're not gonna look like a marshmallow. You're gonna look like a beautiful mother-to-be. You're gonna glow."

"Shut up! I am not!" Brenda bellows into my mother's shoulder.

"Yes, you are! Eric, isn't your sister gonna be a beautiful mother? How could she not be? She's an Ianelli." I know she says this loud enough for my father to hear in the other room; every chance she gets, my mother dismisses the influence of his side of the family on her children. She thinks they're bloodless, slack-jawed bumps on logs, and that my father was the only one who got out and made good. "Isn't she gonna be beautiful, Eric?" she says again, eyeing me sternly.

"Of course you are, Brenda. After all, you're *my* sister," I say, and my mother and I both laugh with forced brightness. We both just want her to calm down; she's like an explosive we're constantly trying gingerly to defuse.

"No, I'm not. I'm a friggin' cow," she says, but at least she's merely sniffling now.

"No, you're not," my mother and I say in unison. Brenda remains collapsed in my mother's hug for a few more seconds, my mother stroking her back and saying, "Baby, baby, shhhhh, it's okay," the whole time, until finally my sister extricates herself, sits down again, and wipes her face with a napkin. She takes a sip of her coffee.

"Whatever," she says.

"That's right," my mother says, shooting me a "Whew!" look and turning back to the salad. She always passes me this look after a fight with Brenda, and I always respond with a twisted little grimace. The look is supposed to say, "Aren't you glad we calmed her down?" but since I'm half-convinced that my mother deliberately riles her up, I can't ever fully share in these looks. It's like my father says to both of them: it takes two to tango.

Now there's a little hush, the sound of the ball game filtering back into the kitchen, and the New Big Fact settles back in around us: Brenda's ten weeks pregnant by Frank, who's now a security guard at one of the state correctional facilities and even though they've been going out since high school, there are no stated plans of marriage. My parents took the news okay; they told Brenda whether she wants to get married or not is completely her choice and they'll support her whatever she does, but I know that more than that is going on in their heads. (Marriage or no marriage, Brenda is having the baby; the "A" word never came up, and in my family, it never will.) Joani and Grandma don't know yet, nor does anyone else except me. My parents told me—they said they knew I was mature enough to handle it. They also said Brenda wouldn't tell me herself because she was too ashamed, and it would be nice if I went to her with a show of support.

So I did. I found her in her room, splayed out on her bed, listening to Black Sabbath and playing with the tassel from her high school graduation mortarboard, which she keeps pinned up on a bulletin board alongside ticket stubs from heavy metal concerts at the Worcester Centrum and Polaroids of Frank, her friends, and herself, usually depicted blitzed out of their minds up at Salisbury Beach, their faces shiny with beer and cancer-inducing suntans. She took one look at me and looked away; obviously, she knew we had been in conference downstairs.

"Hey," I said.

She made some kind of noise into her pillow on the side opposite from me.

"Hey, Brenda," I said, closing the door behind me and leaning against it. "Ma and Dad told me."

"Uh-huh," she mumbled listlessly.

"I just want you to know I'm not judging or anything."

"Uh-huh."

"Why should I? It's great news. It's happy news."

"Uh-huh," she said, unmodulated, as Black Sabbath shrieked on. I'll never know how Brenda listens to that toxic stuff. I only listen to alternative music, like R.E.M. or the Smiths, and I'll admit I also like some old stuff like the Supremes and Billie Holiday. And Madonna, which I try to play down.

"You and Frank were probably going to get married anyway, right?"

"What?" She flopped over and looked at me blankly then, like I was really outstaying my welcome.

"I said you and Frank are probably going to get married anyway, right?"

Then she gave me a huge, sarcastic, big-eyed look and said, mock-portentously, "Time will tell." I was taken aback—Brenda hardly ever talks to me in that cryptic way—and muttered something before slipping out, leaving her and Black Sabbath behind. She called in sick at the card shop three days in a row and hardly left her room, heavy metal blasting constantly from its depths. When she emerged, it was only to go to the beach with her girlfriends and get shitfaced three nights in a row. That's what they were fighting about when I came down this morning; my mother couldn't believe that Brenda would be stupid enough to drink herself blind when she knew she was carrying a kid—in this day and age, no less, when people should know better (which is the same thing she says about Brenda's smoking and my father's high cholesterol intake).

I glance at Brenda across the kitchen table. She's still sniffling a little and patting her face dry. "Are you going to tell anybody today?" I ask her.

"Couldja not be so loud, Eric?" she says. "I don't want them hearing upstairs."

"They're not going to hear," I say. "Grandma's telling Joani the pressure cooker story, and Joani wouldn't understand anyway."

"Don't underestimate your sister, Eric," my mother says. That's what she always says to us about Joani; in fact, it's what we all say to each other: "Don't underestimate Joani." What everybody is waiting for Joani to say or do, I don't know. Stand up on a chair and denounce all of us as hypocrites, fools, woeful underestimators?

"I don't want to tell anyone yet," she says. "Why should I have to tell them until I start to show? They're all just going to judge me anyway and call me a slut."

"Brenda, they are not!" my mother says. "Would you stop being so melodramatic? This is your family, for God's sake. They're gonna support you whatever you do, not judge you."

"Yeah, we'll see." Brenda sulks.

"And besides, do you think you're the first person in the history of the world for this to happen to? It happens all the time now, because there isn't the self-control there used to be among young people."

"Oh, would you not start in with that bullshit again!"

"Fine. Fine. Shut me up. All I'm saying is that this isn't the end of the world."

"Well, do *you* want me to tell them?"

My mother opens her mouth to come back fast, then snaps it shut, considering. "I want you to tell people when you're ready to tell people. If that's today, then fine. We're all gonna stand by you. If that's next week, then fine. If it's when you show, then fine. If you wanna go into hiding from your family, then fine."

Brenda pulls a cigarette out of her pack and holds it, unlighted, in her hand. "How can I go into hiding from my family when Grandma's right here in the house, breathing down my neck and telling me I need to lose weight all the time anyway?"

"Bren, I don't *know*. I'm just saying it's your child, it's your choice."

"You don't want me to tell," Brenda says, moving to ignite the Newport with her big yellow Bic lighter. "You're ashamed."

"Don't you dare light up that cigarette in my house!" my mother says, lunging for the lighter. Brenda slips out of the chair and makes for the screened-in back porch. It's the only place my mother allows her to smoke in the house, but I always smell it coming from her room.

"How can you smoke one of those deathsticks when you're responsible for another human life?" my mother shouts after her.

"Ma, shhhh!" I say. "Think about upstairs." Not a word from the den, where the ball game and the rustling of newspaper goes on.

Brenda sticks her head back in the door, the fully lighted cigarette stuck in her mouth. "Like this," she says, and blows a mouthful of smoke into the kitchen.

"You are *hateful!*" my mother screams back, before Brenda runs out the back porch and around the corner of the house, laughing maniacally. *"Hateful!"* she yells again, before she notices Mr. LaFollette next door trimming his hedges and ducks back into the house, mortified. She slumps down at the kitchen table. "Oh, Eric, honey, what did I do to deserve a hateful daughter like that one?"

She's asked me this a million times. I could give the usual answer that begins, "Brenda doesn't hate you, she loves you; you're just both very strong personalities," but today I just say, "I don't know." My mother's been a geriatric nurse now for over twenty years, and she's fond of saying that she can communicate with a roomful of eighty-year-old infants babbling away in a dozen different dialects of dementia, but half the time she can't communicate with her oldest daughter, a grown woman who speaks perfect English. (Plus every four-letter Anglo-Saxon word ever invented, I should add.)

Now she looks at me across the table and smiles wanly, picking up Brenda's mug and drinking the lukewarm remains. "How come you never give me any trouble?" she says to me. "Don't you *want* to give me trouble sometimes?"

"Don't you already have enough trouble?" I ask.

She laughs. "It's not trouble, it's God's test, right? That's what Grandma always says, right?"

"Yeah, but now Grandma is one of the tests."

She swats my arm across the table in mock horror. "Don't you talk that way about your grandmother. You want God to hear that?" Now we both laugh. I can never tell how seriously my mother takes religion. I mean, from the way she goes to church almost every morning before work, it's obvious that she takes it seriously, but I think it's more of a comfort to her in the midst of all her anxieties, a reminder of her childhood, when she was surrounded by nuns and superstitious Old World grown-ups and everything was conveniently black and white. Whether she really still believes in a strict sequence of transgression, punishment, penance, and absolution is what I wonder about.

"Daddy says you liked Yale, didn't you?" she says.

"Yeah, I did," I say cautiously.

"It's fancy, huh?"

"It's definitely up there."

"But why not Harvard? That's just as good quality, isn't it? Then you could come home on the weekends and we could come see you all the time and—"

"Ma! You know that's not the point of college."

"Well, how would I know the point of college? I went to nursing school. That's not college. It's the start of a life prison sentence in a loony bin."

"Cut it out with that talk. You know what I mean." We've had this conversation before, and I'm holding my ground.

"I know, I know," she says. "I want you to go where you want to go."

"I'm going to apply for lots of scholarships."

"We'll find a way. It doesn't look like we're gonna have to put Brenda or Joani through anytime soon. So we can focus on you."

"Great," I say tightly. It makes me uncomfortable when they refer to me this way, like I'm the last great hope or something.

She glances up at the clock and jumps. "Jesus Christ, Mary, and Joseph, look at the time! Everyone's gonna be here in a little while, and I haven't even made the marinade. Go ask your father when he's gonna pull himself away from that game and start the grill."

I get up to go, but she stops me. "Honey, would you just scratch this little itch on my back? It's been driving me crazy ever since Brenda came down this morning. Ha Ha."

"Yuk, yuk," I say. She's always asking me to scratch an itch on her back. "Where is it? Right here?"

"No, down a little, over to the left. Over a little more. No, back. That's it! Oh, that feels good."

"You think Brenda's gonna tell anyone anything?" I ask as I scratch.

"Why does anyone have to tell anyone *anything?*" She sits up straight in the chair. "We're not politicians. We're not celebrities. What we do in our own little family is our private business."

"Not for long, in Brenda's case."

"Well, we'll cross that bridge when we come to it. Ooh, scratch that harder. Just a little harder."

"Ma, what do you want me to do, use a Brillo pad?" My arm is getting tired from scratching.

She pops out of the chair. "All right, smart aleck, forget I asked. Go ask your father. I'm gonna do the marinade." She disappears into the pantry.

My father is intent on the Red Sox in the den, but he looks up at me when I pop my head in. I slip into my usual voice when addressing him— a little more sober, a little lower, a little bored. "Dad, Ma wants to know when you're gonna—"

Suddenly, there's a burst of excitement and cheering on the TV, a home run or something. "Eric, hangonaminute!" my father says, actually popping out of his chair and squatting in front of the TV so he looks like a catcher. "Ooh, sonofagun! Get it! Get it! *Sonofagun!*"

I watch all this feeling very aloof and slightly disdainful. I know the rudiments of baseball, but I gratefully haven't followed it since I put my foot down when I was twelve and said I wouldn't play another humiliating season of Farm League. Now he looks up, flushed, at my impassive face; a current of civic passion moves from Fenway Park northward to West Mendhem, into our house, right through my father, and stops dead at me. "Big moment?" I say softly to pull him out of his bewilderment.

"Huh? Oh, yeah. Yeah! Evans comes up on second—" He looks at me again, blinks, and in a millisecond he comes to. "Eric. What's up?"

"Ma wants to know when you're gonna start the grill."

"In a little bit. Just at the next commercial. Tell her to relax; no one's coming for another hour and a half." He says *half* the old-fashioned Massachusetts way, with a long *a*.

His eyes dart up to me, back to the TV, back to me as I stand in a kind of brief limbo in the doorway. "Okay," I say. I notice his coffee mug. It's one I gave him for his birthday when I was younger. It's powder blue with a picture of Papa Smurf on it. "You want more coffee?" I ask him.

"Yuh. Sure. Thanks." I pick up the mug. "Are your mother and your sister still going at it in there?"

"No. Brenda ran out the back door with a cigarette. Ma was freaking out."

My father gives what I call his short, philosophical little laugh: "Heh. Your mother worries too much."

"About Brenda?" I ask.

"About everything."

"Don't you think she's got a lot to worry about?" I ask. We're always having these soft, prodding little disagreements; more to the point, I'm always having them with him, trying to find a little chink in his smooth armor of certainty. He doesn't take issue with me, or any of us. He's implacable; he seems beyond us. At least with my mother, I know where I stand. My father doesn't compliment me, and he doesn't criticize either. I'm always wondering what I'd have to do to push him in either direction, if I ever chose to.

"You worry too much, you kill yourself," he says, putting more concentration into wiping his glasses clean than into the thought itself. He's got on his weekend clothes, elastic-waist shorts with snap pockets on the back and a T-shirt advertising a new low-fat cheddar cheese. He's got a lot of T-shirts advertising cheeses, pepperonis, and crackers. He's a salesman for a company that sells those things to restaurants and little specialty shops.

I take his mug back into the kitchen and fill it up.

"When's he gonna start the grill?" my mother asks.

"He says in a half-hour or so. He says there's no hurry," I say. *He* spoken between my mother and me—*he* referring to my father—has some special cadence, some particular kind of weight. I'm not sure what it means, exactly. It's just how we say it.

"He's crazy if he thinks he's gonna get it going in time," she says.

"That's what he says," I say.

"Fine. Let 'im."

I take the Smurf mug back to him and set it down. He's back into the game.

"You're sure you're gonna have enough time for the grill?" I ask him.

"Umph."

I shrug and walk out. Through the dining room window, I see Brenda crouching in the middle of the backyard, sort of rocking back and forth. She's got the cigarette in one hand and both arms wrapped around her middle, and she's looking up at the sky. It looks like she's talking and at first I'm not sure, until I catch a fragment of her voice, in a rising pitch—"and I said no fuckin' way, I swear to God I did"—and it drops down again.

I walk away before more floats back to me. I feel like I can handle our family secrets; they don't surprise me. It's the secrets underneath the secrets that I think would knock me out, everybody's little private dialogue with heaven, or wherever, that I can do without hearing.

Two

We live in the middle-class part of West Mendhem that I've always jokingly called the ghetto, the oldest pocket of town, where saltboxes gave way to little one-plot Greek Revivals that gave way to one-plot Victorians that eventually gave way to one-plot split-levels and Cape Cods like the one we live in. Beyond the ghetto, West Mendhem suddenly uncoils into hills and winding roads, farms, the great lake, and the raw new fourteen-room neo-this-and-that houses that squat in tree-shorn developments with names like Yankee Mews or Goodharvest Homes. Excepting these developments, this is my favorite part of town, where I biked away whole afternoons when I was younger and where I cruise aimlessly now when I'm restless after work, edging my mother's 1979 hatchback close to the shoulder of the road to make room for passing Volvos and Saabs. I like it out here because you can almost forget it's the twentieth century, or you can almost forget this is America, pretending instead that you're in the Vichy countryside, racing along as fast as you can to deliver Resistance plans to some nuns in a remote farmhouse.

Our neighborhood is the buffer zone between the rest of leafy, bucolic West Mendhem and the sooty, decaying threat of Leicester, whose defunct factory smokestacks you can actually see from the windows of our house. When Leicester's "complexion"—as one of my junior high school teachers once delicately put it—started to change in the 1970s, this neighborhood was the first rung a lot of white Leicester families (including mine) could grab in the middle of their frenzied exodus from the old city. Kids who would have grown up little Catholic punks in Leicester instead grew up little Catholic punks just over the border, this while their infuriated parents mourned the loss of their native city and cursed the arrival of the Puerto Ricans, Dominicans, and other assorted boat people who were—*even as we speak*—turning beautiful old Leicester into a filthy warren of drug dealers, knife-wielders, lazy welfare recipients, and other sorts of miscreants. They shouldn't have left so easily, these parents (including mine) would say to each other; they should have stayed, shown some gumption, fought for their neighborhoods. But they didn't, and when they moved into one of the half-dozen towns that ringed Leicester, they stopped going back there to eat, to shop, to pray, or to visit, because by now almost everyone, including the terrified elderly, had left as well.

To me, it's the sleeping giant just at our backs, the once-thriving hulls of black textile mills and Art Nouveau bridges that gird the sluggish Merrimack River, the repository of memories that makes up the history of my dispossessed suburban family and all of my dispossessed suburban cousins. It's where my mother and father grew up, on opposite sides of the river in the days when Italians and Irish had rumbles because they were the only ones to define each other's difference. It's also where my parents met, at a bar just after Thanksgiving 1963, everyone still mourning the killing in Dallas, she with her mostly Italian friends from St. Agnes Academy, he with his, mostly Irish, from City Catholic Prep. She was finishing the nursing program, now disbanded, at Leicester General Hospital, her mind filled with four-color textbook illustrations of nervous systems and clear mason jars of human brains and lungs suspended in formaldehyde. He had just come home from four years in Boston, attending business school by day, and bartending at night, living with two roommates in a basement apartment on Bay State Road, now back to a retired, widowed mother still shell-shocked at the loss of her eldest son, her only other child, in the Korean conflict. (That was our *other* grandmother, the meek one, who died—of nervous exhaustion, I think—when I was ten.)

I've always wanted to know what he said to his friends when he saw her, what she said to hers, duck tails and loafers with pennies on one side of the room, sweater sets and pedal pushers on the other, cigarette smoke and cheap beer coursing between in a show of Roman Catholic daring, and finally what they said to each other. They had lived for twenty-some years in the same city and never seen each other before, but surely he had a friend who knew one of her three sisters or friends. It's so difficult to picture sudden romance between them, something with strings rising in the background, difficult to picture anything other than the worn-in, slightly contentious *"Hey, Art?" "Hey, what?" "Hey, Art?"* back-and-forth by which they ferry what seems to be only key information to each other these days.

They married in May of 1965, then settled back in Leicester, in a three-room apartment just a mile's walk in any direction from everyone they knew, into a carefully budgeted life. They filled the place with just enough affordable Danish modern furniture to make it livable; socializing revolved around weekend excursions to Salisbury Beach or Saturday nights playing cards or Monopoly with my mother's sisters and their husbands, all of whom had no choice but to become best friends. Brenda came in 1966, me three years after, and we moved to a one-story ranch-style house in one of the planned neighborhoods on the semi-suburban western outskirts of the city. Then the big surprise, Joani. My mother sat around watching the Watergate hearings with utter indifference during her pregnancy, concerned only with the proper development of her third child.

We were now a completed family. By then they were preoccupied, like everyone else, with the thought that the public schools were going down, even the relatively good ones of our semisuburban neighborhood, and they followed their friends and their relations out of Leicester and into the provinces, to West Mendhem, where we live today. "Why not?" they said. The time was right—Leicester was changing, we needed good neighborhoods and good schools, and my father had been promoted from bookkeeper to salesman, with a route that kept expanding thanks to his easygoing, no-pressure rapport with the area's shop owners and restaurateurs. He didn't glad-hand them; he asked them about their wives and their kids and their entrepreneurial aspirations while he took his lunch at their bar counters like the other local businessmen; then, somewhere in between, he'd tell them what new cheese wheel or pepperoni stick they couldn't be without. He was a regular guy, not your regular salesman, and they liked him immensely.

Now, at seventeen, to remember growing up in this house, in this family, seems to be about remembering what it was like to be buffeted by currents stronger than myself but not yet knowing how to negotiate them. There was always the purposeful screaming of Brenda and my mother, and the less deliberate screaming of Joani—sick with this or that cold, falling down the stairs, getting some smelly old blanket or stuffed toy taken away from her for washing—and at the center of it all, my father's silence or his philosophical little laugh, "heh," not much more than a hiccup: my father, who seemed capable of endless reserves of patience, or self-removal, a Zen-like quietude surrounding him and his ball game, him and his newspaper, him and his paperwork.

I grew up, somehow, in the middle of it, carving out a narrow private chamber between the outside world of school and beatings and hated baseball and soccer practices, and the Fitzpatrick-Ianelli world of silent men and unsilenceable women. I filled it at first with drawings and funny little lifelike props cut and pasted out of construction paper, then later with books and old movies and magazines and piano lessons, all sorts of faces and voices that blessedly looked and sounded absolutely nothing like what surrounded me at home, in school, around town. There was the soporific drone of teachers, the unspeakable curses of older boys before they threw my schoolbag into the street, the nightly brawls between Brenda and my mother over punky boys or failed classes or Brenda's general bad attitude, the interminable slurred, slow grind of Joani's conversations with herself.

But there was also the strange, archaic, formal, dazzling syntax of Charles Dickens and Jane Austen and F. Scott Fitzgerald, the honeyed, regal comportment of Vivien Leigh and Clark Gable in *Gone With the Wind* or Katharine Hepburn and Cary Grant in *Philadelphia Story*—modes of speech and behavior like I had never seen from anyone in my family or in West Mendhem. In *People* magazine and *Vanity Fair* there were reports of people with inestimable sums of money and schooling and experience, even the reports of some ordinary people who had fallen out of step with ordinariness and ended up having marvelous lives. And from sheet music the elaborate machinations of Mozart and Brahms and George Gershwin, and, even more extraordinary, my growing ability to translate their black markings back into tricky chords and phrasings, on the upright piano we had gotten from my grandmother when she sold her Leicester house, in the living room with the accordion doors shut on either side so as not to disturb the television in the den or the squabbling in the kitchen.

I didn't hide these elements of my private life, but at the same time no one inquired about them. They were largely quiet things, I pursued them on my own time, and it's almost as though everyone observed an unspoken rule of no entry in this province of mine. Either that, or they simply didn't care. I was bookish, I was creative, I was artistic, I was private, I didn't make any trouble. Now I look around my room at the books I've collected, the books I somehow managed to hear about, seek, find, purchase, and devour, and I'm almost shocked at what I've managed to get away with while everyone else was making noise in other quarters of the house. I'm shocked at everything I know that no one knows I know. No one ever said, "What are you reading? What's it about?" It shocks me—no one ever thought to ask.

"Eric, come play patty-cake with me and Joani," my annoying parochial-school fourteen-year-old cousin Bethie Lynn calls back to me as I take off across the lawn in the middle of the barbecue and slip back inside the house.

"Okay," I call. "I'll be right back," but it's a lie. I can't take Bethie Lynn and her little Goody Two-Shoes platitudes anymore. In fact, I can't take any more of my extended family this afternoon: not Grandma and Auntie Reenie, Bethie Lynn's hulking mother, also a nurse, fighting over whether Grandma can have another meatball-and-sausage sub; not unmarried Auntie Lani, who's been hacking up a lung, chaining Virginia Slims all afternoon; not Auntie Winnie, the youngest of the four of them and the manager of a children's clothing store in Methuen, who's running across the lawn in her pink jelly shoes to swat my little bratty cousins Jason and Robbie over the head for beating up on Brittany, the three-year-old daughter of my oldest cousin, Frannie, who thinks she's a yuppie because she's a C.P.A. and told me that going to Yale, or anything other than business school, was a waste of money; not my father and all my sullen, mute uncles who have been playing cards and smoking cigars all afternoon, the cooler full of Michelob Lites right beside them. All I want to do is hide out in my room and finish *A Handful of Dust,* which is on my summer reading list for senior year, and which I happen to be devouring.

I slip out the kitchen and up the stairs. It's nice upstairs, cool and quiet, and I'm thinking that I'll read for a little while when I hear voices coming from Brenda's bedroom. It's Brenda and Frank, her boyfriend, who I guess has been hanging out up there all along, because I can hear the sound of the ball game on Brenda's black-and-white TV.

I stand frozen outside the door. "I can't fuckin' *stand* them anymore today," Brenda says, tense. "Fuckin' Frannie. I know she knows, just from the way she looks at me. She's such a fuckin' snotty bitch."

"Brenda, wouldja cool down?" I hear Frank say. I like Frank okay, I guess, even though he kind of scared me when Brenda first brought him home. He grew up with just his dad in the most run-down part of town, by the old train tracks at the bottom of Main Street, and he probably would've been kicked out of West Mendhem High School for all sorts of things if he hadn't been such a football hero. He's the kind of guy who would've harassed the shit out of me when I was a freshman, except he didn't because I was Brenda's little brother. He even told other guys to leave me alone, and they did—at least, when he was around.

Then it sounds like Brenda's going to cry again. "Oh my God, Frankie, what am I gonna do? I'm gonna start showin' pretty soon. I've gotta tell 'em. Oh my fuckin' God, I can't believe I'm having a baby! What am I gonna do?"

"Baby, baby, shhhh! Take it easy, Bren. It's not what are *you* gonna do. It's what are *we* gonna do. And we're gonna get married, right?"

There's a pause. Then Brenda says, "Yeah, I guess so." She sounds defeated, but maybe that's because her voice sounds muffled through the door.

"Whaddya mean, you *guess* so? We've been talkin' about it all along, anyway, right?"

"Yeah."

"So no better time than the present, right?" Frank sounds much gentler than he usually does, like when he's reminiscing with my father about old Thanksgiving games, or talking about the Puerto Rican *muthafuck-ahs* he has to guard all day at the correctional facility.

"I guess so," Brenda says. "But even if we get married next week, they're still gonna know it happened before."

"So what? So screw your crazy family. Screw the whole fuckin' world. I don't give a shit about what any muthahfuckahs say. Do you?"

"I guess not," Brenda says. She sounds a little calmer now, appeased.

"So what's the big deal, right? We're gonna get married, Bren, and we're gonna have a baby boy."

"Baby *boy?*" Brenda asks, annoyed.

"Baby boy, baby girl, I don't care. Whatever."

"Yeah, whatever."

Pretty soon I can hear them making out, that ungodly smacking sound. It's funny; I'm genuinely concerned about Brenda and Frank, but in a strange way their whole situation almost seems kind of wholesome and old-fashioned to me. Like it's out of *West Side Story,* or that horrible song "Jack and Diane." You know, "two American kids doing the best they can," and that kind of thing, even though I know it's not nice for me to reduce them to a John Cougar Mellencamp song.

It's around seven o'clock now. Most everybody has gone home, except Auntie Reenie, Auntie Lani, and Auntie Winnie. Now they're having the big talk downstairs in the kitchen with my mother. My bet is that no-body wants to take in Grandma except for Auntie Reenie, but the other aunts won't let her because she and Grandma fight too much and Grandma will end up having another stroke, if Auntie Reenie doesn't have one first. Brenda and Frank went off to a movie or something, and Grandma and Joani are taking a nap together in the other room. I think my father's downstairs in the den reading a MacArthur biography, keeping out of everything.

I fell asleep with the book in my hands and had a dream, bits of which I actually happened to remember. I dreamed I was driving around the St. Banner campus late at night in my mother's hatchback. But it wasn't St. Banner in my dream, it was college, and I was looking for the place to register. Finally, I got out of the car—it was freezing cold in the dream, I remember—and I went into some majestic old building, where all these Chinese students were gathered, dressed like they were going to a cocktail party, and they were all playing some huge board game, Monopoly or something. Then it got peculiar, because then *he*—Mr. Snotty Black Guy—got up from the table (he was the only one who wasn't Chinese) and came toward me. He was dressed in Nikes and shorts, like he was ready to run a marathon, and he had a huge stack of folders under his arm. And he came toward me and said, "Did you bring your files? I hope you brought your files." There was also classical music coming from somewhere, something very somber with a lot of strings. And I was at a total loss because I didn't bring my files, or whatever.

That's all I remember of the dream. Now I'm lying here, in that sweat you get when you wake up from a nap in warm weather, and I'm trying to make sense of it. It's college worries, obviously. Cavernous old oak rooms and classical music emanating from somewhere—pomp and circumstance, just like Yale.

Now my mother's calling me from downstairs. "Eric, Phoebe and Charlie are here."

I pop downstairs. Phoebe and Charlie are standing in the hallway with my mother. They look like refugees from a Grateful Dead concert and they've both got these big smiles on their faces like they're about to burst out laughing any minute. They're really only friends through me, but Phoebe said she'd pick up Charlie on the way over, and it's funny seeing them standing there together. Charlie smashed his mother's car against a telephone pole last week and now she won't let him drive. Sometimes I wonder how these two fuckups came to be my best friends, because a fuckup I most definitely cannot afford to be. But I know the answer. They're the only two people at school who I think are funny and interesting, and they're also the only two people who don't think I'm a nerdy intellectual freak. Or maybe they do, but they don't mind.

My mother looks at me skeptically when I come down the stairs. "We're having a little meeting in the kitchen," she says to the three of us, "but there's plenty of food if you guys want to have something on the porch."

"What do you have, Mrs. F.?" Charlie says, his words a little slower and louder than usual. "I'm starving."

"You guys can have a meatball sub, or a sausage sub. There's also potato salad and pizzelle cookies."

"Oh, I *love* those cookies!" Phoebe gushes. "Are those the Italian snowflake cookies, Terry?"

"That's right," my mother says, smiling. This isn't the first time she's seen Phoebe and Charlie in this state.

"They're so *pretty!*" Phoebe says. She's only about five two, but her long, flowing batik skirts and sandals and long, straight, stringy hair make her look even shorter. She sort of looks like what you'd get if you crossed Janis Joplin with a Cabbage Patch Doll, but I don't tell her that. Charlie, on the other hand, is over six feet and still seems to be growing. His flannel shirts and jeans always seem too short for his arms and legs. He's also got the biggest pair of feet I've ever seen, which usually smell because he goes around wearing big work boots without socks, even in the summertime.

"They are pretty cookies," my mother says with a little edge of mockery. She likes Phoebe and Charlie, but she knows they're fuckups and thinks their parents should have exercised a little more discipline with them. Charlie's parents have become experts at looking the other way, and Phoebe's mother and father are too busy running food drives and other charity events through their church. Mr. Signorelli is Italian and Mrs. Signorelli is Jewish, but they both became Unitarians when they got married. Phoebe sings and plays the tambourine in the congregation's folk band that plays in the basement of the church at the Sunday night coffeehouse, which she takes me to quite frequently. The band is called godjangle, with a lowercase *g*.

Now my mother stoops down and fingers the fabric of Phoebe's skirt. "*You* look pretty in that skirt, honey. Did you like the concert?"

Phoebe flings her head back and says in a deep, dramatic voice, "It was *amazing*. I was flying the whole time."

My mother laughs. "I'll bet you were," she says, which makes Charlie start laughing, too.

"Look, guys," I say, starting to feel a little edgy, "why don't we go to Harrington's Roast Beef and get a sandwich. I don't think I can take any more sausage today."

"You told me you *loved* the sausage today!" my mother says.

"I did. I just overdosed, that's all."

"Your brain is turning—to—*sausage,*" Charlie says to me in a Boris Karloff voice, his eyes huge.

"Let's go." I can't take this anymore.

"Why don't you take my car?" my mother says.

"Thanks, Ma." I grab the keys from the hallway table.

"Just call me if you're going to be late. You know I trust you guys."

"Thanks, Ma," I say again, giving her a kiss on the cheek. I know she partly wishes I'd stay in tonight, so she could tell me what happened at the meeting. My mother always needs to debrief, and it's usually with me that she has to do it. "We can talk in the morning," I say.

"I *love* riding in your hatchback, Terry," Phoebe says as we're walking out. "It's so compact!"

"Thanks, Phoebe," my mother says. "The hatchback loves you."

Charlie turns to me and says, "For the same reasons." My mother hears him and laughs ruefully before going back into the house.

"You two are so stoned," I say half-reprovingly as we get into the car.

"It's Phoebe's fault." Charlie adjusts the passenger seat so he can fit his legs inside. "I was just hanging out at home, innocently practicing my new techniques from drum camp, when she comes over straight from the Dead show and fills up a pipe with this amazing stuff."

"This stuff is *soooo* amazing, it's like total goodness and beauty washing over you," Phoebe rhapsodizes from the backseat, before leaning forward and setting the radio to WAAF, where, wouldn't it figure, they're playing more Grateful Dead.

"The show was incredible. I'm definitely taking you to the next one, Eric. It'll change your life."

"I like my life the way it is," I say.

"All you listen to is that faggy alternative shit," Charlie says. "You've got to listen to some classic rock. It's got the best drum shit."

"Dude," I say in a fake surfer accent. I love mocking Phoebe and Charlie's hippie talk.

"How's your scary Mafia family?" Phoebe asks me. She always says we're both lucky that we're half-breeds, so we're not completely under the evil spell of being one hundred percent Italian. "Did they break anyone's knees today?"

"Oh, please!" I laugh. "They *wish* they were Mafia. Then they'd have some real clout. They're just Merrimack Valley petty mercantiles. They don't even own any franchises."

"What was that meeting about, anyway?" Phoebe says.

"It's about what to do with my grandmother. She's staying with us now and they're trying to decide where she should live permanently."

"Oh, my God," Phoebe says. "The last time I saw your grandmother, she said to me, 'You're so cute. You look like a little stuffed elf you hang in the kitchen to keep out the devils.' "

This sets Charlie off on such a hard laughing jag that he starts snorting through his nose.

"Shut the fuck up, Charlie," Phoebe says. "You sound like a fucking 'tard." Then she remembers about Joani. "Oh my God, Eric, I'm so sorry! I didn't mean that."

"Don't worry about it," I say. Phoebe and everybody else are always slipping up around me and using the word *retard*. I tell myself that they're not even remotely thinking of a *real* mentally retarded person like Joani, but it still bothers me a little. I mean, why can't they just remember and use some other word?

"Oh, Eric, I brought something for you," Phoebe says, rummaging around in her big canvas bag. "Here it is."

She passes me a book over my shoulder. It's *Still Life with Woodpecker* by Tom Robbins, which she's been trying to get me to read for ages now. I have this funny feeling I'm not going to like it. I don't know—it just doesn't seem dignified enough for me.

"Thanks," I say. "I've been meaning to get this from you for a while."

"It's *soooo* excellent," Phoebe gushes some more. "It totally changed my life. I mean, Tom Robbins, he's really sharp."

"I can't wait to read it," I say again. "I don't know when I'm going to have time, with school starting Wednesday. Did you guys read anything on your reading list?" Phoebe and Charlie are smart enough to be in the top classes with me, but they usually get C's because they never do any work and the teachers are always threatening to demote them to a lower section. They basically get through because I dictate their papers to them over the phone the night before they're due.

"I read *Howl and Other Poems* by Allen Ginsberg," Phoebe says. "Four times. That's it, though."

"I read *Rolling Stone* all summer," Charlie says.

"How literary," Phoebe deadpans.

"Hey! I read it faithfully, every other week. That's self-discipline!"

"Yeah, that's stoic!" Phoebe hoots, using one of our favorite vocabulary words, and we all laugh. Privately, though, I'm always wondering what's going to happen to these two after graduation. Charlie says all he wants to do is move to Boston and work in a coffeeshop, get in with a good band, and play T.T. the Bear's every Friday night, but I know his parents are going to pressure him to go to college, *anywhere*, as long as it's private and looks bucolic and prestigious. Phoebe says she wants to go to some little semiagricultural school in the Berkshires and major in creative writing, but at the rate she's going, I don't know if she'll get in anywhere. She can't pass math to save her life; she says she has a quantitative learning disability. I wonder why Phoebe and Charlie don't approach the whole matter of the future with as much urgency as I do.

Thankfully, Harrington's Roast Beef isn't too crowded. It's a big high school hangout, and although I'd always much rather be sitting at Algiers in Cambridge sipping an espresso and nibbling at tabooleh, Harrington's has to suffice on those nights when we don't make it into the city, which, unfortunately, is most.

Phoebe and I order ice cream and Charlie gets a large roast beef sandwich with American cheese and barbecue sauce, as well as a large order of fries and a chocolate shake. He always gorges like this when he's stoned, which is often, and I don't know how he still manages to look like a scarecrow. I figure he must have a high metabolism.

Across the room from us are a group of West Mendhem High kids, incoming juniors probably, the girls all squealy in their little pastel shorts and moussed-up hair and the boys looking like little thugs-to-be in their football jerseys and spiky jock haircuts. They're exactly the kind of people Phoebe and I can't stand, which is most people at West Mendhem High, and most people in West Mendhem, for that matter. Charlie doesn't mind other people so much, largely because they don't give him a hard time. Charlie is very go-along, get-along, as my mother says of him, but that's because most of the time in school he's either thinking up drum riffs in his head, or stoned, or both. Sometimes I resent Charlie. I want to know where he gets off just moseying his way through life, never in a hurry, never stressed out, never cynical. I'd like to be that way some of the time, but it seems like a moot point, because I can't see it happening anytime soon.

Now the squealy-thuggy crowd is glancing over at us and I hear one of them say, just loud enough for us to hear it, "Fuckin' freaks."

Phoebe gives them a big shit-eating smile and blows them a huge kiss. They look away, giggling to themselves. "I hate those fuckin' brickheads and their skanky girlfriends," she says, her mouth full of ice cream.

"Why do you let them get to you?" Charlie says.

"Because they *oppress* me," Phoebe snaps back.

Charlie laughs dismissively. "I'm gonna write a song about them for you to sing in my band someday," he says, then, in a yodel, he sings, "Brickheads and skanky chicks / crampin' my style / Brickheads and skanky chicks—" He can't think of a rhyme, so he just sings, "Oh, yeah yeah yeah, baby."

"What about 'Brickheads and skanky chicks / makin' me smile'?" Phoebe sings.

"Or 'Brickheads and skanky chicks / fill me with bile'?" I join in.

Phoebe laughs now, some ice cream dribbling out of her mouth comically. "Or 'so fuckin' vile.' "

Charlie beats out a rhythm on the table. "Or what about 'Brickheads and skanky chicks / Like scum on a tile.' "

Phoebe and I explode now. " 'Like scum on a tile!' " Phoebe says. "That's very sophisticated, Charlie."

"Yeah," I say. "Gorgeous imagery. You hear that, and instantly you think, 'That's obviously Metengarten.' "

"Fuck you two," Charlie says, straight-faced, with about nine French fries in his mouth.

"Oh, Charlie, you're so full of life!" Phoebe erupts out of nowhere, imitating her mother, who grew up in Brookline. Phoebe usually refers to her mother as a dervish, a JAP, a society pig, or a shrew, depending on the latest anecdote involving Mrs. Shapiro-Signorelli and her various church or school-related projects about town.

Eventually, Charlie and Phoebe start coming down off their highs and nodding off. I collect their trash and throw it away, then collect the two of them and we head back out to the car.

It's a muggy, still night, as most of the late summer nights have been, and West Mendhem actually looks pretty, all leafy and shadowy under the moon, as I drive outcountry to drop the two of them off. Phoebe and I are going into Cambridge tomorrow so she can buy school clothes at the thrift shops, and she'll pick up her car at my house when we get back.

"School Wednesday." Charlie groans. "I can't believe it."

"I've got so much work to do this year," I say, more to myself than to either of them.

"If you work really hard, Eric, you can be anything you want to be," Phoebe says from the backseat. Through her drowsiness, I think I hear a little edge of meanness in her voice. I want to ask her exactly what the hell she means by that. But I don't. I just say, "Thanks for the vote of confidence." She doesn't answer.

After we drop off Charlie, Phoebe slumps down in the front seat and chews on her hair. The radio is on softly, the Grateful Dead again, and we're both quiet as I navigate around Great Lake Drive toward her house. I love these moments with her, driving her home, listening to the radio, the lake glinting periodically through the trees, and neither of us feeling like we have to say a thing.

When I pull into her driveway, I turn off the engine for a minute and it's quiet in the car. There are lights on in the living room window, but Phoebe's parents never pop their heads out to check on her when they know she's with me. I think it's because they're hip parents. Phoebe says it's because they trust me.

"Good night, darling," I say.

"Good night, darling."

We share our routine theatrical peck on the lips. Before she gets out, though, she stops, just a few inches from my face.

"I wonder if that'll ever turn into a real kiss," she says, giving me a dopey, stoned, lopsided smile.

"You mean with *tongue*?" I ask in mock approbation.

"With whatever." She's getting really dopey on me.

"Oh, please," I say. "I think you're just using me to get to Charlie Metengarten. He's your big, tall rock-and-roll fantasy."

She lets out a long, exaggerated sigh. "But he's not as clever as you are."

"But he's a rock star."

She just stares at me with that same dumb look for a few more seconds. Then she runs her hand through my hair and whispers, "Good night, little Eric."

"Good night, little Phoebe," I whisper back, mimicking her ridiculous smile, which she suddenly drops. Then she's out of the car and heading up the walkway to her front door.

Driving home, I've got the windows down and the radio on quietly. The air is sweet, and as I negotiate the sharp turns of Great Lake Drive, marked by yellow signs bearing squiggly black lines, I'm thinking about a whole jumble of things: my mother and Brenda fighting, Brenda and Frank fighting, Phoebe and Charlie and their constantly glazed-over expressions. Then there's school, that big airplane hangar building that smells always like foul putty, and then there's Yale, which looks like it can't really exist except as a backdrop for *This Side of Paradise* or *Love Story* or some other movie about rich, brilliant people acting out the drama of their lives. And there's me in this car, finally alone at the end of the day.

I drive by St. Banner, which sits in a kind of vale set back hundreds of yards from the road, barely visible through the trees and accessible only by two long, blacktopped driveways marked on the street by twin pillars of piled-up stone. Glancing away from the road, I can make out the modern buildings, the library and the hockey rink where I played on Saturday mornings when I was young, and around them, the old white clapboard buildings with windows lighted yellow, the buildings that must be where they live. At the bottom of it all is the lake, immense and black, where the rowers practice on fall afternoons and into which I've dived, late on summer nights, with Phoebe and sometimes Charlie, stoned and fully clothed and humming inside with fear and bravado.

Then I swear it's so bizarre, it's like my dream never ended, because I'm driving along and all of a sudden I see this figure walking along the narrow dirt shoulder of the road, head bobbing among the lowest reaches of the overhang from the maple trees. I get up a little closer and it's just who I thought, it's him—it is *he*—from the sub shop. He's walking fast, straight as a rod, almost like he's trying to put distance between him and St. Banner but he can't actually run because that might draw attention. He's wearing a funny cap, like a golfer's, pulled down severely over his head, and a white T-shirt glows against his neck and the surrounding shadows.

My window is rolled open, and I'm slowing down, pulling up closer to him without even really realizing that I'm stopping. He whips around, startled by the crawl of the car. His first look inside is terrified, rabbity. When he sees it's me, his whole face reframes itself in relief, until he pulls it back into that infuriating tight little smile and actually *bows* at me from the shoulder of the road. I've come to a dead stop, and I turn down the radio.

"It's my good man from the pizza emporium," he says, glibly, but not so glibly as the other night, because I've come upon him in flight, or transit, or something. Even as he addresses me, he keeps glancing back down the dark road toward St. Banner, but there are no other cars approaching, from either direction. He doesn't have that studied lethargy he had the night before; in fact, he looks a little bug-eyed, winded.

"What are you doing out in these parts?" he asks me, stooping down, scooping up a handful of gravel in the road's soft shoulder, rolling it around in his palm, like the Greek worry beads that Auntie Reenie hangs from the rearview mirror of her truck.

"I'm dropping off a friend at home," I say, innocent. "What are *you* doing out at this hour?"

"I'm memorizing the terrain, so I can escape one night to a friendly farmhouse on the Railroad."

"The railroad?" I ask.

He rolls his eyes, frowns at me in mock disappointment. "Yes, you know, the Railroad? The *Underground* Railroad? The thing that all you nice Massachusetts-y liberals set up to set me free?"

I haven't thought of the Underground Railroad since we studied it in maybe third grade. "But that was a long time ago," I stammer. Pathetically, it's all I can think to say.

"Ah yes," he says, speechifyingly, hand to his breast, "but it lives on in hearts like mine and yours. Does it not?"

"I suppose it does."

"You suppose it does."

I'm dumbfounded; I don't know how he can snap from utter solitude into this act, perfect grammar and all, caught alongside a road no less, without prompts or cue cards.

"Isn't this past your curfew?" I ask him. I'm idling the car by the side of the road, hoping no one's about to take the corner, especially a cop. You don't pull over in the middle of the night to talk to people you happen to pass on the road, at least not in West Mendhem, outcountry. I know he'd look suspicious. I know *we* would.

He looks at his watch, that expensive-seeming watch that looks like it should belong to a prosperous grown man, not an eighteen-year-old. "As of this moment, I am twenty-five minutes in excess of my curfew."

"Don't you ever worry about getting caught?"

"Of course," he says, so plainly that there's nothing more for me to say about it.

"Where are you going?" I ask him. "Really?"

"To get smokes—at that little store you told me about."

"But didn't you get them last night?"

"Uh-huh. And I smoked them all."

"That's a lot of cigarettes to smoke," I say.

He shrugs, loosing the gravel from his palm and back onto the road. I can hear the crickets buzzing from the trees behind him. Suddenly, he's bathed in light; a car emerges, slows, and curves only to clear my mother's hatchback, and vanishes past. But in this matter of seconds, he becomes rigid and ducks into the side of my car to obscure his face. It's his fault, I think, his choice to be breaking curfew, taking this risk. And yet some part of me is hurt by this, fleetingly protective of him and his immediate instinct to hide.

"Do you want a ride to the store?" I ask him. "I'll take you there and bring you back. You'll get back to S.B.A. faster, and nobody will see you."

He looks at me—suspiciously or what, I can't tell—then glances up the road again. "Very good," he says, low, and stalks around to the other side of the car, slips into the passenger seat, and sits up very straight. He's not much taller than me, but slender, and for some reason I think how odd it is to see his skinny legs, almost bony, stretched out in camping shorts against the powder-blue vinyl upholstery of the car.

I drive on; he's got those long, webby-looking hands clamped over his knees, and suddenly he's not saying a word. We pass the Shell station and Russ Treadwell's ice cream, both closed, both cast in the stripes of security lights, and all of a sudden, it's like I'm driving around in a town I've never seen before, after hours, locked up, and strangely forbidding.

"It's a pretty boring little town, isn't it?" I say, to break the silence.

"Excuse me?" he says in a small voice, staring straight ahead.

"I said, it's a pretty boring place. West Mendhem. There isn't a lot to do."

"Uh-huh," he says, very slowly, like he's thinking hard about it. But he doesn't take his eyes off the front window.

I pull up in front of Cumberland Farms, which seems empty except for the cashier, some acne-ridden high school kid in a Mötley Crüe baseball shirt.

"Here we go," I say, putting the hatchback into Park, leaving on the engine.

He pulls a decrepit five-dollar bill out of his wallet and hands it to me. "Would you kindly go inside and buy me a pack of Camel Filters?" he asks me, tentative and polite like I've never seen him before. "And an Orangina? And something for yourself, if you want it?"

"Don't you want to go?" I ask him.

He points into the store. "That same fellow was in there last night and gave me funny looks. I don't want him to start remembering my face."

"Why not?"

"Well—*because*. Because it's not wise."

"Um. Sure. I'll go," I say, turning off the engine.

He smiles, politely again, and it seems genuine. "Thanks so much— Eustace?"

I laugh. "No. Eric. I'm not some dandy in an Edwardian novel."

Now he laughs—a deep, abrupt laugh that feels to me like we've finally hit on some common point of humor, not a laugh at my expense or his. "I'm so sorry. Brooks," he says, holding out his hand with that funny, grown-up 1950s kind of rectitude.

"I know," I say, shaking his hand in the same phony-hale spirit. "I remember from last night."

In the store, I take from the glass refrigerator a Coke for me and an Orange Crush for him because there's no Orangina. (In fact, I don't think I've ever seen Orangina outside Boston or Cambridge.) At the counter, when I ask for a pack of Camel Filters, the Mötley Crüe kid gives me a curious look. Maybe he recognizes me as someone from school who doesn't smoke. I only vaguely recognize his face; to me, he looks like one of dozens of pimply wastoid underclassmen who skulk around the hallways between classes, going from small engines to gym to earth science, or whatever.

Back in the car, I hand him his cigarettes and Orange Crush. "They didn't have Orangina, so I got you this."

"Oh." He examines the Crush minutely. "Oh."

"What's wrong?" I ask.

"I don't think I can drink this. It's too leaden. It's hypercarbonated. That gives me the twitches."

"Oh," I say, distressed because he seems so distressed. "Do you want me to get something else?"

"No! No. Absolutely not. I'll just—I'll just hold onto this." And he cradles it, somewhat ridiculously, in his arms.

"Are you sure?" I ask, popping open my Coke and starting up the car.

"Yes. I'm quite sure. Thank you, Eric. You're very kind."

Pas de quoi, I say, gamely, and he laughs shortly, but not phonily. Soon, I'm pulling off Route 136 and replaning the hatchback onto Great Lake Drive, under the leaves of maple trees that meet in an almost perfect arch high above the middle of the road. He's packing his cigarettes, but not opening them up, and he's so quiet I'm struggling for something to say to cut the silence. But I don't have to. He speaks first.

"You start school soon?" he says to me.

"Wednesday," I say. "You?"

"As well, Wednesday."

"Are you nervous?" I ask.

"No. I'll do the work, and stay on, or I won't do it, and get kicked out. It's a simple choice. There's not a lot of gray area there. Why, are *you* nervous?"

He sounds disdainful, like he thinks I'm a grind who actually develops stomachaches over homework, which I don't. I get migraines.

"Well, you've got to understand, it's different going to public school. If you want to go to a good college, a really competitive college, it's not like you come with a seal of approval from a place like St. Banner. You've really got to distinguish yourself."

"I see," he says. Now he's got that faintly mocking edge back in his voice. "And what do you do to distinguish yourself?"

My first instinct is to enumerate for him the recipe for success I've enumerated for myself—grades, scores, awards, memberships, good attitude, and so on—but I don't like the feeling that he's ridiculing me again. "You find a cure for cancer in biology class" is what I say.

"Our medical establishment is in safe hands with you, I'm sure," he says in an ultra-bored drawl.

"Thanks," I say, sourly, and then, certainly without having intended to: "Why are you so fucking sarcastic about everything?"

"I'm so fucking *what?* I'm sorry?"

"Sarcastic," I say again. "And cynical. It's like, everything I say, you've got to cut down in some way, like you're some character out of—you know—"

"Out of an Edwardian novel?" he says, so fucking polite and acid I want to kick him out of the car. But I don't.

"*Exactly!* It's like you're incapable of ever being yourself, like you think you're Oscar Wilde or something. You're always onstage."

Somewhat to my surprise, he snorts. "Who the hell are *you* to tell me I'm not being myself?" His voice loses its I'm-so-bored lilt. Suddenly it's just loud, and harsh. "You're some silly-billy townie who served me my pizza and then gave me a lift tonight, probably hoping that I'd tell you more stories about Paris so you can plagiarize me in your stupid college admissions essay."

Then, I can't believe it, I'm so embarrassed I want to cry. "Get the *fuck* out of the car, you fucking snob!" I yell, pulling over to the side of the road. "I'm just as smart as you are, and I didn't get kicked out of two schools, either!"

He actually puts his long webby hand on the steering wheel and forces it back into the center of the road. "Of course they didn't kick you out," he says. "They need their little Ivy League token. But you'll probably end up at B.C. or Notre Dame, or some other place with a lot of dumb Catholic honkies."

"Fuck you! Lemme pull over!" I'm actually on the brink of tears now—I can't believe it, I'm so mortified with myself, because I never cry, and when I say "over," it comes out a big "ovah," and I sound just like the Massachusetts idiot he thinks I am.

"You pull over here, and I'll pull a knife on you," he says, his hand still on the wheel. "You offered me services and now you're going to render them." Then, in a horrible, imitation-slave voice, he says, "I's gonna learn you some responsibility, boy."

I give up struggling—not because I'm scared, but because he's won, he's humiliated me, and even kicking him out of the car right here wouldn't win things back for me. I stop sniffling and wipe my face dry. He takes his hand off the steering wheel and sits back in the seat. I just want to drop him off and never see him again, I'm thinking.

We proceed up Great Lake Drive in silence. I glance over at him once, and he's staring out the window. Then, out of nowhere, he says, "Maybe if you thought I was being *cynical* and *sarcastic* with you, that's because I thought you could give it back."

"Not according to what you just said now," I say, as calmly as him. "You just called me a townie and a dumb Catholic."

"Well, you called me a knife-wielding spook."

"No, I *didn't*," I say, outraged at his lie. But then it dawns on me that maybe he's trying to be funny.

"I'm afraid you did."

"You're right. I'm sorry. I guess my tongue slipped."

He doesn't laugh. Instead, he says, "I don't really have a knife."

"If you're running around West Mendhem in the middle of the night, maybe you should have one. It's a dangerous town."

"I know. Little literary *enfants terribles* joy-riding after dark in their mother's cars."

And—I don't know why—I laugh. It's a funny image.

Now we've approached the stone wall that cordons the St. Banner soccer fields off from the street. "Pull over here. That way I can run across the fields and slip in the back way."

I pull over into the shoulder of the road. "Would you douse your headlights for a minute, too?" he asks, and I do.

I can hear the crickets again in the bushes through the open window, and from beyond the soccer fields, there are squares of yellow light coming from the white buildings where they all live. I think about St. Banner, restful and assured in its green vale, and I think about him, who says he carries a knife but doesn't, and for the first time I think I might understand why he keeps creeping away at night.

"I'm quite ready for my reentry," he says, sotto voce, because it's very quiet now. "My good man, good night."

"Good night," I say, trying to sound a little exasperated, but that's not exactly what I'm feeling.

I'm waiting for him to get out. But he's not getting out. He's staring straight ahead, tightly gripping the Crush can in his hands.

"Eric," he says, low, and my own name has never sounded so strange. Eric—that's my name, people say it all the time, my family and friends, but I never see my face in my name when they say it.

"Uh-huh?" I ask, low, too. I'm shaking, and embarrassed because of it.

"I don't think you're a dumb Catholic."

"Thanks." It's all I can think to say.

"In fact . . ."

"Uh-huh?"

"I think you're quite bright for your demographic circumstances."

"Thanks. I think."

What kind of a compliment is that? I'm thinking. But when he puts his hand over the handle of the door, instantly I don't want him to leave.

"Brooks?"

"Yes?" He sounds weirdly patient, like a tired professor, like he never expected me to just let him vanish out of the car and across the dark soccer fields.

"Where did you say you were from again?"

He takes his hand off the handle and it falls between his knees. We're both staring straight ahead, not looking at each other, and he's not answering the question. In fact, neither of us says anything for what seems like forever.

"Virginia."

He moves his left hand up behind me and I can feel it now against the back of my neck, then his webby fingers running in my hair. I lean my head back against the seat of the car, and it's like some casing around my whole body cracks, the way you can crack an entire mirror by tapping in a nail, once, at the center. It's like I don't have joints anymore, or bones, like I'm made up completely of soft matter, and I'm falling. No one has ever laid hands on me this way before.

"Where in Virginia?" I ask. When I hear my own voice, it sounds like a hollow, dying reed coming up out of some deep swell of terror and anticipation in my gut.

"Coastal Virginia," he says. "In an old city. That's very southern. Um. And beautiful." He's running his hands up into my scalp, back again down my neck and underneath the collar of my T-shirt. I raise my right arm over his left until my hand finds the back of his neck. It feels cool and faintly powdery, and underneath his ridiculous cap, underneath the hair cut short on the back of his head, I can feel the contours of the base of his skull. It's strange to me; it feels so naked, like if he could let me know what the base of his skull feels like, then nothing he can say to me from now on, no bitchery or artifice, can ever cut me again.

"You live there with your parents?" I ask him.

"No. With a great-aunt." With his right hand, he pulls off his cap and puts it flat on his lap, but it's too late. Glancing down, I've already seen why. I'm in the same condition myself, and I know I should be embarrassed, but I'm not, oddly enough.

"You live with a great-aunt?" I ask. I know we're taking our chances; anybody could drive by right now—a proctor, someone I know from school, the cops—and it feels like we're sitting here in suspension until somebody does.

"Yeah," he says, laughing a little. "She's eighty-three. I'm going to get all of her money."

"Lucky you."

"Lucky me. Lucky Brooks." He bends down his head and rests it on the bridge of our arms. I turn off the ignition and lean back in the seat, running my hand through his hair. It's peculiar, though, because in the middle of this, we both actually start to nod off. It's the high beams of another car, rushing forward, that causes us both to jerk forward and duck down in our seats until it's gone.

"I should go," he whispers, so harshly it's almost a hiss, and reaches for the car door. He's immediately tense again, dart-eyed and in recoil, and so am I.

"Okay," I say, turning over the ignition. The noise is horrifying in the stillness. Now he's got one foot out of the car and he's scanning across the soccer fields, looking for watchmen, planning his route.

"Are you still slicing pizzas?" he asks me.

"Just Tuesday and Friday nights during school."

"I'll maybe visit some night," he says, so seriously I feel like he should hand me his business card.

"Don't get caught."

"Don't *you*. You're the one with something to lose, Horatio."

"What Shakespeare is that?"

He scowls. "It's not. Horatio *Alger?*"

"Oh."

"Ah, yes. You've heard of him." Then he closes the door—softly—and in a moment he's picked his way gingerly over the low stone wall, then he's running along the edge of the soccer fields near the woods. He's barely a shadow now, something faint and thumping against the grass in the middle distance of the field. I see him one more time—against the gray night sky, over the final rise at the far end of the field until it dips down into the campus—and then I am utterly alone by the side of the road.

Driving home, I'm preoccupied. I run a red light at the corner of Great Lake Drive and Route 136. A car coming from the left barrels wildly around me. *"Asshole!"* I hear, and catch about four upraised middle fingers flying from the windows as the car speeds on in the dark. My mother would call that a brush with death, but even a second after it's happened, the moment already seems a thousand miles away.

When I get home, the house is dark. Everyone seems to be away, asleep, and I make it up to my room unbothered. *I'm going to make a list of everything I have to do,* I tell myself. I even go as far as opening up a new notebook and writing "To Do: Academic Year 1986–87." But I don't write a thing, because my brain is humming like a crazy man's. I think about how far over the line I stepped tonight, and what if anyone in this house could read my thoughts right now, and do private thoughts leak? Do they show through, the way Grandma says you can't hide a sin, because it seeps through?

But the flip side of that, deeper than that, defiantly and so thirsty for the precise cataloging of movement from just twenty minutes before: I think about the exact pressure and configuration of his hand on the back of my neck and the lineaments of his skull inside my palm, and the tents we each pitched in our shorts, and how mine is creeping back on me now—desire strong enough to summon it back even as the moment recedes—and how your own name can ring out in your head like a siren when somebody utters it plainly in want. And also, kneeling here now in the room where I have slept untouched for most of my life, I feel so loose of limb, like a husk just splintered, like a secret that cracks cleanly out from its heart and along the path of its fibers.

Now I'm carrying this secret on my person, already finding that it's a nerve-racking thing, it's like an explosive; you can't ever jar it or walk carelessly. But as it grows in discomfort, it becomes more exquisite, too, if that makes any sense at all. Because you can't share it with anyone, and precisely for that reason, maybe it's the only thing that's completely yours.

Three

It's a Friday night around ten, and I'm starting to wrap things up at B.J.'s. When I say that, I mean it literally, not idiomatically: I'm actually wrapping up unused tomato halves in saran. There's hardly anyone in here, except for two old men who live in the apartments for the elderly around the corner (they're playing poker and talking about being stationed at some camp in Delaware during World War II) and Jimbo McGoff, who's hunched over, shredding up napkins and talking to himself about dinosaurs, his favorite topic. Jimbo is the town crazy; he rides around all day on his old Schwinn in a trench coat and beat-up wingtips, getting kicked out of Dunkin' Donuts and various stores. Phoebe thinks Jimbo is sexy. She says he looks like William S. Burroughs, and whenever she sees him, she wants to "interview" him about his philosophical beliefs for the school paper. I beg her to leave him alone, and she does, grudgingly. "I'm just fascinated by the way his mind works," she says. "He could be you in twenty years, or me, or any of us."

It's been a trying week, and I'm wondering how I'm going to get through this year and keep my bearings with everything going on. First, school started: the same joyless putty-smelling corridors, burnt-orange carpeting, and particleboard bacon burgers for lunch. All the idiot students look the same, but this year, not only do I have to contend with a new crop of honors-class teachers, I have to get nearly perfect grades in their classes *and* ingratiate myself with them so they'll write me sterling college recommendations. Phoebe and Charlie are in most of my classes; I've already given each of them the plot, themes, and symbolism of *Tess of the D'Urbervilles* so they can write the first English paper on their favorite book from the summer reading list.

The only teacher I find interesting (in a slightly creepy way) so far this year is Mrs. Bradstreet, who teaches honors American history. All the other teachers (guys) in the social studies department talk disparagingly about her because she went to Wellesley, and they all grew up in West Mendhem and played varsity football for the old high school before going to state teachers college and returning to the new high school, mostly to coach varsity football.

The *real* story, which Mrs. Bradstreet told us standing up on the first day of class and reading an essay she had written called "Living Inside American History," is that she *had* gone to Wellesley, in 1965, "like every nice Bronxville girl educated at Emma Willard," but then dropped out to join the Freedom Rides—"which we'll be examining later in the year, and I'll bring in photographic documentation."

Her essay ended there, and she assigned us to write what she called a think piece on the same topic, "Living Inside American History," due Friday. She doesn't tell us how she ended up, rather incongruously, at West Mendhem High, but enough people in school have talked about her for me to know the basic story: somewhere along the line, after her Freedom Riding hippie years were over and she had come to teach at West Mendhem High School, she met Nathan Bradstreet, who's a selectman in town. His family was one of six to settle West Mendhem about three hundred and fifty years ago, and today he owns roughly half of it, with a street, an elementary school, and three Revolutionary War monuments around town, all bearing his family name. Nathan Bradstreet is nearly twice her age, filthy rich but destitute-seeming in his L.L. Bean rags from the 1950s, with no occupation other than his selectman's post, which he's held for twenty-five years.

The conventional wisdom is that Mrs. Bradstreet married Nathan Bradstreet for his money. I don't know if that's true or not, but Mrs. Bradstreet *does* spend every summer in places like Nepal or Bora Bora, *without* Nathan Bradstreet, who doesn't look like he's ever set foot outside West Mendhem for longer than a day. (He'd need a change of clothes.) This past Wednesday, the day she read the essay, Mrs. Bradstreet was deeply tanned and wearing a huge necklace of carved wood gazelles, which Erin O'Rourke (a dumb, cutesy girl in my class) told her was "wicked cool."

"Why, thank you, Erin," Mrs. Bradstreet said in her weirdly measured voice, taking off the necklace and solemnly handing it to Erin for inspection. (To me, Mrs. Bradstreet seems to have the grim, regal bearing of a court royal being carried off to the guillotine.) "It was given to me as a gift by the natives of a village I stayed in this summer in Burundi, helping to build a clinic. It's a symbol of the strength and beauty of mothers."

To which Erin O'Rourke said, baffled, "Oh. Cool," and handed the necklace back like it was infected. "Where's Burundi?" I heard her asking people later.

"Mr. Fitzpatrick," Mrs. Bradstreet called to me from her desk as people were filing out at the end of the first class. When I looked her way, she said something so low and quiet, I couldn't hear her.

"I'm sorry?" I said, stepping up closer to her desk.

"I said, I hear from Mrs. Bissett that you're quite the young bard."

"Oh, God. Whatever. Mrs. Bissett was a great teacher," I said, lying. Mrs. Bissett was my English teacher last year and wasn't good for teaching us how to diagram a sentence.

"You have ambitious postsecondary plans, I presume?"

"I don't know," I said. "I'm looking at Yale."

She gave me a broad, conspiratorial smile, as if the very word *Yale* was a delicious little secret the two of us shared. "Ah, God and man at Yale," she said. "But you've got to watch out there."

"Why's that?"

"Because they're *puckish* at Yale. Everyone," she said, almost like she was reading me a sonnet or something. "At least the ones I used to know."

I laughed. "I don't think of George Bush as very puckish," I said, glad for a chance to let her know that I understood the meaning of "puckish."

"Mr. Fitzpatrick," she said, pointing her pen at me. "I think you are grossly overcalculating my age."

"Oh," I said, flustered. "I didn't mean that. He just came to mind when you said Yale. I wasn't insinuating you were contemporaries."

"No," she said, then, after a pause, "nor soulmates. You're not a Reagan Democrat like the rest of this community, are you?"

I laughed again, slightly bewildered. "I'm politically apathetic, like the rest of my generation," I said—jokingly, but more or less honest.

"We'll have to change that this year."

"I wish you luck."

"Good day, Mr. Fitzpatrick."

"Good day," I said awkwardly, mimicking her formal tones. She smiled—indulgent bordering on condescending, I thought—and I slipped between two dividers and out of the space.

Outside in the corridor, Phoebe and Charlie were having some whispered, giggly-looking conversation against Phoebe's locker, which she had already plastered with photographs of Jerry Garcia, Charles Bukowski, and Airplane-era Grace Slick.

"I'm not interrupting anything, am I?" I said when I approached them.

"You're so paranoid, Eric," Charlie said, looking away. "We're not the fucking KGB. You gotta chill."

"We were just talking about what a kook Mrs. Bradstreet is," Phoebe said. "Why is she writing essays for *us*? That wasn't about American history. It was *her* neurotic D.A.R. history, that's what it was."

"She just told me Yale was very puckish, then she asked me if I was a Reagan Democrat," I said.

"Why did she ask you that?" Charlie said.

"I don't know," I said. "I feel like she's set on watching me this year or something."

"That is scary shit!" Phoebe said.

"She's hot for you, Eric," Charlie said.

"Delightful. Are you two ready for English with the sparkling Goody Farnham?" We've nicknamed Mrs. Farnham, our new English teacher, Goody Farnham because we're reading colonial American writing and her pinched face, severe hairbun, and apparent total lack of joy in the world of literature remind us of a butter-churning Puritan wife.

"Go on without me," Charlie said. "I've got to hit the john first."

"What were you two whispering about?" I asked Phoebe again as we headed off to English class in Learning Pod 4A.

"Nothing," she said, irritated, walking faster than usual.

"It didn't seem like nothing."

Finally, she stopped and looked at me. "Well, if you must know, it was a very small something."

"What?" I said.

Phoebe squirmed a little in embarrassment. "Well, what do you think?" she said, looking away from me.

"Oh my God!" I said, low. "Are you two— I can't believe it."

"What?" she said, embarrassed but also enjoying the revelation. "We're nothing—really. Or maybe we are. How the fuck should I know?"

"Did you get together?"

"Sort of."

"When?"

"Last night. I taped a Dead show that he wanted for him and I brought it over."

"And?" I couldn't believe that my two best friends—who only knew each other, barely, on account of me—had gone ahead and hooked up behind my back.

"And what? He asked me if I wanted some pot in his room and we had some. And then we fooled around a little. What's wrong with that? Charlie's great. He's cooler than all the other sausages in this school. He's got excellent taste in music and he's got hair like Jackson Browne."

"Charlie is excellent, Phoebe, but he's not *sharp.*"

"He is, too, sharp," she said, indignant. "He just hides it under all this stoner stuff. He doesn't bend over backwards proving he's sharp all the time, like *some* people."

"Oh, I wonder who you could mean by that?" I said, suddenly feeling very crummy.

Phoebe gave me a funny look. "I'm sorry, Eric. I didn't mean that. You *know* who I like better between the two of you. You know who makes me laugh, and challenges me, and truly appreciates my singular sense of humor. But I gave Charlie a vibe and he gave me one back. You never give me a vibe back."

"I'm sorry. I didn't know I was supposed to be your personal pleasure orb."

"Fuck you!" She kicked me clumsily in the shin and stalked into class.

All through English with Goody Farnham, Phoebe, Charlie, and I kept exchanging glances: Charlie looking apologetic at me, me looking baffled and suspicious at Charlie; Phoebe looking sourly at me; Charlie and Phoebe looking sheepishly at each other, when they could manage to do it at all. My crummy feeling seemed to seep out of a little cavity in my stomach. The two of them together didn't feel right to me at all; I felt like they had gone behind my back and deliberately betrayed me, especially because I thought that Phoebe and I had always had a sort of understanding. Of course, we weren't together like *that*— that would spoil it, we always said—but otherwise we considered ourselves virtually married. We called ourselves F. Scott and Zelda Fitzgerald, James and Nora Joyce, Virginia and Leonard Woolf. We were partners in crime, we said. We called each other darling. We shared everything.

My crummy feeling only worsened when Goody Farnham announced that as a mandatory class assignment we had to enter a youth essay contest sponsored by the *Boston Globe* called, repulsively, "What I Cherish in America." The idea was that despite poverty, crime, the threat of nuclear annihilation, rising taxes, and terrible diseases like AIDS, there was still a lot to love about the United States, and who better to remind everyone but the rising young people of the nineteen-eighties? The top three winners would get to read their essays at some V.I.P. dinner in Boston and First Place would also win a personal computer to take to college. Goody Farnham told us she didn't care what we wrote about, as long as it was typed, double-spaced, and submitted to her in two weeks.

"If we can pull a winner out of this class, even just third place, that looks great for West Mendhem High when the accreditation team comes around next year," she said, stifling a yawn and latching back a tendril that had escaped from her skin-tight bun. "And it also looks great on a college application. So just crank something out and I'll put them in the mail next week."

With that, she steered us back to Cotton Mather, about whom she actually seemed to have a notch more than her usual cursory commentary.

I was personally furious that Goody Farnham would waste our classroom time using us as pawns in a mercenary game, but I also needed her for a recommendation in a few months and couldn't afford to risk her goodwill. So I said nothing and jotted the assignment—imbecilic title and all—down in my notebook. Then I went back to brooding at Phoebe and Charlie, feeling crummy that I obviously hadn't picked up my cue when Phoebe chose to send me a vibe.

Things got even stranger that Thursday. I was at home, helping Joani with homework in the den as my mother and father watched *The Cosby Show* and Grandma fell off to sleep on the couch, her ragged snores beginning to annoy us. (Nobody has come to a decision about Grandma yet, so she's still with us.)

We heard the front door slam. Brenda walked into the middle of the den and stood there like a totem pole. She still had her little name tag from the card shop pinned to her shirt.

"I can't believe it," she said once, in a strained half-whisper. "It's like a nightmare! I can't believe it."

We all looked up while *Cosby* prattled on, and Grandma stirred from her nap with the crashing noise of an interrupted snore.

"Honey, what is it?" my mother said, scared. I knew she was thinking something had gone wrong with the baby.

"You remember Kerrie Lanouette, that slutty girl I graduated from high school with?" Brenda said, collecting herself a little.

"Slut," Joani repeated, and broke out into hysterics.

"Watch your mouth," Grandma said through a yawn.

"Isn't she working at the package store on 136 now?" my father said. "I went in there the other day on an account and she was behind the counter."

"She was," Brenda said ominously. "She was. But not anymore."

"Why not?" I said.

"Because—because I was at work tonight, and Kathy Fanuele comes in, whose father's a Statie, and she tells me that this afternoon they found— Oh, my God, this is so *sick!*"

"Joani, honey, will you go in the kitchen and bring Mummy another cup of decaf?" my mother said.

"I wanna hear!" Joani whined.

"Joani, don't be a brat!" my mother said. "Get Mummy a cup. You can have a Ring-Ding and some milk if you want, over the kitchen table. On a plate!"

Joani lumbered up and padded out of the den, rolling her eyes.

"They found *what?*" I said again, even though I already had a good enough idea.

"They found her *body* all—mangled up—off a dirt road in Harold Porter State Park today."

"Jesus Christ," my father said, low.

"Jesus Christ, Mary, and Joseph!" my mother said. "Now I'm gonna have nightmares for a week."

"You think *you* are!" Brenda said. "I'm already having them, and I haven't even gone to bed yet."

"That's what the world is comin' to," Grandma said, fully awake now, and unfazed. "Every day, it's rape this, murder that. I can't watch the news no more. You know whose fault is it, don't you? God forgive me, it's those damn P.R.'s that took over Leicester."

"Ma, stop it!" my mother said, distracted.

"God forgive me, it's true," Grandma said.

"Kathy said her father said there was a witness who saw Kerry walking down 136 after she got out of work this morning," Brenda said. "And the witness said she was walking down 136 with some dark-looking guy."

"Oh, for God's sake," my father said, but I couldn't understood what he meant.

"Brenda"—my mother lowered her voice and craned her neck toward the kitchen to see if Joani was out of earshot—"did Kathy's father say it had also been a—you know—"

"A rape?" Brenda said bluntly.

"Yeah, if you have to shout it out with Joani in there," my mother snapped.

"Kathy said her dad said that's what it looked like, but they've got to examine her, and give her, you know—"

"The autopsy?" I said.

"Yeah, that. But Kathy said her clothes were all ripped off."

"Oh, good Lord," my mother said, and she and Grandma both crossed themselves.

"What the hell was she doing in Harold Porter anyway?" my father said. "It's right on the Leicester line, it's totally deserted. Nobody goes in there now except for drug dealers. It's not a family picnic place like it used to be when I was a kid."

"Some kids from West Mendhem High hang out there at night to drink," I said, "but they go in big groups."

"How should *I* know what she was doing in there in the middle of the day, anyway?" Brenda said, bristling. "I'm not her keeper. She was always kind of a slutty lowlife anyway, always hanging out at the Showcase Cinema and the mall with guys from Leicester and Methuen."

"It's not fair to call her a slut just because she socialized in a lower economic bracket, Brenda," I said.

"Oh, shut up, Eric. You know what I mean," Brenda snapped at me. "Anyway, Kathy thinks she was seeing some Puerto Rican guy and she didn't want anyone to know about it. She should have known better. I called Frank at work and told him about it and he said the same thing. But isn't it *horrible!*" She slipped back into the aggrieved mode with which she had entered the room. "It's like, this could almost happen to *any* girl. It's like, even West Mendhem isn't safe anymore."

"I told you, that's what the world is comin' to. It's the devil's work," Grandma said again, as though we had all missed her point the first time.

"So what are they doing about it?" I asked.

"Kathy said the West Mendhem and Leicester police were teaming up and searching all over Leicester looking for guys that fit the description of the person that the witness saw Kerrie with."

"All they know is that he's a dark-skinned guy?" I said. "That's, like, two-thirds of Leicester."

"Kathy said they also said he was kinda fat. Not fat, like, but kinda beefy. And I think she said he had a beard, too."

"That's a big help," I said. "Aren't they going to look in West Mendhem and other places, too?"

Brenda shrugged. "I don't know. I guess so. Anyway, Kathy said the

Leicester Tribune and even the *Boston Globe* were on the story and it's gonna be on the front of all the papers tomorrow. And Kathy also said that her mother's so upset that this kind of stuff is leaking into West Mendhem that she's going to organize some kind of rally on the Common on Sunday afternoon. Some kind of 'Take Back Our Town' rally, where everybody speaks out against the crime and drugs that are coming in from Leicester."

"That's good," Grandma said, nodding. "You gotta stand up and fight this stuff. That's what we would have done in the old days." Nobody had any idea what she meant by that, so we just let it pass.

"Everybody should just take a deep breath and calm down first," my father said, his usual exhortation in any crisis short of an earthquake. "One little incident doesn't mean the Puerto Ricans and the others in Leicester are coming in to take over."

"Art, would you call this just a 'little incident'?" my mother said sarcastically.

"Terry—"

"What?"

"Why do you wanna give me backtalk like my kids give me backtalk?"

"I'm not giving you *backtalk.*" My mother looked like she was going to explode. "I'm just saying, maybe this is more serious than you think. Joani!" she called into the kitchen. "Are you gonna bring me my decaf, honey?"

"Tonight, I'm prayin' twice as hard for God to stop the world from comin' to this," Grandma said.

Joani padded back in, sloshing coffee in a mug with one hand and carrying a Ring-Ding on a plate with the other. "Isn't anyone gonna tell me nothing?" she said.

"Gonna tell me *anything,*" I said automatically, but too harshly, and Joani blushed furiously without repeating my correction, which she usually does. I felt bad and gave her a squeeze on the fanny, but she didn't smile. And a creepy kind of quiet set in, with all of us sitting there, waiting for something to happen, and *The Cosby Show* blared on.

Brenda was right. The story made the front page of both the *Tribune* and the *Globe,* with Kerrie Lanouette's tacky-looking high school graduation picture and stories that said state and local police were searching greater Leicester (that's the term they used) for a dark-skinned man who fit the description. Even worse, all the Boston news stations covered the stories as well, with thriller-movie-style camera shots zooming over the very dirt road off which they had found Kerrie's body. There was even a horrible interview with Kerrie Lanouette's parents in front of their ranch house with the Virgin Mary statue on the lawn and Kerrie's haggard mother bawling on about what a good girl her daughter was, how she had loved collecting teddy bears and stuffed animals, and how excited she had been because she had just gotten her first Cabbage Patch Doll. (These struck me as strange preoccupations for a twenty-year-old woman, but I guess Kerry hadn't had a lot of other things in her life to bring her pleasure.)

"Good girl!" Brenda spat, watching the news with me. "What a crock of shit! She was the biggest friggin' slut West Mendhem High has ever seen."

Brenda was also right about the protest. That following Sunday afternoon, about two hundred people—mostly parents, but a lot of kids, too, including some of my classmates—congregated on the West Mendhem Common and took turns speaking into a megaphone, saying things basically along the line of "We worked hard to be able to move to West Mendhem, and we didn't move here to watch our children get abducted and mutilated and our property values go down." Nobody came out and specifically accused the Puerto Ricans, or the Dominicans, or even Leicester in general; it was more like "those who would like to see West Mendhem go down the tubes just like their own communities" and that sort of thing. No one in my family went to the rally; we've never been really involved in town affairs. It was Phoebe who told me about it, who said the whole thing was so bourgeois and racist she almost puked. She accompanied her mother, she said, who went as a representative of the Unitarian church, hoping to make a little pitch about harmony and understanding and the need for open dialogue between the two communities. But, Phoebe said, she never got a chance. Kathy Fanuele's mother, who had organized the rally, kept pushing Mrs. Shapiro-Signorelli's name further and further down the list on her clipboard, until dusk came and they cut the speaking short.

Other than a lot of random shouting, Phoebe said, the upshot of the rally was this: they were going to put up posters of Kerrie Lanouette's high school graduation picture all over town, with an inscription that read: "Kerrie Lanouette, 1966–1986. We Won't Forget," and start a scholarship fund in her name. They were going to print bumper stickers that read "I Support a Crime-Free West Mendhem." They were going to lobby for a staff increase at the West Mendhem Police Department at the next town meeting, so all-night patrol cars could cruise the parts of town that bordered Leicester. There were other things they said they were going to do, and over the next few weeks, then months, they did them: they picked up their children after sports practice and dance practice and student council meetings, because they didn't want them walking home in the blue-gray West Mendhem dusk. They would have started locking their doors at night, but they did that, anyway, so now they bought alarms for their cars and their houses. And what had been a murmur of fear, which piety and guilt repressed, became perfectly audible conversation—accepted fear, justified loathing, a topic of the day in stores, on street corners, after church. People started saying they finally knew why the Irish pitched such a fit over the forced busing in Boston ten years ago. They said you had to see the threat in your own backyard before you realized.

Meanwhile, the search for the killer continued, and images of Kerrie Lanouette's dazed teddy-bear face started appearing everywhere, in store windows, in the corridors of schools, on telephone poles—in such profusion that if you squinted in the blue-gray dusk, they almost seemed to float in the streets, populating West Mendhem like a copycat army of townie girls rubbed out even before they reached majority, dispossessed of the storybook riches of growing up, growing old in a sepia-perfect New England village.

Walking home from school today, I passed a little group of mothers hanging the first crop of posters of Kerrie Lanouette. They didn't take me by surprise, because the high school was already one big beehive of talk about the murder. Kids in classes had told the teachers they couldn't focus on the lessons that day because they were so upset, so—whether this was genuinely true or whether it was a way out of classwork for a warm Friday in the beginning of September—every class turned into a little speakout. A few teachers and a handful of girls said that whether or not Kerrie Lanouette was going out with a Puerto Rican from Leicester didn't matter, because she was still a victim of a horrible crime, but most, including girls, said she asked for it by going off into the woods with some stranger. Ms. Mahoney-Smith, a music teacher who lives with her sculptor husband in Rockport, wants the health classes to do a segment on rape awareness, but already Mr. McGregor the principal, an overweight army vet, is resisting. He says the word "rape" shouldn't even be coming up in a "learning environment." At any rate, everyone's buzzing.

A Volvo passed by with a sticker for St. Banner on the back, probably the vehicle of some proud local parent whose kid was a dayhop at the school, a townie charity case. And I thought of the sweet, muggy smell of shrubbery by the side of the road near the stone wall of the St. Banner soccer field from a week before—and I thought that it was my shift at the sub shop in a few hours. My stomach flopped, and I got that strange feeling that I was walking around a town I didn't know, and that feeling didn't pass until a little kid on a Big Wheel came plowing down the sidewalk and almost ran me over in my distraction.

I wasn't halfway into the house when Brenda, holding the keys to her Mazda, yanked off my backpack, threw it down in the hall, and pulled me back outside.

"Ma's making me go to Grandma's apartment and get more clothes and some other stuff," she said, stalking toward her car. "You gotta come help me."

"I wanted to take a nap before work tonight," I said.

"You can take it later, but you gotta come now. I hate prowling around that smelly apartment by myself."

Helplessly, I got in. Brenda popped in a Led Zeppelin tape and roared off toward I-95, to the apartment complex where Grandma had lived ever since she sold her big house in Leicester fifteen years ago.

"Brenda, why does Grandma need more clothes?" I asked, turning the music down just enough so I could hear myself think. "Ma can just wash the stuff she has, and she's probably going home soon, anyway."

Brenda hit the dashboard with the side of her fist. "You really wanna know why we're getting more stuff for Doris?" Brenda always calls Grandma by her first name, Doris, when she's talking just to me.

"Do I?" I asked.

"I don't think so, but I'm gonna tell you anyway. It's 'cause, guess

74

who's coming to live with the lucky Fitzpatrick family?"

"Are you serious? Permanently?"

"Indefinitely. At least, that's what Ma said, anyway."

"But I thought Ma and Uncle George and everybody else were working this out."

"Well, it looks like they did. Duh!" Brenda said sarcastically. "They had a huge phone call marathon this morning when I was at work, and this is what they decided. That for right now, anyway, Doris was better off with us than in her own place or in a home."

"What did Ma say about that?"

"What could she say? You know Ma. She's not as ballsy as Auntie Lani or Auntie Reenie and she doesn't whine her way out of things like Auntie Winnie. She just said to me, 'Everybody's got responsibilities, and this is one of mine.' And that she thought maybe it would be good, because Doris could cook and stuff and watch Joani while she's at work."

"What does Dad think of this?" I asked.

"He said, 'Fine, fine.' You know him. He's so fuckin' dead to the world, he doesn't care one way or the other."

"He's not dead to the world, Brenda. He's just got a very laissez-faire attitude about things."

"Like I said." Brenda shrugged. "Dead to the world."

I let it go. "What about Grandma? She doesn't mind giving up her place?"

"Doris?" Brenda said, more sarcastically than before. "Doris? She couldn't be happier. She says now she gets to be surrounded by her favorite daughter—she's calling Ma her favorite daughter now—and three of her beautiful grandchildren, even though I know the woman can't stand me. And she says she's gonna make Joani into a real Italian cook, and a seamstress and a wonderful homemaker, even though maybe Joani should concentrate on learning how to *add* first, don't you think?"

"Brenda!"

"Well, it's true! I mean, who the fuck needs school when you have Doris Ianelli living in your house, pretending it's the old country and helping you beef up your dowry?"

It occurred to me that Brenda could be very cutting when she wanted to, but I didn't flatter her by letting her know it. "What are *you* gonna do over the next few months, now that she's going to be around every day?" I asked. I figured it had to be on her mind.

"I'm just gonna tell her I'm getting fat from all her delicious pastafazooli meals. And then, when it *comes*—" Brenda suddenly stopped and violently popped the Led Zeppelin out of the deck. "I'm sick of this fucking tape," she said, and popped in another.

"Yeah?" I asked.

"When it comes, I'm gonna tell her it was an immaculate conception. She'll believe it, she's so fuckin' religious. She'll believe anything, if you tell her Jesus did it."

"She's not *that* religious," I said. "When you start to show, she's gonna know."

"Well, maybe I'll go live somewhere else until it comes," she said.

"You could go live with Frank. Maybe you two could get a place together. You're going to be doing that anyway, right?"

"I'm sure it will all work out" was all she said. Then, out of nowhere, she asked me, "Eric, are you going out with your little Jewish friend?"

"Her name's Phoebe, Brenda, and she's only half Jewish. You always call her my little Jewish friend. It sounds very anti-Semitic."

"What?"

"It means not liking Jews."

"I don't have anything against the fucking Jews," she snapped at me. "You're always looking for a fight, Eric. I just wanted to know if you two were, you know, going out or something, because you spend so much time together."

"We're just friends," I said, sullenly. I didn't feel like telling her about Phoebe and Charlie. Somehow, telling people that my two best friends had started going out made me feel like an underdeveloped eunuch.

"Oh," Brenda said, giving me that I-don't-really-care-about-your-business look. "Well, it's nice that you have girl friends. I mean, you know, girl *friends*. Not girlfriends."

"I know what you mean," I said.

"Anyway, I was just curious."

"Is your curiosity sated?" I asked.

"Huh?" she asked, pulling into the parking lot of Grandma's apartment complex.

"Is it satisfied?"

"Huh? Yeah. Sure."

First, Brenda pulled all of Grandma's mail out of her box—mainly bills, grocery store circulars, and parishioner bulletins from St. Agnes's Church—and stuffed it into her pocketbook. After fumbling with the key combinations for a moment, we got into the apartment, which smelled, as it always had, of Grandma: a funny mixture of oven grease, oregano, mothballs, and Oil of Olay. It hadn't been cleaned in a while, and a particularly thick layer of dust lay on everything—the old cedar furniture, the dozens of graduation and wedding photographs framed and propped up on doilies, the colossal old hi-fi with the straw weaving over the speakers, the huge, maudlin-looking crucifix hanging over Grandma's bed. I had to agree with Brenda: it *was* a little depressing, a whole framed legion of smiling children and grandchildren, even Jesus himself, collecting dust, waiting for Doris Ianelli to return and beam complacently back at them.

Brenda pulled an old suitcase out from under the bed, blew off the dust, and flung it open on the bed. "Ma gave me a list of stuff to get," she said, pulling a piece of paper out of her pocketbook. "What's first here? Underwear. Okay." She opened the top drawer to Grandma's dresser, pulled out a clump of plus-size panties and bras, and dumped them into the suitcase.

"Don't you want to count them out and fold them?" I asked.

"What difference does it make?" she said, throwing in a pile of nylons, even more sloppily than before.

"I don't know. Ma's gonna be mad when she sees that mess." I went over to the suitcase to start putting things in order.

"Eric, just let me fuckin' do it!" Brenda screamed at me, slamming the top of the suitcase down over my hand.

"Jesus, Bren, that hurt! What are you, on the goddamned rag or something?" I yelled back, rubbing my hand, before I even knew what I had said.

"That is so fucking funny, you asshole," she said to me in a low voice.

"Brenda. I'm sorry. That was stupid."

"Just forget it," she said, suddenly looking wildly around the room before she landed back down on the list. "Look, Ma says here she wants some books, and there's a whole pile under the stereo in the living room. Why don't you go pick them out, being the literary one of the family? I'll get the rest of her shit in here."

"All right," I said, desperate to make up for my gaffe. Sure enough, underneath the hi-fi, I found books—dozens and dozens of paperback romance novels with covers of uncorseted women held captive in the arms of huge, strapping shirtless pirates and royal-looking types. I laughed out loud to discover that Grandma had such prurient reading taste, and I spent about ten good minutes picking out about a dozen of the trashiest titles I could find.

Finally, I scooped them all up in my arms, hoping Brenda would get a kick out of my choices. But in the doorway of Grandma's bedroom, I stopped. Brenda was sitting on Grandma's bed, her back to me, holding and staring at our parents' wedding picture, which Grandma kept on her dresser. I heard her make a funny kind of croaking noise, and before I could tell if she was crying or not, I slipped back out into the living room and sat in the rocking chair for a few more minutes, pretending to be engrossed in one of the Harlequins.

"Brenda, you've got to see these books Grandma's got!" I finally yelled, trying not to sound too fake-cheery, and when I went back in the bedroom with the books, Brenda was looking busy, folding up the underwear and putting it back neatly in the suitcase. She was trying to look as though she'd never stopped packing, although when I glanced over to the top of the dresser, I noticed that our parents' wedding picture was skewed out of place from the rest.

"Oh, yeah? What's there?" she said with a little I'm-pretending-to-be-interested smile.

"Look at this pulpy stuff!" I said, putting the books down on the bed. "She's got tons of these in there under the stereo."

"Shit." Brenda laughed without really seeming to see.

I started helping her fold Grandma's enormous underwear and she didn't object. We were both quiet for a little while, until, not stopping her folding, Brenda said to me in her matter-of-fact-sounding voice, "Eric?"

"Yeah?"

"You know how when we were little, Grandma was always, like, 'If you do that, you're gonna go to hell'?"

I laughed. "Yeah?"

"I mean, do you think she really believes that shit?"

"It's what she's been taught to believe, and she's probably never questioned it," I said.

"Well, I mean, that's what we were taught, too. I mean, do *you* believe it?"

I laughed again. "Well, I guess—no, of course I don't believe it. That's just ridiculous Catholic doctrinology. It's just a control mechanism. You know what they say, Brenda: religion is the opiate of the masses."

"Who said that?"

"Marx."

"Mark who?"

"Marx. Karl Marx. The founder of Marxism—you know, like communism, like in Russia. He believed that religion was just a device used by those in control to keep the poor in their place."

"Oh," Brenda said, looking slightly annoyed. "Well, that's not exactly what I meant."

"Oh. Well, what did you mean?"

"I mean, do you think if— Okay, say, if Ma had gotten pregnant with me before she got married, do you think she ever might have thought of *not* getting married—and just having me anyway?"

I put down Grandma's underwear and looked at Brenda. She was still folding, but she glanced at me with her matter-of-fact face.

"Well, that's hard to say. I wasn't there. I couldn't have been in her mind if that had happened."

"But, do you *think?*"

"But Brenda, she supposedly loved him. I mean, she wanted to get married." Then I laughed. "And even if she hadn't, she probably would have anyways, she's so into duty and responsibility and all that stuff. Why?"

Brenda looked uncomfortable, even vaguely miserable, like she wanted to run to the bathroom and puke. Instead, she sat down on the bed and started rocking and making creaking noises, running her hands through her big hair. "Why? *Why?* Eric, I don't know why."

I put down the underwear and sat down next to her, wanting to put my arm around her, but feeling like she might throw it off if I did. Instead, I decided to be direct.

"Brenda, do you want this kid?"

"What?" she almost screamed, throwing back her head.

"Do you want it? Him? Her? Whatever?"

"I'm twenty-one years old, for God's sake!"

"I know."

"Do I *want* it?" Suddenly, she was crying all over the place, as late-afternoon light filled up the room through Grandma's sheer nylon drapes and the big maudlin-faced Jesus looking down on us like the moderator of a panel discussion. "Yes! I want the fucking kid! I want to be a fucking *mother,* all right? I think it would be *nice."* I grabbed a handful of Kleenex off Grandma's bureau and handed them to her, and she used the whole wad to clean herself off, violently. "And I want to get out of the fucking card shop and go to computer programming school like Kathy Fanuele and get a real paycheck and get my own house—and have a *real life!"*

"So?" I said, trying to be as bright and optimistic as possible, just like my mother usually would. "What's stopping you?"

"I don't know!" she bawled again. "I don't fucking know!"

I decided to lay it all on the line, since nobody else would. "You don't want to marry Frank, do you?"

She looked at me, horrified, and wiped the tears off her face as if Frank was going to walk in at any minute and her crying would be an admission of guilt—or lovelessness. "I didn't say that!" she hissed.

"But you don't, do you?"

"I don't know! I just—I don't feel for him like I did in high school. I know he's sweet and he works hard and he's Italian, and all that. And he loves me, and he can't wait for the baby, but—I don't know." Then she looked at me, seriously, as though she really wanted me to concentrate. "Eric."

"Uh-huh?"

"There are just a *lot* of things that Frank doesn't get."

I wanted to say, "No kidding," but I didn't. "Like what?" I asked instead.

She looked at me, exasperated. "Like—Eric, like he said that when the baby came, I could bring it by the jail and he could show it to his work buddies. I'm not bringing any fucking baby into a jail! But I don't say that. Instead, I say, 'How am I gonna do that if I'm at work, too?'

And he goes, 'You don't have to keep that stupid job when the baby comes. You can stay home with it and I'll work more overtime.' And I'm thinking, *How do you even know I want to stay home with it all the time?* Maybe I'll want a break from it. Maybe I'll want to leave it with Ma sometimes. Or even Grandma, if she doesn't scare it to death. But Frank isn't laid-back like Dad, you know? He's fuckin' bossy. He thinks he's got the right way to do everything."

She picked up with the underwear, frowning. She had stopped crying and now she just looked worn out and bewildered. I decided, again, that if I didn't say something to her, nobody else would, including her friends.

"Bren?"

"Yeah?"

"It sounds like you've got to tell Frank you don't want to get married. Not just yet, anyway."

"Oh, Christ. How am I going to tell him that?"

"You've just got to tell him, point blank. Just say that you weren't expecting to get married so soon, and just because the baby's coming, that shouldn't be an excuse to rush it. Say it's only because you love and respect him so much that you're not jumping into a situation that might hurt you both later. There. Doesn't that sound good?"

She looked at me like I was crazy. "Eric!"

"What?"

"He's gonna think I'm a fuckin' freak. Everybody is! Just going ahead and having this baby and shutting out the father?"

"You're not shutting out the father. Frank can still see the baby whenever he wants. I mean, the right thing to do would be to split the taking care of the baby down the middle."

She let out a big, raggedy laugh. "Oh, no! No fucking way. I'm bringing up that kid, or nobody at all. Frank wouldn't know how to change a diaper if he practiced for six years."

"Then wait six years until he knows how to change a diaper, then marry him. I guess by then, he wouldn't need to change a diaper, would he? Unless you two have another kid."

The thought of that seemed too much for Brenda, who just stared at me blankly, and blinked. "Look," she said. "Why don't we just drop this, okay? I'm sure it's all gonna work out. Let's get outta here. This place is giving me the creeps." She crumpled up the list, stuck it in her pocket, and started zipping up the suitcase.

"Are you gonna talk to him, Brenda?" I asked again, feeling like I had to push the issue a little.

She sighed, exasperated. "Yeah, I'm gonna talk to him. When the time is right."

"When is the time going to be right?"

"Would you just drop it!" she yelled, and I did.

We were both quiet in the car until Brenda said blandly over the music, "I suppose it could be worse. I could be Kerrie Lanouette, right?"

"That's a morbid thought," I said.

"But then again, Kerrie Lanouette doesn't have any problems right now, does she? She's sittin' pretty somewhere."

"Brenda," I said, fed up, "you *don't* want to be Kerrie Lanouette."

"I guess you're right," she said.

Neither of us said anything for the rest of the drive home.

Four

Before I can negotiate another thought about my world as I know it—
a riot of thoughts that includes wondering where Sal keeps the extra
saran I need to finish wrapping the tomato halves—I see him: a slender
figure walking fast, hunched over, across the parking lot, straight toward
the plate-glass front window of B.J.'s, where he stands and signals me
from the outside, pointing to his watch. It's ten-thirty and Jimbo and the
card-playing old men are still here, but their backs are to the window
and Jimbo is engrossed in his napkin-shredding. It only takes me a second to hold up all ten fingers and then one more, to signal eleven
o'clock, and he smiles wildly at me and he's gone.

He came, I think, *he didn't forget,* and I can't say, frankly, that I've forgotten either—through everything, through the distractions of school
and family and murder—I can't say I've forgotten even once since the
last time I saw him. I'm flying through my close-shop chores and at ten
minutes to, the two old men gather up their cards and leave, without a
word to me, and I'm over at Jimbo's table, picking up his napkin shreds.

"I've gotta close up, Jimbo," I say. "You gotta go home now."

"Naw!" He laughs toothlessly. "*You* gotta go home now, Admiral. I
gotta stay and fight T. Rex!"

"No, Jimbo, you've gotta fight T. Rex at home. I've gotta close up,"

I say, smiling back, thinking, *Get the hell out of here, you crazy idiot.* It only takes a little more doing on my part before I'm guiding Jimbo out the door, he all the while babbling about the impending duel with the mighty T. Rex, and then he's on his old Schwinn and off in the night toward his mother, or whomever, whatever he calls home.

I shut all the lights except the ones behind the counter and start giving the tables a second wipe-down, to pass the time, but the hit radio station calls 11:03, and, in tandem with that, he's there again, on the other side of the glass door, gleaming in a white striped shirt and khakis and the same loafers shined to distraction. He's got something in a paper bag under his arm, and he's beaming tonight.

"Hey," I say, unlocking the door and letting him into the darkened shop.

"Good evening," he says, and he puts his hand over mine on the door-knob and we hold them there, just for a second, me peering out across the parking lot to see if anyone has seen, but it looks deserted.

"You're so dressed up tonight," I say.

He hurls himself into a chair and throws his legs up on a table, as though this is home to him, as though he's been here a million times before. "Friday night is all-campus formal dinner, with prayers and candles and the idiotic glee club singing after the meal. You have to wear a coat and tie, but I slipped mine off before I came." He peers around the darkened, fake wood-paneled shop. "Can I have a drink? A Sprite or something?"

I get us two Sprites from the soda fountain behind the counter (which is not against the rules, I tell myself, because Sal says I can have all the drinks I want from the soda fountain. I'm doing nothing against the rules) and sit down across from him. He takes one sip from his drink, grimaces, says "Syrup," and doesn't touch it again.

"Where have you been since ten-thirty?" I ask him. I'm starting to worry about him creeping all over town.

"I hid out in some shrubs near these apartments right behind here. Two old guys walking by almost saw me, but I ducked down. I blend in, in the dark," he says, preeningly.

"Not in that shirt you don't. You look like a sitting duck."

He leans in toward me and lowers his voice. "I took it off," he says, "and stuffed it in my pants."

"Oh," I say, blushing, which is what he wanted, I suppose, because he laughs, robustly. He pushes the paper bag across the table toward me. "I stole you a book from the library."

"From the West Mendhem Library?" All he needs, I think, is to get picked up for theft in the middle of West Mendhem. That would be the end of that.

"Of course not. From the J. Archibald Sloan Memorial Library of St. Banner Academy. Thirty-two thousand volumes and an international array of periodicals." Tonight, I'm noticing, he seems to be talking somewhat more to me and less to himself.

I pull out the book, and he laughs again when I see the title. It's an old hardcover copy of *Ragged Dick* by Horatio Alger. Inside, there's a stained yellow bookplate that says, "Property Sloan Library, St. Banner, 1924."

"Thanks," I say, wondering how much the gift is or isn't supposed to be a joke on me. "I haven't read any Alger yet."

"He's the patron saint of boys like you. Now you can write your college essay on how *Ragged Dick* inspired you to shoot for great heights of success."

Now I know the joke's on me, and I'm a little annoyed. "Don't *you* want to shoot for great heights of success?" I ask him. "You're the one who's going to one of the most prestigious schools in the country. You're the one with everything going for you."

He's quiet a moment before he looks away and says, "Yes. I am charmed."

"So why don't you want to shoot for great success? Isn't that what you're trained to do up there?"

"My dear Mr. Fitzpatrick," he says, minutely examining his watch. "I *am* a success. I've already been successfully ejected from two of the finest institutions of secondary education on the Eastern Seaboard. And if I can maintain my dizzying record of success, I'll have been kicked out of the third by the end of the academic year."

His logic flabbergasts me. "You're *trying* to get kicked out of S.B.A.? I don't understand you."

"Actually, I'm trying *not* to get kicked out this semester, so I can go back to Virginia for the holidays and not upset my great-aunt, who will surely keel over and *expire*—in a genteel, lace-curtain darky sort of way, of course—if she receives one more letter of termination about me just before Christmas. No. If I get myself expulsed, I'll do it toward the end of second term, so I can leave directly for Paris from Boston and entirely avoid facing my great-aunt's broken heart."

"You're going to *Paris* this summer?"

"Most likely, yes."

"For the whole summer?"

"That depends. I may go to Florence as well. Or Greece, maybe." He looks at me sharply. "Why? Are you wondering why I don't work in the summers, like you?"

"I guess you don't have to, right?"

"Precisely." He pulls out a cigarette, lights it, inhales, blows the smoke out extravagantly through his nose, and taps the ashes into his untouched cup of Sprite. Only then does he lean over to me and enunciate quietly, "Because I am *very very filthy rich.*" Then he throws back his head and laughs.

"So?" is all I can think to say. And all of a sudden I'm getting a sick feeling that, in a funny way, has nothing at all to do with him. I shouldn't be here with him; it's wrong; I don't even know him, and even though we haven't done a thing, I know—looking at him look at me, with some bombastic U2 song blaring in the background, Bono screeching "Sunday Bloody Blah-blah-blah."—*Oh, shit*, I think, *I know where this is going. I know exactly where this is going.*

Then, as if I've just told him all this, he draws my hands away from myself and pulls them toward the center of the Formica tabletop and puts his own hands over them. And he says, "I'm filthy rich. And you, Eric Fitzpatrick, are going to Yale University, which is certainly more than I can say. And you are getting the holy hell out of here."

"Thank you," I say, like an idiot, and suddenly, looking at his hands clasped motionlessly over mine, I start to cry, and with that, it's like everything's mixed in—my home, my parents, my pregnant sister and my retarded sister, my brain-dead friends and good-for-shit hometown. It's like they all come chasing up out of the pit of my stomach and I upchuck them all over the table, in front of him. And then I can't believe it, I'm not crying, I'm sobbing, and I know I must sound like a choking fool.

"Look at you!" he says, laughing. "You're a mess! The little plugger,

Eric Fitzpatrick, is a mess." And then he starts to sing, "Don't cry for me, B.J.'s Sub Shop / The truth is, I never left you. . . ."

"Cut it out!" I say, but he's laughing now, and I can't help it, so do I. Then he takes both my hands up to his mouth, and he's kissing them all over, and I don't know whether to be horrified or to do the same. I'm still blubbering, and he seems so intent on my hands. And I take just one of his peculiar slender hands in my own, and draw my head closer to his, hunched in, and hold his fist to my eyes and forehead, and he does the same. I'm quieting down, then, and we just stay that way for what seems like forever, in the dark, scored only by hit radio. I can smell his breath—it smells like cigarettes and some kind of pungent wood, maybe cedar—and I can hear it too, short and constrained, like he's in a bush, hiding, which is exactly the way mine sounds, too.

Finally, he whispers to me, "Do you want to go somewhere?"

"Uh-huh," I whisper back, but I can't seem to make it sound quiet enough.

"Okay," he whispers. "Lock up. Let's go."

I've done my work. I throw out our paper cups, stick the Horatio Alger book into my backpack, turn off the radio and the remaining light, and in a minute we're both stalking across the parking lot toward my mother's hatchback, lying, thankfully, beyond the scope of the security lights buzzing in the silence from high above.

"What's this?" he says, fingering the little St. Christopher medallion hanging from the rearview mirror, as I start the car and pull out of the lot and onto Main Street.

"It's St. Christopher," I say, trying to sound derisive. "He's the patron saint of travel."

"You mean he's sort of like the secretary of transportation for Catholics?"

"Sort of. I didn't put it there. It's my mother's. She's superstitious."

"Oh," he says, leaving it be. "What would your mother say if she saw you right now?"

"I don't know," I say, annoyed. "I'd say I'm hanging out with a friend. She wouldn't care. She's not prejudiced or something, if that's what you mean." I try to sound righteous, because I know my mother would have a million questions if she could see me right now.

"I didn't say that," he says.

"No. But maybe you were implying it. I can read between the lines."

He laughs, sounding contemptuous to me. "*Can* you?" he says.

Here we go again, I think. I don't answer. Instead, I say, "What would *your* mother think?"

"I don't know. She lives in Amsterdam, I think. Or Berlin now, maybe. I haven't seen her in about—oh, dear—I guess about five years."

"Oh," I say, ashamed for asking. "I'm sorry."

"I might look her up when I go over there next year," he says matter-of-factly, rolling down the window and lighting a cigarette. "I think she might be amenable to lunch. Or drinks."

The whole idea of wondering if your mother is willing to meet you for drinks in Amsterdam is so bizarre to me, I don't say anything except another "Oh."

"Aren't you going to ask about my father? No boy can become a man without knowing his father, *n'est-ce pas?*"

That makes me think of my own father, Arthur, whose own father died when he was three. *Is my father not a man?* I think to myself, but in an academic way, in the back of my mind, as though it were an essay question on an English test. What I say is: "You don't have to tell me about him if you don't want to."

"It's not that I don't want to," he says evenly. "I just don't know that much. All I know is, he did some import-export thing because he couldn't get hired at an American bank. He went away on business, and he never came back, but he sent me a calculator. I remember, they had just come out, and it was huge, the size of a notebook, made in Korea, and he had had my initials engraved on the back. But that was the last from him, except for checks every month, I found out recently, even though Auntie Fleurie didn't need them. But it was my mother hoarding the checks, and in a year she left, too."

"She left without saying good-bye?" I gasp. I can't believe the pathos of this story.

"No. She said good-bye. She dressed me up in a little seersucker suit and took me out to a swank restaurant. She drank a lot, and I had three Buck Rogerses. She told me she was going on vacation and would be back in one month. But she didn't come back in a month."

"And that's the last time you saw her?" I ask.

"No. She visited a few times, and Auntie Fleurie and I went to see her once in Amsterdam. The last time she came back to Virginia to visit I was thirteen. I was happy to see her—she took me out to dinner again, and bought me a new suit for it—but she and Auntie Fleurie had a *ripping* fight. Two educated Negro ladies tearing each other apart in three languages, *such* drama. Then, *poof!* Gone again. Auntie Fleurie hates her now."

"Do you?"

He glances at me, then turns to the window to exhale. "How can I hate her? I don't even know the woman. She could be any woman I might pass walking down the street in any major European metropolis. Maybe she's Diahann Carroll on *Dynasty.* Maybe she's Phylicia Rashad."

"On *Cosby,*" I say absent-mindedly, and he scares me half to death by laughing out loud. "Yes!" he exclaims. "On *Cosby!* Oh, Lord! Maybe that's my mother!"

I can only laugh, nervously, I'm so taken aback by this outburst, which strikes me as a little psychotic. He throws his cigarette butt out the window and says, calmly now, "No. I don't hate her. What's to hate? Amsterdam is a hell of a lot more interesting than Virginny. So is London."

"So your Auntie Florie raised you?" I say.

"Not Florie, darling. Fleurie. Like *fleur,* you know, the French for 'flower,' like *fleur-de-lis?*" He's lisping now, getting bitchy, deliberately trying to annoy me. Maybe he thinks I don't know those disgusting stereotypes. Well, he's wrong; I do. Everybody does.

"I know the French for 'flower,' thank you," I say.

"I'm sure you do."

I decide to let it pass. "So your great-aunt raised you?" I ask again.

"Hmmmm," he says, exaggeratedly, as though he's considering the question. "Hmmmm. Housed me. Fed me. Clothed me. *Educated* me, even—expensively, as you can attest. But raised me? Not really. Not terribly. I spent most of my time hiding from her. And Auntie Fleurie is so goddamned dignified, in her big old house with a portico and eighteenth-century wallpaper—she wouldn't debase herself to come look for me. So, no, in answer to your question—and, I will add, a most *keen-minded* question—she did not raise me. Nobody did. I raised myself."

We're silent for a moment before he asks, "Now, Mr. Fitzpatrick, the question remains: Who raised *you?*"

"It's more like, who's *raising* me," I say.

He pounces right back. "All right, then. Who has *raised* you and who continues to *raise* you?"

He's sounding so ridiculous, so arch and professorial, I can't help but laugh a little. And before I can think of a cleverer answer, something approaching his own, I just give him the honest one: "A lot of people."

This doesn't seem to give him pause. "And do you share their values?" he shoots right back.

It seems like such an obvious question, and yet I've never really considered it before. In some ways, I don't even know what it means. "Well," I answer carefully, "I guess about some things, no. And about other things, I guess I do."

"Such as?"

"Well, I don't know. I guess about family. Feeling that your family is very important to you, and you don't let them down. And that you support your family in whatever they do, and they support you." Even halfway through saying this, I feel like a cornball, but I mean it, I think.

"I see," he says, starting to finger the St. Christopher medallion again, much to my dismay; I start feeling some sort of frontal attack coming on. "And do they support you in all your endeavors?"

I think about my mother and about Yale, and how she had said, "We'll find a way," and how, even if they had never introduced me to my interests, they certainly had never stood in the way, and I say, "Uh-huh. I guess on the whole they do. Basically, they don't bother with me."

"I see," he says, then: "What *are* your people, anyway? I presume Irish, this being Massachusetts?"

"Irish," I say, then, "Dirty micks," but he doesn't laugh.

"And is that it? You look swarthier than just Irish."

"And Italian, too, on my mother's side. But I try to play that down."

"I see," he says, still professorial. "So here we have the red-nosed people of Eire, surely the dumbest people in the world, with the possible exception of a few drunks who fucked the Blarney Stone, like Joyce and Yeats. And then we have the brilliant race behind Mussolini and the Holy See—and the *Godfather* movies, which completely glorified cold-blooded murder in the name of *family*, as you say—and let's see, what else? Oh, of course, scungilli! Delicious scungilli! And Chef Boyardee!"

I don't even know what scungilli is, but I'm still vaguely pissed off, partly because I'm embarrassed enough about the Italian side of my family and have always been grateful to have gotten my father's last name instead of Ianelli. All I say is, "It's not correct to refer to Italians as a race. They're an ethnicity, maybe, or a nationality. But not a race."

"Oh, yes, they are!" he exclaims. "They're a race. They're a race to the finish line, to see who can eat the most scungilli before Judgment Day, before the Big Thunderclap!" And he smashes his hands together—"Ba-boom!"—and I'm beginning to wonder all over again if he's psychotic. And then he quiets down and he says to me, settling back in the passenger seat, his cigarette finished, "You needn't worry, Mr. Fitzpatrick. You transcend your race."

I scowl. I almost want to say to him, flip, *"You transcend yours,"* because he's like no black person I've ever seen—or white person either, for that matter, or *any* person. He's more like a character out of some novel, or a play, he seems assembled out of so many pieces. But I don't say that. I don't think that would be wise. Instead, I say, "Thank you, Mr. Jefferson Tremont," and I hope that's flip enough for him.

"My lord!" he exclaims. "You remembered the entirety of my last name. *Quels* retention skills. You'll ace the SATs."

"I already have," I say, and then I can't help but laugh a little at my own arrogance. It also buoys me to be a little grandiose for a minute, like him.

"Have you?" he says, and laughs, too. "Well, seize the day!"

The little digital clock on the dashboard reads ten to midnight; without even really thinking about it, I've been driving back past St. Banner, through the outskirts of West Mendhem and well into Boxford; without even calculating, I've been wanting to get us both out of West Mendhem, beyond my realm of familiarity, and his, because when I'm with him there, it feels a little spooky; it feels like a place I've never been. I'm pulling off rural Route 133 now, onto a semipaved road that leads to a small lake in the woods where Phoebe and I go sometimes. (Once we went there in the spring and read Emily Dickinson aloud while eating fresh strawberries, and declared ourselves pretentious.) He seems to be pricking up his ears in the seat next to me now, peering out into the leafy darkness.

"Where are you taking me, Mr. Fitzpatrick?" he asks with mock trepidation. "All sorts of untoward things could happen in a remote spot like this."

"We're not so far from St. Banner, actually," I say, enjoying this moment, being in control, picking the locale. "I just wanted to get out of West Mendhem. There's a pretty little lake down at the end of this road where I come sometimes."

I pull the hatchback halfway off the path and into the woods, and shut off the engine. Now there's dead quiet, here in a pocket of clearing in yet another ancient Massachusetts burg known only for its proliferation of horse stables and antique stores, but that's all somewhere else, and long gone to bed, like the rest of the world. There are goddamned crickets, though, just like the other night by the roadside near St. Banner, a whole singing society of them.

We're walking now down the path, down the little slope to the rotting wooden pier that sits on the lake, the flat feet of his sockless loafers louder on the gravel than my sneakers, sounding so acute, like a kind of dare. " 'Whose woods these are I think I know. His house is in the village though,' " he says, sotto voce. "I bet you had to memorize that in elementary school, didn't you?" he says to me.

"No," I say, and before I can elaborate, there's a horrible commotion in the bushes to our left, and some kind of shapeless furry thing— an opossum, I think—runs across our path. I jump back about six feet, with a hiss. But he never moves, just watches it run across the pathway with curious detachment, as if he nearly falls over woodland creatures all the time.

"Are you quite all right?" he asks me a moment later, archly.

"That thing was the size of a beagle," I say.

"Thank God you're a country boy," he says, and we keep walking.

The pier doesn't creak when we step onto it—it's too sodden—and in the dark the small lake looks black and forbidding, like oil, except for the patches covered in lilypads, which glint silver now. On all sides, there's a wall of fir trees and weeping willows, and behind us, the car and the road are obscured over the rise in the land. It's like we're in a kind of hollow.

"It's pretty here, isn't it?" I ask, just wanting him to agree, to say a simple yes and not make much more of it.

"This is so," is what he says, so calmly, looking over the surface of the lake, and I can't see the temperament of his eyes in the dark, whether they're mocking me or not. Then he pulls something out of the pocket of his khakis—a joint. He smokes it the way he smokes cigarettes, indifferently, not greedily like Phoebe or Charlie, or, I guess, on those occasions when I join in, me myself.

"*Vous voulez?*" He offers the lighted joint to me. I pause for a moment and he catches it and says, "I won't fink on you when you're up for a Supreme Court nomination in later life. I won't fink on you about anything."

"That's okay." I take the joint and inhale, trying to play it cool. "I hate politics. They bore me."

He takes back the joint, seeming actually to be considering my words with some consternation. He takes another hit—holding the joint between his second and third fingers, I notice, which I've never seen before, but it's actually rather elegant—holds, exhales, then smiles. "They bore me, too. You know that? They really do. They don't get anybody anywhere. He takes yet another hit before he hands it back to me. "Anyway, I believe in the trickle-down theory. I really do agree with Reagan on that. It only makes sense. Everything trickles down. Money. Love. Hate."

"Rain," I say, laughing, and he laughs, too: "Of course, rain, brilliant! Everything trickles down!"

The pot is creeping in around me now—it's obvious; I can feel it. A warmth is starting to prickle from the top of my head down my spine, and an exquisite buzz is filling up my head, smothering out all sounds save the two of us standing here, snickering. He doesn't seem to be affected; he's still got that same disdainful half-mask smile on his face, and he's concentrating it on me. For the first time, I'm feeling it without daring to think it: he is handsome behind his little glasses; there's something geometric and assured and smart in his face, and his right hand, holding the joint delicately, seems to say as much about his intelligence and his profound contempt; he discriminates against everyone, including me, because why shouldn't he, with such perfect, self-possessed hands? Thoughts I guess I might have had from the start, anguished, but now they're seizing me with complete sovereignty, utter clarity, uncomplicated by dread. Or, better, my dread is choked off in narcotic acuity.

Then we're facing each other—how do people find themselves in those positions without having maneuvered to get there?—and he's got his hands on my waist, under my T-shirt. "Oh, baby" is what he says, bringing my ear down to his lips, "you're gonna have it all."

"You're such an idiot," I say back. "You already have it all. You just waste it." My hands are on his shoulders now, unbidden by me, buzzing. It's an awfully warm night, come to think of it.

"Uh-*huh,*" he says, and that's it. We're on the ground now, kissing each other's brains out. Later, I'll realize it was my first kiss, but now, it just feels like an extension of the conversation. Later, I'll wish I could say that he played me, that he handled me wherever he wanted to handle me, that I didn't even know what was happening, but it would be a lie.

Stopping for a minute, divested of shirts and buckled belts, he asks me, "Have you ever done this before?"

"No," I say. I guess I basically know what he means. "Have you?"

"Uh-huh."

"Who? Someone at S.B.A.?"

"No. Someone in Virginia. Last summer."

"Who?"

He laughs, viciously. "The poor fool who comes to tune my aunt's piano. He's forty-six, with a wife and kids. He's a loan officer at the bank and he tunes pianos on Saturday mornings to calm his nerves. He's of complete shabby-genteel lineage, and if you didn't know that, you'd think he's condensed-milk white trash! But he's not. He's an absolute angel, and he *adored* me."

I don't know if he's making this story up or not, it sounds so outlandish. So I venture: "What happened?"

"What happened?" He settles his head against my stomach, crosses his hands over his chest and looks up at the sky. His short, scrubby hair feels itchy and almost—weirdly—comical against me, and lies there like a funny dark meteor against my stomach. "What do you *think* happened?"

"Well, I don't know," I say. "That never happened with me and *our* piano tuner."

"That never happened with you and anyone, am I not mistaken?" he asks, turning his head and nuzzling his face into me like I'm a throw pillow, but I can't say I don't like it.

"No," I say. "Not until tonight, I guess."

"Never with *une petite fille?* One of your little striving, poetry-loving friends from town?"

That makes me think of Phoebe, and then Phoebe and Charlie, and I wonder what Phoebe would say or do if she could see me now. (I wouldn't want her to, I think. I wouldn't want anybody to see me now.) And all I say is "No. Not yet, anyway."

He laughs, and it sounds derisive to me. "Aren't you going to tell me?" I ask, wanting to change back the subject.

"What's to tell? It was last summer. I was just back from Paris. Fleurie was at a church meeting, and Mr. Stockley the tuner was downstairs under the piano. So I went down and sat on the settee and watched him and asked him about his tuning business. And then he asked me all about Paris and I told him. And it looked like he was going to cry, he wanted to go so badly. He asked me if I had seen the *Mona Lisa* in the *Louver.* That's how he pronounced it, Louver, like a louvered door."

I laugh, glad I'm able to be in on this joke instead of outside it, which I too often seem to be with him. "And then what?"

"And then. And then I said yes, I had seen the *Mona Lisa* in the *Louver,* and he really wasn't missing anything because you can't get that close to it anyway, and he was just as well off buying a postcard and maybe taping it up near his desk at work where he did his accounting work. And then I asked him how to tune a piano, and—what then?—oh, precisely, he had an enormous coughing fit, and I brought him a glass of water because it was Saturday and the maid had the weekend off to go see her sister in Charlotte, and then he said, 'You gotta get right down here if you want to see how it's done.' And that's what I did."

"And?"

"And what? Good Lord, you're a Curious George."

"What did you do?"

"What do you think? We did exactly what we're doing right now." He's quiet for a minute, then says, "Only more."

I'm starting to get that prickle again, not far from where his head is, and I wonder if he can tell. "Well, what does that mean, exactly, 'Only more'?" I also don't know how I'm bringing myself to ask such a question.

He rolls over until his chin is digging into my stomach, and he looks at me with his eyebrows arched high in his forehead. "Do you really want to know?" he asks me, and he seems gentler and more deferential than ever before.

"Um. I guess so. I mean, yeah."

Then he ratchets his head down a few inches, and in a minute he's pulling down the zipper on my shorts—efficiently, without a lot of fuss— then he's pulling down my briefs, which I can only assume smell wretched from a long night of manual labor. But then, in a minute, when he's lost to me and everything else in his singular pursuit, all I'm thinking is that I have never known anything could feel so good, not a back-rub from Joani, not the last line of the greatest book ever written. I can't take my hands off the top of his head, and eventually, I'm so consumed with curiosity that I sit up and swing around and lunge for his khakis the way I imagine a quarterback—or fullback, or halfback, or whatever—must lunge for the ball in the crucial final seconds of the game, leading the team to sweet victory.

"Good Lord," he exclaims, surfacing for a minute. "Can't you just lie back and enjoy yourself?"

"I am" is all I can say before I start in, before he starts again.

When it's over—first me, with him just on my heels—and I'm furiously running my tongue around inside my mouth to make sure everything is still there, he says to me, "Do you know what the piano tuner said to me right after this?" He's lying back, flat, receding, his head lying smack against the rotting planks of the pier, looking different than I've ever seen him before, drugged and unpoised, like I've caught him in the moment when he's about to fall asleep.

"What did he say?" I ask. I'm sitting up now, pulling my briefs and shorts back on, feeling funny down there, like I've been skinned, and in my head bewildered whether or not I should feel bereft now, and fallen, or simply not bother.

"He abandoned all pretense of petit-bourgeois gentility. The Louvre was the last thing on his filthy little mind."

"What did he say?"

"He said, 'I wish I could stuff your beautiful black cock in my mouth every day, first thing in the morning and last thing before I go to bed.' "

It's a shock to me, not the sentiment itself, but to hear him of all people say it. I don't say anything myself. I don't know what to say.

"Don't you?" he asks me, and I look at him, expecting him to flash me a preening smile. But he doesn't. He looks perfectly serious, and for some reason, that makes me take the question literally, makes me think about the crazy logistics of that: every day, twice a day. "That would take some doing to pull off in my house," I say. "Especially with my grandma living with us now, because she's up at the crack of dawn saying her rosary."

He just looks at me, and smiles thinly, and then I smile, feeling foolish, and then he reaches over to me and says, "Come here, child," and he doesn't sound sarcastic at all. Then, sitting Indian-style, he puts his arms around me so that I can't see his face; it's resting on my shoulder behind my head, and he doesn't say a word. Staring into the pond now, I realize I'm still quite stoned, and what does this mean, this silent embrace? But then, with my arms around his naked warm back and half his scrubby, angular head against my face, it's perfectly all right just to stare out at a black pond glinting silver with lilypads. And it's all right to pretend that it all begins and ends here, there is no tomorrow, no next month, no next year, no West Mendhem, Massachusetts, no Arthur, Terry, Brenda, Joani, Grandma, aunties, uncles, cousins, teachers, Phoebe, Charlie, no Kerrie Lanouette and all her floating facsimiles. Nobody, living or slain, tonight or tomorrow, but the two of us, black and silver, in a pocket of silence.

"So—*are* you?" he finally says to me, not moving.

"Am I what?" I ask, still staring out.

"You know. What I asked you the first night. I asked you if you were or not."

"Oh," I say, remembering, and feeling that this time, it's okay to answer honestly. "No. I don't think so. It's just a label anyway, right? I hate labels."

"Uh-*huh*," he says, slowly.

"Why? Are you? I don't care if you are, you know."

"It doesn't matter what I am," he says. "I don't stay in any one place long enough for it to matter. It remains immaterial. *Splendidly* immaterial."

"But it must matter to *you,*" I say. "I mean, not just that, but everything. If you don't have a sense of self, I mean—I mean, if you don't have a sense of identity, then how can you function in this world?" I realize, vaguely, that I'm invoking ideas I've only encountered in English class—ideas that I frankly haven't given much thought to, myself, outside of tests and essays for the literary magazine—but suddenly they seem incredibly important to me, very real and relevant. I think, *Imagine thinking it doesn't matter who you are!* My mother and all the aunts would have a fit over that. They would say, "You're Italian, that's what you are, and you're an Ianelli."

But he doesn't seem agitated. He just says, "No, it should matter to *you.* You're not going anywhere, not immediately anyway—and even when you do, you've got to come back. You have got to deal, my friend. That's my privilege: I don't have to."

I want to tell him how wrong he is, how he won't escape it, how it will catch up to him, how he will always feel incomplete until he finally sits down and takes the time to look himself in the face. But I'm catching on to him now: that's exactly his problem. He doesn't know how to sit down and just do *anything;* that's why he keeps getting kicked out of schools. He's a procrastinator and lazy, a classic underachiever. I didn't say it first, he did, and now I'm beginning to believe it.

So I sigh, exasperated. "If you say so," is all I say.

Then, suddenly, I feel him go completely rigid, and I wonder if he's seen somebody, since he's facing toward the pathway.

"What is it?" I say, tensing myself, not daring to turn around. *This is it,* I'm thinking, *it's the Boxford police, or the Staties,* and I can't even begin to count the number of laws we've probably broken tonight.

He doesn't say a word. But then he relaxes and begins uncoiling himself from me, carefully. "It's nothing," he says. "I got a funny cramp." Then he's lifting me up—we're standing now, starting positions resumed—and he kisses me one more time, cleanly and briefly, on the mouth (I still can't reconcile myself to the sensation), and then he says, "We'd better get you back."

"It's Saturday tomorrow," I say. "I don't have to be up."

"Well, *I'd* better be back, before a proctor gets up in the middle of the night to go to the lav and decides to do a surprise two-thirty A.M. bed check. Come, come. Let's go back to the car. Look away, great lake," he whispers, flourishing in the direction of the pond. He pulls another cigarette out of his shorts and lights it.

Hastily we dress and trudge back to the car. Still stoned, I'm super careful backing out down the gravel road and onto Route 133 heading back toward West Mendhem, but he obviously trusts me, because he smokes on, out the window as before, oblivious to the mechanics of reverse-driving down an unpaved wooded road in the middle of the night.

Just shortly after passing the sign announcing West Mendhem, sixteen-something-something, I see it again, the Kerrie Lanouette poster, even this far out of town: first on a tree, then a telephone pole, then pasted to someone's roadside mailbox. Of course I can't make out the particulars of her face in the dark, but by now I'm so familiar with it—everyone is—that I could probably spot it from half a mile away.

"Oh, God, there she is again," I say aloud.

"There's who?" he asks, vaguely, still smoking away from me, out the window.

"A poster of this girl from West Mendhem who they found all slashed up in the state park. My older sister sort of knew her. Everybody's on a witch-hunt now to find some Puerto Rican guy from Leicester to blame it on."

"Good Lord," he says, exhaling, indifferent.

"I can't believe you haven't heard about it. It's been all over the paper and the news every day for the past week or so," I say.

"Well, you know us at St. Banner Academy. We're our own little universe. Besides, they don't let us read anything except for *The New York Times,* and I don't presume it was *that* big a story."

"I guess not." We drive on in silence, me careful on the roads and probably slower than usual, until, about a half-mile before we get to even the edge of the S.B.A. campus, in the middle of the woods, he puts a hand over my own on the steering wheel and says, "You can let me out here. I'll walk the rest of the way."

"That's crazy," I say. "It's got to be a half-hour walk from here, and it's the middle of the night. You could get run over. Let me just drop you off where I did before, and I'll turn off the headlights."

"No, Eric, please," he says, gripping his hand tighter over my own on the wheel, almost literally steering us over to the side of the narrow pitch-black road. "I want to smoke another cigarette before I reach Mendhem—"

"You can smoke it in the car," I say. "You've already had two in here tonight, anyway, one more isn't going to matter."

"—and I really don't want to take any chances that the car will get seen."

"Brooks, someone could come along and clip you right off the road." But by this point I've drawn the car to a stop, or rather, he has, and he's already got one hand on the latch.

"I've got a white shirt on," he says.

"That's not what I mean," I say, frustrated. "Nobody would be visible walking along Route 133 at this hour. The turns are too sharp."

"I'll be fine. I'll cut through the woods. Just me and the tigers and bugger-boos and creepy-crawlies, and rattlesna—"

"Why are you so self-destructive?" I suddenly lash out, and I can't believe how much I sound like my mother, rebuking Brenda, or Joani, or (occasionally) me. "It's almost like you *want* to make trouble for yourself. Why?"

"That's not true at all," he says airily, drawing on the cigarette, but I can see he's edgy, ready to spring from the car. "I take impeccable care of myself."

"No, you don't!" I protest, as though I'm pleading with a problem child. "You take stupid chances!"

"Don't talk to *me* about taking chances, Hester Prynne," he says, wagging his finger in my face.

"Oh, shut up!" I say, but now I'm laughing, and before I say another word, he grazes my lips with his, jumps out of the car, and runs across the headlights and toward the woods. Then he stops and turns around.

"When again?" he calls. *"Mardi soir?"*

I nod, dazed, and before I can call him back to say, But what *are* we? or Why are we doing this? or Won't you *ever* get caught?—or Will *I?*— he leaps over the guardrail and vanishes into the dense woods.

I'm freaked driving home, still stoned, and moving at a crawl for fear that I'll miscalculate distance, but it's so late no cars pass me or approach, and when I get into town, there are no yellow lights in windows in my neighborhood. None but the lighted square of our own den window. Creeping into the driveway and gentling the car door closed behind me, I hope desperately that my father forgot to turn out the light before sleepwalking up to bed. But when I slip inside through the back door, ease off my sneakers, and try to pad silently up the stairs, I have no such luck.

"Eric?" from the den. It's my mother, and I'm still half-baked.

"Uh-huh?" I call back, trying not to sound too loud or too weird.

"Get in here."

"I'm really tired, Ma," I call, poised, panicking on the lowest step.

"So am I. Get in here."

My mother is on the couch in her nightgown, looking waxy and haggard in the nearly two A.M. light from the lamp. Home Shopping Club is on the TV, but she's turned the volume almost all the way down, and the changing shots—product, hostess, product, hostess—cast different volumes of light on the walls. One look at her, and I only hope that please, in a million years, crime isn't written all over my stoned face.

"Eric, where the hell have you been?" she says, looking exhausted, and I hope this is going to be brief.

"Ma, look, I'm sorry," I say, and then I plunge right into my next vice. "Phoebe came by toward the end of work and we hung out all night."

She lets out a short, mean laugh, which scares me, because she's never mean with me, really. "How can you look me in the face and just lie like that?"

"Huh?" I say, like an idiot.

"Eric, Phoebe called here at half past eleven to see if you were home. The phone ringing woke up Grandma."

"I know," I say, feeling viler by the second as my improvisatory lying limbers up. *What is happening to me?* I think, sickly, but what I say is, "She didn't come by till around midnight because I told her that Sal was gonna make me work late tonight."

"Oh," my mother says, sounding more tired than angry or suspicious or anything else. "Well, then why couldn't you have given me a call and let me know you were gonna be out? You know I don't mind, but I want a call. I called Phoebe's house after midnight and woke up Mrs. Signorelli, and she said Phoebe wasn't home yet. Why do you want to scare your mothers to death?"

"I'm sorry, Ma," I say, emphatically, so grateful the exchange is over. "We went to IHOP in Danvers and just lost track of the time. You're right. I should've called. I'll fill the car up with gas tomorrow morning."

She waves dismissively, and yawns. "Eric, I don't care about the gas. I just don't want you to make me sit up all night and worry. I've got enough to worry about right now."

"Ma, come on," I say, leaning down to kiss her good night. "Everything's gonna be fine."

"Yeah, sure," she says, accepting the kiss and running the back of her hand across my forehead, a gesture she's reserved for me since I was little. "You're a good kid, Eric. Don't make me wait up like this again. I need my sleep."

"All right, Ma, sorry. Good night."

"Good night, honey."

In my room, in bed, I want to sleep, I'm so fried and tired, but I can't. It's like, things he said, things I said, and things we did, they keep converging and diverging in my head, like they're on separate loops of tape and they keep looping over and over again. There's "Baby, you're gonna have it all," and what did he mean by that? and "I take impeccable care of myself"—such a lie!—and, worse, "Don't talk to *me* about taking chances"—and, oh, God, what chances did I take? Did anyone see us, leaving the sub shop and driving outcountry? And I have to call Phoebe tomorrow and tell her please to tell her mother that she was with me the night before just in case our mothers run into each other in the supermarket, and what will I tell Phoebe when she asks me where I was? (I'll lie again, of course.)

And then there's *that*—that fetal moment with him, curled up there like two babies, and I'm getting hard again just thinking about it. And then I want to jerk off, but I can't because I'm afraid my mother's still awake and she'll hear me and *know* I'm truly sick, and then, turning on my bedside light and grabbing my notebook, I want to write about it, I want to sort everything out on paper, but I can't, because someone might find it, even if I threw it out later, even if I tore it up in a million pieces; someone in the house—Joani, probably, just for fun—would probably find it and piece it back together and hang it with a magnet on the refrigerator door for everyone to see.

So instead, wanting to write myself to sleep, I remember that stupid essay I've got to write for Goody Farnham, for the contest—what is it?—"What I Cherish in America," and I think about how dashing it off now, in this delirious state, would be perfect justice to a stupid, mercenary assignment I don't even *want* to be a part of, and won't Phoebe and Charlie think it's funny that I—Eric, Honor Society me, perfect student—wrote an assignment when I was *stoned*, and in some stupid way I anticipate their approval, and their laughter. So I turn the notebook to a fresh page and write at the top, in huge, exaggerated letters, feeling cocky and full of contempt, "WHAT I CHERISH IN AMERICA."

Then I stop and think for a moment, and the only thing that comes to mind, unbidden, her chorus of photocopied faces, is Kerrie Lanouette, and I write:

> *Just a week ago, right here in my bucolic New England hamlet of West Mendhem, a good half hour northward from the dangerous urban pulse of Boston, a murder took place. It was a local girl, a girl with a face full of hope and wonder, a girl with dreams of a life full of love and happiness and contentment, perhaps even big dreams, dreams of changing this unhappy little world for the better, of touching everyone she met with her generous, radiant smile. She could have been your sister, or mine, or your high school sweetheart, or maybe your best friend. She could have been any girl, really.*
>
> *But now she is gone, her body found maimed and exploited, in a public park meant for picnicking and bird-watching and other pursuits that bring families together, whatever their station in life. Already, her loss has rung like a gong throughout our little town, posters of her dream-filled face covering every street corner, every storefront, as a reminder of this vessel of youth and hope that we have lost—lost to eternity, to Heaven, perhaps. Many people say the culprit was a person of foreign complexion from the poor city next door, Leicester, where dreams have lain dead for some fifty years now. Many people say they will not rest until the culprit is apprehended, and made to pay due justice, and*

peace of mind is again restored to the uneasy little town of West Mend-hem.

At this point, I stop writing, read over what I've already written in the breathless space of five minutes, and decide where I should proceed. *I need a main point,* I tell myself, not even knowing what the main point of this is. But I keep on writing, mechanically, loving the feel of this abandonment, feeling like it's the nastiest thing I've ever done, and that words really do have the power to hurt:

> *But even before this provocatively titled essay was assigned me, I had already been thinking about what I* [and I underlined the "I," dramatically, three times] *cherished in America, and this exciting and thought-provoking contest only gives me pause to commit to paper thoughts I had long been yearning to express. And I have decided that what I* [underlined, again, now four times] *cherish in America is just this—*

Here, I stop again, wondering where this could possibly lead. But I know where it's leading—toward cliché, toward something affirming and positive, where all my high school essays lead, toward something that tastes like crap in my mouth because I doubt all of it so thoroughly, because I feel like it's got nothing to do with me, and all I want is a one-way ticket out of this land of stultifying niceties and good intentions and unspoken bitternesses, embodied in my teachers and my family and everyone I've ever known here. And I write this, hating with all my heart, and feeling so good to hate, so good that the words just spill out onto the page like puke:

> *What I cherish is that the spirit of Kerrie Lanouette, this young expired woman, lives on—it is unquenchable, it is a flame that burns deep, inextinguishable, in the hearts of all young people in America, regardless of race, color, creed, or physical handicap. It is a flame that says, You may kill me, but you cannot kill my smile, you cannot kill the ineffable fire that makes me me, that makes me me despite those who would try to remake me, or unmake me, or make me any less than me. It is the*

flame that our forefathers first carried when they arrived on these very shores of New England, the flame of their incredible pride in the face of persecution, the flame that ignited an entire nation and made it great, the flame that made it burn into the long nights of despair and destruction, the flame that even today, Anno Domini 1986—in the face of poverty, and crime, and sickness, and social unrest, and sometimes what seem to be unconquerable woes—still flames on, illuminating everywhere the nooks and crannies of hope, the hope you see in whole cities, towns, states, and regions, the hope you can still see in the face of a young girl from West Mendhem, Massachusetts, the flame that will not die, that says you may snuff me out, for a moment, but I will be back to flame on, flame on, flame on!!!

Then I pause again, reeling, my entire right hand cramped and throbbing; and I collect myself and I write:

It is an American flame, yes, and it is my flame, and the late Kerrie Lanouette's, and yours as well. And in many ways, this American flame is the flame of all nations, just as the very utterance "America!" still rings, in all corners of the earth, as a call to truth, justice, and something uniquely, inalienably right. It is the flame of divine liberation and human dignity, and it is what I cherish most in America, even in this troubled year, 1986. For it is the flame that guides all nations, casting blessed, burning light upon the way whole nations live. [Here, I make a new paragraph, for effect; I can hear the roar of this pause as "The Battle Hymn of the Republic" sounds beyond.]
The way whole nations thrive.
The way whole nations love.

> Eric Arthur Fitzpatrick
> Senior, West Mendhem High School,
> West Mendhem, Massachusetts

I slam shut the notebook and chuck it across the room near my backpack—the final flourish. I don't want to look at it again. Now my digital clock says three in the morning. I put out the light and get back under the covers, but it's cold, so I climb out again to close the window. There's someone prowling in the backyard, I think, someone who looks to have been walking with a limp, in a striped white shirt, hastening toward the bush, frozen now in my gaze—but it's not, it's the humanoid shadow a tree makes against a hedge. Still, it's creepy to look out there. There are cold snaps coming on, shorter days; there is fall coming outside this house.

November 1986

Five

❖

After I fell asleep that night, the night after he and I went to that little pond in Boxford, I kept having dreams that turned to nightmares. I would wake up sweaty and spooked, and stare around my dark room and out into the dark yard, until I fell back asleep, and then the dreams would start again, turning to nightmares, scaring me awake, and so on like this until the sun started coming up. In the dreams, I was with him, hiding out in secluded places, in a forest or a car or, most strangely, in our old cottage at Hampton Beach, and while we made it together he was saying the most astonishing things to me, explicit things but said with his usual gravity, and more strangely, I was saying them back. And then what would happen was, we would become concentrated on each other, to the point where we were all wrapped up together, naked, limb for limb, in a contortion impossible to unlace on a moment's notice.

That was always the exact point where the dream would turn into a nightmare, because suddenly there we were, in the same position, but somewhere else, in broad daylight, like my backyard, or in the hallways at school between classes, or, worse, in the middle of the auditorium during an assembly, and whole hordes of people were watching us. There were kids from school screaming, "Faggots! Faggots!" and their parents, looking away, saying to each other, "Oh, I'm gonna be sick." In one nightmare, Phoebe and Charlie were there, getting stoned, making out, and wearing little matching John Lennon sunglasses, just smiling smugly like they had known it all along. But worst of all my family was there, my whole family, with my mother bawling and begging me to stop (but I couldn't, because I was stuck to him) and my aunts and Bethie Lynn trying to console her, saying, "Terry, it's okay, he just wants attention, he's always needed to be different," Joani looking bewildered and terrified like she didn't understand why her brother was at the center of a riot, Brenda actually leading on the chanting pack, screaming the loudest, and my father staring at me with absolute disgust, then looking away, then staring back, then looking away, until, finally, he just stalked away, past a whole pack of other dads wearing West Mendhem Booster Club baseball caps just like him who kept laughing and saying, "Sorry, Art, real sorry about your son." And then about half a dozen football players started to come toward us, saying, "We're gonna kill you homos," and all their jeering girlfriends behind them, and even Mrs. Bradstreet and Mrs. Farnham standing together, frowning and saying, "It's too bad, he was going to be our first at Yale in nine years." And Brooks stuck to me, naked, saying out of the corner of his mouth, "Can't you disentangle yourself from me?" and me struggling like a madman, screaming, "I'm trying! Can't you see I'm fucking trying?" And then, of course, it was like any nightmare: I woke up, saved at the last minute, telling myself, *It could never happen. I wouldn't let it happen.*

And yet. And regardless. That night was two months ago. It's November now, nearly Thanksgiving, the ground is freezing, and since then I've seen him a lot—something like every other day until just last week. Even though he was arrested, and let off, and he's on probation at St. Banner, even though so much insane stuff is going on here at home, and in West Mendhem, that I can hardly keep my mind on what I'm supposed to do, even though I *am* doing what I'm supposed to do, although I'm doing it like a sleepwalker, dazed and vaguely amused that I'm actually getting it done, even cocky, maybe, but God, I hope not, because pride will bring me down faster than anything else; if I slip for just one minute, I'm a goner. But it's like everything else is a kind of cyclone—it's so noisy I can hardly hear myself think—and at the center, in the only quiet place, there's him, Brooks, and me, and it's such a bizarre, cut-off part of my life that I can't even believe it *is* my life. I'm convinced I'm playing out some part in somebody else's life, or some movie they've never made, and never will make. And yet. And regardless. It's the only part of my life when I feel wide awake, when I feel like there's some other Eric Fitzpatrick. Not the "Eric!" I hear from the bottom of the stairs at dinner, not the "Eric Fitzpatrick" Mr. LeFebvre calls out during attendance in homeroom every morning, not the "Eric honey," "Eric sweetie," "Eric you asshole," "Hey Erky" I get from my mother and aunts and sisters, but another Eric, who's yet to exist, who *might* exist in five years, or ten, twenty, God knows when.

And him, Brooks. It's so funny now to think back to that first night at B.J.'s, and to think back to how he intimidated the hell out of me, with his low, measured voice that held everything, including me, in contempt, and his endless name-dropping, about books, about art, in French (and a little Italian, too), in a code I only feebly understand. This guy couldn't be real, I thought, but now, thinking back, the funny thing is, he was. And he still talks like that, like nothing—probation, or whatever—is going to wreck him, but now I know better than to let him scare me.

He can't leave campus anymore; he can't take the chance, or they'll kick him out, for good. (In fact, now all he does is stay in his room, or at the library, and read all the time, and he tells me that he is excelling, especially because the work is idiot's work compared to what it was at Exeter, and he'll probably win all the departmental awards at the end of the year.) So now we have a new place: the barn where they used to keep the rowing sculls until they built a real boathouse right on the lake. The barn, at the far end of campus on the other side of the soccer fields, is deserted, with lofts you can climb up into, a perfect place to meet. We've also worked out a new system: after school, when I'm through with meeting for the newspaper or the yearbook or the literary magazine (or when I'm pretending to be detained with them), I'll call the pay phone in his dormitory, and someone will call him to the phone. Then I'll say, "Can you meet this afternoon?"—which he usually can, because the mandatory after-class athletic requirement that he chose is building sets for the school plays and the head of the drama club at St. Banner is a narcoleptic—and he'll say, "Yes, when?" And I'll say, "In fifteen minutes, the usual place?" and he'll say, "But of course," or something like that. And then I'll say, "Should I bring you cigarettes or anything?" and he'll say yes or no, depending, and then he'll say, "Don't get arrested," and I'll say, "You neither"—because it's become a joke after what happened, *Don't get arrested*—and we'll both say, "See you soon," and then I'm off in my mother's hatchback, heading outcountry toward St. Banner.

When I get there, I park deep into a dirt road, and then I skirt the woods on the border of the school, until I sprint across a corner of the grounds, timing it so that all the soccer players are after the ball in the direction opposite from me. The barn is big, and drafty this time of year, and still smells faintly of hay and manure from way back when St. Banner was still farmland, and the only light is that let in by the small window at the very place where the pitched roof joins and by the occasional cracks in the wood. I climb up the grotty old ladder into the loft, the one way in the back, and I wait for him. (Sometimes, peering through a break in the wall, I can see him stalking toward the barn from the other end of campus, backpack slung over his shoulder in case anyone should ask him where he's going; then he'll tell them he's going down to the lake to study, because it's more conducive to absorption there, more Thoreauvian, and they leave him alone, because they think he's a freak: very "bright," but "troubled.") From below, then, in the shaft of light from the open door, I hear it, low and tentative—because we don't know who else might use this barn as a hiding place—"Hello?" and I'll lean over the edge of the loft, expelling old, gray shards of hay, and call, "Up here."

Up here is where I see him first, climbing up in school clothes: loafers, khakis, a blazer, a striped shirt, a tie in his backpack. His first question to me is always, "Did you get here all right? Did anyone see?" and mine to him is the same. He'll smoke, cigarettes mostly, pot sometimes, which I don't do here because later in the evening, I have obligations: family, homework, school applications. We'll bring each other things: he brings me a book, or a magazine, or a tape he's made. (He listens to strange things; a few weeks ago he brought me a recording of these chanting monks, which I actually like.) I'll bring him cigarettes, or some snack he can't get at school (Toffee-Fays, on which he seems to subsist, eating them delicately one after another), or, once, socks and underwear because, embarrassed, he wrote me a check and told me that he was in short supply and his great-aunt was becoming too addled to remind the housekeeper to pick them up and send them to him.

We fool around up here; a few times, we've fallen asleep, and when we woke, it was getting dark outside, and cold, and we both sat up with a gasp. We talk in a kind of half-baked, wandering way, as though we're both too tired for talking, as though hiding out here is activity enough. When I'm up here, the last thing I want to talk about is school, or home; I think it bores him, and when I'm here, it all seems rather boring and far-off to me, as well. He'll ask occasionally how my college plans are going—in the most offhand way, because he professes to hate the very institution of college—and I'll answer offhandedly, too. When I ask him about his summer plans, it's always the same answer: "Paris, *probablement.*" He says he'll probably finish the year out respectably after all, though he could care less; he's just doing it because that's the path of least resistance. After that, he says, he might just stay in Paris and get work in a café and maybe settle there, and never come back. Do you know any cafés that would hire you? I ask him, and he says if Paris hired Josephine Baker, they'll hire him. He says he's staying on campus for Thanksgiving, and, of course, before I ask him to my house, I think better of it. He says he's going back to Virginia for Christmas Day, and then after that, with his holiday money, he'll go to Barbados, alone, for January. And do what, alone, I ask? "Get lost," he says.

My last visit up there, last week, he got stoned in front of me, morosely, as though I were hardly there. It was frigid inside the barn at four o'clock, colder than it had yet been. Outside, dimly, we could hear the shouts from the soccer fields, hoarse cries that seemed to suspend for a moment and then get sucked up into the tremendous, precise cold of the air above the fields.

"Listen to those idiots," he said curtly, before taking a tremendous first hit and sitting cross-legged, his eyes closed, letting the smoke settle in his lungs for several seconds before exhaling. "Running around like *orang*utans in their little shorts. For what? For a *ball?* That's unfathomable to me."

"Why are you in such a bad mood today?" I asked him, feeling suddenly very depressed, very alone, holed up here with somebody nobody else in my life even knew existed and watching him float away.

"I'm not in a bad mood," he said dully, taking another drag, concentrating entirely on his joint. "I'm just fine. How are you?"

"Right now?" I asked. "I've been better."

"I'm sorry to hear that." He shrugged his shoulders at me.

"Maybe I'd better go," I said. "You've got your pot, anyway."

"Thanks to the lovely rolling papers you brought me."

"Yeah, right." I reached across the loft floor for my backpack.

"You don't have to go yet, Eric," he said, putting his hand on top of my backpack. "Maybe I want your company."

"Maybe if you wanted my company, you wouldn't get stoned when I come all the way out here to see you. My own friends do that to me. Why should I take it from you, too?"

"Maybe I'm more than just a friend to you."

"Oh, *really?*" I couldn't help spluttering. "What *are* you? Are you my mentor, because you throw books and classical music at me, because I'm a townie and you want to cultivate me?"

"Oh, please," he says, rolling his eyes. "You're so self-dramatizing. You're a little suburban boy who's going off to Yale. You're the goddamned American dream. Will you ever drop this illusory sense of yourself as this poor working-class ethnic?"

"Well, what did you mean, then? Did you mean that we're—that we're *boyfriends* or something?" The word felt very thick on my tongue, and utterly absurd to say.

"I didn't say that," he said, his voice so rich with what sounded like contempt, and I knew he was glad that I had said the word, not him. "I was thinking more along the lines of special friends. You know, like Gertrude and Alice."

"Who?"

"Stein? And B. Toklas?"

"Oh. Well, this is West Mendhem, Massachusetts, not the Lost Generation," I said, proud of my quick recovery.

But he didn't say anything back, didn't even smirk. He just took another long hit off his joint, which had been incinerating in his hands, and stared over the ledge of the loft, down toward the vast, moldering space below.

"Brooks, I probably should go. I've got a lot of work tonight," I said, reaching again for my backpack. "I'll call you next week, okay?" I stood halfway up in the loft and started to brush the dirt from my pants. It was already becoming night outside, and in the barn, I was losing his face in the gathering gloom.

"Would you stay with me for just a few more minutes?" he asked, sounding weirdly hoarse, like he had caught a cinder in his throat. "I'll put this out, all right?" And he carefully extinguished his joint on the floor of the loft. "There. Now, would you just grant me that much?"

His voice sounded so strange and disembodied in the dark that it caught me off guard. I laid down my backpack and sat next to him on the floor. "Okay. If you really want me to," I said tentatively.

"Please. Thank you."

"Okay."

For what seemed like the longest time, neither of us said anything. I knew he was looking away from me, over the edge of the loft, and I could hear his steady, reedy breathing. I started to worry that something was wrong with him; it wasn't the first time we'd been together when he had gotten stoned, but before I had hardly been able to notice the difference; he still always seemed talky, glib, sarcastic. Now it was as if he had crawled into some hole in the ground, as if he was falling deeper, and I was standing at the top of the hole, looking down, losing sight of him.

"Eric?" he finally said, sounding weirdly tentative and scaring me.

"Uh-huh?"

"Do you utterly—loathe yourself?"

"Loathe?"

"Yes."

"You mean, do I *hate* myself?"

"I believe 'loathe' is a synonym for 'hate,' yes." He was still looking away from me in the dark; I could feel it. I could feel his entire body leaning away from me and toward the edge of the loft, leaving me in a kind of dark vacuum all my own.

"Well, I get upset at myself, yes. I think there are a lot of things I do that I could do better. But I can't say that I *hate* myself, no. Hate is a pretty strong emotion, don't you think?" (That's what my mother has always said: "You don't *hate* anybody. Hate is a strong emotion.")

"Yes," he drawled. "It certainly is."

"Why?" I asked. "Do *you* think I do?"

He didn't answer for the longest time. Then he said, "No. I don't. Not yet, anyway. But you might learn to, if you give it time."

He was making me nervous now. "I don't think that will happen. I think I just need a change of scenery, that's all."

"You're right. You're absolutely right."

"Why, anyway? Do *you* hate yourself?"

He laughed softly, eerily, as if he was hypnotized. "Don't be ridiculous," he slurred. "What's to hate, right? What's to hate? That's a strong emotion." It was then that I saw it, even in the dark. He was sitting cross-legged, and he started leaning rightward, toward the edge. One whole side of him rocked off the edge.

"Brooks, what the fuck!" I hissed, grabbing him by the arm and pulling him back up. He was dead weight in my hands, and in the dark, as I yanked him back away from the ledge, I swore I saw him smiling at me.

"You're so fucked up!" I said to him, propping up his head with one hand. "You almost rolled right over the edge. You've got to stop getting stoned. You're worse than Phoebe and Charlie."

Now he couldn't stop the soft, drugged laugh; it came out of him like hiccups, spasmodically, the way Joani used to sound when she choked on her juice and my mother would have to whack her on the back to make her stop. "Eric, you saved my life." He giggled, putting his hands up to my face. I pulled away, kneeling beside him. "That's awfully sweet."

"You're a fuckup" was all I could think to say. "You've got to get it together."

He just giggled more, looking depraved in the dark, and reached for my belt buckle. "Come on, let me suck your dick. You wanna suck my big dick, Eric? You haven't done that in a while. Wouldn't that be nice?"

I shoved his hands away. "Shut up, you idiot!"

"You wanna take me home for dinner? You wanna take me home for dinner, and lemme suck your dick at the table? Hey, Mr. and Mrs. Fitzpatrick! Hey Grammy! Guess who's coming to dinner? Sidney Cock-sucker!" He couldn't stop laughing. Suddenly, I wanted to cry, I was so unhappy, and I desperately wanted to leave.

"Come on, Brooks, get up," I said, tugging at his right arm and reaching for his backpack. "You've got to get back to the dorms. You should just get in bed and sleep this off. You'll feel better in the morning."

"No," he whined. "I want to fuck your brains out, Eric. Don't you wanna get fucked, you little dago faggot? Just like that little girl they thought I fucked before I sliced her up?"

"Brooks, shut up and get the fuck up!" I said, clenching my jaw and yanking at his right arm. "You've got to walk across that campus and get to bed and not make a scene, or you're gonna get expelled."

"Naw. Lemme sleep right here."

"You can't. Somebody might find you. And it's cold."

"It ain't so cold, Eric."

"Yes, it is. Now get your bag and come on. I'll go down first, and I'll spot you."

"Aw, Jesus Lord!"

"Get up!"

Somehow, by pulling and tugging, and strapping his backpack onto his shoulders, I got him on his feet and led him toward the ladder, where he missed the last five rungs and fell on me. Outside in the cold, behind the barn, he lost his playfulness and receded, again, blank and unreachable, hands in pockets.

"Can you get back all right, or should I sneak back with you halfway?"

"I'll be just fine, thanks," he said, deathlike, not looking at me, staring off toward the white clapboard buildings with their squares of yellow light.

"Can you get back all right?" I asked him again, holding his elbow. I didn't know why I asked again, but looking at him looking away from me, concentrating intently ahead of him at nothing, I felt the emptiest, sorriest pit in my stomach. What I felt then was a kind of terror—faintly for me, but much more acutely for him—and the deepest, deepest gratitude that I wasn't him, the deepest regret that we had ever met, and the deepest, edgiest resolve that I wouldn't toss him away.

He was freezing on me, turning to stone in my grip. I wondered what kind of horrible chorus, what kind of white noise, was screaming in his head, and I desperately didn't want to know, and I pulled him closer toward the barn and reached up and kissed his frozen, unmoving lips, and held him, awkwardly, while he stood there with his arms at his sides, like a tin man.

"Brooks, are you listening to me? Please get back safe. I'll call you to-morrow, okay? Get a good night's sleep."

"Okay," he said, looking over my shoulder, past me, God knows where.

"Good night, Brooks. You're my special friend, okay? Like Gertrude and Alice, just like you said."

I thought he smiled faintly, but it could have been at anything. "Okay."

"Get back safe. Good night."

"Nighty."

I gave him a little shove in the right direction, and watched him start off toward campus, walking stiffly, hands in pocket, his whole body tilted forward—the gait of either an awkward young boy or a rheumatic old man. When he was well ahead of me, I was seized with fear that he might pass out cold on the abandoned soccer fields before he made it back, and I ran forward to watch him. He didn't look back once, and I stood at the top of the rise as he descended into the vale, onto a gravel pathway, in the direction of two girls with flowing blond hair who gave him a wide berth as he scissored past and around behind the long row of white clapboard buildings.

I ran back to the car and sped home, stuffing the afternoon and thoughts of him away as I did every afternoon, so I could walk in the house with a clean face. And I entered a house so busy with its own pre-occupations that, as I did every other night, I got away with it—coming in the back door, setting the table for dinner, sitting through dinner, then later, in my room, plowing through assignments—but behind it all, I couldn't shake the sight of his dazed, stoned face and his low, slurred voice, saying things he didn't even know he was saying, telling me what he wanted us to do.

But I'm getting ahead of myself. That was our last meeting to date, al-most two months after that night on the pond in Boxford. The day after *that* night, a Saturday afternoon, the house was quiet. My mother had taken Joani grocery shopping, Brenda was at work, Grandma was ei-ther sleeping or saying her rosary in Joani's bedroom, and I could hear my father snoring on the couch in the den with the sound of an old war movie on the television. All afternoon, immersed in college application forms and essays, I had managed to put the night before out of my mind so I was twice as startled to see the headline at the bottom of the front page of the *Leicester Evening Tribune,* which was lying by the front door in the hallway.

"St. Banner Student Questioned by West Mendhem Police in Connection with Lanouette Murder," ran the headline. I peered into the den to make sure my father was asleep, then took the paper into the kitchen and sat down queasily at the kitchen table.

The West Mendhem police picked up a St. Banner Academy student they said they found walking along Great Lake Drive, about a mile from the prestigious private school, this morning at about 1:45 A.M., according to Police Chief Ryan McElroy. The student, who was found off campus several hours after St. Banner curfew, was taken to the West Mendhem police headquarters, where he was questioned by the police, then claimed at 3:12 A.M. by St. Banner officials, who are putting him on probation for violating school curfew regulations.

Officer Anthony DeMarco said he was making his nightly rural patrol when he stopped Francis Tremont, 18, a senior at St. Banner Academy, for questioning approximately halfway between the St. Banner campus and the Boxford town line. Tremont attributed his late-night walk to anxiety from academic pressure and insisted he was on his way back to campus, but he was taken back to police headquarters for questioning because, according to DeMarco, he fit the description of the primary suspect in the murder of a West Mendhem woman, Kerrie Lanouette, which took place in Harold Porter State Park two days ago. "It was standard procedure," said DeMarco, who said that in addition to an ongoing investigation into the murder by West Mendhem, Leicester and state police, officers have been instructed to take in for questioning anyone fitting the current description.

Tremont repeatedly insisted that he did not fit the description of the man in question. (The composite drawing depicts a dark-skinned man, presumably in his thirties, heavyset, with a slight mustache. Tremont, who is black, is slight of build, clean-shaven and several years younger than the suspect.) Austin Trilby, dean of students at St. Banner, also pointed out the lack of resemblance and confirmed that Tremont had been in his first day of classes the afternoon the murder is presumed to have taken place. After Trilby's promise that Tremont would be disciplined for breaking curfew, the two were escorted back to campus. Tremont has no previous criminal record.

"He was a bright kid, very educated, very polite, and we felt real bad about having to take him in," Chief McElroy said today. "But everybody's in a panic about this killing and if we spot someone who fits the description walking around West Mendhem in the middle of the night, we can't just let it go. Besides, he was breaking curfew, and he shouldn't have been doing that. He could've gotten run over."

The search for the suspect in the Lanouette murder continues, say local and state authorities, but so far there are no new leads.

At first, all I could feel was relief that he had gotten off so easily, that (presumably) they hadn't questioned him about where he had been, and that he hadn't mentioned my name. *I told him not to walk home,* I thought to myself, remembering my plea just before he ran out of the car and into the dark. *Why does he go around looking for trouble?* I seemed to linger on the word *trouble,* and some kind of chill started settling in around me, a danger sign. What was I doing in the middle of the night with this guy I hardly knew? He had fled the car; he *could* have been going off to kill someone—but no, he wouldn't do that, he wasn't a murderer, he was too bookish. Now here I was, linked to Kerrie Lanouette's murder, however tenuously, and my next thought was that if I were smart—which I was, ostensibly—I'd be getting out of this before it went any further.

I warmed up some leftovers in the microwave, trying to decide what to do. I knew it probably wasn't right for the police to take him in just because he was black, but I had to be honest: if *I* had seen some lone black guy walking down Great Lake Drive in the very middle of the night, I would be suspicious, too. Now he was in trouble at St. Banner, they'd probably kick him out, and he'd go—where? Home? (But he really didn't consider it home.) Paris? To find his mother?

I crept up to my parents' bedroom, closed the door behind me, looked up the main number at St. Banner, and dialed it. It was a Saturday; probably no one was in the office and I'd have to sneak up there and try to find him, which might create even more problems. But someone picked up the phone.

"Admissions, St. Banner, may I help you?" said a woman's voice. It wasn't a local voice. The woman had that rich, accentless, TV way of talking that everybody up there had. She also sounded bored, and indignant at being interrupted.

"Yes." I cleared my throat. "I'm trying to get in touch with Brooks Tremont."

"Brooks? Do you mean Francis Tremont, one of the students?"

"Um . . . yeah. Francis."

"I see," she said, and paused. She sounded immediately suspicious. "Well, he lives in Goolsbee House across campus, and there's only a pay phone over there."

"Oh."

"Yes. Can I take a message and pass it to him?"

"No," I said, too shortly, but the thought of him calling my house terrified me. (Whoever answered the phone would wonder about that voice immediately.) "I mean, I'm an old friend from Virginia, and I don't even know if he'd remember me." Then, for authenticity, I said, "I ran into his great-aunt a while back and she told me he was at boarding school up in Massachusetts." I said all this taking great pains to conceal my own accent.

"I see. You're a friend from Virginia." She didn't sound convinced at all.

"That's right. But I'm away at school now, too. I'm at—Middlesex," I said, because that's where Charlie was supposed to go, but he didn't get in.

"Oh, *really?*" The woman perked up, suddenly entirely familiar. "How's Kratsy? Is he still there?"

"Um, I think so. I just started this year, just like Francis did at St. Banner."

"Well, I hope you have Kratsy for classics. He's a *marvelous* teacher. Would you ask him, please, if he remembers Susannah Bailey? I was

Trey's little sister, class of '79. Would you tell him I'm on staff now at Mendhem? He'll be absolutely *furious!*"

"Susannah Bailey, class of '79," I said dutifully.

"That's right. Trey's little sister. I'm so happy you're at Middlesex! It's a wonderful place. Will this be your first New England winter?"

"Yes, it will."

"Well, I hope your folks sent you long johns and a good coat, because winters here are killers. But Middlesex is beautiful at Christmastime. They put candles up everywhere."

"Thanks for the advice. I can't wait to see it."

"Mmmmmm," the woman cooed happily on the other end of the line.

"So, can I call into that phone over in Goolsbee House? I'd love to catch up with Brooks—Francis."

"Oh, of course. He may be out of the house right now in a meeting, but you can give him a try." And she gave me the number, which I scrawled down on the back of a bank envelope.

"Thanks a lot, I said. "I'll look around for Kratsy for you."

"Susannah Bailey—" she began again.

"Class of '79," I finished. "I won't forget."

"Goody! 'Bye now." And she hung up.

I checked out my parents' bedroom window to make sure my mother and Joani weren't pulling in yet. *Is that what everybody at Yale is like?* I asked myself, and then, *What did she mean, Brooks might be in a meeting? They're kicking him out. He's getting kicked out.* I felt queasy again as I dialed. After about sixteen rings, some random guy picked up the line.

"Is Francis Jefferson in?" I asked. He told me to hold; he'd go see, he mumbled. He sounded either very fatigued from studying, or stoned.

I waited for what must have been about five minutes, picking up bits of grunted conversation in the background (they all sounded stoned there) and constantly watching out the window for my mother's car.

Then, finally, "Yes, this is Francis."

He sounded so businesslike I couldn't help a grunt of laughter. "You told me your name was Brooks."

"Who is this?"

"Who do you think it is?"

"I'm sorry. I don't recognize the voice."

"It's *Eric,*" I said, closing the bedroom door behind me. "Your friend from last night?"

A pause. "Ah. Mr. Fitzpatrick." Another pause. "May I call you back? I'm in conference at the moment."

"You can't call back. I'm—I'm going out in a minute. I won't be here."

Silence on the other end of the line. *Did I lose him?* "Listen, Brooks—or Francis, or whatever—I just saw the newspaper. I read about the police."

"Oh, really?" he said, casually, as though I were talking about someone else. "That was an unfortunate business, wasn't it? I'm presently paying the piper."

"Are you okay?"

"I'm quite intact. Your local police force is very cordial. They almost seemed to hold me in awe. They told me they didn't think anyone of my hue went to Mendhem."

"Of your *what?*"

"My hue, Eric. You know, as in 'hue and cry'?"

"Oh. Well, are you okay?"

A laugh from the other end. "Yes, I'm quite fine. They were perfectly gentle with me. Thank you for your concern."

"I mean, is everything okay at school? Are they going to let you stay?"

"Um. That's currently being negotiated. I'm supposed to make a fervent plea for forgiveness, but I can't seem to muster the fervor. I'm already dreaming of cathedrals and the Louvre."

"But you *should* make a plea. Don't you want to at least finish the year out? Otherwise, you'll be in high school forever. Don't you want to finish?"

A big, weary sigh from the other end. "Well, I suppose if it means that much to you."

"It doesn't have anything to do with me!" I snapped. "But you don't want to be in high school for the rest of your life. That's so depressing. Don't you want to get on with your life?"

"Who says I have to stay in *this* godforsaken place?"

"But you have finish high school. Even if you don't go to college—fine, that's your choice. But everyone needs a high school diploma. Otherwise, you're not good for anything."

"My dear boy, I am *loaded.*"

"That's not going to get you everything!"

"Oh, dear, you *are* awfully conventional."

"Thanks a lot."

"I'm just kidding. Listen, Eric, if it allays your fears at all, I think they're going to take pity on me. They asked how to get in touch with my parents, and I said that I honestly didn't know. Then they asked about my aunt, and I said she was going senile and the whole issue would just confuse her. I think they see me as some sort of foundling. I think they feel like I'm their responsibility, God forbid. Their project, and they want to rehabilitate me. They're demonstrating an enormous amount of Yankee guilt."

"Oh. Well, that's in your favor."

He laughed. "I suppose so."

Then neither one of us said anything, and there was a funny silence over the line. I wondered if he was thinking at all about the night before, if he even remembered it, or if he wanted to just forget all about it. *I* wanted to forget all about it—in the light of day, it seemed like a disjointed, murky dream—but at the same time I didn't, and I didn't want him to, either. It was wrong, it was not supposed to happen, but for him to pretend it didn't, to pretend he didn't know me that way, seemed like the worst kind of fakery.

"Why did you tell me your name was Brooks? The paper said Francis, and so did the woman at the main office."

"My name *is* Brooks," he said. "It's my name for myself. I picked it."

"Then who's Francis?"

"It's my father's name. It's my given name. I reject it."

"Oh. Where'd you get Brooks from?"

"Gwendolyn Brooks, my mother's favorite poet. Cleanth Brooks, my favorite literary critic. Well, one of them. It seemed appropriate."

"Oh." I didn't know what else to say. "That's a nice name. It's aristocratic-sounding."

He laughed. *"C'est moi.* What's your real name?"

"Eric. It's my only name."

A mock gasp. "What? You mean you didn't give me a pseudonym to protect yourself?"

"Why would I do that?"

"What if I wanted to blackmail you? I could destroy your life, and all your dreams."

I started to feel a little ill again. "You wouldn't do that," I said, wanting to sound breezy, but not really feeling it.

"Hmmmmm. How can you be so sure?" Then, before I could answer, "No, you're absolutely right. I think now I want to have as little as possible to do with the whole wonderful world of West Mendhem. I don't want to make the papers again. I can only handle so much celebrity."

"That's good," I said weakly, before another long silence. *It's time to get off the line*, I was thinking to myself, but I didn't know what to say, how to end it.

"My dear boy?"

"Uh-huh?"

"Why, exactly, did you feel compelled to call me?"

The question hit me with a kind of sick thud. *I shouldn't have called* was all I could think. "Why did I call you?"

"That was the question."

"Well—I don't know. Because I just wanted to make sure you were okay. I was worried they were going to kick you out. Isn't that reason enough?"

"Don't you have enough to worry about in your own whirlwind life? Yale awaits you."

"Oh, shut up. You know, this might be hard for you to believe, but maybe despite all our differences I consider you a friend."

"That's so sweet! A boy raised on *Sesame Street*."

"Oh, shut the fuck up! Do you even *have* any friends?"

"I guess I do now, whether I like it or not," he said, before bursting out laughing.

"Jesus Christ, shut up!" I started to get the same furious, blubbery feeling I had gotten before with him, that second time in the car when he said he had a knife. "Why do you always have to be like this? You're so fucking—"

"Look, Eric, I'm sorry."

"Fucking *sarcastic,* like everything's a—" But then I stopped short. My mother and Joani were pulling into the driveway; in a moment they would need help with the groceries. (They'd be blabbing, blabbing, blabbing, and this would hang over me, unfinished.) I cleared my throat. "Look, I gotta go, my mother's home—"

"Eric. Eric. Eric." He sounded serious now, but I could hardly hear him, I so badly wanted to get out of the bedroom. "Eric—"

"I gotta get out of here. Off the phone."

"Eric. You're my friend. You're my friend. We're friends, okay?"

"Eric!" I heard my mother scream from the front door. "Come help with the bags!"

"Hurry up, Erky!" Joani yelled after her.

"I'll be down in a sec!" I yelled back, then, into the phone, "Okay? Gotta go!"

"Eric, did you hear what I said? I said we're friends."

"Huh? Okay, that's good. Don't worry about it." I could hear Joani coming up the stairs, slowly, huffing like an old woman. I was starting to sweat.

"Do you want to get together again?"

"What?" I barked into the phone, too loudly, disoriented. Downstairs I heard my mother yell again: "Eric, get down here! Everything's gonna melt!"

"Do you want to get together again? I can't leave school, probably, but you could sneak over here."

"Okay. That sounds great."

"Phone, all right?"

"All right. Great. Great. 'Bye."

"Good-bye, dear boy. Don't let a simple—"

Joani flung open the bedroom door, breathing heavily, looking flushed from the grocery trip and the flight up the stairs. I hung up the phone. "Who're you talking to, Erky?" she asked coyly, standing there sucking on a Popsicle.

"Just Phoebe," I said, frozen for a minute before her.

She smiled at me with the Popsicle still in her mouth. "Ohhhhh," she said, singsong. "You guys are in love."

I exhaled, smiled back, moved toward her and scruffed her on the head. "That's right, Joani. Phoebe and I are madly in love. We're gonna run away together and get married. You guessed it. How'd you get so smart?"

She just shrugged, loving the game, with the goddamned Popsicle still in her mouth. I bolted down the stairs to get the groceries, shaking out my head, shaking out the phone conversation and all its loose ends, shaking out the booming sound of his voice in my ears, even though his voice was beginning to stick there between meetings, even though I was beginning to hear it clearly there now, even when I was alone.

Again, that was all back in September. It's November now, colder, with holidays coming. We've discovered that old, cold barn, and, like I said, it seems to be the eye in the middle of a hurricane. So what can I do? I hope and pray that no one finds us out, and I should probably know better. But I still go.

Six

❖

It's a Saturday afternoon about a week before Thanksgiving, and I'm working an extra shift at B.J.'s (Sal needed someone up front while he fixed the walk-in in the back room), trying to slice mushrooms and read *The Waste Land* at the same time, which isn't easy, when the phone rings. I turn down the radio and pick it up.

"B.J.'s. Can I help you?"

There's a pause, then: "Eric?"

"Yeah? Bren, is this you?"

"Yeah. I'm glad you picked up."

"Are you home or at work?"

"Um. I just got home." Brenda sounds strange, like she's been crying or something—or she's about to. "Nobody else is here. They're all out somewhere."

"Oh," I say, and she says nothing. "Bren, are you okay?"

"Listen—actually, I was kinda hoping you could come home for a minute. I gotta go over some stuff with you."

"Bren, what do you mean? I'm at work. Can't you come here? What kind of stuff?"

"Just—*stuff!*" Brenda says with a snort. There's another pause while

I hear her trying to pull herself together. "Look, I had a big fight with Frank last night—"

"You did?"

"Yeah. It was really bad."

"Did you finally tell him no wedding?"

"Yeah, and he freaked out. He was really drunk. He said to me, 'I know you're fucking some other guy, and I'm gonna mess you both up,' and he totally wouldn't believe me when I said no way. Then he said he wasn't gonna leave me alone. He said he was gonna come take the baby as soon as I had it, and he was—he said he was gonna slap all kindsa lawsuits on me and stuff for being an unfit mother, and—and—oh, I don't—just scary shit." I can hear her start to cry again.

"Bren, take it easy," I said, low, turning the radio back up so Sal can't hear me. "Frank was just talking stupid because you took him by surprise and he was drunk. He's not gonna do that stuff."

"Anyway, Eric, that's not all of it. I'm takin' off, and I need you to come over here and help me write a note. I was up all night. I can't think anymore. I can't get my head straight."

"You're taking off? Where are you going?"

"Look, I'll tell you when you get here, okay? Just say—just tell Sal you gotta drop me off somewhere. Sal's cool, right?"

"No, Bren! Tell me now. Where the hell are you going?"

"I'm goin' to live in Billerica with this friend of mine, Lori, that I work with. She's got her own apartment there, and she's real nice. She's Italian."

"Brenda, what does that have to do with anything? Look, you can't just move out when you're pregnant. What'll Ma think? She'll freak out."

"Eric, you idiot, don't you get it?" Brenda hisses at me. "I can't take any more of this! Frank is gonna be all over my case, and Ma's at work all the time anyway, and Dad is so weird, it's like he won't even talk to me, and when he does, his eyes get all leaky. And *Doris*"—she spits out the word—"Doris is prayin' for me night and day 'cause she thinks I'm going to hell. And everybody around town is looking at me funny. I can't take this fuckin' town anymore!"

"Well, what about me?" I say softly. "Can't you just talk to me about this? Can't we just talk through this?"

"Oh, Eric, look—" She sounds exasperated, like she called for a specific favor and her patience with me is wearing thin. "Eric, you know you're my favorite, but—but you're all in your head and shit. It's, like, you give me all this intellectual advice, and—and then I take it, and look where it ends me up."

"Bren, you didn't *want* to marry Frank just now. Don't blame me for that."

"I know. I'm not sayin' that," Brenda says. "I'm just saying I need a girlfriend for this. And I gotta get away from the family."

"Bren, look, Sal's working in the back. Can't you just come down here and have some lunch with me, and we'll work this out?"

"Eric, *no!* I'm outta here today. Are you gonna help me or not?"

I'm thinking that if I don't get to Brenda fast, Ma will beat me home and there'll be a serious fight. "Hold on," I say into the phone. Then I call back to Sal, asking him if I can take off for a half hour or so to give my sister a ride somewhere. He yells back that I can, and to pick him up a pack of Salems at Cumberland Farms, and to say hi to my sister for him.

"All right, Bren. I said I'm coming to pick you up."

"Thanks, Eric. You're excellent."

Sal comes out to relieve me while I'm getting my coat. "Make sure you lock up your car when you leave it," he says to me, wiping his hands on a dirty rag. "You hear the news on the radio this morning about the old lady?"

"No, what news?" I ask, distracted. I'm thinking about getting to Brenda as soon as possible, and defusing a potential disaster.

"Old lady—a Mrs. Haley, I think her name was. Lives way out-country, almost into Boxford. Two fuckin' assholes broke in and woke her out of a sound sleep. Then they tied her up and gagged her and cleaned out her house."

"That's horrible," I say, knee-jerk, but I've only got one ear on Sal.

"And the poor old lady stayed like that until the meter man came around this morning and heard her moaning. It's a wonder she didn't have a fuckin' heart attack before he got there."

"Did they catch the guys?" I ask.

"No, not yet," Sal says darkly. "But I bet you can guess what she said they were."

"No, what?" I ask, making for the door.

"Fuckin' spics, that's what. From Leicester, probably." He just stands there, nodding slowly at me. "Ohhhh," I say, fake knowingly, but I'm really just wanting to get to the car.

"Things are comin' to a head, buddy," he says, picking up where I left off with the mushrooms. "They are comin' "—and he chops emphatically—"to"—another chop—"a *head*." One final chop. He just looks at me and keeps nodding meaningfully.

"I hope not," I say with a wan little smile, and leave. It doesn't surprise me that Sal and Frank were good buddies in high school.

When I get home, Brenda's upstairs in her room, packing stuff into one of my father's suitcases, clothes and cosmetic stuff everywhere, and I wonder why it is that whenever I have a private confrontation with Brenda these days she's packing a suitcase.

"Hey," I say, coming into the room and standing over the bed.

"Hey." She only glances at me for a second before looking back down at the suitcase. She doesn't seem hysterical anymore, just resolute. I think I see a bruise or something on her left cheek, but her head is bent down, and I can't really tell. It could just be makeup smudged from crying.

"Thanks for coming," she says, not looking up.

"It's okay," I say. "I gotta get back pretty fast, though. Sal just heard about another Hispanic-related crime on the radio, and he's exacting revenge on the mushrooms."

"Wow," Brenda says, rolling up clothes and stuffing them in the suitcase, and it's obvious that she didn't hear a word I just said.

"Ma thinks we're all having dinner tonight," I say carefully.

Brenda laughs sharply, and shrugs. "Yeah, well—"

"You sure about this, Bren?"

She looks at me, smearing her hands across her face. "Uh-huh" is all she says. She's weirdly subdued, resigned. She looks beat up, if not literally then inside. Suddenly, standing there, watching her pack up her things in her usual slobby way, getting fatter every day, I start to feel like if I don't think of something else fast, I'm going to cry, which will *really* piss Brenda off. So I say, "What did you want me to do for you, again?"

"Huh?" she says, too loud, as if I'm distracting her, and staring me blankly in the face.

"Didn't you say on the phone you wanted me to help you write a note or something?"

"Oh. Yeah. So I can leave it for Ma and Dad. They'll find it tonight, but don't let on like you knew I was goin', or anything. Just don't make a big deal about it."

"Brenda," I say, trying to sound sensible, "it *is* a big deal, whether I make a big deal out of it or not. They're not gonna be happy."

"They'll deal," she says flatly, getting a notebook and pen from the top of her bureau. "They've got other stuff to worry about now, anyway. Grandma, and Joani, and putting you through school. I'm gonna try to get a temporary spot at the franchise of the card shop in Billerica, so I'm not around town."

"Oh, Jesus Christ," I say. "What about the baby, and the doctor's appointments and stuff?"

"I'll come back for that. Billerica's only fifteen minutes away."

"Are you sure you don't want to wait to leave until tomorrow, and talk to them tonight?"

"No. I want you to help me write this note. You can write it and then I'll copy it out before I go. I gotta get my thoughts straight. I can't make sense of anything talking to anyone anymore. No one in this family listens to anyone, anyway."

"Thanks a lot."

"You know what I mean," she says, annoyed. She seems to lose her place in the packing and walks over to her dresser, where there's a statue of a little baby Jesus dressed in a crown and a genuine lacy white gown. Grandma gave it to her for her First Communion, and it's been on her dresser since then, surrounded by hair products and some of Frank's old football trophies and other stuff. Brenda's probably never thought to put it away somewhere. Now she picks it up and fluffs out the little gown and blows dust off of it before putting it back, at a funny angle.

I decide not to press her any further, at least not yet. "What do you wanna say in the note?" I say, opening up the notebook and uncapping the pen.

"Um," she begins, coming back to the suitcase, "I don't know. Well, first of all, that I talked to Frank and that the wedding plans are off, at least for now. And that if he calls, everyone should just say that I'm taking some time off and I'll get in touch with him when I'm ready."

I scrawl all this down. "Like, when is that?" I ask. "Three weeks? A month?"

"I don't know. Probably longer. Just leave that part blank."

"All right. What else?"

She sits down on the bed for a minute and rubs her hands absentmindedly over her belly. "Um. And that I'm not doing this to hurt anyone, but I've got a lot of stuff to sort out in my mind right now, and I need some peace and quiet. . . ."

I take this down dutifully, and when I look up, I catch her looking at me expectantly, as though she's impatient for me to record the rest. "Uh-huh?" I ask.

"And that even though Ma and Dad have been pretty good about this, not freaking out and everything, I don't think anyone really knows what I'm going through right now. I don't think anyone really understands."

Then, all of a sudden, I look up at Brenda, who's staring out the window with this far-off look in her face, and I want to shake her, she's making me so angry. It's funny, I don't even know where the feeling's coming from, because I've always been Brenda's supporter and confidant and I've been worrying a lot about her lately—but suddenly I look at her, and, right then, I think she's the most selfish person in the world.

I probably shouldn't say it, but I'm feeling kind of harsh, so I ask, "Brenda, does it ever occur to you that you're not the only person in the world with problems? Or even in this family?"

She looks up at me, betrayed and defiant. "What the fuck is *that* supposed to mean?"

"I mean, maybe you're not the only person in this family who's going through tough stuff right now. What about Ma?"

"What about Ma?"

"Maybe she's really stressed out," I snap back, my voice rising higher than I want it to. "Maybe she's worried about how she's gonna take care of Grandma, and Joani, and keep her job on top of it. And maybe—even though you can't believe it—maybe she's worried about you, and she wants you to be around so she can look after you. She's just not saying anything about it to you because you've been so cold and distant lately."

"I can't help it!" Brenda says. "This is how I feel!"

"And what about Dad?" I go on, ignoring her. "Don't you think he *wants* to reach out to you? Do you really think he sits there reading the paper and watching TV and he's not thinking about it? Because if you do, you're wrong. That's what his leaky eye is—that's how he expresses his emotions. But you've always been so sarcastic and mean to him, he's terrified of opening up to you. And you're his oldest kid!"

"I'm not mean to him!" Brenda protests. "I just don't know what to say to him."

"What about 'How was your day?' instead of your usual 'Hey, Art'?" Before she can answer, I plow on. "And then Joani! Bren, our sister is *retarded*, she can hardly read, who knows how long she's gonna be around, and you don't give her the time of day!" I don't know where this is all coming from, I'm scaring myself as I say it, but it's the first time in a long time I've blown up at anyone in my family, and it's giving me this scary excellent feeling, like I could go on forever.

When I brought up Joani, Brenda started crying all over again, but now she looks me full in the face and shouts, "Who the fuck are *you* to say this to me?"

"I'm your brother, that's who, and I've always been there for you. You know that," I say righteously, calmly, wanting to steer this whole conversation away from me. But she keeps screaming.

"I know you have, okay? What do you want, a fucking *medal?* You're already got enough anyway! You've never had a fucking problem in your *life!* You just glide through everything, and you're everybody's pet, and you never make any trouble, you're like—you're like a fucking robot!"

"Brenda, shut up, okay?"

"Well, you are! And you tell me I have to stay around for my family, but what are *you* gonna do next year? You're gonna go off to little la-di-da Yale or Harvard or wherever the fuck you're gonna go, and you're not gonna give a *shit* about us. You're gonna hang around with a bunch of hippie Phoebes and Charlies and just let us all sit here and *rot!*"

"You're talking like an idiot, Brenda," I say, but I'm not feeling as righteous as I was a moment before.

"Why do you think Ma keeps her stupid job, anyway? 'Cause she *likes* it? No! She's been a nurse for twenty fuckin' years, and she's sick of it. It's because they don't make enough to put you through school on Dad's job alone, and Ma can't make that kind of money doing anything else."

"That's total bullshit. She does it because she loves it. It gets her out of the house."

"That's not true. She's doing it so she can send you to school, so you can have everything you've always wanted. She told me so."

I stare back at Brenda narrowly. "She did not."

"Yes, she did."

"When?"

"What, when? The exact day? The exact minute? I don't remember. A few weeks ago."

She's standing over me on the bed, her arms folded across her chest, looking triumphant. I don't say anything, because I don't know if she's lying or not, and I can't prove that she is. But if she isn't, I feel like shit—and she knows it now, and she knows that lying or not, she's quelled me.

"Eric, look," she says to me, softer now, sitting back down on the bed. "I didn't mean to say those mean things. All I'm saying is, how can you tell me to think about other people when you don't even know what it's like to have any problems to deal with? You *never* have any problems at school. You *never* have any problems with Ma or Dad. You haven't even had a girlfriend yet. You don't even know what it's like to be in *love*, never mind try to figure out if you're still in love with somebody or not. So all I'm saying is, how can you tell *me* how I'm supposed to feel over what's going on in my life? I don't even know where I'm going in life. You're all set."

I look at her, stunned, then away. I don't feel angry at her anymore, or anything—just a funny kind of blankness. I want to yell back in kind, to say, "What the fuck do you know about anything? What the fuck do you know about my life?" but I'm paralyzed; even if I wanted to say something, it would never come out.

She just stares at me with this look that says, "I'm sorry, but I'm not sorry," and then she gets up and goes on packing. I go into my room and write out the note, then bring it back to her as she's trying to close the zipper on the suitcase.

"Here's the note," I say, holding down the top of the suitcase for her.

"Thanks," she says, hardly looking at me again. She opens up the notebook and starts copying down the note, concentrating as she writes. "You're such a good writer, Eric," she mumbles without looking up. "This says everything I feel."

"It's just a little note," I say.

"It's so good, I hope they think I wrote it."

"I tried to keep it simple. I don't think they'll notice anything funny about it."

She finishes copying it, signs her name with her trademark big flourish, rips the page out of the notebook, and folds it up.

"Thanks," she says. "Now I gotta get my stuff in the bathroom."

"I should get back to the shop."

"Okay." She stumbles toward me, giving me a mechanical hug and kissing me on the cheek. "I'll call soon. I promise. Don't worry about me."

"Okay." I hug her back, holding on even when I can feel her pulling away. My heart is beating in a funny panicky way; there's something going crazy in there I want to let out so badly.

"Bren?"

"Yeah?"

"You're wrong about me. I swear to God you are. I'm not perfect. I'm not, I swear."

She smiles, kisses me again. "Whatever. Just forget that shit, okay? I was just pissed off."

"But I'm *not.*"

"Okay," she says, faintly impatient. "Don't worry about it." She stands back from me, still smiling. "Everything's gonna be fine, okay?"

Something in me gives up. "Yeah."

"I'll just leave the note on the kitchen table, and it'll be like you weren't even here. Like you never knew I was leaving, okay?" she says, going into the bathroom and rummaging around in the closet. "That way you don't have to lie or anything."

"Okay," I say, standing outside, half hearing her.

"You still there?" she says a moment later.

"Yeah."

"You better get back to Sal."

"All right. 'Bye, Bren."

" 'Bye, hon. I'll call you soon."

I go back out to the car. Later today, I'll have to fake that I didn't know she was leaving. I'll have to arrange my face and the pitch of my voice into that expression and cadence that say, *"I know nothing."* What I think to myself is that when the time comes, doing that—playing dumb, playing innocent, playing someone with no party to anyone's machinations, even my own—shouldn't be a problem at all.

Brenda was wrong, of course, when she thought her leaving would be no big deal. I was in the family room staring blankly at MTV when I heard my parents come in; the sound of my mother's cheery "We're home with steaks!" when they came through the door made me briefly ill. I forced myself into the kitchen and listened to my mother, still in her nurse's uniform, babble about some funny thing that had happened at work while my father unpacked groceries; the whole time, Brenda's letter—*my* letter—sat innocently on the kitchen table like a mail bomb waiting to be opened.

"Where's Joani? Where's Bren?" my mother asked brightly. "We gotta put on the steaks!"

"Joani's at Eddie's," I said, truthfully enough. "Isn't Bren still at work?"

"She gets off Saturdays at three," my mother said. "What's this?" she said, picking up the letter and unfolding it. She hadn't read for more than ten seconds before she said "Get this out of my sight," dropped it back on the table, and walked upstairs like a zombie. We heard the bedroom door slam, and, in a moment, the sound of her bawling from within.

"What the hell is that?" my father said, picking up the letter and pulling out his reading glasses. He mouthed it silently as he read.

"What is it?" I forced myself to say, convinced that I reeked of phoniness.

"It's from your sister," he said, dead. "She moved out."

"What?"

I'm certain he looked at me keenly for a moment, his eyes narrowing and leaking behind the glasses, before he said it again, in a deadpan that made my blood chill: "She moved out. She's sick of all of us, and she's movin' out." He shrugged. "Fancy that, huh?" he said with a weak laugh, his eyes glassy, then walked upstairs. I heard the bedroom door open, then close, softly.

I picked up the letter, looked at my words in Brenda's fat handwriting, and said aloud, "I hate you." But I didn't know if I was saying it to Brenda, or myself, or both.

Brenda didn't come home for Thanksgiving at Auntie Lani's, even though Frank stopped by, hoping she'd be there. Of course, her absence dominated the day, even though no one spoke about it directly, which probably would have been much easier to take. Instead, the aunts clucked over my mother and hugged her, saying, "These are the times to get through," which made my mother nod tightly because she couldn't stand their pity.

Now Christmas is coming, and none of us are feeling yuletide. My mother took second shift at the nursing home through the holidays, so she doesn't get back until eleven o'clock, and since this is also the big season for cheese and cracker sales, my father comes home late every night as well. These days, everybody eats at odd hours from big platters of lasagna and manicotti that Grandma makes. She's become the de facto head of the household, and she's thrown herself into her job: when she's not cooking, she's showing Joani how to sew or praying for Brenda over her rosary beads.

Brenda has called once, on a Sunday night, and I didn't get to talk to her. Instead, I sat at the top of the steps and heard my mother's side of their brief conversation, just long enough for my mother to try to keep her cool, lose her cool, inveigh against Brenda's selfishness, and get hung up on by Brenda. Since that phone call, my mother hardly mentions Brenda, and when someone else does, her face darkens, as does my father's. Joani wants to know when Brenda's coming back, and I tell her soon, soon, and when she does, she's going to be *really* fat, because she's having a baby, and you'd better not laugh at her, Joani. And Joani promises gravely not to laugh, so reverent has the Ianelli family made her toward the process of baby-making.

But no one really talks much about Brenda openly, and there's a funny kind of civility to this house now, without her blasting music and her predictable screaming matches with my mother. It's as though Brenda's become some kind of ghost, as though invoking her aloud will bring bad luck. I wonder over the instinct in my family to fill Brenda's absence with silence instead of talking it into habitability, the instinct to treat her leave of absence—a minor thing, a temporary thing—like the gravest betrayal, like a kind of household death.

"The age of anxiety has come, and now there will be no peace," Charlie intones dramatically. "West Mendhem is now paying the price for its years of evil depravity."

"In the end, the hate you take is equal to the hate you make," Phoebe says.

"Do you really think all this stuff is that simple of an equation?" I ask.

"Totally," Phoebe says. "Don't you understand the laws of karma?"

"Fuckin' A," Charlie says. "What comes around goes around."

"Exactly," Phoebe says, brushing hair out of his eyes.

The three of us are sitting in study hall together in the cafeteria, talking low at a far table so that Mr. Parker, this period's study hall monitor, doesn't separate us. We're talking about what Phoebe, in typical hyperbolic fashion, calls "the local Armageddon"—what everyone around town is calling a crime wave, even though since the murder of Kerri Lanouette, to date unsolved, there have only been a handful of events, like the robbery of that old woman out by Boxford and a few other random incidents, like car thefts. All these things could have been carried out by anyone—God knows they could have been carried out by West Mendhem kids themselves, bored and restless on a Friday night—but people in town seem more and more convinced that it's all coming from Leicester, that slowly, inexorably, the invisible barriers that separated West Mendhem from the neighboring city for so long are crumbling, and that this is just the first stage in the transformation of West Mendhem into a *jungle*, which seems to be a popular metaphor these days around here.

The paper has begun publishing nightly boxed "Security Tips" ("Always leave a light on in your window when you're away late at night, or even the television!" and "Don't open the door for a delivery man or meter reader until they've shown you full and proper identification"). Lots of people are talking about buying a gun—"Just a little one"—to lock up in their nighttables, away from the kids, and in masses, the weekly "Lord hear our prayer" call-and-response always leads off now with "For the safety and sanctity of the young and old in our community, in the streets, and in our homes."

So "Exactly," Phoebe says, looking away from her dog-eared copy of *Siddhartha* and brushing hair out of Charlie's eyes. He blushes and shakes his hair back into his face, dopily, like a dog, when she does so. "All these years, people in West Mendhem totally *dick over* these Hispanics in Leicester. First they leave the city, and destroy the economic infrastructure, and then they won't even allow housing to be built in West Mendhem that these Hispanic families can afford, so they can send them to decent schools—if you wanna call *this* shithole decent—and get out of their shitty cycle of poverty and despair. And now they're uprising, and they're coming after their oppressors. I, for one, am surprised that it didn't happen sooner."

"You can fool some people sometime," Charlie starts to whisper-sing in a horrible Rastafarian accent, miming steel drum on the cafeteria table, "but you can't fool all the people all the time."

"Metengarten, keep it down," Mr. Parker barks across the study hall in the voice he usually reserves for when he's reffing bombardment in gym class. There's a little ripple of laughter in the cafeteria directed at our table.

Phoebe makes a jerking-off gesture behind Mr. Parker's back—she's hated him ever since he flunked her in gym for wearing clogs—and looks gravely at Charlie, then me. *"Exactly,"* she says again, and they share a portentous glance, my two stoner revolutionary friends.

Phoebe and Charlie are still seeing each other, although the relationship seems to be more about taping Grateful Dead concerts for each other and having stoned sex than any real philosophical bond. There was tension between the three of us for a while, until one night when we all got high in Phoebe's parked car. Charlie went off into the woods to piss, and Phoebe and I finally had it out. I said I felt like the two of them were conspiring to edge me out, but then Phoebe said that, completely to the contrary, they wouldn't even be able to go out if they didn't have my endorsement, which they did, didn't they? And that I was their biographer, their chronicler, and someday I would write the story of their great romance ("It'll have epic sweep, like everything you'll write," Phoebe said brightly.) And that she and I weren't a good romantic match, anyway, that I needed someone less bohemian and ethnic, more urbane and aloof—a woman to worship as well as love, like Daisy Buchanan, or Ellen Olenska from *The Age of Innocence*.

Then she said, "Charlie might be my spatial lover for the time being, but you'll always be my mind lover," and she kissed me on the head. I guess that was what I wanted to hear, but it was too late to pursue it, anyway, because Charlie came back to the car, oblivious, as usual, to the tension. He fiddled with the radio until he found "Lisa Says" on WFNX, turned it all the way up, and we sang it at the top of our lungs all the way into Lowell, to which we drove for no good reason other than that it was Jack Kerouac's hometown.

"Why do you necessarily think that *everyone* in Leicester wants to destroy West Mendhem, and that no one in West Mendhem is capable of doing this stuff themselves?" I ask Phoebe now, fed up with her Sandinista talk.

"Oh, come on, Eric," she says. "It's the age-old class struggle. If you have, you want to keep it, and if you have not, you want to get it."

"But why do you think Leicester is filled completely with have-nots?"

Phoebe looks exasperatedly at Charlie, who goes back to doodling skulls in his notebook. "Eric, let me introduce you to a basic fact," she says in her annoying singsong schoolteacher voice. "In this society, most *dark* people are poor and oppressed, and the object of their resentment is usually—" and here she gestures comically around the cafeteria— "white people!"

"Phoebe, that's not always true," I say.

"Okay," she says, "you name me two nonwhite people you know in West Mendhem who don't fit that bill."

"But everybody in West Mendhem's white," Charlie interjects, too loudly, earning us another shush from Mr. Parker and another round of titters.

"That's not true," I say. "What about Akhil and Malini Patel, and Jennifer Hsu?"

"They're Oriental, or Middle Eastern or something. They don't count," Phoebe says.

"How can you say they don't count?" I ask. "They're not white."

Phoebe looks at me like I'm the biggest idiot of all time. "Eric, their parents probably work for some electronics company on Route 128. I'm talking hardcore seriously oppressed minorities that are caught in a vicious cycle of poverty and hunger and stuff. You know, drugs and welfare and babies and all of that. Let's face it, *they're* the have-nots, and they're all just across the border."

"Well, you're right," I concede to Charlie, "there aren't a lot of them in West Mendhem. But it's not as though rich black people or Hispanic people don't exist."

"Name one you know," Phoebe says.

"Michael Jackson!" Charlie bursts out, then buries his head in his arms and laughs convulsively at his own stupid joke.

"Yeah, right," Phoebe says, "and your other good friends Lionel Richie and Oprah Winfrey and Vanessa Williams."

"And the Cosby family," I add.

"Of course, the Cosbys," Phoebe says. "All good friends of yours, right, Charlie?"

Charlie looks up. "Yo, word up." Then he starts gurgle-laughing again.

Suddenly the school secretary's voice crackles over the intercom: "Eric Fitzpatrick please report to the principal's office. Eric Fitzpatrick please report immediately to the principal's office."

Now Charlie laughs twice as hard, and Phoebe looks at me wide-eyed, as does the rest of the study hall, including Mr. Parker. My legs go weak and my heart is suddenly pounding; I've never been called to Mr. McGregor's office before in my life.

"What the fuck do you think that's about?" Phoebe says.

"I don't know." I stand up and gather my books. "I wasn't expecting a summons."

"Maybe Ray wants to discuss the meaning of life with you," Charlie says, still finding everything wholly amusing.

"Maybe," I say blankly, pushing in my chair.

"Come to my locker and tell me at the end of seventh, okay?" Phoebe holds out her hand to me.

I take it limply. "Okay."

As I walk out, a few kids, stupid underclassmen, make low you're-gonna-get-it noises. "Hey," Mr. Parker announces, deadpan, "zip 'em up or I'm gonna write out some yellow slips."

It's the middle of fifth period, the halls are completely empty, and all the way to the office, I'm terrified, thinking, *What is it? What is it?* And then, halfway there, I stop cold and think: Does this have to do with *him*—Brooks? Did someone see us together one of those afternoons— or that night he was picked up—and they've just waited until now to do something about it? What if the police are going to be in there, and they want to question me? Then I just start walking again, and I think I'll just play it cool. I haven't done anything wrong. If they saw us together, I'll just say we're friends. I'll say we met—we met in the town library, and we're working on—we're starting up a joint literary magazine between S.B.A. and West Mendhem High—to promote good relations, or something like that. *Nobody could have seen us together like that,* I'm thinking, determined. *Brooks isn't a criminal, except for some drug use. And they can't touch me.* Still, when I step inside the glassed-in anteroom to Mr. McGregor's office, I'm shaking and there's sweat running down my back and armpits underneath my shirt.

"I got paged," I say to Miss Laski, the hunchbacked old secretary, and she calls through to Mr. McGregor on the intercom. "Eric Fitzpatrick here for you."

I hear Mr. McGregor's booming ex-marine voice crackle over the speaker: "Send 'im in."

Miss Laski wheels around in her chair. "You can go in, Mr. Fitzpatrick," she says, sarcastic, and I swear that when she looks at me I can see twin portents of doom in her eyes.

When I go into Mr. McGregor's office, there's a virtual powwow taking place: Mr. McGregor sitting behind his desk, some authoritative-looking WASP-y guy in a navy blazer, horn-rimmed glasses, and shiny loafers sitting opposite him, and on the sofa Goody Farnham my English teacher and, of all people, Mrs. Bradstreet. Then I notice they're all *beaming* at me, and my dread turns to general bewilderment.

"Good afternoon, Eric," Mr. McGregor says to me, amiably enough, which makes me suspicious. He's always been nice to me in a stiff sort of way because I'm on the Honor Society and a bunch of committees, but Phoebe and I have always thought he was a military fascist and I've always made a point of being as chilly to him as I possibly can be.

Goody Farnham greets me, looking like her hairbun is about to burst off the top of her head, she's smiling so broadly, and Mrs. Bradstreet, too, has her eyes fixed on me like I'm some kind of museum exhibit. The WASP-y guy in the horn-rimmed glasses is also smiling at me like an old uncle or something, like he's known me all my life. He turns to Goody Farnham and Mrs. Bradstreet and says, "He looks like a man of letters."

"Oh, he's always had it in him," Goody Farnham chirps back, perched on the edge of the sofa.

"Sit down, Eric," Mr. McGregor says, indicating the empty seat near the WASP-y guy.

"Am I in jeopardy?" I say, sitting down, and everybody bursts out laughing so hard I almost miss the seat.

"You just might be," the WASP-y guy says heartily. I notice he doesn't have a local accent, but one of those rich-sounding voices, and I wonder if he's from St. Banner.

"Well," says Mr. McGregor, turning to WASP-y. "Would you like to tell him?"

"Why don't you?" WASP-y says. "You're his principal, after all. His patron, so to speak."

Mr. McGregor turns back to me and folds his hands across the table. "Good news, Eric. Do you remember writing an essay for Mrs. Farnham for a *Boston Globe* competition? 'What I Cherish in America'?"

For a split second, I think back to the night when I wrote that essay, how I was still half stoned, who I had been with that night, how writing it had felt like such a great, nasty fuck-you. I had passed it in and then put it completely out of my mind.

"I do," I say now to Mr. McGregor. "I gave that piece a lot of thought."

"That much was evident," WASP-y guy says. "We gave it a lot of thought, too, Eric. It gave us pause. That's why we picked it out of two-thousand-some entries across Massachusetts as the first-place winner in the 'What I Cherish' competition." He gets out of his seat and extends his hand to me. "Congratulations, Eric. You're quite the wordsmith, and one of the last of the humanists, to boot."

Everybody is smiling at me like I'm a prize dog, and my first instinct is total shame; I want to tell them all that they made a mistake, that I wrote the essay as a joke, that I didn't mean any of it. I want to, but I don't. Instead, I take WASP-y's hand.

"Thanks," I say. "Wow. I wasn't expecting it."

"We were," Goody Farnham says. "I showed it to Mrs. Bradstreet, and we agreed it was the best piece of expository writing we had seen from a student in twenty years."

"Congratulations, Eric," Mr. McGregor says, extending me *his* hand across his desk, nearly crushing mine in his boot camp grip. "It's nice to know WMHS has actually got a brain trust to draw on."

"Oh, God," I say, blushing, feeling like an idiot, but already I'm thinking maybe the essay was better than I thought; maybe I *do* deserve the prize. What was it about? All I can remember is, something about Kerrie Lanouette's murder and the spirit of America.

"Eric," the WASP-y guy says to me now. "I'm Philip Coe, in charge of special programs at the *Globe*. I've been running essay contests like this for some twelve, thirteen years now, and I must say, never have I encountered a prose style quite like yours in a high school student. What are your influences?"

"Oh, he loves literature," Goody Farnham breaks in, demanding my attention.

"Well," I say, feeling like Eddie Haskell, "I guess I have great teachers." Everyone breaks out in more laughter—Goody Farnham looks like the Puritan husk has just fallen right off her—and WASP-y Philip Coe sputters, "Well, I *see!* Now here's a savvy kid! But I mean, what are your *literary* influences? Your favorite writers."

"Um," I say, warming to the conversation, "I like J. D. Salinger. And, oh, I don't know, F. Scott Fitzgerald and some Henry James. I like social critics a lot," I say, feeling very discerning.

"And Whitman?" Philip Coe says.

"We're reading Whitman right now, aren't we, Eric?" Goody Farnham puts in.

"Yeah, I guess Whitman, too," I say. "Ebb and flow, right?" and Goody and Mrs. Bradstreet laugh approvingly.

"I *thought* so!" Philip Coe says to Mr. McGregor, who nods dumbly. "I could detect a love for Whitman in your essay. In its rhythms, and its sweepingness, and its—oh, damn, you know, its *humanity*. Where are you going to school next year?"

"Yale, if they're smart," Mrs. Bradstreet says. She's hardly said a word before this, but she's been eyeing me curiously the whole time—like there's some little secret the two of us share, like she helped me engineer this coup—and it's making me uncomfortable.

"Don't *say* that to a Harvard man, or I'll have to revoke your prize," Philip Coe says, and everyone laughs again, harder. "Oh, well," Philip Coe says, sitting back down. "It's Harvard's loss if you don't apply. But anyway," he says, pulling a manila folder out of his battered leather briefcase, "let's get down to business. Now, the *Globe* is going to announce the first-, second-, and third-place winners on the front page the Sunday after next, just in time for Christmas. We'll be running your piece alongside a story and photo of you, so a staff writer will be getting in touch with you soon to set up an appointment. Maybe they can get a shot of you standing in front of some local monument, or something comparably spirited."

"Maybe in front of the World War One Memorial on the Common," Mr. McGregor says.

"Now, Eric," Philip Coe continues, completely ignoring Mr. McGregor. "You know you win the Apple PC to take to Yale, pardon me"—and he stops to fake-spit over his left shoulder, and everyone laughs again, dutifully—"and, further, how's your public speaking?"

"I haven't done much lately," I say. "Why?"

"Well, you know, part of the prize package is that you get to read your piece in front of the *Globe* heavies and about five hundred invited guests, including your family and teachers, of course, at an awards ceremony and dinner in Faneuil Hall just before the holiday. My office is handling all that, but I promise you, we will *not* be serving chicken with the skin on, *nor* a fruit cup for dessert."

"That's going to be a thrill," Goody Farnham says, looking heavenward.

"I'd better get a new tie," I say.

"That's a wise idea," Philip Coe says. He picks up his battered briefcase and starts to pull on his Burberry coat. "In the meantime, I must get back to the desk before I hit the afternoon rush on 93. And you, Mr. Fitzpatrick," he says, shaking my hand again, "must prepare to become a local celebrity, which should be at *least* as exciting as four years in the halls of Old Eli." He hands me his business card out of his breast pocket. "Consider me your handler. You call me if you have any questions. Otherwise, I'll probably see you next at the awards ceremony. You'll be getting an official invitation on engraved *Globe* stationery from our dear editor-in-chief very shortly. And to you fine educators, I wish you a joyous holiday season." He shakes hands with Mr. McGregor, Goody Farnham, and Mrs. Bradstreet, all of whom murmur back niceties to him; they seem completely mesmerized by his presence, which I must say *is* rather overwhelming. "You should be very proud of your young charge."

"We *are!*" Goody Farnham giggles, and with a final squeeze of my shoulder, Philip Coe dashes out the door. A moment later, from Mr. McGregor's office window, I see him throw his briefcase in the back of a little Subaru and drive away.

"Oh, Eric!" Goody Farnham erupts the minute he's gone, and actually leaps forward to give me a little hug, a most un-Calvinist gesture. "You're bestowing *honors* upon the English department!"

"You're the one who made us enter, Mrs. Farnham," I say.

"But *you're* the one that married sentiment and word and made them sing," Mrs. Bradstreet says, standing back from us, in her unnerving, measured la-di-da voice, still giving me that look that says "It's our secret." Now she's really starting to bug me; I want to ask, *What the hell are you even doing here? You're not my English teacher; you're social studies!* But of course I don't say that; I just smile and try to look self-effacing.

"Eric, why don't you go into Mr. Fazzi's office and call home with the good news?" Mr. McGregor says. "He's away at a conference, and I'm sure your folks would like to hear about it."

"I've got to get back to study hall," I say, wanting to seem dutiful and humble, like I don't deserve special favors.

"Oh, for God's sake," Mr. McGregor says, scrawling something down on a piece of notepaper and handing it to me. "Here's your dispensation. Give this to old Parker."

"Thanks, Mr. McGregor," I say. Everybody knows Mr. McGregor dislikes Mr. Parker because Mr. Parker humiliated him on the field in the faculty touch football game last fall.

"I'll see you in class, Eric," Goody Farnham says, all a-twinkle. "Exciting weeks ahead."

"I'll see you in class, as well, Eric," Mrs. Bradstreet adds, but from her it sounds more like a threat than a pleasantry.

"As usual," I say, aiming to sound a little arch, and slip into Mr. Fazzi's office, which is dark and quiet and weirdly exhilarating to be inside. Mr. Fazzi is the vice principal and his four sons, who used to give me wedgies in junior high school gym class, are all star athletes; his whole office is cluttered with their trophies and pictures of them in various uniforms, but there isn't a single scrap of what looks like work anywhere to be seen on his desk. I sit down in his leather chair and dial my mother at work. When she comes to the phone and I tell her the news, she yelps with excitement, then she says she'll call Grandma to have her make eggplant parmigiana, my favorite dish, for dinner so we can all celebrate. And she says she'll get someone to fill in for her at work, and that I should be home by six. Then: "Bye-bye. I'm so proud of you—you really cheered me up!" and there's just the tone on the line, and I'm alone in Mr. Fazzi's office.

I know I should take Mr. McGregor's pass and go back to study hall and tell Phoebe and Charlie the news, but I still can't believe I wrote a bullshit essay and somebody actually bought it. And it seems like such a wicked secret that I want to tell it to somebody who'll really appreciate it, but I don't know who—and then I look at the phone, and suddenly, right in the middle of Mr. Fazzi's office, right in the middle of fifth period on a Tuesday, I want to call *him*, Brooks, and tell him all about it, I want to laugh with him over it because I think he'll get a kick out of it. It occurs to me that I haven't even seen him now since the time when he got stoned and almost fell out of the loft, and how that scared the hell out of me, and how I tried to push him to the back of my mind and concentrate, concentrate on everything else—but since then, that last picture of him walking stoned across the soccer field, back to the dorm, has kept pushing itself into the front of my mind every day, when I least expect it. What he said to me that last time, about whether I *loathed* myself or not (not hated, *loathed*), and what he tried to do to me when I was stoned, comes hurtling back into my head at the strangest times—in the middle of class or a yearbook meeting, when I'm helping Joani with her homework or doing my own, when I'm brushing my teeth in the morning, or late at night, exhausted, getting ready for bed.

Even though he's probably in class, I pick up the phone and dial his dorm. It rings eight times before someone finally picks up.

"Goolsbee," someone says, flat.

"May I speak to Brooks Tremont, please? Francis Tremont?"

"May I ask who's calling?"

I pause a moment. "Eric," I say. "His friend Eric."

There's a pause on the other end of the line, then there's the old familiar broadcast-news voice, the voice that sounds like skeptically raised eyebrows. "Oh. Hello there. This is Brooks."

I'm taken aback. "You don't sound like you," I say.

"Who do I sound like?"

I don't know how to answer that. "Why aren't you in class?"

"Latin canceled due to instructor's gout. I'm reading in the common room."

"Oh. Well, how have you been?"

"Of no consequence, really."

He sounds totally deadpan, like he hasn't been thinking of me at all, couldn't care if he ever sees me again. "Really?" I say, laughing nervously.

"Really. What about you? You've been in absentia lately. I actually didn't know if I'd be hearing from you again after the way I conducted myself that last time."

"Oh, that?" I say, relieved. "Forget about it. People get that way."

"I was *truly* wretched, wasn't I?" he says, almost gleefully.

"You weren't that bad," I lie. "You could have called me, you know."

"No, I couldn't. You never gave me your number. I think you didn't think it was wise to let me know how I could reach you."

I'm embarrassed because he's absolutely right; I've always been afraid of him trying to call me at home. "I'm sorry," I say. "I've been going crazy with stuff here—with my sister taking off, and school. But I've been meaning to call you for a while."

"Mm-hmmm," is all he says.

"Really," I add.

"As you've made clear."

"How are you, really?" I ask again, desperate.

"Of no consequence, as I've made clear."

"Are you going home—going to Virginia for Christmas?"

"Yes, to illness. My auntie is poised to expire."

"I'm sorry," I say. "I guess that means you're poised to get a lot of money."

"Do you really think I'm that mercenary and shallow?" he snaps. "Do you honestly think that's what I'm thinking about right now? The woman is *dying*, you know—not pleasantly, either."

"I'm sorry," I say, shaken. "It's just that—that you always joked about it, and stuff."

"You should learn when to read between the lines of a joke."

"Well, I'm sorry," I say again. He doesn't answer, and I begin to wonder if it was such a good idea to call in the first place; maybe, having let a month pass, I should have just forgotten about the whole thing.

"I just found out I won a big contest," I spew recklessly.

"Oh, really?"

"Uh-huh. I got first place in this *Boston Globe* essay contest called 'What I Cherish in America.' We had to do it for class. I wrote it as a total joke. I actually wrote it that night after we went out to the lake."

"Is that so?"

"Uh-huh," I rush on. "And then today this guy from the *Globe* shows up, and they're gonna publish the essay and I have to read it at this big dinner at Faneuil Hall. Isn't it a riot?"

"Terribly," he says. "How exciting for you."

"But I wrote it as a *joke,*" I say again. It's important to me that he understands this.

"I'm sure you did." That's all he says. I'm sorry I called.

"Listen," I say. "I've got to go to my next class; I'm calling from school. Have a good Christmas, okay? I hope your aunt's okay—or—you know—okay?"

"Well—"

"Okay? I gotta go."

"Eric, listen, can you meet today after school?"

Now I can't believe what I'm hearing. "Today?"

"Well, yes. You know. In the usual place?"

"Well, I've got to be home by six. My grandma's making dinner for me—for us—to celebrate this contest."

"Well, you could come just for an hour or so. Say around three? Do you have any engagements after school?"

"Well—sort of. But I could get out of them."

"So, three then? I promise I won't ingest any behavior-modifying bromides."

"Um—I guess so. The usual place."

"Yes." The bell goes off outside in the hallways, scaring me half to death, and in a minute I can hear the din of students barrelling their way through the hallways.

"All right, then. I'll see you at three. Ciao."

"Ciao—'bye," I say, and hang up. I apologize to Mr. McGregor for taking so long as I pass by his office.

"Listen to the loudspeaker on your way to class," he says to me with a sly smile. "I've got a surprise for you."

As I'm walking to class, Miss Laski's zombielike voice comes on the loudspeaker. "Your attention, please, for a special announcement from the principal's office. Senior Eric Fitzpatrick has placed first in the *Boston Globe*'s statewide essay contest with his informative essay "What I Cherish in America." His essay will be featured in the paper a week from this Sunday. This is a special honor not only for Eric, but for West Mendhem High School. Please be sure to congratulate Eric on this notable achievement. Thank you for your attention."

I pass a group of kids in my class, some guys on the hockey team and their girlfriends. "Congratulations, big guy," they say to me, pounding me on the back and mussing my hair. "Eric, congratulations, that's so exciting, you're so *smart!*" their girlfriends squawk at me, big-eyed, gasping.

"Thanks," I say, dazed from the pummeling. We go our separate ways. When they turn the corner, I hear them all burst out laughing.

Seven

It feels strange to be driving out to St. Banner at this time of day. I haven't done it in nearly a month, and it's much colder now, the middle of December, and even though it's only three in the afternoon, the light already seems to be bleeding out of the sky, the color of wet undyed wool. Taking Route 136 outcountry, I pass several old white houses that already have Christmas lights in their windows and strung around their bushes and trees. I feel like I am fleeing civilization, fleeing festivity, on this, the first afternoon of my celebrity. But as I turn into the familiar pathway near the far outskirts of St. Banner and park the car off the gravel, half in the woods, the old thump in my chest starts up again, and the funny tingle in my stomach, perhaps stronger, because I haven't made this trip in a month.

Soccer season is over and the fields are deserted. Now, stripped of greenery and athletes, St. Banner looks lonelier than ever, more like an old, out-of-the-way sanatorium than a school, and I feel minuscule and paranoid as I trudge across the hard-packed earth of the field sidelines, bent forward into the wind, walking toward the horizon below which unfold the buildings and the immense lake. The old barn looks the same, but when I pull back the colossal wooden door it lets out a ghastly shriek that I don't remember it ever having made before.

I close it behind me. It's slightly warmer in here than it is outside, but not much, and the darkness disconcerts me; the tiny windows high above took in more light back in the fall. Inside it's completely silent.

I stand in the middle of the barn and squint up toward the loft. "Hey!" I shout-whisper sharply. No answer.

"Brooks?"

Again, no answer. I look at my watch. It's only seven past three; he mustn't be here yet. I take the old ladder, careful to lean forward as I climb so the weight of my laden backpack doesn't throw me back down. At the top, I stare into the dark recesses of the loft.

"Hello."

"Shit!" I almost topple back down, I'm so startled by his voice. Now I can make him out: he's sitting Indian-style in a far corner of the loft, absolutely still, like someone practicing meditation, or something, lost inside the biggest, bulkiest knitted sweater I've ever seen, jeans, and knee-high rubber waders. He's got some sort of open shoe box in front of him, and, in his hand what look like photographs and scraps of things.

"Didn't you hear me from down there?" I ask, climbing into the loft, pulling off my backpack and standing over him awkwardly. It's funny: we haven't seen each other for some time; I'm reabsorbing his face, his posture, his voice, everything about him. He looks—I don't know— gaunter than the last time I saw him, but maybe that's just because he's swallowed up in his ridiculously huge clothes, like someone pressed at the last minute into playing an old New England salt and hurried into the garments of someone twice his size.

All he does is look up at me slowly and nod, like a kid who's just been clocked, and then finally, in a voice that's hardly there, he says, "I did."

"Well, then, why didn't you call back?"

"I'm sorry?" Looking blanker still.

"Why didn't you call back when you heard me call?"

He looks down at the pictures in his hand. "Because I didn't hear you."

"*What?* Brooks, you just said you did!"

"I'm sorry," he says, not looking up. I'm still standing over him, wondering what to say, when I notice that the pictures are shaking in his hand. (They're old photos, I notice absurdly now, making out dim figures in black and white.) Pretty soon his whole body is shaking, and in a moment I hear a horrible racking sob come out of his chest. Then he drops them back into the box and throws his head into both his hands. Suddenly he's just *weeping*, his whole body shaking and rocking, sounding like he's never sounded before, and, terrified, I get down on my knees beside him. I think I can smell marijuana on him, but I don't think to ask about it.

"Hey. Brooks, come on. What's wrong?" I put my cold hand on his shoulder; I can feel it shaking through the scratchy huge sweater.

"Brooks. Come on. Talk to me," I say. I begin to wonder what I was thinking when I said today I would come; I begin to think I've wandered into something too deep for me to handle. But when he just crumples further into himself, all I can do is move the shoe box from between us and put my arms around him, and think *Just let him ride it out. That's what he did for me once. It's only decency.* At first he stays as he was; then he extricates his arms from under me and puts them around me and, still crying, lets his head fall onto my chest and then into my lap. He keeps on crying and I stroke his head, sitting awkwardly on my knees and staring into the darkness of the loft, aware of the cold, and we stay that way a long time. And then he stops crying, and we're both absolutely silent and still, and he finally looks up at me from my lap. I wipe the wet off his face, and then we both just look at each other, blankly, until he says, "Eric."

"Yeah?"

"Come here."

And I lie down beside him on the freezing loft floor, my backpack and his shoe box somewhere down below our feet, and we both just start running our hands over each other's faces, still staring at each other, and I'm beginning to feel very old, but in a grimly content way, like an adult, and I'm wondering to myself: *Is this what it feels like to have thoughts too grave and tender to express, so grave and tender that it feels wrong to express them? Is this what responsibility feels like—or am I fooling myself?* But before I can really worry about it, he pulls my head close to his (his hands are curiously warm on the back of my neck) and pretty soon we're sucking face for I don't know how long, maybe nearly half an hour, but I don't really know because I'm not keeping time. It's as if everything that's happened since the last time we did this falls away, as if it all was just a prologue to this happening again, a series of exquisite points on a time line, and I'm wondering how we've gone so long without, why I thought it was best to go without, or how I thought I would, or how anyone possibly could, especially through this long approaching winter.

"Hey," he says.

"What?"

"Feel this." And he puts my hand over his pants, and I go, "Oh," and in a moment I'm pulling his stiff thing out of his jeans and he's in my pants pulling out mine with his warm hand. Then we're sucking face again, furiously, and we both stop a moment to slobber all over our own hands and smear the spit over the top and shaft of each other's things, and I'm thinking I'd pass up a *million* stupid essay prizes just to be able to do this with him every day—no, not even every day, every *week*, maybe, every *month*. We've each got our other hand down underneath each other's shirts, and we're kind of holding each other up and staring down at ourselves (our right arms making an **X**) and then back up at each other, with our legs sticking straight out and our pants down around our knees, butts freezing on the loft floor. And suddenly I feel myself hit the top of the hill; I go completely stiff and hold my breath and pretty soon I'm spewing in festive white ribbons onto my bare legs, all over my shirt, and onto the floor.

"Oh, my God, beautiful," he says, still completely stiff, and I sit him up, facing forward between my legs and I pull off his sweater and shirt, lock my ankles over his, throw my left arm around his chest, run my right hand across the spew on my legs, place it back on his cock, and start jerking him off, faster and more aggressively than before. And now that I'm over the hump myself, so to speak, I can't get over how incredible it is just observing him go through the same arc of pleasure, hitting the top of the same hill, and, exclaiming, "Ex—*traor*—dinary!" stiffen his back against my chest and send his own white ribbons out before us, straight out, four shots plus, in as clear and unequivocal a trajectory as my own.

Then I lean back, and so does he, and we just lie there for a few minutes, breathing hard, not saying anything, and then finally he puts his hand on my cheek, and he whispers, "I missed you."

"I missed you, too," I say. And I startle myself because I can't believe how much I mean it.

He sits up and wipes himself off with his shirt, although even by now, in the cold, everything's mostly crusted up, and he pulls his jeans, shirt, and colossal sweater back on haphazardly, and I do the same. Then he pulls over the shoe box and settles the two of us into a corner and grabs the old army blanket that he brought up here some time ago, and drapes it over our laps and knees.

"I brought this up here to show you," he says, placing the box on his lap, actually looking kind of shy.

"What's in it?" I ask—gently, trying to encourage him.

"It's photos and clips and things that I took from my auntie's house when I came away. She's been saving this stuff all these years, even though there's no love lost between her and my mother, or my father, for that matter. I don't know if she ever intended on giving this stuff to me—maybe as a graduation present or something—so before I came up here I slipped away with it. The purloined shoe box."

"Indeed."

"Here's my mother." He hands me a page from some fashion magazine dating back to the late sixties. "She used to be a model before she married Francis. Her name's Viola, but everyone called her Vi." He pronounces it "Vee," like the letter.

It's a striking, almost intimidating photograph of a lithe, beautiful black woman in a crazy flowing pink pantsuit, legs pitched wide and perched on tiny heels, arms thrown out, askew, above her head, and long hands (like his) flung out, Catwoman-style. Her hair is pulled back tightly on her head, like a sleek black cap, and I try to look beyond the spidery false eyelashes and Cleopatra makeup to see in her eyes if I detect a resemblance to him. I do; it's a dueling look, a look that says, "Just *try* to best me, because you won't."

"She's beautiful," I say, handing it back. "Why did she quit?"

"She got knocked up. With me. She was supposed to go back to Virginia and become a schoolteacher when she graduated from Spelman, but then her mother died and she freaked out. She didn't want to live with Auntie Fleurie, so she packed her things and moved to New York, and waited tables and lived in the YWCA. She walked into a fashion magazine for colored ladies one day, looking for a job, and they asked her if she wanted to pose for a shoot. And that was that. The whole 'Black is beautiful,' the whole exotic thing, was starting up, and she got plenty of work."

"I can see why," I say.

"Then she met Francis at a party—he was just starting up his own little outfit at the time—and they started seeing each other, and he knocked her up. Then they got married. I was born, and for a while, we all lived happily ever after in a walk-up on West Ninety-sixth Street. He started traveling down to the Caribbean on business, and she'd take me into the park every afternoon. She became friends with all the Negro nannies, so all these little white East Side babies were my first friends. Then my father didn't come back from a trip; he sent a letter instead saying that the more he went away the more terrified he became of coming back. And that this time, his terror finally had gotten the better of him. And that we would be provided for. So my mother packed us up and we moved back down to Virginia to live with Fleurie."

"Did your mother go crazy when your father left?" I ask.

He purses his lips. "I don't really remember. I was too young, and when I was growing up, the name *Francis Tremont* was spoken in a poisonous whisper, if at all. All I remember is one thing, really: my father left behind all of his ties in New York, dozens of them—gorgeous ties, too, designer ones, Yves St. Laurent, Pierre Cardin. My mother would get them for him for free because of modeling, because he was starting his own business and couldn't afford to buy good ties himself. And my mother brought all those ties back to Virginia with her, and over the years, Auntie Fleurie ended up sewing them all into quilts. Some of the quilts she'd sell at church fairs, but a fair amount ended up around the house. Growing up, that was how I knew that Francis Tremont had indeed actually existed, because his ties were everywhere."

"Shit," I say. "That's eerie." I'm trying to take it all in: beautiful mother, New York City, the Caribbean, a globe-trotting father in exquisite ties secured for free. It's almost more than I can process.

"Rather." He hands me another photo, the kind that comes in a cardboard frame you can prop up on a bureau. "This is him, Francis, right after graduating from Cornell."

"Wow. Cornell?"

"That's right. He was from the North, upstate New York, very solidly bourgeois. His father owned some kind of glue factory, I think, and his mother was a nurse. He was confident; I remember that about him, he was fierce—and *big*. He played football for Cornell. He was also Phi Beta So-and-So, but he still couldn't get a job with any New York City finance outfit. My mother told Auntie Fleurie it was discrimination, but Auntie Fleurie said, 'No, child, that isn't discrimination, it's Francis being too cocky for his own good.' Auntie Fleurie never liked Francis; she thought he was one of those uppity, squawk-talking *integrated* Northern niggers."

The word hits me like a slap, and I look at him, surprised, but he just shrugs. I open up the frame: there's a formal black-and-white photograph of a seated man in a thin-lapeled black suit, hands folded over one crossed knee. Brooks is right, he *is* big: squared-off, not attenuated like his son, and he isn't so much handsome as capable-looking. He's smiling decorously in the photo, but in his eyes, behind the horn-rimmed glasses, I think he looks a little stunned, like he's there more in body than mind.

"He looks imposing," I say, handing it back.

He puts the picture back in the box and closes the lid. "I suppose so. I don't remember." And he slides down and drops his head into my lap and looks up at me blankly.

"Is that who you were thinking about when I came in?" I ask, running my hand over the top of his head.

"Huh?"

"Your father? Your mother?"

"Sort of. But it's hard to think of Francis in anything but the abstract, since I haven't heard from him in about twelve years. I guess it would be nice to see the lovely Vi, but she's becoming more and more of an abstraction in my head, too. I wonder if she'll come back for Fleurie's funeral, which should be any day now. She's got to, I suppose."

"Brooks?" I venture. "What are you going to do when your auntie dies?"

"I don't know. Meet with the executor of her will, I guess. I suppose you want to know where an old black lady in the South got all her money, hunh?"

It seems like he wants to tell me—it seems like he wants to tell me a lot of things tonight—so I say I guess it's crossed my mind.

"You know how in those romantic, lying movies about the Old South, Ole Massa's on his deathbed, delirious, and he gives over all his land to Big Sam, or Jiminy, or whichever good darky didn't desert the farm with all the other no-good niggers when the Yankees came through?"

"I guess so," I say, although I can't actually remember any movies where this occurs.

"Well—believe it or *not*—that's actually what happened on Fleurie's side of the family, although I suppose it wasn't quite as simple as that. Somehow the land came down to Fleurie and she lived on it for a while, but she got tired of the White Lords of the Magnolia, or whatever the fuck they called themselves, coming around and burning the crops down. So she finally sold it, for a fraction of what it was worth, but a goodly sum nonetheless, and she built herself a fine house in the city. And she educated herself and she became a lady of standing in the community. *So there.*"

I don't know whether he's mocking his aunt or not—I don't even know what parts of the story to believe—so all I say is "Wow. That's impressive."

"It *is* impressive, isn't it?" he says, mocking *me* now with his saccharine golly-gee voice. "And a few years ago Fleurie got herself a nice sympathetic white law firm to execute her estate when she popped off. So they're the fine fellows I'll have to meet with—imminently."

"And then what?" I ask.

"And then since they're my custodians, I'll have to convince them to let me take the money and run."

"Run to where?"

"What have I said before? To Paris, city of eternal light."

"Aren't you ever going to go to college?"

"Not if I can help it," he says, reaching down under the blanket into his pocket, where he withdraws two cigarettes and lights them simultaneously. "Here," he says, handing one to me.

"You know I don't really smoke."

"Oh, for Chrissakes, just take it. You look sexy with a cigarette. I can pretend you're Holden Caulfield. You'd like that, wouldn't you, you little prep-schooler manqué?"

"What does that make you, then?" I ask, lipping the cigarette tentatively.

"A lost cause," he says, exhaling.

"Would you shut up with that again?" I say, annoyed. "I've told you a million times, you've got everything going for you. First of all, you're—"

"Oh, Eric, for God's sake, *you* shut up!" he exclaims, sitting up and putting his hand over my mouth. I'm taken aback, and I let out a muffled "Hey."

"What was that for?" I ask when he uncaps my mouth.

"Eric," he says, putting his hand up against my shoulder and pinning me, effectively, to the wall. "There is something you simply must understand, once and for all. I don't *want* your idea of success. There's nothing in the world that I'd like less than going off to some constipated school like Yale or Harvard or Amherst"—he makes a special, exaggerated point of dropping the "h," prep school style—"or *whatever*, and hanging around a bunch of brain-dead idiots like the ones here for another four years. I don't *want* it. I don't want to be a Rhodes Scholar, I don't want to be a lawyer, I don't want to be an investment banker. I don't want anything to do with anything you could even remotely call an American success story. I just want to get out of here; I don't ever want to be picked up by the police for walking at night again; I *love* walking at night. I just want people to leave me alone."

He's got his eyes fixed on me and his upper lip is curling. I'm a little hurt, because I feel implicated in everything he's telling me he hates, but I say it anyway: "Do you hate everybody just because they're white?"

"No, I don't hate everybody just because they're white," he says, mimicking me, sneering. "I've had just as few black friends as white ones. I hate everybody because they're idiots."

"Well, then, why do you stand me? *I'm* white, and *I* want to go to college. And I guess I want to be some kind of American success story."

"You already are," he says acidly. "You won the big *Boston Globe* high school essay contest. You're the new Eleanor Roosevelt."

"Oh, shut up," I say. "Can't you give me a straight answer?"

"Why do I put up with *you*, you want to know?" he says, crushing out his cigarette. "Because you amuse me. Because I think on some level, you honestly believe that the more books you've read, the more places you've been, the more intellectual sheen you can accrue, the happier your life's going to be someday. You think you're going to get out of your miserable little Dickensian town and go to Yale—and then, God knows where, New York! London! Paris! And you're going to be the life of the party. You really *are* a Horatio Alger hero, but you believe in the currency of cocktail banter instead of the currency of money. And I guess I find that sweet—"

"That's about the most condescending thing I've ever heard!" I say, but he ignores me. He really seems to be on a roll now.

"I find it sweet, and I also wonder if we'll ever meet again in a few years—maybe in London! Or Paris, darling!"

"Would you stop that stupid lisp?"

"At some smashing party on the cliffs at Antibes, and you'll finally tell me that now you know I was right when I told you that, all the way back in dreary West Mendhem in that chilly little barn."

"Told me what?" I ask.

He looks away for a minute, lights another cigarette.

"Told me *what?*"

"You really want to know, Eric?"

"Yes!"

He grabs me by the chin and talks right into my face, like I'm a child. "That you're not going to have a happy life, Eric. And neither am I. Maybe that's why I'm drawn to you. Because I'm a loner here and you're a loner right in the middle of your own family, your own town, or why would you be consorting with me? They don't pass out happy lives to boys like us, Eric."

"Boys like what?"

He laughs out loud. "Oh, good Lord, would you finally stop lying to yourself? What do you think we just did up here an hour ago? Eric, when you picture yourself in ten years, who do you see yourself with?"

"What do you mean, *with?* I don't know. Friends, I guess, like I have now. Like Phoebe and Charlie."

"I mean *with* with. Who do you see yourself getting into bed with every night? Who are you fucking, Eric? Where are you putting your cock, other than into your own hand? Or into a pound of chopped liver?"

I push him away. "I don't want to think about this stuff right now."

But he keeps on. "I mean, you tell me you're so very devoted to your mother and your grandmother and your knocked-up older sister and your three million cousins, or kissing cousins, or whatever they are—your whole tribe. Well, Eric, what would they *say* if they could have seen you a minute ago, jerking off a black boy? What if I got it on tape, and I sent it to them?"

"You wouldn't do that," I say.

"Of course I wouldn't, but you're missing my point. What would they say? They probably wouldn't say anything. They'd probably just hold a big cross up to your face and excommunicate you from the family, if they didn't stone you first."

"I think that's a little extreme," I say with a scowl.

"And what about your teachers, and the terribly prestigious *Boston Globe?* Do you think they'd like to know about the private life of their star contest winner? You want to take *me* to your awards ceremony?"

"*Très drôle,*" I say feebly.

"Eric, all I'm saying to you is *Think about your life.* Why are you killing yourself to please these people who would rather erase you from the books than let you be yourself?"

Now *I'm* the one who explodes. "What the fuck do you want me to do? Tell my whole family and my whole school to fuck off, and run away to Paris like you? Well, I'm sorry, I can't. I don't have a trust fund! Why do you think I work so hard? It's not to please them! It's so I can get the hell out of here and go somewhere more—more—I don't know—*progressive.* I hate it here, okay? Is that what you want to hear? I'm *not* a trained puppy, though! I'm not Ragged Dick!" And I'm just about to start bawling, he's made me so unhappy, but he breaks out laughing, convulsively.

"How can you say those horrible things to me, and then start laughing?" I ask, aghast.

"I'm amazed at your ability to start crying every time you feel like you've been slighted, like you're Vivien Leigh in the final shot of *Gone*

With the Wind. It's almost like you can see the close-up of your tear-stained face and hear the orchestra swell up behind you."

"You're an asshole," I say, which makes him laugh harder.

"All you need is a big radish in your hand to complete the picture."

"What about you?" I finally say. "You almost flooded us out of this loft today."

"I missed my mommy," he says, deadpan. "And I was still a little stoned when you got here."

"Then you broke your promise to me."

"I promise that's the last promise to you that I ever break," he says, lifting up the army blanket and throwing it over the two of us, easing us down into a lying position.

"Yeah, right." I wrap my arms around him under the blanket, lace my legs inside his, bury my mouth in his neck.

"Solemn promise," he says, pressing against me.

It feels good under here, and I realize I'm tired. "I've gotta leave soon," I mumble. "It's gotten dark outside."

"Stay five minutes," he says.

"All right," I say. "Five." And we settle into each other against the cold and I close my eyes and start to doze off, as the phrase "Don't fall asleep" starts repeating itself in my head until it becomes a bloated, disjointed chorus.

"Eric," he whispers, and I mutter, "Uh-huh," and he whispers, "Je t'aime," and I grab him tighter and mutter back, "Je t'aime aussi."

I dream we're accepting the award together, but not the *Boston Globe* award, some other award. I don't know what it's for, but we're on stage together in an enormous hall, before a huge adoring crowd, getting a standing ovation. We're dressed, in this dream, in black tie, and there's no hostility coming from the crowd, only great waves of mirth and approval. I hold the award aloft, and hold out my hand to him, smiling, and he accepts it, smiling devilishly, and leans in, kissing me on the cheek, and whispers underneath the roar of applause, "We've arrived."

It's freezing and pitch dark in the barn when I wake up with him sleeping beside me. I look at my watch; the digital glow reads 12:30 A.M. "Oh shit!" I yell, and he wakes up with a start.

"Who is it? What, what?" he says, groggy, panicked.

"I've gotta get out of here," I say, throwing off the army blanket, groping around for my backpack.

"What time is it?" he asks, coming to.

"It's after midnight!"

"Oh, good Lord."

"I've got to get out of here," I say again, frantically lacing my shoes. "I was supposed to be home for dinner tonight. They must be freaking out! I'm dead! Why did you ever let me fall asleep?"

"I didn't tell you to fall asleep," he says.

"We can't do this anymore." I grope on all fours toward the ladder at the edge of the loft. "What the fuck am I going to tell them?"

"Why don't you wait a minute and figure that out before you just run out?" he says, so matter-of-fact I want to hit him. "You're already eight hours late for dinner. Another five minutes isn't going to make a difference."

"Oh, shit!" I say again. "No. I can't wait. I've gotta go. I'll figure it out on the way home. I hope the car's still there."

"Aren't you going to help *me* figure out something to say? I'm in deep shit, too, you know."

"I'm sure you'll think of something," I snap, lowering myself onto the ladder.

"Will you call me and tell me what transpires?" he asks. "Don't you get *anything?*" I want to yell at him, but I don't. "I'll try" is all I say; then I scurry down the ladder, out of the barn, and out onto the terrifying dark of the soccer fields. Thankfully, the car is where I left it. I race home along the deserted roads, trying to formulate a story in my head, hoping that maybe there's some chance they just thought I was caught up at school, putting together the next issue of the newspaper or something, and forgot to call home, even though I know it's a slim chance.

Which it is. When I get home, the lights are on in the house and my father's car isn't in the driveway. I haven't even turned off the car when I see the front door fly open, my mother standing there, still dressed in her nurse's uniform. I swallow, and brace myself.

"Where the hell have you been? Where the *hell* have you been? We

165

thought you were dead!" my mother is screaming at me before I'm even in the door.

"Ma," I say, wedging past her and throwing down my backpack in the hall. "Just let me explain, okay?"

"You damned well better explain," she says, pointing a shaking finger at me. She looks like she's either going to strangle me or start crying. I notice there's a plate of half-eaten eggplant parmigiana on the kitchen table, and a platter full of the stuff sitting atop the stove. "I have been on that thing all night," she screams, pointing now to the phone, "with *everyone*. Phoebe, Charlie, your teachers, your *principal*, Auntie Winnie, Auntie Reenie, *everyone!* And your father is out right now with the *police* driving all over town trying to find you. We thought you were murdered—or kidnapped—or God knows what."

"Ma," I say, gritting my teeth. "I'm okay. Would you just let me explain?"

"Go ahead. I'm waiting. I haven't heard anything yet." She's rooted to the same spot in the middle of the hallway. She's got huge black circles under her eyes and she looks absolutely possessed. In the living room, the lights on the Christmas tree twinkle serenely; they forgot to turn them off after ten o'clock, like they usually do.

"Would you just let me *talk?*" I yell.

"Go ahead and talk!"

I pause a moment, then plunge in. "I went to see Brenda—"

"That's bullshit!" my mother cuts me off viciously. "I called Brenda and she said she hadn't seen you all night. How can you just look me in the face and lie?"

"Would you let me finish?" I say. For some reason, the sight of the Christmas tree is making me feel incredibly sad as I go on with this lie; so far, this hasn't felt like any other Christmas season I've ever had. "I went to see her, but I never got there."

"What?"

"I wanted to go get Brenda and see if she'd come to dinner tonight, to celebrate," I say.

"Well, then, why didn't you just *call* her?"

"Because I thought if I called her, she wouldn't listen. I thought I'd go to the card store and try to talk to her there."

"She wasn't even working this afternoon," my mother says, coldly.

"I didn't know that. I thought I'd take a chance. But then, on the way there, I took the wrong exit or something and I pulled into this parking lot at a shopping plaza to ask somebody directions."

"And?"

"And then—I don't know. I just felt so incredibly tired all of a sudden that I put back the seat and lay back, just to rest my eyes. And I fell asleep."

My mother looks at me like I'm crazy. "And you slept for, what—*eight hours?*"

"I don't know what happened," I say, feeling as though I'm over the worst part of the lie. "I just—crashed so hard. When I woke up, it was totally dark and the parking lot was empty. I looked at my watch, and I thought it must be wrong. But then I heard the time on the radio in the car and I freaked out."

She just looks at me, stunned, and then she finally laughs, a long, harsh laugh that sounds like a rip. "Well! Well, I am so glad that *somebody* is rested, because your father and I certainly aren't."

"I'm sorry, Ma. I didn't know what happened."

Then she looks at me, and her whole face crumples—it's like her whole body crumples—and she walks past me and says "Oh, Eric," and sits down at the kitchen table, throws her head down on her arms, and starts to cry, exhausted. "Oh, Eric. Oh, baby. Do you *know* you had me and your father worried sick? I thought one of the sickos had gotten you. I thought, *That's it. I've lost my daughter, and now I've lost my son, too. God must be punishing me for something.*"

"C'mon, Ma" is all I can say. I can't go over to comfort her because I feel too disgusting.

"Grandma's been praying all night," she says, looking up at me, bereft, her face stained with tears. "She made this nice dinner and everything."

"I'm sorry, Ma," I say again, weakly. It's becoming a mantra. "I'll tell Grandma I'm sorry."

"And you'd better go upstairs and wake up Joani and show her your face or she's gonna have nightmares all night. She was terrified."

"Okay," I say, suddenly feeling insanely hungry—but too guilty to ask for food.

We hear cars outside. My father comes running in, saying hoarsely,

"Any word?" Then he sees me, like I'm an apparition, and he says, "Oh, God."

"He just got back," my mother says dully.

"Kid, where the hell have you been?" he says, out of breath. Now I'm really scared, but I give him the nutshell version of the lie. He just looks at me like I've completely unraveled, then he says, "I gotta tell De-Marco he's back," and he steps back outside. Meanwhile my mother doesn't look at me, just stares blankly at the half-eaten plate of eggplant parmigiana.

When my father comes back in, he takes off his coat and gloves, unplugs the Christmas tree, and pours himself a glass of scotch. My mother goes on staring at the plate. Then my father comes back in the kitchen, puts down his scotch, and just stares at me—not in anger so much, it seems, but bewilderment, like he doesn't even know me. Tonight, they both look older to me than they've ever looked.

"Would you mind telling us how you managed to sleep in a cold car for eight hours without waking up?" my father asks me.

"I don't know," I say, trying to seem as astounded as he is. "I just closed my eyes for a minute, and next thing you know . . ." (At least, I think to myself, there's some truth in the story. Even if I was at St. Banner, I wasn't awake.)

"Eric," my mother says, "is there something wrong that you're not telling us about?"

"I don't think so," I say. *Keep it simple*, I'm thinking.

"Do you have too much work at school?" my father asks.

"No more than I usually do. I guess I was just more tired than I thought I was."

"Maybe you should go to Dr. Dineen," my mother says, feeling my neck for swollen glands. "Maybe you have mono."

"I don't think so," I say. "But I'll go if you want me to."

My parents just stare at each other. Nobody says anything as my mother gets up, puts some eggplant parmigiana on a plate for me, and puts it in the microwave oven. For moments, the only sound is a warm atomic whir. My father holds his drink; my mother sits back down. I wish they'd both just go to bed, but they seem to be holding out for something.

"Eric. Honey," my mother finally says. "We're all tired these days, and stressed out. There's Grandma with us, and Brenda gone, and all the crazy stuff going on around town. I know it seems like in all the commotion we tend to forget you, because you never give us a problem. But you gotta know: if something's bothering you, we want to hear about it. We really do."

"That's right," my father adds, looking into his drink, and their entreaty catches me so off guard, moves me so deeply, that for one split second I want to just collapse, just tell them all about him and be out with it; I've been keeping it in for almost four months now. I feel something balling up in my stomach and rising to my throat—not nausea, really, but a greater release, and it's just about to come out, now unbidden by me, more like a natural ejection, beyond prudence, beyond reason, when my mother says, "Is it something between you and Phoebe? You can tell us, honey, you know," and the pressure in my throat evaporates, and I come hurtling back down to earth.

"No, it's not. Honestly," I say. "I guess it's just school pressure. And missing Brenda."

My mother takes the plate out of the microwave and puts it down in front of me with a fork and paper towel for a napkin. "Honey, we all miss Brenda—"

"We do?" My father laughs, setting the ice in his drink astir like tiny bells. (He jokes that the house has never been so peaceful, but the other night I found him lying on Brenda's bed in her bedroom, staring straight up at the ceiling. When I asked him what he was doing, he said he had come in to look for his glasses, until I pointed out that they were in his shirt pocket. "So they are," he said, putting them on, and continued to stare at the ceiling, unfazed by me.)

"Yes, we *do*," my mother says firmly. "She's our oldest, and she's having a baby. And Eric"—she puts her hand over mine—"I know how protective you are of your sisters. That's one of your many wonderful qualities."

"I just wish Brenda would figure things out and come back," I say mechanically, my mouth full of food.

"She will," my mother says. "She will. In the meantime, we've just got to keep it together around here. We all have work. And now your prize. And there's always Joani to watch. Now, will you go up there and let her know you're back before she starts having nightmares? And then *get some sleep,"* my mother says, squeezing my face and taking away my finished plate.

"Okay," I say, glad to be dismissed. "Good night, Ma." I kiss her quickly on the cheek. "Good night, Daddy," I say absently, picking up my backpack.

My father laughs. "Daddy?" he says. "That's a blast from the past."

I'm embarrassed that I called him that in my absent-mindedness. "I'm sorry. I'm tired," I say. "Night, Dad."

"You don't have to apologize," my father says, but I'm already halfway up the stairs.

I creep into Joani's bedroom, where Grandma is snoring away in the dark, and stand over Joani's bed. She's sound asleep and looks so angelic and serene that I hate having to wake her up, but I'm afraid if she starts screaming with nightmares (as she's been known to do) at three o'clock in the morning, it will be my fault. I rub her arm lightly and whisper into her ear.

"Hey, Joani baby—"

She opens her eyes, oblivious for a moment, then focuses on me. "Erky," she says, holding out her arm. "Come here." And I lean in further toward her and she puts her chubby arm around me and kisses me on the cheek.

"I just wanted you to know I was okay," I whisper to her. "Go back to sleep before Grandma wakes up, okay?"

"Okay. I sewed an apron today."

"That's great. You can show it to me tomorrow. Go back to sleep now, okay?"

"Okay. I love you."

"Love you, too."

I creep out, into my own room. I know I'm going to be a basket case tomorrow, and I haven't even done the five or so hours of homework I was supposed to tackle tonight, but all I can think about is those old photos, that glamorous woman and that handsome man, and how it happened that they both came to leave him. And I think about what he said about us both being loners, and, brushing my teeth, I start to think, in a creepy kind of way, that maybe he's right: nobody really knows me, including my mother and Brenda, including Phoebe and Charlie, even my teachers, Mr. McGregor and old Mr. WASP-y What's-His-Name from the *Boston Globe*. (If *he* really knew me, I think, he never would have given me that award.)

I get into my own bed, safe and sound for now, I suppose. And I'm wishing he could be here, too. Or better, I'm wishing I could still be back there, up in that loft, freezing, with him.

Eight

❖

The contest awards ceremony was tonight, the last Friday before Christmas. I had to put on a coat, tie, and loafers, and drive into Boston with my mother and father, Joani (looking sweet and uncharacteristic in a dress), and Phoebe (who said she wanted to come so she could hear how bad the second- and third-place speeches were). Grandma wanted to come, but my mother had to convince her she wasn't up to the late night. I'd called Brenda at work earlier in the week asking her if she wanted to come, and she said she'd try to make it. Then, Thursday night, she called home and said she had been put on the schedule at the card shop for Friday night, at the last minute. I gave her the benefit of the doubt.

The ceremony was in some enormous room inside Faneuil Hall, complete with gilt and towering windows and marble floors, a colossal Christmas tree, pine boughs, and tiny lights everywhere for the holiday season. First, there were opening speeches: the editor-in-chief of the *Globe*, who talked about the power of the written word in such trying times; then WASP-y Philip Coe, who talked about the history of the contest and looked about as suave as ever in a red tartan jacket; then a thin, exceedingly jaded-seeming nun in a tailored suit, talking about the methadone clinic she ran in Roxbury and the meaning of the word "ministry" in the 1980s; then a rookie for the Celtics who had pulled himself out of the ghetto somewhere and up into the pros, talking about pride and dignity and self-reliance; he got a huge welcome from the audience (including my father, who seemed more excited than I could remember him being in a long time) and, when he was finished, a standing ovation in which Phoebe and I joined, although neither of us had ever heard of him before.

A jazz band played swing versions of Christmas songs after that, and they served a fancy dinner (something with chicken, which meant that Phoebe, being a vegetarian, ate only her vegetable medley). Then Philip Coe got up and announced that the top three winners would now read their essays, starting with third place. "This is it," my mother whispered, beaming like my father, and Joani held my hand underneath the table. Even Phoebe seemed to be chomping nervously on her hair. I felt inside the breast pocket of my coat to make sure my typed copy of the essay was there.

The third-place winner was a skinny black kid with big, square-framed glasses who was leaving the tough neighborhood of Roslindale and going to M.I.T. on full scholarship next year, the oldest of nine fatherless kids and the first in his extended family to go on to college. What *he* cherished in America, he said in his speech, was that anyone, even a poor inner-city kid like him, could get a top-notch education and achieve success as long as they worked hard and stayed out of trouble. That's why America was so much better than Europe or Japan or anywhere else, he said, where only a select few got to go on and pursue their dreams; *here*, he said, anyone could truly be whatever he wanted to be, which was why America was truly a democracy. He concluded by actually *singing* the last two lines of the national anthem, in a deep, wavering voice that sent the audience into wild fits of applause. Standing in front of the crowd, the kid burst into tears and said "God bless you!" into the microphone, spurring the audience to clap and holler twice as hard. The kid seemed so transported he just stood there at the podium while the applause raged on, until Philip Coe had to escort him gently back to his table, where he collapsed into the arms of his mother and younger siblings. Phoebe raised her eyebrows, giving me a look that said, "My goodness!" and I started wondering why that kid hadn't received first place instead of me.

The second-place winner was a gawky, pale girl from Framingham, with big moussed hair like Brenda's, who clattered up to the podium with a walker. In a horrible, grating South Shore accent, she began her essay by relating how, back in the summer, she had been driving to her job as a cashier in the supermarket when a drunk driver in a minivan came careening around a corner and smeared her little compact up against a telephone pole, knocking her unconscious and breaking nearly every bone in her body. She was in a coma for three weeks and traction for several months, until she was finally able to go back to school while taking intense physical therapy. In the meantime, her family's parish had raised money to cover half the hospital bills, the nurses took turns reading Judy Blume books to her to bring her out of her coma, and her classmates had even voted her Homecoming Queen in absentia and shown up en masse the night of the dance to crown her in her hospital room. What *she* cherished in America, she told the audience, was that despite the fast pace of contemporary life, community and compassion still existed; people would still band together in times of crisis to feed the hungry in Ethiopia, or fight against evils like apartheid, or even save the life of someone like her. She finished her essay by explaining how her physical therapist, Debbie, had inspired her to pursue her own career as a therapist next year at Framingham State College. If I thought they couldn't have cheered louder than they did for the kid from Roslindale, I was wrong, because they did. About half the people in the audience were crying, too, including my own mother.

After the girl from Framingham had clattered back to her seat and the applause had died down, Philip Coe finally rose to the podium, and there was silence in the great hall. My mother put her arm around me, my father nodded at me deeply across the table and whispered, "Stand up straight," and Joani squeezed my hand so hard I had to squirm away.

"We chose our first-place winner because, never in fifteen years of administering this contest, had we come across prose that moved us quite as strongly as it did in this instance," Philip Coe said soberly into the microphone. "I think you'll see why in just a moment."

I turned to Phoebe, whose face was actually flushed with anticipation. "I can't read this," I whispered to her. "It's bullshit."

"What do you mean?" she whispered back. "You won first place."

"But I didn't mean any of it. It was a *joke*. It's mean and sarcastic."

She shrugged. "Nobody knows that. Just read it like you mean it. Be *sincere*."

The rest was like some fantastic, sped-up dream sequence. Philip Coe announced my name. I heard "—happy to introduce Eric Fitzpatrick, a senior at Mendhem—I'm sorry, *West* Mendhem High School," and then in what felt like a rocking ocean of applause, I was threading my way between tables, sweating, shaking, until I had reached the podium, standing under harsh light and staring down at a sea of encouraging, expectant faces. Way in the back, I could see my own table, Joani's head bobbing like a little banner of support, and across the room I could see where Goody Farnham sat, erect and alert in her seat, next to her equally Puritan-looking husband. But as for the rest, looking out at them, all I could think was *They're going to see right through me. I'm a liar, and they're all gonna see it.*

My hands were shaking badly, but I managed to pull out the essay, unfold it, and smooth it down on the top of the podium. The room was so quiet that the most muffled cough flew up into the air and reverberated against the ceilings. I swallowed a lump in my throat and, startled by the sound of my own voice coming out of the loudspeakers, eeked out the first sentence of the essay, the one about Kerrie Lanouette's murder. Immediately, a grave murmur of recognition shot through the entire room—the murder had been in the news and the papers across the state for months now. Originally, I had only wanted to get through the essay as quickly and unremarkably as possible, but now, buoyed by this instant ripple of response, I calmed down a bit and settled into the cadences, actually growing to like the sound of my own voice over the loudspeakers, to the point where I was experimenting with different inflections just to hear what they sounded like.

The funny thing was, after about the first paragraph, still flushed and sweating, I started to have a weird sort of fantasy, right there in front of hundreds of people. I started to believe that the essay was actually about me and him, Brooks, that it was a declaration, or a confession, that somehow I was appealing to all these people, including my family, Goody Farnham, and Phoebe, but also the state representatives, and media celebrities, and sports figures in the audience, to recognize us, and understand, and absolve us, even embrace us, in the name of American liberty and justice, and the great river of Christian charity. And when I got to the part where I had to repeat the word "flame" over and over again, it struck me as so funny—but a joyous kind of funny, like I was sharing the joke with everyone—that I actually laughed aloud, which evoked a funny trigger laugh in the audience (I actually heard Joani's inimitable shriek-laugh float up above the rest). And then, toward the end, feeling elated, feeling this extraordinary warmth and trust between me and all these good people of the Commonwealth of Massachusetts, I slowed down and deliberately counted out the pauses between the final lines:

"For it is the flame that guides all nations, casting blessed, burning light upon the way whole nations live.

"The way whole nations thrive." (And I actually choked a bit before uttering the final line.)

"The way whole nations love."

There was total silence; I looked out into the room and it seemed that every face was hanging in the balance of my next breath, slack-jawed, luminous. And at that moment, I heard him clearly in my head—"Baby, we've arrived," whispered in my ear—and a wave of exhilaration and joy rushed up my back and over my head, like breakers at high tide on Hampton Beach, and with tears mounting in my eyes, blurring my vision and turning the whole room into a muddy collage of green smudges and white-light pinpricks, I leaned forward and rasped into the microphone, "Thank you."

The applause didn't build; it crashed over me, instantly, like a wall that finally gives way to the overflowing river outside. All the people in the room rose to their feet, and in the middle of their deafening ovation, whistles, and hollers, through the haze of my tears, I could make out Philip Coe, aglow with proprietary good cheer, Goody Farnham, striking her hands together like tiny cymbals, my own family, my parents, my mother, transmitting to me *What a day to be an Ianelli!* It felt like all the disparate pieces of my entire life had finally come together, a splendid fusion, and even though he wasn't there, he was, blindingly, he was part of it.

I couldn't feel my legs—they felt somewhere far, far below me, as though someone had untethered my upper region, my head and heart, and they were floating somewhere high above—but I managed to leave the podium and weave my way back toward my family, through tables of people who were still on their feet, applauding me, blanketing me in a quilt of smiles and good wishes. A middle-aged woman, about my mother's age, stepped out, grabbed me by the arm and stared right into my eyes, her face red with the heat in the room. "You have a gift from God," she said sternly, almost remonstratively. "Don't waste it."

Only after I smiled dumbly, putting a hand over her arm, and said, "Don't worry, I won't," did she let me go.

My mother embraced me when I had finally wended my way back to our table. "You were the best," she whispered to me. "You were definitely the best." A wringing handshake from my father and a booming "Nice job!" From Joani, cries of "Erky!" and kisses. Even Phoebe hugged me and said, "You sounded so evangelical!"

"I didn't expect that to happen," I told her, dazed.

She laughed. "I thought you said it was bullshit."

"I thought it was!" I protested. "I guess—who knows how people are going to react. It ended up moving *me*. I'm so embarrassed."

"Don't be."

Philip Coe made closing remarks, the band swung into "Jingle Bell Rock" (in the spirit of the moment, my mother grabbed Joani and jerked her around in a jitterbug for a moment before restoring herself), and they unleashed us. We could hardly get past the table for the well-wishers; first, Goody Farnham and her husband, who proclaimed to my parents, "He is a voice. He really is a *voice*," then parents, whose praise didn't throw me, but their children as well—teenagers, my own age, who approached me with awe and respect, not the usual malice, and *that* threw me. Then reporters from papers around the state, asking me questions as my parents, the Farnhams, and Phoebe gathered around me like a half-shell. What inspired the essay? ("I don't know; I guess Kerrie Lanouette's murder, but it mostly just wrote itself.") Where are you off to school next year? ("I don't know; Yale, I guess, if they'll take me.") Do you want to be a writer? A priest? You'd write great sermons. ("I guess I'd have to say a writer, some kind of writer. I've never thought about being a priest.") "He's always had a way with words," my mother shared with the reporters. What do I think is the biggest social problem facing our society today? (To which I responded, absurdly, "Yuppies. Materialism.")

On the way home in the car, first, there was jubilation, all of us puffed up on the shimmer of the evening, and the applause, and the reporters. My mother marveled over how "elegant" everyone had looked; Joani insisted that I was going to get my own TV show, just like Michael J. Fox on *Family Ties* (on whom she has a big crush); Phoebe told Joani to hold still while she tried to work Joani's too-short, too-fine hair into little reggae braids. My mother told me that my delivery was electric and gave her shivers. And then my father asked, "Why'd you start cryin' at the end, though?"

"I did not!" I snapped, indignant.

"It looked that way, from where I was sitting."

"I think it was just the strong lights made it look that way," my mother said. To which my father merely hiccupped "Hmph" and we all became silent. It was late now, nearly midnight, and Phoebe and Joani fell asleep on each other's shoulders, in the backseat with me, and my mother cocked her head back in the passenger seat. In the rare silence of sleeping women, sleeping girls, my father and I didn't talk. He drove on; I slumped down so as to be invisible to him in the rearview mirror, and feigned dozing. Instead, I stared up at the black December sky unfurling above Route 95 between Boston and West Mendhem. Some of the delirium of the evening began to fade; the sky, bright with the stars of the Advent season, seemed to be a clarifying agent. And I started feeling profoundly foolish for my delusion. I *had* cried, in my oddly seized moment of joy. *He wasn't there*, I told myself now, in the creeping cold of the car. *He couldn't be there, no matter how badly I wanted him there.* And I curled up into myself, crawled back into the husk that I felt I had shed for just one night, because the more time I spent thinking about him, the more obvious it became that he could never, never appear before anyone but me.

Christmas crept up, spooking me. When I was younger—twelve, thirteen—I took a tremendous amount of comfort in Christmas. It always seemed like no matter what depths of ridicule or alienation I was suffering at school (or out of school), the holy season filled me with warmth and goodwill; I felt close to the colonies of tiny lights strung around trees and bushes; the voices of Brenda Lee and Perry Como that seemed to whisper out of every corner; the luxurious practice of reading O.Henry or Dickens in the living room under the tiny lights of our own tree. Christmas seemed to welcome me when nothing else did.

Not this year, in which I felt oddly banished, as though Christmas were a pure thing, a celebration of the honest and the good, that I was marked not to attend. One night shortly after the awards ceremony, I found myself walking home late from school (having stayed to cobble together the end-of-year edition of the newspaper, complete with my scathing predictions for New Year 1987), extremities freezing despite boots and gloves, breath crystallizing ghoulishly in front of my face as I walked. A full mile before I reached home, not far from the town library, I had a vision of what I'd find there: leftover meatballs congealing in a pot on the stove, both my parents, exhausted, my father bent over paperwork, Joani and Grandma knitting, whirring (Grandma turning Joani into some warped 1950s ideal of domesticity, and for what?), and a dark room, collecting dust, that used to belong to my hell-raising older sister; in every room, dry heat billowing out of low metal radiators painted beige.

I looped back toward the old brick library, its tall windows casting white panes of light on the ground below, fished a dime out of my pocket, and put it in the pay phone outside the building.

"Goolsbee." It was some stoner's voice, slurred, the pitch-perfect music of indifference.

"Could you get Francis Tremont for me?"

"Aah. Lemme see if he's still here. He mighta gone home early on break."

The sound of a receiver falling from an in-house pay phone, swinging in space, like a hanged man. I waited for three minutes, into the recorded warning of termination, put in another dime, waited, was warned again, redeposited, still waited. Finally I heard the clanking sound of someone retrieving a receiver from thin air.

"Mr. Godfrey? I'm so sorry, I was packing and making arrangements—"

"Brooks, this isn't Mr. Godfrey."

Then him, perplexed: "It isn't?"

"No. It's Eric."

The usual silence, then, quieter: "You're catching me at a bad time. My auntie died this morning."

"Oh. I'm sorry." Suddenly I could have kicked myself for choosing this of all nights to call.

"Well—" Another pause. "I thought you were Mr. Godfrey. He's the executor of her will. My guardian now, until I'm twenty-one. He arranged a flight home for me, and my housemaster's driving me to Logan tonight to catch it."

"Oh. All right, I won't keep you, then."

"I'm starting my Christmas break early. It goes until the middle of January."

"Are you coming back?" I said, fighting back a plummeting feeling.

"Presumably. I don't think I'll get a red cent out of Godfrey if I at least don't come back and finish the year."

"Oh," I said again. "Well, I guess I'm glad that you're coming back."

More silence, then, faintly ironic, "How are *you?*"

"I'm okay," I said, not wanting to talk about myself. "I'm really sorry about your aunt. I know you liked her."

"Did you pay a terrible price for our last catnap?"

I laughed. "Not really. Well, sort of. My parents had the cops out looking."

"Not *them* again."

"Yeah. I told them I was driving to see my sister—"

"What, the pregnant one? The runaway?"

"Yeah. That I was driving to see her, and I pulled over because I was lost, and closed my eyes for a minute and fell asleep."

He laughed thinly. "A likely story."

"I know. Did *you* get in trouble? Did you sneak back in okay?"

"I did. The proctor himself had sneaked away that night, too, though not for the same reasons. Into town, I guess, to watch the hockey game at a bar."

"That was lucky for you," I said.

"Wasn't it, though?" he said wearily. "I wonder if it ever expires."

"If what does?"

"One's *luck.*"

"Oh, yeah." There was another silence, and a gust of wind against the brick front of the library that reminded me how cold the night was.

"The falling asleep in there that night?" I ventured into the void. "And the getting in trouble?"

"Yes?"

"It was worth it," I said. "I had a really good time that night."

"Oh, you did? You like being dressed down by a misanthropic doomsayer who tells you how miserable your life is?"

"I don't mean that part of it," I said. "I mean, you know—the part before. And seeing your pictures. And falling asleep was nice, too, even though it went on too long."

"Yes, falling asleep was nice," he said briskly. "And thank you for looking at my memorabilia. I guess I'm the real keeper of the family archives now."

"I guess you are."

More silence. I wanted to tell him how much I missed him, that I had been thinking of him at the awards ceremony, that it had almost been like he was there, in some funny way, but I said nothing. "Well!" he finally sang. "More packing awaits me."

"Okay."

"Happy holidays to you and yours. I'll see you in Anno Domini 1987."

"Who are you going to spend Christmas with?" I suddenly asked, horrified at the thought of his having to spend the day alone.

He laughed. "My dear boy, I am about to spend Christmas with more of Fleurie's immediate kin and next of kin and friends and fellow church ladies than I've ever seen before in one sitting. They're going to turn her house into one final revival meeting before it goes forever into my trust. So I don't imagine I'll be alone on Christmas Day—although I'd prefer it to making nice with hundreds of living fossils in their holiday finery from the Reconstruction era."

"Well, I'm glad you won't be alone," I said.

"*You've* gotten awfully solicitous of my welfare."

"I guess I have."

"Are you quite all right, Eric? Where are you, anyway? Are you outside?"

"Uh. Yeah. I'm in front of the library. I was doing research."

"I see. Well, I return the sixteenth of January. If you call then, I'll be back in Goolsbee House, all right?"

"All right," I said, unable to believe I wasn't going to see him for a month. "I will."

"All right, then," he said, sounding hesitant, sounding like he wanted to get back to packing. "Good-bye, my dear boy."

"Good-bye. Brooks, I'll miss you."

Silence. Then, melodramatically: "But you must be *strong*. Let no one know your private grief!"

"I was serious," I said.

A clearing of the throat. "I know. I'll miss you, too. So 'bye for now." And then a click on the other end.

I stared at the receiver for a moment and then hung up. It was almost eight o'clock and I still didn't want to go home. I walked the fifteen minutes down Main Street to B.J.'s Sub Shop, empty despite the come-hither tinsel and cardboard-cutout Santa face I had taped up in the window during my shift last week. Inside it was bright and warm. Sal was surprised to see me on one of my nights off; I told him my house was noisy and I needed a quiet place to do my homework. He lowered the radio and wiped down a table for me, and I lost myself in trigonometry. Sal served me an Italian sub, a Coke, and, from the display rack, a bag of Ruffles and a Little Debbie brownie, all on the house. Except for that, he didn't bother me at all, just kept reading his car magazines, and I thought about how decent people could be when you most needed it, even people like Sal, whom I had always thought of as Tony Danza's evil twin brother, even when they didn't have a clue as to what was bothering you in the first place, even when they probably wouldn't want to know.

Christmas Day was disconcertingly warm, but it rained most of the day, compounding the strangeness of our second holiday without Brenda. She wouldn't come to Auntie Lani's house, just over the border in New Hampshire, where the Ianellis and the timid in-laws of the Ianellis have gathered every Christmas to exchange presents. My mother, who usually gives the best presents, was so distracted this year that she ended up buying everyone easy-assembly wine racks she got on sale at T. J. Maxx. Everyone professed to love their wine racks, but later in the day, after dinner, I overheard a whispered conversation between Auntie Winnie and my cousin Frannie.

"Poor Terry. She didn't even scrape the whole price tag off my rack, so I know she got them at T. J. Maxx," Auntie Winnie said to Frannie. "She never used to overlook something like that before."

"I know. The poor thing," Frannie said. "She's not herself these days."

"I know." Winnie made the clucking sound all the Ianelli women make when they're discussing someone's bad fortune. "It's because of that Brenda."

"I know," Frannie said. "She's breaking Auntie Terry's heart, and I don't even think she knows it."

"And at Christmas, too," Auntie Winnie added.

The only other thing that happened was that Grandma almost had another stroke playing a too-lively game of patty-cake with Frannie's daughter, Brittany. The pace had accelerated considerably, until suddenly Grandma turned chalk white and started clutching her heart and calling out for the Holy Mother. There was complete fear and chaos for about three minutes, while Auntie Reenie screamed at Grandma to take deep breaths, dispensed her heart pills (which Grandma had forgotten to take that afternoon), and put her to bed. As usual, during the entire incident, my father and all my uncles were playing cards in the other room and never even knew it happened.

Grandma stayed to spend the night at Auntie Lani's when my parents, Joani, and I departed for home in the late afternoon to open our presents, as we do every year. As we approached the driveway, even through the rain, Joani called out "Look! It's Brenda's car. Brenda's come back!"

We found her in the kitchen, drinking coffee out of her old mug with the chipped silver "B" on the front, a shopping bag full of presents at her feet, big with pregnancy, but wearing a pretty holly-flecked red jersey maternity dress, looking rested and actually happy. She had had her huge, towering mane of big hair cut into a short, flipped-back style that actually made her look kind of chic. The second Joani saw her, she ran to her and grabbed her around the waist, heedless of the baby, saying her name again and again. I was so happy to see her I felt something catch in my throat, but I only stood there in the hall with my parents, taking her in.

She gently unlaced Joani and stood up a little nervously, smoothing down her dress over her belly, keeping her arms there, as though she wanted to hide, or protect, her progress. "Hi. I used my old key to get in."

"That's okay, honey," my mother said, almost in a whisper.

"I didn't forget, you know? I mean, I remembered this is the time we open the family presents. So I brought mine, okay?"

"We're glad you came," my father croaked, his right eye leaking waterworks.

Brenda fidgeted. "So—hey. Merry Christmas."

Then my mother just lost it—I saw her whole face crack open, heard the rumble coming up in her throat, until she burst into tears, ran to Brenda and hugged her so tightly I thought they were going to flatten out the baby. "Oh, baby, oh, baby, oh, baby, don't ever just leave us like that *again*, do you understand? You scared the living hell out of me," and Brenda, bawling now, too, just saying, "Oh, Mommy, I'm sorry," and Joani, holding onto both of them now, blubbering too, for the hell of it. I got teary-eyed, too; I couldn't help it. I caught my father's eye, but I didn't care; he was red with pent-up emotion, but he couldn't let it out, and I was fiercely glad not to be like him at that moment. I stood there and smiled at the spectacle of my mother and two sisters through my own haze.

Finally Brenda poked her head out from the clump and looked at me. "Hey you, the big literary celebrity, get ovah here." And I joined them in their cluster, and we all sniffled and laughed and cried, and my father went upstairs to turn on the electric candles in their windows. When he came down in a moment, when Brenda, Joani, and I were pouring eggnog and slicing up cheese and pepperoni, I heard my mother talking to him in the hallway.

"So, are you happy to see her?" she asked.

"Um-hmmm," I heard him say, that forced devil-may-care voice with the edge of "Don't probe me."

"She looks beautiful, doesn't she?" my mother said, combing her hand through my father's hair.

"She certainly does, Terry. She certainly does."

"She loves you, you know. She just doesn't know how to show it. And neither do you."

"Terry, c'mon," with a deeper edge.

"Well, it's the truth."

"All right, honey. Whatever you say."

"Now, let's have a nice Christmas night with all our kids in one place, okay? We don't know how long we're gonna have her back here for, so let's just have fun, okay?" And I heard his peevish note of compliance—"that's exactly what I want, too"—and I heard her lips smack his cheek.

The night and the rain crept on; we opened our presents, modeled new clothes for each other, listened to the warped Christmas albums my parents had bought in their first year of their marriage, drank more eggnog. There was a fragile atmosphere that made us all pass the night with our senses more acute than ever before—the knowledge that momentous things had happened that year reconfiguring us, that we might be reconfigured still, but that for the precarious balance of this night, we would count our blessings, make happy, and defer talk of 1987 until tomorrow.

Brenda trundled an exhausted Joani up to bed around nine; in a rare recreational spirit my father challenged me to a game of cards, and we played, near-silently, while my mother and Brenda rustled through maternity gifts in the other room, talking of baby accessories and Brenda's progress and skirting the broader issues of what she planned to do with her life, and where she planned to do it, and with whom. At about nine-thirty, the phone rang, a chilling caw in our otherwise cloistered night. I peered into the next room.

My mother looked troubled. "I hope that's not about Ma," she said, going into the kitchen. Brenda waddled into the den and looked over my father's shoulder at his hand of cards.

"Jesus, Art, what a killer hand!" she said.

"Oh, yeah?" my father said, looking up at her. "Whaddya think I should throw next?"

"Lemme see," Brenda said, resting a hand on my father's shoulder. "That one," and she pointed.

"That's patently unfair!" I said. "No special consultation, unless it's on both sides."

"If we're gonna have special consultation," my father said to me, "I want your sister. You can have your mother. She was never any good at this up at the beach." And I noticed Brenda laughed and her hand briefly grazed my father's shoulder, again, before it settled back on her stomach.

My mother came into the room, frowning. "Brenda, that was Frank. He said he wanted to come over to see you, to give you your Christmas presents."

Brenda's hand fell from her stomach and her face chalked over. "What did you say to him?"

"Well, I told him we were getting ready to go to bed, and maybe he could come by tomorrow—"

"And?" Brenda said, tense.

"And he said he'd just come by for a minute, and he was leaving right away."

"Oh, shit!" Brenda said, turning away from us.

"Well, look, Terry," my father said, throwing down his cards. "Just call him back and tell him he can't come over tonight. Or I'll call him myself. Christmas is over. It's too late to go passing around presents at this time of night." Frank and my father get along really well; they love discussing football stats and playing cards together, which is why the tone in his voice took me back.

"But he said he was leaving right away," my mother said, looking guilty. "He just about hung up on me. I think he's on his way here now."

There was a split-second silence before Brenda said, "That's it. I'm outta here. I was gonna spend the night, but I've gotta get outta here now." And she hustled into the living room to start collecting her presents.

"Bren, honey, hold on a minute," my mother said, pleading, following her. "Can't you just see him for a minute, to swap presents? Just a minute, and then he'll go, and it'll be just us again tomorrow?" My mother had her hands on the presents in Brenda's arms, trying to take them away from her.

"No, Terry!" Brenda snapped. "I can't swap presents with him, because I didn't *buy* him any presents! I didn't have any intention of seeing him! And how dare you say it's okay for him to come over just because you want us to get back together again?"

"I *didn't* invite him over!" my mother protested. "He wouldn't let me get a word in edgewise! He strong-armed me!"

"Hey, hey, both of you, take it easy!" my father called out, ineffectually, because Brenda was already in motion, up the stairs to retrieve her things, my mother chasing after her. My father and I heard a door slam, then the resigned footsteps of my mother coming back down the stairs.

"Jesus Christ," my father said, collapsing back onto the couch, looking at me. "Can't we have just one night of peace and quiet in this house?" I didn't know how to answer; I just looked at him and shrugged.

My mother reemerged in the doorway. "She thinks it's me. She thinks I told him to come over. But I didn't! It's not my fault. Now what am I gonna do?"

"When he gets here," my father said, finishing off the rest of his Manhattan, "we're gonna tell him that Brenda left because she's not ready to see him yet. And that she'll call him when she's ready, and it's her right to see him or not to see him when she wants. And that's that."

The three of us sat there, saying nothing, until we heard the sound of Brenda in the hallway, and rushed to her. She had on her coat and a ridiculous-looking ski cap pulled down over her ears, and two Jordan Marsh bags filled with gifts.

"See ya later," she said, kissing us all brusquely. "I'll call you soon."

"Brenda," my mother said, standing in her way. "Don't go. You can just stay up in your room, and we'll tell Frank you already went back."

"Nope, no good," Brenda said. "He'll see my car. And I gotta work tomorrow anyway."

"Brenda, *please!*" my mother pleaded, clutching her arms.

"Sorry, Ma, you blew it. Now let me outta here. 'Bye, guys," Brenda said to us; then, with some awkwardness, she maneuvered herself and the two bags out the front door, into the cold drizzle.

"You're gonna slip and slide on the roads!" my mother called back to her. "You're taking a big risk!"

"I'll be fine," she called back. In a minute she was in the car, streaking out of the driveway and down the road toward the highway. My mother closed the door, her face tight with withheld tears, and stalked upstairs, leaving my father and me standing bereft in the hallway. The grandfather clock struck eleven-thirty.

"You wanna go finish the game until Frank comes?" my father said, trying to sound casual, but I knew he was nervous because his right eye was leaking a streak right down his cheek.

187

I was tired, and depressed now, and wanted to slip up to my room, but I sensed he wanted someone to hang out with him while he waited for Frank, so I said sure. But he fouled his next two hands purely out of distractedness, and I think he was almost relieved when, ten minutes into our resuming, the front door bell rang three times in rapid succession. "I hope he hasn't been drinking," my father said, getting up to answer the door, and I followed him, hanging out in the living room, just beyond sight of the front door.

"Hey, Mr. Fitz, Merry Christmas! It's a wet one, huh?" I heard Frank say after my father opened the door. He sounded cheerful, but too cheerful, as if all his pleasantries were just preface to coming face to face with Brenda. He also sounded too loud, and thick-voiced, the way he always did when he had had too much to drink, something I had witnessed during his visits to our house on many previous holidays.

"Hey, buddy, Merry Christmas," my father said back, fake-genial and cautious. I could tell he hadn't budged from the doorway, nor was he letting Frank in. "Long time no see, huh?"

"Yeah—well, whatever," Frank said. "That's the whole point of the holidays, huh? Making the rounds?"

"Absolutely," my father said. "Absolutely. Problem is, you were on and off the phone so fast, you didn't give Terry a chance to tell you that Brenda's not here. She had to go back earlier tonight. She was afraid the streets were gonna ice over."

There was a pause, then Frank started in, more slurring than before. "No, no, no, Mr. Fitz, wait a minute. Mrs. Fitz told me Brenda was still here."

My father laughed, thinly. "Well, what happened was, Terry got tired out, so she went up to bed, and when she answered the phone, she thought Brenda was still here. But Brenda had taken off a little while before. Tell ya what, Frank? Why don't you leave your presents here, and we'll get 'em to Brenda, and she'll call—"

"Oh, come on, Mr. Fitz, don't give me this bullshit!" Frank whined. "I know she's here. Now, come on, I always thought of you as a friend a mine. I helped you install your back deck last summah an' everything."

"Frank, you are a friend. That's why I'm bein' honest with you and tellin' you Brenda's not here. Now, why don't you be a good kid and leave your presents here and she'll give you a call when she's ready, good enough?"

"No, it fuckin' isn't!" Frank bellowed. "Mr. Fitz, I don't know what the fuck is up. I love your daughter. She's havin' my baby. And I wanna marry her, but now she won't have anything to do with me!"

"She's goin' at her own pace, Frank," my father said, trying to stay calm.

"She hasn't even called me since she moved out! It's like she thinks I'm a fuckin' leper or somethin', and I'm gonna infect the baby."

"Cut the melodramatics, Frank," my father said. "She doesn't think you're a leper, and you're gonna see her soon enough."

"But I wanna see her *now!*" Frank shouted, and I could hear the heavy scrape of his boots as he tried to let himself inside.

"Hey, punk, you're drunk!" I heard my father say now, in the same harsh, staccato voice he always used with Brenda and me when he used to get really mad at us. "Now go home and get some sleep."

"Lemme inna fuckin' house—" was the last thing I heard Frank say before my father slammed the door shut and locked it, twice. After that I heard Frank's garbled cursing from outside and the sound of his fists rattling the storm door. I stepped into the hallway.

"What are you going to do about him?" I asked. "Should we call the police?"

My father sneered. "Just let him blow off his steam. He'll leave soon enough."

"You think so?" Outside, Frank was still muttering and banging on the storm door.

"Yeah," my father said, after a pause. "Just ignore him. He'll leave when he sees he's not gettin' any attention."

"Okay." And we both stood there, listening to Frank blubber on outside in the drizzle.

"I'm pooped, Eric." My father let out a big yawn. "Can we pick up that card game tomorrow?"

"Sure," I said. "I think I'm gonna play some solitaire before I go to bed."

"All right," my father said hesitantly. "Just turn out all the lights when you're done. And if this one rings the bell again"—he jerked his thumb toward the front door—"ignore it."

"Okay," I said. "Well. Good night. Merry Christmas."

My father laughed his little philosophical laugh: "Heh. Merry Christmas." I leaned over awkwardly and kissed him good night on the cheek. He laughed again—"Heh"—before heading up the stairs.

In the living room, I collected the dirty glasses and put them in the dishwasher in the kitchen. Then I fixed myself a bowl of Raisin Bran, went back into the den, turned on the TV to what must have been the fourteenth showing that night of *It's a Wonderful Life*, and turned the volume all the way down. It was the scene where Jimmy Stewart and Donna Reed are listening into the same phone receiver, and she's starting to cry. And then he grabs her and talks right into her face, and they start making out like crazy people. For some reason, watching them kiss soundlessly made me incredibly sad—as though imagining what they might be saying was more moving than hearing their actual words—and I ate my cereal and watched the movie like that, in silence, for about the next half-hour, whereupon I finally put my cereal bowl in the dishwasher, turned out all the lights, and readied to go up to bed.

When I turned out the light in the hallway, I heard a rustle on the front steps outside. In the dark of the vestibule, I peered through the windowpanes of the front door. Frank was still sitting there on the wet steps, looking directly up at me, his face red and puffy with drinking, the bag of gifts wet and deflated by his side. The minute he saw me, he jumped up, mouthing, "Open up. Open up." "I can't," I mouthed back. (The truth is, I've always been a little afraid of Frank. He's got a big square head, and little black eyes that can look mean, and a crew cut, and he's still built like a linebacker.) Then his face just dropped, and he just stared at me, blankly, and I realized that not only had he been drinking, he had been crying, too. "Hold on," I mouthed to him, creeping halfway up the stairs to make sure everyone was tucked away, then putting on my coat and shoes. Softly, I slipped outside into the drizzle, and closed the front door behind me.

"Hi, Frank," I said, leaning against the railing, looking down at him. "I'm sorry. I can't let you in."

"Hey, Eric. Long time no see," he mumbled, looking away. He seemed to have calmed down now; he actually seemed contrite. "How ya doin'?"

"I'm all right. How about you?" He just looked at me and laughed balefully. "Merry Christmas," I said. He looked at me and laughed again, replacing his head back in his hands.

"Why don't you go home to bed, Frank? You're going to catch pneumonia out here."

He looked up at me and squinted, trying to focus on my face. "Eric, would you please just level with me?"

"Over what?" I asked. I couldn't get over this image of Frank. Only three years ago, he had been West Mendhem High's star linebacker, a complete picture of cockiness and bravado racing down the field or swaggering through the halls. Now here he was, a prison guard, sitting out crying in the rain, drunk, on our front steps on Christmas night.

"Over what do you think? Over Brenda."

"What about her?" I asked. I felt bad withholding information from Frank, but I had to remember my allegiance lay with Brenda, and I had to protect her best interests.

"Is she in there?" Frank asked.

"No, Frank, I swear she's not. She went back to her apartment earlier tonight."

"Where's that?"

"I don't know. She wouldn't tell us."

"Bullshit," he said into his knees.

"I swear, Frank, I don't know," I said feebly, because of course I knew exactly where she was. "I tried to find her myself, and I got lost," I added, thinking how ironic it was that two different lies could converge, creating a fabric of story that almost resembled the truth.

He looked at me hard—I wondered if he was going to bully me into telling him—then he just seemed to give up and looked into the palms of his hands. "I only wanted to give her these presents, you know. And some presents for your folks."

"I know," I said, trying to sound sympathetic, which I actually was, to an extent.

"So, you saw her, huh?"

"Um, yeah. For a little while tonight. Then she had to go back. She has to work tomorrow."

"Yeah, you told me. So, how is she?"

"She's okay, I guess," I said, feeling like it wasn't smart to tell Frank that she was doing particularly badly or particularly well. (And she *had* seemed to be doing just okay.)

"How's she look?" Frank asked, his face beginning to brighten.

"Good, I guess. She cut her hair."

Frank laughed. "She did, huh? It looks good?"

"Yeah. It's very stylish."

"Oh, yeah?" He laughed again, then stopped. "I always told her her long hair looked beautiful. I guess she didn't believe me."

"That's not necessarily true," I said. "Maybe she just wanted a change." I started wondering how I could end the conversation and get Frank home without hurting his feelings. It was cold and damp outside, and I was beginning to regret having come out in the first place.

"She big yet?" Frank asked, patting his stomach.

"She's definitely getting there," I said.

"Oh, yeah?" Frank virtually squealed, laughing again. "Whaddya think of that?"

"Well, that's what happens when girls get pregnant, Frank. They get bigger."

He didn't get my sarcasm. He just kept laughing, saying, "I guess you're right! I guess they really do! Hey, does she know if it's gonna be a boy or a girl?"

"I don't think she's looking into it. I think she wants to be surprised."

"Yeah, yeah," Frank said, entirely amenable to the idea. "That's right. Be surprised. *I'll* sure be!"

"So will we all," I said. "Hey, Frank, why don't you go home and get some sleep? It's really wet out here. And I gotta go to bed, too. I just came out to see if you were all right. I'll take the gifts in, if you want."

"Yeah, okay, Eric." He stood up, the back of his pants soaked. "You gotta tell me one thing, though," he said, handing me the sodden bag of gifts.

"Uh-huh?"

"Why's your sister doin' this a me, huh? Come on, tell me. I know you two are close. I know she tells you stuff, an' stuff. Why's she doin' this?"

"Frank," I said, trying to sound firm, "I don't know exactly why. All I know is that Brenda's sorting some stuff out, and when she's ready, she's gonna talk to you. She plans to, believe me."

Everything I said seemed to go right over his head. "But why can't she talk a me, now, huh? What'd I do was so bad to her?" He was right up close to me now, expelling his beery breath in my face. I remembered the mark on Brenda's face that looked faintly like a bruise the day she moved out, and I wondered if Frank *had* done something to Brenda that was so bad, after all.

"Frank, it's not that you necessarily did anything bad," I said, stepping away from his face. "It's just that I don't think Brenda was expecting a baby so soon, or to get married so soon, and she needs some time away from everyone to think things out."

"Even away from me?" Frank asked.

"Even away from you," I said. "You shouldn't take it so personally."

Frank threw his head up in the air and let out the closest thing a human being could emit to an animal roar. "What the fuck do you mean, *I shouldn't take it personally?* You wait until your girlfriend is five months away from having your kid and you haven't seen her, and—and she won't talk to you, you don't even know where she *is*, and someone says to you, 'You shouldn't take it personally.' What would you wanna do to that person, Eric?"

I didn't want to know what Frank wanted to do to me, so I just said, "Look, Frank, I'm sorry. That was really stupid. What I meant was, Brenda's not running away from *you*, per se. She's trying to reconcile her own issues."

"What?"

"I mean— I mean, she's running away from herself."

"Exactly. That's what I've been thinking all along. She's running away from her problems."

"Exactly!" I said, too emphatically. "She'll come around."

Then Frank got silent again, just staring out into the street. By this point, my own head was wet with drizzle, and I followed his eyes out into the street, the blacktop shiny with rain—and for the briefest instant, I wondered what kind of Christmas, what kind of funeral, they had had in Virginia; was it tropically warm? had it rained?—and I thought that this was the gloomiest Christmas I had ever experienced.

"Eric, I love her so much." Frank spoke out of the silence, still looking out into the street. "And I love that kid so much, even though I've haven't seen him yet." (I thought it best not to remind him it could be a her.) "An' all I want is for the three of us to be happy together, just like the two of us used to be, plus one more."

"I know, Frank," I said. Then his voice started to rise; he started crying again, and all I wanted to do was get away.

"I saw my sister's little baby kids today," he said, his own voice becoming strangely babylike as he spoke. "And I played with 'em all day—Annie and Peter, Petie, we call him—'cause I wanted to prove to myself that I could be a good father. An' I wanted Brenda to be able to see me, so she'd know the same thing. And you know, Petie, the boy?"

"Uh-huh?"

"I pretended he was mine. I tried to get him to call me Daddy."

"Well, that's okay, Frank," I said, feeling like a therapist. "It's okay to pretend things."

Then he turned and looked me straight in the eyes, beer breath on me again. "You know, Eric, I'm not like you—"

"Uh-huh?"

"I didn't do very good in school. I never cared. An' I'm not goin' off to some fancy college to become a big-time doctor or lawyer or whatever. I'm a prison guard, okay? Plain and simple. That's probably what I'm always gonna be."

"It doesn't have to be that way."

"That's not my point. I don't care if that's all I'm ever gonna be. I've accepted it. But the difference between us is . . ." And he looked at me again, in a shrewd, cold, analytical way that completely took me aback.

"Is? Yeah?" I said.

"Is that you've got a whole shitload of stuff goin' for you. But if I lose your sister and my kid—then I've got nothin'. Nothin'. And do you know what it feels like to have nothin', Eric?" He was whisper-spitting in my face now.

"No," I managed.

"It feels like shit. It feels like fuckin' shit."

Then he picked up his bag of gifts and started down the steps without saying another word to me. Halfway down, he slipped and almost fell, and I almost called out, but he caught himself, and I thought it best not to say a word to him. I watched him as he made it to his minitruck, turned over the engine, and sped off in a nearly straight line down the deserted street.

When I got inside, cold and wet, I thought that maybe I should call Brenda, but then decided that would only scare her; also, it was after midnight. But sitting at the bare kitchen table, I desperately wanted to talk to someone—not about Frank, really, but everything. I wanted someone to know that I wasn't the only person in the world without a story to tell, that I wasn't merely an observer and chronicler of other people's lives, that I wasn't an emotional vacuum or some kind of sick emotional leech. I thought about calling Phoebe; she would definitely still be up, listening to new tapes that she got for Christmas. I stared at the phone for a long time, thinking about what I would say, how I would frame my story, how she might react, how I'd respond to all her questions, and how she would support me in my anguish forever after. Finally, I picked up the receiver and dialed her private line, connected to her bedroom.

"Hello?" I heard, and something that sounded like Cream in the background. I also heard the click in my throat when I tried to speak, to identify myself, but nothing more than that came out.

"Hello?" from Phoebe, more annoyed, then: "Merry Christmas, you fuckin' pervert," and she hung up.

Silently, I replaced the receiver. Then I stared at the phone a long time, thought of calling back, explaining myself and my reluctance to speak, and then starting all over again. But I didn't. Instead, I went into the living room, lay down on the sofa, and stared at the darkened Christmas tree, glistening blackly with tinsel, until I fell asleep, and dreamed of an unmarked southern funeral—decorous, genial, and gray with warm rain.

January 1987

Nine

❖

It's about four in the afternoon, that last corridor of light in the dead center of the winter when the sky goes a charcoal color, and a few fat, solitary flakes of snow are falling out of it and onto the windshield of my mother's hatchback as I gun the motor out of the high school lot and onto the little network of slender old farmers' roads that eventually spill into Great Lake Drive. I usually feel numb this time of year, mid-January, but I'm keen and alert today, having fled school right after the last bell, telling Phoebe I had to go take care of my grandmother and would she please make excuses for me at the literary magazine meeting.

Well, that was a lie. Grandma is staying with Auntie Reenie for the week because my mother is burnt out, and right now, this very minute, I'm driving in the middle of a threatening snowstorm toward St. Banner, to meet him in the old familiar place, this being my first visit since way back in December, since before his auntie died and he went home for winter break, since before the *Boston Globe* dubbed me the Voice of Youth—since before a lot of things. But he's held over, strangely; it doesn't feel as if his face, his voice, his crummy attitude, and snide remarks have blunted at all in my mind. In an odd way, it's like he's been with me the whole time, like a mean, funny little imaginary friend, constantly commenting into my right ear on everyone around me, nearly provoking me to laugh—or sneer—aloud, in the presence of others. When I called him last night, when he told me he had just gotten back, he hadn't even opened his bags (*valises*, he actually called them), when he said he had forgotten since Exeter how *absolutely gloriously suicidal* New England Januarys made him, I heard the old sneer, sneer, sneer. And I felt like I had to apologize for the state of the weather in Massachusetts in January, that it was a reflection on my stock, my lineage, my non-upwardly mobile tribe.

I park the car in the usual hidden spot off the road and gather up my scarf and gloves; it's going to be frigid in that barn. My heart is pounding as I make the old sprint across the soccer field, now completely iced over and looking like the remote Alaskan tundra (or what I imagine that would look like), and for one split second I wonder if it's smart that I'm starting this up again, now with all these good developments going on—fame and all—and then I remember that in the middle of all this, there's only been one person I've been wanting to talk about it to for the last month, and just before I slip inside the barn, I think: *Okay. I'll play it by ear.*

Someone stored old crew shells in here over the winter break; they're lying right side up along the far wall, and for some reason, they remind me of a picture of Egyptian mummies' tombs I remember seeing when I was a kid, and that freaks me out a little. It's silent in here and I take my usual position underneath the loft.

"Hey there," I call up, audibly, but scared as usual to be too loud. Nothing. I wonder if, for once, I've beaten him to the meeting place.

I call up again, a little louder. "Are you up— Shit!" Something comes hurtling down from the loft, something square, and it hits me on the forehead, knocking me back a bit, then falls on the ground in front of my wet boots.

"What the fuck?" I say aloud. It's a package, wrapped in fake Victorian Christmas paper, topped by an enormous, ridiculous-looking bow. Then I hear it—hyena laughing from the recesses of the loft—and I'm pissed off, and my stomach flips over, delicately, with a thrill.

He sticks his head over the edge of the loft, looking down at me, still laughing his brains out, he thinks it's so funny.

"Did I *clock* you? I didn't mean to. That's my Christmas present to you. Airmail," and he starts laughing all over again.

"You got a haircut," I say, stupidly. I should cuss him out for being immature, for throwing gifts out in midair, not knowing whom they're going to hit. I should ask him if he's ringing in the new year by getting stoned again every afternoon. But I'm so happy to see him, it's as if my only, my secret happiness has been restored, and all I notice is that he got a haircut, very close to his scalp (it was getting bushy before he left, because he wouldn't trust it to the "cretin" elderly white barber in downtown West Mendhem), and he looks so intelligent and evil-minded and handsome, like nobody else I know.

"You noticed," he says, saccharine and phony-flattered, running his hand over the top of his head. "It's terribly military, isn't it. But I couldn't look like a Black Panther–in–training for my auntie's funeral, could I? Nor would I want to, I suppose." He runs his hand over it again. "It's severe to the touch. *Il faut que tu le touches.*"

I laugh. "I'll come up," I say, picking up the package, as about a thousand other things in my life seem to evaporate behind me, somewhere outside, away.

"No, wait," he says. "I'll come down. I want to stretch." He comes bounding down the ladder, about ten times more herky-jerk than usual. It's like he's lost his old wary, measured, I'll-never-move-too-fast quality; he's behaving like a little kid—hyper.

"He-llo," he chimes, hopping directly in front of me.

"*You're* chipper."

"It's 1987. New year, new frontiers. And I am now a very, very wealthy colored boy. My wealth *engulfs* me."

I laugh again, but my feelings sharpen. "Lucky you," I say, shrugging.

"Oh, lucky for *both* of us," he says, and he grabs the waist of my overcoat. "Well, Seigneur Fitzpatrick?" And I blush and say, "Well, *I* don't know," and then we start making out, more aggressively than ever before because I'm trying to make up for a month of not even touching him, and I put both my hands up on his head and clamp them there, over his stark skull.

"It *is* severe," I say, and, blown into my mouth, he says, "Severe times call for severity." More fooling around, then: "Aren't you going to open your package?"

"I guess I owe you a Christmas present," I say, pulling off the ridiculous bow, not knowing what to do with it, depositing it gingerly in my coat pocket.

"Nonsense. From now on, you are merely going to accept my gifts and edify yourself."

I don't know what he means by that, but I'm not sure I want to, so I go on opening it up. "Did you wrap this?" I ask him.

"Della did," he says.

"Della?"

"Fleurie's housekeeper. It was one of the last things she did before she packed her bags after thirteen years of service and moved back to her sister's. Weeping the whole way, of course. For Fleurie."

"It's very rococo," I say of the package, trying out a new word.

"Della was very rococo."

Inside, it's a copy of *A Moveable Feast* by Ernest Hemingway, the old kind of hardback, with woven covers, fraying a little around the edges. The pages are yellow, smelling like cedar, and inside, fading, someone's written in a spidery, calligraphic hand: "April 1961. To lovely Vi. He hath made every moment a 'feast' in your life. Give thanks!!! xxoo F."

"Fleurie gave that to my mother when she went off to school. It made my mother go to Paris the summer after her freshman year. That started the trouble with her. She never wanted to come back."

"I haven't read it," I say, keeping it to myself that I hate Hemingway.

"Of course I *loathe* Hem," he says—as though he knew exactly what I was thinking—picking up my backpack for me, slinging it around his shoulder, marching us back up the ladder, into the loft. "Disgusting creature. Everyone in Paris, Gerald and Sara Murphy, Gertrude, F. Scott and Zelda—oh, Lord, poor Zelda—they all wasted their time on him, because he convinced them he was a genius. When he really was a huge fraud."

"I totally agree," I say, even though his whole assessment goes rather beyond the amount of thought I've given to Hemingway.

"How*ever,*" he says, shaking out the old army quilt for us to sit on. "If you haven't been to Paris—"

"I haven't," I say sourly, before he can say something condescending.

"I know, and that's just fine. If you haven't, you must read it for that reason alone. If you want to know what it was like to have been part of a particular crowd at a particular time and place."

I like the sound of that: a particular crowd at a particular time and place. It doesn't just seem to mean particular as in *specific,* but as in *particular*—discriminating, like all these people had certain qualities in common, and if you didn't have those qualities, they didn't let you in. "I don't feel like I've ever been part of a particular crowd at a particular time and place," I say. "I've never really had a crowd."

"Neither have I," he says airily, pulling out his cigarettes, lighting one, offering a drag to me. (I take it, uneasily.) "Then again." He exhales.

"What?" I say, fighting back the dizzies.

"That's not to say we couldn't *start* one. You know, start our own particular crowd. Members only, of course."

"Where?" I scoff. "Here?"

"Oh, *please.* I don't mean here. I'd never bother. I meant more—" He looks away from me, examining the burning end of his cigarette. Then he says in a big, grandiose voice: "I meant, *we* could become to the Paris of the eighties what F. Scott and Zelda and Gert and the brute Hemingway were to the Paris of the twenties. What you do, my dear boy, is you go there and you just plant yourself in front of a café and you wait for *other* disaffected Americans to walk by—and you say to them, *'Bonjour, mes Américains?* Did you find the motherland as dispiriting as we did? Would you like to drink and debauch yourselves into oblivion for the rest of your life here with us? You would? *Très bien.'* And that's it." He snaps his fingers. "You have yourself a bona fide expatriate scene."

"I didn't know there was a formula for it."

"Of course," he says, as though I'd ever think to doubt him. "It's that simple. And *we* could set it in motion. *We* could be the pioneers. *You and I,* Eric," he says, all mock-poignant, grabbing my hands in his and holding them aloft.

"New frontiers, right?" I say.

"Precisely."

"I think I'd better get out of West Mendhem and see America before—"

"Why?" he cuts me off. "It's all the same piece of shit."

"Oh, I know," I say, trying to keep it funny. "But I'm sure to a hick like me, even—I don't know, even New Haven would seem exotic."

He looks at me, looks away, starts to extinguish his cigarette elaborately, in a neat drilling motion, on the rotten loft floorboard. "Maybe so," he says, indifferently, putting an end to the conversation, a closer approximation to the sullen version of himself I remember from last year, and I wonder where this whole exchange went awry.

"Well," I say. "Thanks for the book. I can't wait to read it."

"Don't mention it," he says, engrossed in trying to tear a loose thread out of the seam of his wool pants.

"It was really your mother's, huh?"

"You read the inscription yourself," he says sulkily.

"I know. I just mean—you don't want to keep it for yourself?"

"I have more books of my mother's in storage at Fleurie's house than I know what to do with. They're just sitting there growing mold, along with everything else until I decide with Godfrey what to do with it."

"Who's Godfrey?"

"My trustee," he says, and I say, "Oh," remembering suddenly the time I called for him at Goolsbee House right after his aunt died, and he thought I was Godfrey calling. "He's watching over the house right now."

"What do you think you're going to do with it?"

Then, in the most casual tones possible, he tells me he's trying to decide whether he should sell it (what Godfrey recommends), or go back down to Virginia after he leaves St. Banner to live in it, renting it out until then—he would sustain "the family seat," he says, scoffing. Then he tells me that, under his aunt's will, Godfrey won't give him his own whopping inheritance until he turns twenty-one or graduates from college, whatever comes first—but that in the meantime, he's stashed away enough of his personal allowance in the West Mendhem bank to live very well, "outside of indentured schooling," for quite some time, thank you. And as for "*le* grand sum," he has goods on Godfrey that could free up the money sooner than Godfrey thinks. He tells me all this in the meanest, most cryptic and suddenly indifferent way possible, leaving me completely unwilling to prod further. Besides, the whole financial side of his life seems so complicated to me, attached to so many strings, that I don't think I can truly fathom it. I'm wondering whether next week's B.J.'s check is going to be enough to cover the fees on my remaining college applications.

"So, those are my options," he concludes, smugly, fiddling with another cigarette he's yet to light. "A brilliant array, wouldn't you say?"

"You *are* going to finish out the year here, right?" I venture.

He laughs. "Just for the sake of appearances, so Godfrey can get me off his goddamned mind. Then I'll slip away someplace very lovely and very remote this summer, before Godfrey even knows I'm gone. Then"—he pauses, lighting—"I'll play it by ear. To use a rotten cliché."

"Where do you think you'll go?"

"Mmmmmm." He deliberates a minute, burlesquing, his head cocked. Then he looks me straight in the face. "Bimini." And he explodes laughing.

"That sounds nice," I say, faintly, because I've never heard of the place before—it sounds generally Polynesian, but I don't know for sure—and for the first time, his smart little esoteric responses to everything I ask him are beginning to annoy rather than intimidate me.

Eventually he stops laughing and muses over his cigarette, with this galling self-reflective half-smile that seems to say, "Isn't it a shame, Brooks, that we've got to enjoy all our own jokes, because *he's* not equipped to understand?" "So, I've become quite the celebrity," I say, finally, to change the subject.

"I know," he says. "I found your essay in a back issue of the paper in the library here."

"You did?" I ask, suddenly sick with the thought that he's read it. "How did you find it?"

"Do you really want to know?"

"I mean, how did you come across it?"

"You told me to look for it, back before the holiday, remember?"

"Oh—I guess so. Well . . . what did you think about it?"

"It's very lyrical," he says.

"You think so?"

"Certainly. Too bad it's not about anything. It's like a Victorian strolling garden. All arabesques and ornamentation"—he flails his arms about over his head—"and no real sequence. No arc."

"It does, too, have an arc!" I say, offended, because ever since the night I read the piece at the awards ceremony, it *has* had a private meaning to me. It's about him—I'm not exactly sure how—but that's what it's come to mean to me, even if I'm not about to say as much.

"Well, what the hell is it? I sure as hell didn't see one."

"It's pretty obvious, I think."

"Well, I don't think so," he says calmly, dragging on the cigarette. *(How can anyone smoke so much?* I think, then, absurdly, it strikes me that he and Brenda would at least have their chain-smoking in common.) "So what's it about?"

"It's about *racial harmony,*" I say, haughtily. "Is that so hard to see?"

He lets out a long "Mmmmmmmm," pretending he's just been enlightened. "You know, now that you mention it, I completely see that. It's completely clear to me now. Clear as day."

He's being an asshole, and I decide not to press. "I certainly hope so," I say, still trying to sound suitably miffed.

"It completely slipped my mind that you are Mendhem's—"

"West Mendhem's," I correct him.

"West Mendhem's, of course. That you are, after all, West Mendhem's premier authority on matters racial. You even have your own rich trove of personal miscegenation experience to draw from."

He thinks I don't know what that word means, but I do. "Shut the fuck up," I say.

He spits a mouthful of smoke out into my face. "No, Mr. Fitzpatrick, why don't *you* shut the fuck up? That stupid fucking essay wasn't about *racial harmony* and you know it. It was you showing off your flashy, unctuous public high school vocabulary."

"Fuck *you!*" I stand up, grabbing my backpack. "I don't have to take this from you." I'm screaming now, I realize—and even more startlingly, for the first time, he's screaming at me.

"Why don't you sit the fuck down and take it anyway? Maybe it'd be good for you. You never have to *take* anything, do you, Eric? You just cut out. You just cry—and go home."

I want to stay indignant, and I'm trying, really trying. "What right do you have to say that to me?" I flip back at him after only a moment's pause. He looks composed again, sitting there Indian-style, looking up at me. Then I notice the cigarette between his fingers and I see that he can hardly hold it still. Then I look at the very edge of his head, where the thin film of stubble scrolls over his scalp, and it's shaking, too, and something in me gives way. "What did I ever do to you to deserve that kind of talk, Brooks?" I say, dropping my backpack, sitting back down.

He doesn't move, just stares at me, perplexed; then he looks down through the space between his khakis. "I just think you need to learn to take some things."

For a second, I want to press him; I want to tell him that I don't even know what he's talking about; I want to ask him what he means specifically, *specifically,* because I think there's a lot of stuff I "take" in my life—if I'm interpreting him the right way—a lot of stuff he could never even know about, Mr. Rich Jet Set Jefferson Tremont. But I don't. I just sit there, looking at him in the crowding darkness of the loft, wondering how I got so wrapped up in such a freakish scenario.

"I saw my mother at Fleurie's funeral," he says matter-of-factly, out of the silence.

"She came back?" I ask, trying to match his tone: *no big deal.*

"Yeah," he says, listless. "Briefly. To honor Fleurie, she said. And to settle her share with Godfrey. She said she would've stayed longer, but all of Fleurie's sisters and friends were giving her such shit for being a deadbeat mother, deadbeat niece, deadbeat relation, that she couldn't stand it any longer. She also said she hated Virginia—the South—well, America, in short. She said she didn't know how to *be.* La-di-da."

"How is she?" I ask. "Still beautiful?"

"Oh, yeah, you know. 'Handsome's' the word. Very 'Forty isn't fatal.' Very 'Wisdom has made me beautiful.' She's married now, to some Belgian guy. He's short; she showed me a picture."

"Very Hercule Poirot?"

He laughs halfheartedly. "Sure, whatever. She's a 'party planner' now, she says. A hostess or something—whatever that means. She goes into old châteaux and palazzi and decides where the string quartet should go, and where the Japanese lanterns should go, and who should sit next to what ambassador. And then she has three-by-fives about all the guests that she has to memorize, and she goes around all night introducing people."

"In Amsterdam?" I ask, glad for my recall.

"All over. 'René and I jump around,' she says." He waves his hand up in the air. "They're in Rome right now. And Paris for half the summer, then Barcelona for the second. Busy, busy. I don't even know how Fleurie's friends managed to track her down, and she didn't tell me. She was . . . *oblique* with me, about a lot of things."

"She was?" I say. *Oblique:* vague, unknowable, obscure.

"Yeah. She said she was glad I was out of the South. And she said I look like my daddy now, and that scared her."

"She said that?" I'm surprised. That doesn't sound like a nice thing for a mother to say to her son.

"Yeah. And then she said she was sorry she left me to my own devices. And she wants to catch up. And did I want to come to France this summer, even though René and I probably wouldn't get along, because René thinks all Americans are coarse dogs with stunted aesthetic faculties? But maybe I could change his mind."

"So? Are you gonna go?"

He doesn't answer at first. Then: "We'll see. Maybe I'll just pass through, not make a bother of myself. I wouldn't want to put off René."

He says "René" with an exaggerated, guttural accent, pulling up phlegm in his throat when he says it. He coughs and looks at me sheepishly, and we both laugh. It's getting late; I'm thinking I should go, because I'm swamped with homework tonight, and I can't afford to be showing up well into the evening anymore, especially after my close call last month. But it's not so freezing in here anymore; it's like we warmed up the loft with our fight—like calisthenics—and it's nice just to be sitting here with him, in coat and gloves, not saying anything, like we did a lot last fall. He's not even stoned, I think, and I'm grateful for that. He extends his leg and kicks my boot sloppily with his own.

"Let's go somewhere," he says.

"Now? I have to get home."

"Not *now,*" he says, frowning. "I mean—what are you doing this Saturday?"

"This coming Saturday?" I ask, quickening.

"This very one."

"Nothing," I say, even though I promised to take Joani to the mall, to the fabric store to help her buy material for a spring dress, which is going to be her biggest project to date. But I figure there's a way I can get out of it; I'll say there's an open house for prospective Yalies at some alumnus's house in Wellesley or Marblehead, or something.

"Let's *go* somewhere," he says. "Anywhere—I don't even care. I've got sign-out privileges for the whole day. I'm so sick of this goddamned icebox shack. Let's get out in the *world,* Fitzy," he says, kicking me again.

"Hey," I say, inspired. "You wanna go to Boston? Or Cambridge? We could go to all the bookstores—and the record stores. And maybe we could have lunch at Au Bon Pain, and see a movie at the Brattle or something?"

"What are you going to say if you see someone you know?"

"No one I know goes to Boston, except for Phoebe, and she and Charlie are going to some hippie concert up in Vermont for the weekend. And what if we did see someone I knew, anyway?" I add, feeling impetuous. "I'm allowed to have other friends, right? I'm allowed to go into Boston when I feel like it."

"The world is your oyster."

"Okay," I say, standing up. "Okay. Excellent. I'll pick you up around ten, how's that? I'll pull up on the street, okay, and you can watch for the car from here, okay? That way no one will know who you're going off with."

"Brilliant," he says, but he's not getting up off the ground, and he suddenly seems less excited than he did a minute ago, as if he's handed the whole project over to me.

"Okay," I say, slightly confused, still eager. "I've gotta get home now, Brooks, okay? I'm glad you saw your mother. I'm glad she wants you to come see her." I'm wondering if there's anything else I should say in valediction; he doesn't seem to be preparing to see me off.

"Would you help me up?" he asks me, extending a hand.

"For God's sake," I say, fake-exasperated (*We're getting away, we're getting away!* is what I'm thinking.), and I help him up on his feet. As soon as he's up, he sinks both his arms around me, taking me by surprise ("Emph!" I go, taking in breath) and pretty soon we're knocking up against each other, pushing our tongues around in each other's mouths. "Oh, man," I exhale, despite myself, and he suddenly withdraws.

"What is it?" I say, looking at him.

"You're bad news for me."

"What the hell does that mean?" I exclaim, laughing, even though he's not. And he looks at me, and shakes his head, and, to my relief, he finally laughs, and says: "Oh, *scratch it.*"

And then his hands are on my belt buckle, and mine are on his, and our pants snag on our knees for only a second before they make the drop down to our ankles—and then, without trying, we're doing a funny little dance, right in place. It *is* funny: it's like, I'm always forgetting about the sex part, like this is a *friendship,* like you shouldn't be doing it in the first place. And then he reminds me, and I'm like *Here we go again,* and then we're both working away, and pretty soon it's over and we're both a big mess, like now, kneeling here. And that's when I look at him, and he looks back as if he has no recourse, as if someone pulled all the little pins and pulleys and props out of his face, and it says nothing to me but: "Hey." And it's then, with glop everywhere, and him looking so temporarily possessed of nothing, that I love him best.

Phoebe calls later that night, when I'm plodding my way through a French exercise on the *passé simple* and anticipating Saturday. (Joani almost wouldn't speak to me until I told her I'd take her to the fabric store on Sunday.)

"Hi," she sighs when I pick up the phone in my parents' bedroom. "It's over."

"What's over?" I ask, but I think I already know.

"What do you think? Me and Charlie. The affair of the century."

Secretly, I'm ecstatic—I never liked that my two supposed best friends were going out, and I want to tell Phoebe that she was always much too smart for Charlie anyway, even though Charlie is, of course, an "excellent person," as Phoebe has always insisted. But I don't. "What happened?" I ask instead.

"Oh, I don't know," Phoebe says, sounding bored already. "A lot of things. Do you know, I copied Charlie a beautiful Diane DiPrima poem and he didn't even know who she was?"

"*That's* why you broke up with him?" I laugh, feeling vindicated.

"Well, not just that. A lot of things. I just think we operate on different levels, that's all."

"Hmmm," I say, lying low. "Interesting."

We're both quiet for a minute, then: "Anyway!" she says brightly. "I guess it's just me and you again—conspirators in living, right?" (She got that phrase out of some old book.)

"I guess so," I say, faintly wary. "But I mean, we're all gonna stay friends, right? I mean, you and Charlie aren't not speaking, are you?"

"Well," she fumbles. "He's a little pissed at me right now, but he'll probably be over it by tomorrow. You know Charlie. He's got the memory span of a dog. All that grass."

"I guess so," I say, uneasily.

"So, anyway," she says again. "You wanna go into Cambridge this Saturday? I wanna trade in some records. And we haven't gone in a long time, you've been so busy with college stuff."

"*I've* been busy! You've been busy—with Charlie. That's why we haven't done anything lately."

"Well, whatever. I guess we're both to blame. Anyway, you wanna go?"

"I can't," I say shortly. "I promised Joani I'd take her fabric shopping, so she can make her big dress."

"Well, let's take her with us. We can go to the fabric store on the way in, or on the way back. C'mon, it'll be fun. We'll introduce Joani to bohemia. Maybe we can get her to shave her head and get a nose ring."

"I can't. When I go out with Joani, I've totally got to focus on her. She takes up all my energy."

"Oh," Phoebe says, sounding taken aback. "Well, what about Sunday?"

"I gotta go to my aunt's house," I say, completely riffing. "It's my cousin Bethie Lynn's birthday."

"Oh. Too bad."

"Sorry."

"Whatever." Neither of us says anything, which is really bizarre, because when Phoebe and I talk, there's usually never a quiet moment. Finally, she says, "So, are you psyched to sit on my social activist mother's Unitarian panel?" (Phoebe's mother has organized a "racial healing" panel at their church, scheduled for two weeks from now, in which she hopes to bring all the mothers of Leicester over into West Mendhem so everyone can start finding "common ground" and defuse the mounting revolution.)

"That should be pretty funny," I say.

"It should be, now that you're the new voice of peace and love. If only everyone knew that you're a total Ivy League yuppie-in-the-making."

"I'm not a yuppie!" I snap. "I hate them. Wanting to make a lot of money and wanting to live in an intellectual community are two different things."

"Jeez, I'm *sorry,*" Phoebe says. "I was only kidding. I don't think you're a yuppie."

"Good, 'cause I'm not."

Another pause. I'm starting to feel vaguely sick to my stomach; I don't like the way our conversation is going, but I don't know how to end it. Finally, she speaks again: "So, did you hear the latest town proposal to deal with the crime and everything?"

"No, what is it?" I ask sullenly. (They still haven't found the Kerrie Lanouette killer, although there have now been about nine suspects, all Puerto Rican, and they've all been smeared all over the front page of the *Leicester Tribune,* one after another, only to be released, or whatever, because their fingerprints didn't match up, or something.)

"Now these selectmen are saying they want to change the borders of West Mendhem, and pull them back from Leicester, so that when the Leicester people start moving into the fringes of West Mendhem, they won't *be* in West Mendhem. They'll still be in Leicester. Can you believe that?"

"They're total bigots," I say absently. "They'll never do it. You just can't change borders. Don't you have to go through the state for that?"

"They say it's not because they're racists, it's because of property value." Phoebe sneers. "Like they're two different things."

"Hm." Then we're not talking again.

"Eric?" she finally says.

"Yeah?"

"Do you hate me or something?"

I'm startled. "What?"

"Well—like—I mean, ever since the Charlie thing, I feel like you've kind of come to—*hate* me, or something. And it's really fucking me up, okay, 'cause fuck Charlie! You're my best friend. I love you, okay?" She's choking on her words, and in a minute, she's crying, her jagged sobs excruciatingly distinct through the phone wires. The minute she says, "I love you," this weird wave comes over me, and in a second, my eyes are welling up and I'm closing the bedroom door so Joani won't hear me crying. And suddenly I hate myself for being short with Phoebe, and I want to talk to her—really, really *talk*—so bad, it's like I've got a knife in my chest.

"Okay?" she's saying again. "Are you even listening?"

"Feeb, Feeb," I'm saying into the line. "I'm here. I don't hate you. I swear to God that has nothing to do with it. You're my best friend, too."

"Well, then, why have you been such an asshole to me? It's like you're trying to punish me or something, and I *love* you, okay? I love you more than Charlie—you fucking idiot!"

"Oh, Feeb, I know it. Look—I'm sorry I've been this way, but you have nothing to do with it."

"Well, then what the fuck is it?"

My heart is booming in my throat; I feel like I'm getting near that precipice I've backed away from before, but this time I feel closer to it than ever before. "It's just—I'm really fucked up, all right? I don't know what's going on in my life."

"Well, *why?*" she says, and I'm thinking *Shit, shit, shit!*, watching myself on the precipice, advancing a step, retreating two, like some manic dance. "I mean, you're, like, the smartest person I know," she goes on. "You're, like, number three in your class and you're probably going to fucking Yale next year. You're gonna be some great writer or cultural critic or something. I don't even know if I can get into some stupid commune farm college in Vermont. So—*what?* Eric, why are you bawling all of a sudden?"

"I don't know!" I spit into the phone. "It's like—I don't even know who I am. I just want to get the fuck out of here."

"Do you think you're manic-depressive? My mother is, you know."

I want to scream into the phone, "No, you idiot, I'm not manic-depressive"—and so forth. But I don't. "Maybe I am." I pull back, pull myself together. "I don't even know anymore."

"Look," she says. *"I* want to get the fuck out of here, too. I hate this stupid town. So let's just stick together, okay? We've only got a few months left."

"I know," I say, dead.

"So can we please be platonic lovers again?"

"We'll always be."

"I really need you, Eric. Don't hate me."

"I don't hate you. You know we're best friends."

"I know. I just needed to hear it." We're silent again; then she starts laughing. "Oh my God! Did you see when Goody Farnham came into class today, and she had all those little sesame seeds caught in her teeth? I thought I was gonna puke! Charlie kept, like, picking at his teeth right in front of her, and she was *totally* oblivious—"

"Feeb?"

"Yeah?"

"Joani's calling," I lied. "She needs my help with homework or something."

"Oh. Okay. You wanna meet in the library tomorrow before homeroom? I've got some new poems to show you."

"Okay."

"All right, darling. Good night. I'm glad we talked."

"So am I. I'll see you tomorrow."

For a long time, I just sit there on my parents' bed, staring at a picture on their wall. It's from when we all went to Disney World, when Brenda was about ten and I was seven and Joani was only about two. We're all three making faces at the camera: Brenda and me pulling on the fronts of our T-shirts, pretending we have boobs, and Joani sticking out her tongue. I remember on that trip, I was dying to go into the Haunted Mansion, but when we finally did, I covered my eyes the whole way and screamed, I was so terrified. Now I just look at that picture—I look at myself at seven—and I stare and stare, looking for a clue.

Ten

"It must be exciting for you to go to Boston, cradle of democracy," he says in his usual *je m'en fiche* drawl, passing me a bruised pear and a biscuit that he stole from the St. Banner dining hall. This, as I pull onto 93 South on this unseasonably warm January morning with the ice melting off the blasted granite on either side of the highway, as we sit next to each other in my mother's hatchback—my seatbelt strapped, his not—as we make our great getaway.

Snot-ass, I think, accepting the breakfast awkwardly with one hand as he fiddles with the dial on the radio, changing it from my favorite alternative music station to a classical one. But I don't say that. Instead, I say, "It's actually no big deal. I go in a lot. I know my way around pretty well."

"It's sort of like your Athens, isn't it?" he persists. "Your Mecca?" He's settled the dial on some horrible modern piece, Bartók or something, the kind of thing I cringed from when I used to take piano lessons.

I sigh, pointedly, to let him know I'm not amused. "If you want to think of it that way, fine."

"My, my," he says through a mouthful of biscuit. "Not a morning person, are you?"

"Not with a prick," I say, pulling into the left lane and accelerating.

"Good Lord! Why the ad hominem attack?"

"Well, why do you have to be such a jerk, Brooks? 'It must be exciting for you to go to Boston,' listen to you! You know, we're alway from St. Banner and we're away from West Mendhem. You can ease up, okay?"

I glance at him. He's sitting up straight, biscuit in midair, looking at me, startled. *"Je m'excuse,* Mr. Fitz."

"Fine," I say. "Just don't mock me, for one day, okay?"

He doesn't say anything, until, "Did you have a hard time getting out today?" Questions like this have become a kind of mantra for us: "Where did you say you were going?" "Where did you say you had been?" "Was it hard to get away?" Sometimes I think what we have most in common is that we're both always lying about our whereabouts.

"Not really," I say. "I told them I was going to this all-day program for prospective Yale people at some alumnus's house in Weston."

"Do they have those for people who haven't even gotten in yet?"

"I don't know. But my parents wouldn't know if they did or not, anyway, so what does it matter?" I answer, then feel slightly disgusted with myself that I would exploit their ignorance of such matters so brazenly. "How about you?"

"I had weekend privileges, so I signed out for Boston. Come to think, I hope no one notices I wasn't on line for the bus." (He means the bus St. Banner charters to take people into Boston on Saturday; I've seen it coming through town before, late on Saturday afternoons, full of preppies with bags from Brooks Brothers and Copley Square.)

"Why do I feel like we're on the lam?" I mutter, instantly wishing I hadn't said it.

"Oh, please." He *tsks* absently, taking my hand off the gear shift and pressing it up to his lips.

"Come on, they can see us in the other cars. And you've got crumbs on your lips," I say. He wipes his lips in my palm and says, "Not anymore," laughing.

We park on a side street in Cambridge and walk to Harvard Square. It's an excellent morning, bright and warm, and already the Square is running over with the usual assortment of aging tweedsters, skate punks, weekend arty types, students, dirty bums, Rastas, and born-again megaphone nuts. It's funny, I'm thinking: here's the first time we've ever been together in front of lots of other people, but no one is paying particular attention to us, no one is giving us a problem. I start loosening up—my jaw, which I've been grinding ever since I left the house this morning, stops aching—and I think he does, too, because out of nowhere, he starts getting chattier and jokier than ever before, making funny comments about people we pass and about things we see in windows. In Wordsworth Bookstore, he seems to know something about every book on display, and even though I'm impressed, I start getting angry and jealous, wondering where people actually manage to *get* all the knowledge they get, and why don't I know where to find it? He ends up buying three theory-type books (I can't even understand the stuff that goes on the jacket flaps), all by some French guys, as well as the latest copy of some little magazine, *Grand Street,* and I'm just grateful when he checks out my selection—*Best Short Stories of 1986*—and chooses not to pass judgment.

While we're apart, rummaging, I watch him from the end of an aisle: he's sitting on the floor, poring over some fat book, with about six others stacked up next to him. I have a thought about him, and it comes back when we're back outside, and he's talking more easily than he's ever talked before, pointing at things, telling me little scraps of information about the architecture of buildings we pass, and about the history of the Abolitionists in Cambridge, and about where the Transcendentalists would hang out when they were all at Harvard together. And the thought is that he's too *big* for St. Banner, and definitely for *any* one place, and probably for me—but it's that thought that makes me want him like I've never wanted anyone before, and makes me desperately want to match him mind-for-mind if it's the last thing I do, even though I'll probably never be able to do it.

For lunch, I take him to Bartley's Burgers, my favorite place in Cambridge (I'm ridiculously happy to be able to name a place over him, for once), and the whole time we're there, ordering food, eating it, waiting for the check, we're kicking each other around under the table, surrounded by all sorts of people, totally pushing our luck, keeping straight faces, which seems to be the best joke of all. Just once, when we're laughing too shrilly at something, we catch a woman nearby glance at us, then away, mutter something to the man she's with, who looks, mutters back, and they both look away.

"Do you think we threaten the social order?" he asks me, gravely.

"*Us?*" I ask, amused. "I don't think so." "Threaten the social order" is a phrase that makes me think of serial killers, or those animal-rights terrorist groups that bomb cosmetic companies because they test on rabbits, or child molesters who dress up as clowns.

"But wouldn't it be fun to be a kind of modern-day Leopold and Loeb?" he asks me.

"Who's that?" I ask back (I'm used to it now), and when he tells me, I tell him no, that wouldn't be fun at all. He says I'm priggy and Catholic, and don't I know that there are no fixed morals, that morality is relative? And I say there *have* to be morals, or otherwise there'd be chaos, and you can't just go around killing people just to see what it *feels* like. And all he says, lighting up a cigarette, is: "Oh, please." Of course I know he's joking, which makes it okay.

Later in the afternoon, we drive into Boston and park the car near the Public Gardens. We roam around the Boston Public Library, him scrutinizing the marble and the molding and grabbing my coat sleeve and saying over and over again, "Weren't McKim, Mead, White *brilliant?*" and me just thinking that the whole place smells peculiar. When we come outside, it's getting dark, and colder (we button up our coats), and even oddly barren-seeming for the middle of Boston at four o'clock on a Saturday afternoon, but we walk the entire length of Newbury Street anyway, until we've walked all the way to the Christian Science building, which looks particularly forbidding in the gathering dusk. He says he wants to smoke a cigarette, and we sit down on a bench, but before he goes ahead and lights it, he puts his arm around me, and I look around one hundred and eighty degrees, but we seem to be pretty much alone, and I put mine around his, and we both just sit there looking across the plaza at that stone behemoth.

I pull in tighter toward him and put my gloved hand on the back of his head. "Today was really nice," I say, thinking that pretty soon we'll have to get back in my mother's hatchback and drive back to town and go back to meeting in that stupid, freezing barn.

"Wouldn't you like to do it every day?" he asks.

"Where?" I laugh. "Here?"

"No, not here. Paris."

I laugh again. "Hello?"

"You wanna come spend the summer in Paris with me? Open invitation."

I laugh again, a little hysterically, but he doesn't. "Brooks—come on. I can't."

"Why not?"

"Because! Because I have to make money for school, for one thing. I'm gonna get a job during the day and keep working at the sub shop at night. I can't afford to go to Paris."

"I'll pay your way, fool, and I'll get us a place. And I'll get you a job in a café or something, and you can pocket the money. The exchange rate's going to favor America this summer. I checked it out."

Now I'm getting antsy. "What would I tell my family? That I'm going to Paris to live with some guy they don't even know?"

"No," he says, rolling his eyes. "Use the brain God gave you. Tell them you applied for some exchange program—"

"I can't do that!"

"You applied for some exchange program, and you're going to be living with a nice Catholic family. I'll make up all the documents. I'll even pretend to be the family and I'll send you fake photos and letters in that funny squiggly French handwriting. We'll pull off the perfect hoax."

"Brooks, come *on*—"

He turns around full on the bench and looks at me. "And do you even *know* how much in heaven you will be? Do you even *know* what Paris is like in the summertime? We'll go to the top of Montmartre at night, where the basilica is, and we'll bring a bottle of wine, and we'll look down on the whole city. And on weekends, we'll rent a car and we'll drive out to Normandy and visit these *extraordinary* old châteaux. We'll go to Monet's house, Giverny, it's a tourist trap, but *you've* never seen it, and—"

"Brooks, would you cut it out? I can't go and you know it."

He catches his breath, pulls out a cigarette, lights it, exhales. "Eric, listen to me. Just one more time, okay? At the end of the school year, I am leaving St. Banner, going back to Virginia, selling my auntie's house for as much money as I can get, leaving the country, and never coming back. Now, I am very very kindly extending to you the opportunity to come with me, gratis, even if it's only for one pathetic little summer. This is it. Last chance. Now, I'd advise that you think about the opportunities for travel that you're realistically going to have in your life, and—"

I'm feeling faintly panicky now, glancing around to see if anyone is watching. "Look, Brooks, couldn't you come back up here and get a place in—in Cambridge or something, and I could come in on weekends—"

"No!" he explodes, scaring the shit out of me. "I'm not living like some secret faggot waiting for my secret faggot white boyfriend to come down from the suburbs every weekend to fuck around in secret all weekend and go back into hiding for the rest of the week. Not in this country. Never. My mother knows what the fuck she's talking about."

"But Brooks, what about *my* family—"

"Fuck your family! Don't you get it? I'm giving you the chance to get away from your family—just *once*—so you know what it's like to maybe live your life without running around hiding from your family all the time. Don't you hate it? Or does some perverse masquerading part of you get off on it?"

"Shut up, you know I hate it. It's just—they need me. My mother needs me. And my sisters. I mean, my sister's having a *baby*. And they'd freak *out* if they ever knew about this."

"They already do," he says, looking away.

"What?"

"They already know. I sent them a letter. I told them everything."

"Fuck you! You did not!" He just looks at me, one eyebrow cocked. "Brooks," I say, feeling ill, trying to sound threatening. "You'd better be kidding."

"I'm not," he murmurs. "I posted it Thursday. They should have received it today—while you were at the Yale brunch."

"Fuck you!" I scream at him now, standing up, my head spinning. "How the fuck could you do that? How could you destroy my life? Where the fuck—"

"Oh, shut up and sit down." He scowls at me. "Do you really think I'd go to the bother to destroy your life? I didn't send any letter, so stop flattering yourself."

I'm relieved, but I don't sit down; I'm not going to be his puppet. "You can find your own way home," I say, wrapping my scarf around my neck. "You can take the fucking St. Banner bus with all your friends. I'm going back." I start walking across the plaza back toward Newbury Street: one step, two, three, half a dozen, waiting for him to call back.

"Of course, I always *could* send it," he shouts.

I turn. It's not because I'm afraid of him, I swear; it's because I just want to look at this fucked-up mutant of a human being—and he just sits there and stares at me. And I stare back at him, and he does the same, for what seems to be the longest time, we just look at each other, until I start to feel like I'm part of a surreal tableau: it's like, I don't feel myself anymore, and this plaza in Boston could be as far away as Moscow or Beijing, and this isn't my own life anymore, but someone else's—another person's fucked-up story. And when he doesn't move, just keeps staring, I finally walk toward him, and when I'm standing over him, I pull him up by the lapel of his overcoat and put my arms around him and sink my face underneath his scarf, in his neck. And he holds me back, underneath my coat, and I'm thinking, *Okay, I give up.*

I don't know how long we stay like that, but when we stop, it's completely dark outside, and frigid, and we start walking back along Newbury Street like we're in a kind of vacuum. Dimly, I know there are people around us—yuppies on their way to fancy dinners, punk kids loitering in front of the record stores—but it's like they're on one side of a glass, and on the other, it's just us, silent, but totally wrapped up in some new shared knowledge, some revelation I can't even name.

Back in the car, on the highway, flying over the Tobin Bridge with the lights and towers of the city receding behind us, everyone everywhere else part of the noisy celebration of a Saturday night, this silent pact doesn't end. It's the strangest feeling, like we're sinking together into some vortex, almost like we're underwater, like we decided to take some wordless trip together. My instinct is to get off the road, to turn in somewhere, and when I see an exit for Burlington, I take it, unaccompanied by a word from either of us. We're on a commercial strip now, and it rises up—a Day's Inn, glowing orange sign in the foreground, and behind, the low-slung chalet—without a search or a summons, like we willed it without even trying. I pull into the parking lot and turn off the engine. Two kids run in front of the hatchback, screaming, and behind them, their loping parents, dragging luggage, but again, they seem murky and muffled on the other side of a glass. My head is filled with the sound of my heart thundering; I'm shaking so hard I wonder if I'll be able to walk, and when I finally look at him, he's staring straight ahead out the window. It's dinnertime at home, I'm thinking, but the thought and the image that attends it flash across my mind so fast they're like a passing wave of tremens.

"You wanna?" I finally manage to say, and my voice sounds tiny to me, a thousand miles away.

He doesn't speak, he just nods, and when he puts his hand over the door handle to open it, I catch it shaking like a madman's. Stepping out of the car, he trips, scraping the knee of his pants on the pavement, and when, off-center myself, I ask, "Are you okay?" he doesn't answer again, just nods and weaves ahead of me toward the restaurant and the adjoining lobby.

Inside, in the empty lobby, there's a girl behind the desk—high school age, college age, I don't know because I won't look her in the face. I stand there, examining the fringe on my scarf, while he murmurs something to her and passes her his credit card, and the minutes that she takes to process the card and return with it and a key, that he takes to sign his name (once, then twice in another place) are bloated and excruciating, like going down under anesthesia. Finally, he turns to me—"Okay," he says—and we're stalking down a long, rust-colored corridor, into an elevator, up three flights—"Three sixty-two," he says, and I nod—then up a long, rust-colored corridor until a door marked 3-6-2. Key in the lock, turn on the light, close the door behind, coats on the bed the size of a small island. Over the bed, there's a piece of art: a lake, a boy feeding fish from a silver pail to a spaniel standing on his hind legs—an enormous paint-by-numbers.

"Art for art's sake," he says, nodding toward it, sitting on the edge of the bed, unlacing his hunting boots. I start to do the same, but stop halfway to pull the blinds on the window. Outside, there are tiny lights strung along the highways and semi-industrial hills of Burlington, each light denoting a household in mid-supper. It's dinnertime in Burlington, in the state of Massachusetts, in America, and I have never felt so beyond the common fold of the living, so keenly and irreversibly an outlaw, as I do right now.

I pull off my boots, my sweater and shirt, my trousers, pelting them in a heap on the rust-colored easy chair. I'm almost completely naked now, and so is he, and it occurs to me that although we've been naked together before, we've never before been so in a realm of so much space, so much light—so much opportunity just to examine each other with whole yards between us, and to consider what it would take to traverse the space in between.

"I never thought it would get to this point, did you?" I ask.

He's sitting on the edge of the bed in his underwear, looking down, twisting at his undoffed sock. "I can't say in good faith that I didn't ever once entertain the thought," he says, standing up, snapping off the light, and stumbling toward me, stumbling toward him, in the sudden dark.

It's just after midnight when we check out, hair wet, clothes disheveled, and another excruciating tenure with the lank-haired girl at the desk, who is as terrified of looking up at us as I am of her. Going out to the car, walking fast, businesslike, not talking because it seems to be the craziest redundancy at this point, I'm wondering dumbly how not to file this away, how not to stuff it in a chamber at the back of the mind, wondering how to keep alive in the deadening tide of the schooldays and schooldays to follow—wondering if it's possible at all to do that without losing your mind.

"I'm screwed, probably, when I get home" is all I say pulling out of the parking lot.

"What's new?" he says, thumbing back into shape a cigarette that crushed in his pocket.

"That was funny," I venture, wondering what's the grammar for this kind of talk. "It's like it wasn't you, sort of. Do you know what I mean?"

He laughs, and I think it sounds sort of mean, but maybe I'm misinterpreting. "Well, did you feel like *you?*"

"Sometimes," I say. "But not the whole time."

"Well, you didn't feel like you to me."

"Is that a compliment?" I ask.

"I guess you can read it that way if you want to."

"Oh, thanks."

"Oh, *s'il vous plaît.* It's a compliment."

I pull off the highway fifteen minutes before home and take the back roads through Boxford to St. Banner. Pulling up by the side of the road, it's the idling of the engine of the hatchback that tells us to move it along, which relieves me, because I don't know the special protocol of this moment.

"Well—good night," I say, taking a few of his fingers in my hand awkwardly.

"Et cetera, et cetera," he drawls, flicking away my hand. "Are you coming with me this summer or not? I've got to start inquiring about a place."

"I'll see if I can figure out a way," I say, startling myself.

"I'm sure you can. You seem to have an infinite talent for duplicity."

"It's not infinite, believe me."

"Sure it's not. Call me Monday." He closes the car door—that prudent half-slam—and sprints over the stone wall, across the thawing soccer fields.

Driving home, approaching the common in the center of town, I see a play of spinning red lights in the trees. When I get to the intersection in front of the old Unitarian church, there's a whole scene going on there—cop cars, ambulances, unintelligible voices over megaphones, a few old women who have come out onto their front porches, shivering in nightgowns and robes. A cop is standing in the middle of the street with a huge flashlight, and when I slow down, he comes hustling over to me, swinging the flashlight like a billy club.

"What's wrong?" I ask, rolling down the window. It's Officer DeMarco, the one who picked up Brooks way back in September.

"Nuthin'," he snaps at me, his mouth full of gum. "Little accident, that's all." Past him, past the roadblock, I make out medics loading a stretcher into the ambulance. There are other cops there, shouting at the medics, harsh.

"A car accident?" I ask.

"Nah, just a little accident. You gotta get on now. Can't go through this way. Gotta go back the long way on Great Lake."

"Is that person all right?"

"Yanh, he's gonna be fine. Don't worry about it. Get home now." De-Marco hustles off, the blockhead, flailing his big phallic flashlight.

When I get home, to my dismay, my parents are up in front of the TV in the den. "Where the hell were you tonight?" my mother barks before I'm even in the room.

"Some of the other guys at this Yale thing asked me if I wanted to go into Boston with them when it ended," I say. (I prepared that one the minute I sped away from St. Banner.)

"You're selfish," she says, getting up and snapping off the TV. "Self-ish, running around and having your fun. I just hope you're not think-ing of breaking your promise to your little sister tomorrow. On top of everything else, it'll break her heart." Then she stalks out of the room and up to bed.

"What was that all about?" I turn to my father.

"She's just upset," he says. "Your grandma went into the hospital again today with another heart attack, and it doesn't look good this time. She's all hooked up and she's not talkin' right. I think your mother wanted you to be here to baby-sit Joani, but instead she had to take her along to the hospital."

"Oh, God, I'm sorry. I didn't know."

"How were you supposed to know?" my father says, getting up un-ceremoniously and putting his TV glasses back in their case. "Just make your mother happy tomorrow and make a nice day for your sister, okay?"

"Of course," I say.

"How was your Yale thing?"

"It was okay. I met some cool people."

"That's good." I think I catch a kind of frown from him, but maybe it's just me seeing things. "I'm pooped. 'Night," he says, and lumbers out of the room.

I aim the remote at the TV, turn it on, stare at it for a minute—it's a televangelist—turn it off, and just sit. I think about my grandmother, all hooked up, and Brenda, knocked up, and me—completely fucked up. Then I think about Room 362, and what went down on that island of a bed in that dark room, the lights of the highway vigilant pinpricks outside, and I feel like if I sit here and think about it any longer the living room is going to get so hot they're going to think there's a fire going on downstairs. So, forgoing my coat, I slip outside through the back door and run around the house into the evergreen bushes that stand tall up against the dark dining room windows, and, freezing, I crouch down there like a crazy man, and unzip my pants and do what it takes until I'm no longer on the brink of conflagration. Then I zip up and stand there and wonder what I could possibly do to steady myself before I go back in the house, and, knee-jerk, I start to say a prayer—the Hail Mary, which my grandmother taught me when I was young, which always used to be my favorite prayer. But halfway through, I say to myself exactly what he would say to me—"Oh, *please*"—and I stop dead—"blessed art thou amongst women"—and creep back inside, taking care not to slam the door.

The next morning, Joani and I are downing cereal together before we take off for the fabric store when Phoebe calls.

"My mother wants to know if you can come to an emergency meeting tonight, to represent youth—along with me," she says.

"I thought that panel thing was two weeks from now."

"It *is*, but this is an emergency meeting."

"Why?"

"You haven't heard yet?"

"Heard what?"

"About last night?"

"No!"

"Oh, my God! Eric, last night, some kid—some teenager—some Hispanic guy from Leicester—was wandering around West Mendhem, around the common. I don't know what the fuck he was doing, but the cops are saying of course he was here to steal cars or something—"

"Oh, shit, I think I saw this," I say.

"Don't say *shit!*" Joani screams with glee from the kitchen table.

"And Eric, listen: some guys—some West Mendhem guys—beat the living shit out of him and left him on the common as good as dead. Can you believe this?"

"Is he dead?"

"He's in the hospital, like, holding on by a thread. I just heard the latest update on the radio. They said, like, they jumped on his head with work boots. They totally smashed in his *brain.*"

"Oh, shit. Do they know who did it?"

"Don't say *shit!*" Joani screams, louder.

"No, they have no idea. Some old lady who lives on the common said all she saw through her window were these four white guys, like, pounding this thing on the ground and jumping all over him."

"I saw this last night, Feeb. I totally saw it. I was driving home by the common and I saw them putting this stretcher in an ambulance, and when I asked the cops what happened, they said there was just a little accident, and I should get the hell home."

"They're totally complicit," Phoebe sneers, then: "But that isn't it, though. There's, like, a *riot* going on in Leicester right now. All the people—the Hispanics, the Puerto Ricans, all the guys—they're running around in the streets and overturning cars and setting fire to this whole neighborhood. You know, Essex Heights, where everybody makes packie runs, because they don't card you? It's totally going *up in smoke.* There are arson squads there and all these people are screaming that they're sick of being persecuted in their own country, and that this kid—Jesús, I think his name is; how's *that* for irony?—that he was a basketball star and a good kid and, like, a total hero—"

"Why are they wrecking up their own neighborhood? Why haven't they come into West Mendhem, if this is where it all happened?"

"Eric!" Phoebe sounds appalled.

"I mean, not that I want them to, but wouldn't that be a more effective statement? Like a siege?"

"I don't know why they didn't come here first, but there are Staties all over the place surrounding West Mendhem, and Mendhem, too, because those are the two places all the Leicester people said they were gonna hit next. You can't even go in or out of West Mendhem without being stopped. And there are riot squads all over Leicester wearing these scary space-droid outfits. It's on the news. Haven't you turned on the TV this morning?"

"No," I say. I want to snap on the little TV on the kitchen table, but I'm afraid it'll scare Joani, so I don't. "I can't believe this is happening. It's so pointless."

"I told you this was coming," Phoebe says sternly. "And you know that reporter from the *Leicester Tribune,* the one that interviewed you for the essay contest?"

"Patty Gerrucci?" I say, remembering the fake yuppie and how she annoyed the hell out of me with her second-rate Brenda Starr affectations.

"Yeah, her. Well, this was just on the news. She drives with a photographer right into the riot neighborhood in Leicester to get the big scoop on the story—I'm sure she's thinking *Pulitzer, Pulitzer*—and they see the car coming, and all these guys start screaming, 'White bitch!' and chasing after it, and Patty pulls into reverse and goes flying back down the street, driving for her life. Isn't that a riot?" Phoebe's laughing now.

"Bad pun," I say, but the image of Patty Gerrucci, dressed for success, fleeing the bloodthirsty masses does make me laugh. "So what's gonna happen now?"

"It's insane. All these civil rights lawyers are on TV saying they're gonna represent the family of this kid, this Jesús, and that this is going to be one of the biggest race cases of the past thirty years. Of course the state investigators are gonna launch a full search for the thugs—they're gonna be all over the high school, talking to people—even though that fucking pig McElroy is saying he's sure it couldn't be any of the nice kids from WMHS, and they're probably from Methuen or something. And of course, everyone they show on TV from West Mendhem is saying this is God's justice for the whole Kerrie Lanouette thing, like it's some kind of good karma. Can you *believe* this?"

"We're, like, the new Birmingham or something," I say, trying to be detached about the whole thing.

"Yeah," Phoebe muses, even though I'm not sure she gets the reference. "Anyway, you've gotta come with me to this thing tonight. My mother's talking to the Hispanic churches in Leicester, trying to get some community people to show up, even though their English isn't very good and all she knows is a little French from when she was at Simmons College twenty-five years ago. But anyway, you've gotta come. We'll sit together up on the panel."

"What am I supposed to say? I'm not a fucking riot expert."

Joani whips around to me from her cereal. "You're in deep doo-doo."

"Talk like a grown-up," I say to her absent-mindedly. She calmly opens her mouth and shows me her masticated Frankenberries before turning back to the bowl.

"Everyone knows you as the voice of youth now!" Phoebe says. "Just say that everyone's blowing this all out of proportion, and that we've gotta find a way to get along, and stop the violence. I'm probably gonna read a passage from *Jonathan Livingston Seagull,* or something. And god-jangle might show up, too, and we might sing some Spanish-language folk songs, if they can find any."

"That is so tacky," I say.

"No, it's not!" she says, miffed. "We're trying to find some common ground, here, Eric."

"What time is this thing at?" I ask. "I've gotta take out Joani, all the way to this fabric store in New Hampshire."

"Seven o'clock at the Unitarian church. It's an open meeting. They're announcing it on the TV and the radio. Meet me down in the lounge at five to seven so I can practice my reading on you."

"I don't have to read my stupid essay again, do I? I'm so sick of that thing."

"No, just speak from your heart."

When we get off the phone, I tell Joani to sit tight for a minute, then I go into the den and turn on the TV. Phoebe's right; on all three channels, they've interrupted the usual programming to risk their lives and report from Leicester. For the first time, I get really scared. It's true, the place is a mess; you can see fire and black smoke rising out of the windows and roofs of those old dilapidated triple-decker tenement houses where my parents used to live, and you can see the chassis of cars belly-up in the street, and garbage strewn all over the filthy snowbanks. Big packs of Hispanic guys with bandannas and high-tops, even a few girls, are running up and down the streets, coming right up to the cameras (which are hand-held and swooping all over the place) and swearing and throwing bottles and rocks and stuff, blasting big boom boxes, screaming in English things like "The whities, we're gonna come burn down ya nice houses and rape ya fucking daughters"—the TV censors are bleeping like crazy—and screaming things in Spanish that I can't understand. Then they cut to the correspondents, who all seem at a remove from the action, with smoke billowing in the distance, like they're reporting from Beirut, and they're all earnest and grave, saying how they don't see any imminent letup, because when the riot squad scares the kids out of one neighborhood, they just take off for another and start rioting all over again. About every five seconds, they say they haven't seen racial violence like this since the busing crisis, and they say that people in the Mendhems should stay indoors, behind locked doors, and stay tuned.

Then they cut to the kid's family. His full name is Jesús Antonio de la Costa, age seventeen, a senior and starting center for the basketball team at the derelict Leicester High School. He also loved Lionel Richie and home ec class, they tell us, and might have had an athletic scholarship to Villanova. And they're all standing out on their broken-down front porch in the middle of the cold, about half a dozen weeping women backed by about fourteen screaming, weeping kids and two very old men. His mother, a tanklike woman in a housecleaning shift with a large, pliant face that looks oddly like my own grandmother's, says in very broken English that he was a good boy, that ever since her husband died he was the man of the house and he looked after his grandma and his uncles and aunts, and his six younger siblings and his eight cousins, and he cooked them all rice and beans and fish and chicken because she was away at night cleaning offices. And that she had nothing against white people, we're all God's children, but it wasn't right that four punks should beat him up just because he was out taking a walk under the stars. He liked to leave the house at night and walk, she said, and talk to God about his future, and what he should do, because the house was cramped and he said he needed the quiet and the cold to talk to God, even though he could never stand the cold in Massachusetts, where he had lived since they moved from Puerto Rico—no, not San Juan, the country—when he was eight. And that the doctors said it didn't look good, he had suffered massive—oh, what's the English? "Brain damage"? That's it—his brain was squashed, and his soul was probably already going up, and up. And she held up a picture of him in a frame, and the camera pulled in close, and it was murky, but I could see that he was skinny, with a thin pencil mustache, wearing one of those horrible skinny leather ties, and he obviously hadn't had braces—and his mother and all his aunts begin echoing each other in Spanish, and English: "Yes, that is correct. Up, and up. That's why his name is Jesús"—and all of a sudden, I'm crying, and I feel like only half of it is for him.

Joani comes in with a milk mustache and I snap off the TV, pretending I've got some lint in my eyes. I wipe the milk residue off her mouth with my sleeve, and say, "Get your coat."

Outside, it's a warm, sunny day again, but I can see a kind of gray haze hanging over Leicester to the north. "What's that?" Joani wants to know as we get into the hatchback and she starts fiddling with the radio dials to find hit radio, and I say, "It's probably from the old factories."

Phoebe's right again; when we get to the intersection, there's a whole blockade of state police cars, and one of the cops is walking up to cars—traffic seems to be backed up for a mile—and interviewing the passengers at the window before he lets them pass.

"What's going on?" Joani asks.

"Maybe there was an accident or something."

"I hope they let us through. We gotta get to the fabric store before it closes."

"Joani, it's eleven o'clock in the morning! We have the whole day."

"Mark my words," she says, imitating our mother.

I roll down the window of the car when the cop approaches us. He asks us where we're going, and I tell him we're getting on Route 28 to go to the fabric store so my sister can buy fabric to make a spring dress. He asks us where we're from, and I say West Mendhem, and when I ask him why it matters, he just tells me not to make any trouble, and to get onto the highway immediately instead of taking the junction ramp a few miles into South Leicester.

"You know what's goin' on, don't you?" he asks me reprovingly.

"Yeah," I say quietly, not wanting to stir Joani, and he lets us pass. A few yards up ahead, I pass a tableau: a family, a Latin-looking family, on the side of the road: mother, father, three kids, all with sleds, probably heading to Haggard's Hill in West Mendhem (it's a national preservation zone, or whatever), and a cop has encouraged them out of their rusty gold-colored, seventies-looking Maverick and asked them to show identification. I peek around at the faces in the cars around me, chalky white faces, and everyone looks grim and taut with anxiety and disgust.

"What's goin' on?" Joani asks, craning back to look at the family on the road.

"I said, I guess there was some sort of accident."

In a moment, we're on the highway, and I'm glad to be speeding away to New Hampshire, away from the smoke and the bottlenecked streets. In the fabric store, Joani is a whirligig, flipping through the little notebook she brought with her that contains dimensions and other stuff I don't understand, virtually running from bolt to bolt, asking me what I think of this fabric and that fabric, and I keep saying, "That's pretty," without even hearing myself, because I'm trying to sort out all these other images in my head. It's the image of Jesús Antonio de la Costa walking the streets of West Mendhem late at night, and of me hugging the curves of roads outcountry going to places I shouldn't go, and him, of course him, doing just the same in his gleaming white shirts, and all three of us just walking casualties waiting to happen—

"Joani, would you *shut up* for a second?"

She looks up at me, stunned, as if I'd slapped her, and before I realize that I spoke out of nowhere, before I can say I'm sorry, I was distracted, I watch her face contort into that awful silent grimace—like toddlers right after they've fallen flat on their face, that horrible stunned sliver of silence—and then she wails like a siren and starts bawling at the top of her lungs.

"Joani, Joani, baby, I didn't mean that. I swear I didn't! I was off in space—" I plead, and I crouch down to hold her in my arms, but she's thrashing away.

"Where's my grandma? I want my sister! I want Brenda—and Ma!" she's screaming. By now, we're surrounded by about three frumpy matron types—the types who were smiling all over us a few minutes ago with those Isn't-she-cute? looks—and they're all asking "Is she okay?

Should we call an ambulance?" No, I say, trying to be polite and cavalier, she doesn't need an ambulance, she's just tired and stressed, big sewing project, it means a lot to her, and we'll be fine. And then I whisper to her, "C'mon, baby, don't make a scene," and I realize with a kind of terror that that's exactly what my father would say in the same situation: *Don't make a scene.*

"Why'd you get mad at me? When's Grandma coming back, huh? I want her to come with me," Joani says, still crying and snorting.

"She's coming back pretty soon," I say, holding her again, and this time, thankfully, she doesn't shove me away. "You can go with her next time, okay? I'm real sorry what I just said. It's like, I wasn't even talking to you. It's more like I was talking to myself, get it?" We're both sitting on the floor now of this huge store, surrounded by odd-smelling columns of poly-blend fabric in spring colors, with a piped-in Muzak version of "I Say a Little Prayer" in the background, and I'm thinking, miserable, *What the fuck is going on everywhere?*

She sniffles, looks down at her notebook, then asks reasonably: "Brenda should be coming back pretty soon, too, huh?"

"Pretty soon, I guess," I say, fiddling absently with the zipper on her parka. "Maybe in a month or two."

"Is Grandma gonna die this time?" she asks without pause.

"I don't think right away. Eventually, yeah. We all are. But not right away. Grandma's very tough, you know."

She stares at me dully, half a finger in her nose. *She's on to me,* I'm thinking, way in the back of my head, and I've got to have her on my side, if it ever all comes down.

"Joani?"

"Uh-huh?"

"You still love me, right?"

She looks alarmed. "Uh-huh," she says, nodding her head vigorously.

"I mean—you don't think I'm a bad person, do you?"

"No. You're very, very good. I just wish you didn't yell at me now."

"I'm sorry for that, okay? Now, look: let's finish up here—let's pick a really, really pretty color and a print, something that's gonna make you look really pretty—and then we'll go to Micky D's for lunch, okay? We'll get the apple pies for dessert, okay?"

"That's what you said you'd do anyway," she says, faintly exasperated.

"Right," I say, stymied. "That's what I said. And that's what we'll do. So let's get everything you need and go to lunch, okay?"

"O-*kay*," she says, flat, and she turns away and runs her chubby white hand down a bolt of yellow easy-care sailcloth, then frowns and checks it against her notebook.

They've put out most of the fires in Leicester but patrol cars are still running around arresting gangs of kids, the news reports that night as I'm getting ready to leave for the Unitarian church. My father tells me to be careful on the roads, and to park behind the church if I can rather than in front. "Uh-huh, uh-huh, uh-huh," I say, heading out the door, picking my way around Joani, who's tracing out a pattern on the family room floor.

"Someone called for you, asking where you were tonight," he calls after me.

"Who?" I call back, my hand on the screen door.

"I dunno. I think it was Charlie. I told him you were gonna be at the big meeting."

"Is Charlie going to the meeting?" I call again, momentarily stayed. "That doesn't sound like him."

"He didn't say. He just said thanks a lot, and hung up."

"Oh." I stand there in the doorway for a moment. "Well, okay. See you later tonight."

"See ya," he calls back.

When I pull up to the lighted church, there are so many cars parked in front *and* back—the plain-model American cars of the people like us who live downtown and the navy and steel-gray Volvos of the richer people who live outcountry—that I have to turn the hatchback around and find a place farther down the street. "Lock your doors," an old man says to me when I get out of the car and trudge behind him into the lobby of the church. The look on his face—tense, incensed, afraid, guilty, stubborn—is the look on the faces of most of the people jamming the lobby of the church when I walk in, and I can hear them comparing accounts of what they've seen on the news or heard on the radio all day, in low voices, as if they're stunned, as if they can't believe this is happening virtually in their town, like this is only supposed to happen in Roxbury or Dorchester or other bad parts of Boston. It seemed like everyone's here, not just the horsey liberal Unitarians but all the Catholic Leicester exiles like my own parents (who aren't here, obviously, but they wouldn't be here, anyway; they hate this kind of thing and they never go to Town Meeting). Everyone's standing around in little knots, buzzing, buzzing, buzzing, with occasionally a jarring laugh or a qualified smile, and it's funny to see these two different groups of people together here (because they never would otherwise) in this plain-looking, Puritan-like church completely bereft of the stained-glass windows and mournful statues of the stucco St. Matthew's Roman Catholic on Main Street, to which my own family defected after they left Leicester and Gothic old St. Agnes's behind.

Most of the people here are adults, but I recognize a few kids my age from school. Some of them have even refastened their stupid Kerrie Lanouette memorial buttons back onto their coats, and I want to tell them that Kerrie Lanouette is last year's news, and this is a whole new chapter. There's Phoebe's mother, Judy Shapiro-Signorelli, bustling about with her clipboard, nodding gravely and saying over and over again, "Did I give you a copy of the agenda?" There are a whole bunch of old ladies here and some of them have even gone so far as to bring their rosaries and walk around clutching them like desperate lucky charms. I see Mr. McGregor, my principal, and Charlie's parents in their matching plaid car coats, and my old piano teacher, Mrs. Hartong, who must be pushing a hundred now, and Goody Farnham, her bun no looser for a Sunday night in crisis, and everyone looks dazed and sallow, congregated here under the harsh fluorescent lights of the church lobby, because no one has ever congregated in a church before in the middle of a riot, as far as I know. Suddenly, I catch weird Mrs. Bradstreet standing listlessly next to her husband, craggy, muddy, rich old Nathan, the town selectman. When she sees me, her mouth drops open and she looks as though she's about to come over to me, but I smile thinly and duck off down the stairs in search of Phoebe before she can catch me.

In the basement, where someone's set out coffee and apple juice and whole-wheat doughnuts (*How* very *Unitarian*, I think, in spite of myself), Phoebe is over in the corner with the members of godjangle, three bearded guys in their thirties who own a landscaping business in Box-ford, and they're rehearsing some ridiculous peace-and-harmony song, but Phoebe stops her relentless alto when she sees me and rushes over.

"I'm so glad you came," she says, hugging me, smelling overwhelm-ingly of patchouli, like if she wears enough, she'll immunize herself from the coming revolution that she's predicted. "Isn't this *amazing?* Can you believe my mother organized all these people?"

"I didn't see any Hispanic types upstairs," I say.

"Well, that's what tonight is *about.*" She shrugs. "To brainstorm ways to get over the communications barrier so we can stop all this crazy shit from happening again." She grabs a doughnut from the refreshments table and breaks it in two, offering me half.

"Why don't *we* learn Spanish and *they* learn English?" I say, begin-ning to grow uncomfortable with the entire thing. (For some reason, I can only think about what Brooks would think of all this, and I have a suspicion he'd call it pretty pathetic.) "Don't you think that would be a good place to start?"

"Oh, that's not *too* reductive, Eric." She scowls back at me.

"Well, it's *true!*" I say, getting more upset than I thought I would. "I mean, Feeb, your mother's great for doing this, but nobody in West Mendhem even *knows* any Hispanic people in Leicester. They don't even *see* them, except for maybe the checkout girls at the supermarket at West Mendhem Plaza, and nobody even goes there anymore, they're so fucking scared. So how are we all supposed to get together and talk? The people in West Mendhem don't even want them coming in to town, and nobody's going over there, that's for sure. Should they do it via satel-lite or something?"

Phoebe just rolls her eyes and says, "Think globally, act locally."

"Feeb!" I laugh. "What the hell does that have to do with anything? I don't even know what I'm supposed to do up there tonight."

"Didn't my mother give you a copy of the agenda?"

"Not yet."

"She will. You're just supposed to sit up there with me and be the youth and speak up when the spirit moves you. Try to say something constructive."

"Oh," I answer. I don't know what else to say.

"You want to hear this Corso poem I'm gonna read while godjangle plays?" she asks, pulling a piece of paper out of the pocket of her overalls. I shrug "Sure," but then I say, "Just let me go to the bathroom first, okay?" and I split, ostensibly to go to the bathroom, but more to decide whether I want to make a quick getaway. I'm halfway up the stairs when I nearly crash into Mrs. Bradstreet, who sort of looks like an earthy-crunchy mummy, still completely encased in her Nepalese-looking wrap coat and black knit cap.

"Mr. Fitzpatrick," she says, standing above me on the half-lit stairs.

"Hi, Mrs. Bradstreet," I say, trying to maneuver my way past. "I'm just rushing to the bathroom before things start."

"Can I talk to you for a second first?" Her voice is measured, as usual, but eerily insistent, and in the dimness of the stairwell, her expression seems devoid of clues.

"Um. Sure," I say, not knowing what else to say, and she leads me into the minister's cluttered office at the top of the stairs, where she closes the door behind us. Outside, I can hear the steady drone of residents waiting for the meeting to come to order, and the feeling of being in here with her, quarantined from them, gives me a chill.

"Is this about my Yale rec?" I ask, hating her silence. "Because if you're busy, I can give it to Goody—Mrs. Farnham. If you're busy."

"No, Eric," she says, giving me the weirdest smile, almost like she's sorry for me or something. "I've already written you a glowing dissection and put it in the mail. I took quite a lot of time with it." She shocks me by pulling out a pack of cigarettes, lighting one, dragging on it, and setting it down in the brimming ashtray on the minister's desk.

"Would you like a cigarette?" she asks me, handing me the pack.

"No thanks. I don't smoke."

"Are you sure?" she asks, with that same terrifying half-smile on her face. "I'm not going to tell anyone."

"I'm sure, thanks," I say. She just goes on smiling, her head cocked as usual to one side, and fiddling with the cigarette.

"Mrs. Bradstreet, have I done something wrong?"

She laughs again, still smiling. "No, Eric, you haven't done anything wrong. This is a Unitarian church, you know. You're not defined here by your transgressions."

"I know," I say feebly, but inside I'm screaming to get out.

"I just wanted to remind you," she says.

"Thanks."

She blows a huge mouthful of smoke up to the ceiling, then stubs out the cigarette, hardly touched. Outside, I can hear Phoebe's mother's voice over the PA system, a general hush, then the shuffle and scrape of people taking their seats in the boxed pews.

"They're starting outside," I say, inching back toward the door.

"Eric. Eric."

"Uh-huh?" My hand is grazing the doorknob. All I want to do is slip out of the church and back into the car and drive home as fast as I can and mind my own business for the rest of my life.

"I saw you in Boston yesterday."

What I feel is a sick thud of inevitability, like I saw that line coming the second she laid eyes on me tonight—no, not then, the minute she laid eyes on me that first day in class, like she *saw* me, not in Boston, but just generally *saw* me, from the very start. I'm shaking, I can feel sweat beginning to creep down my back and under my arms, right under my shirt and sweater, and my first instinct is to excuse myself and run, but I don't. I can't, now. I've got to get through this.

"You did?" I ask, trying to tame my voice. "Where?"

"Downtown."

"Oh, yeah?" I manage a smile, and she returns it. "You go in a lot?"

"I do."

"To the museum?"

"To the museum, and other places. The bookstores. Galleries. I have friends there, too, from younger days. But mostly just to get away—"

"Completely," I say, faking a bond.

"And to think."

"Me, too," I say, emphatically, thinking that maybe she only spotted me, fled to Boston, just like here, just to get away for a day, just to sort things out.

"Who's your friend?" she asks, meticulously casual.

"Huh?"

"Your friend. Whom I saw you with. The young African-American man."

"Oh!" I nearly shout. I'm a mess, but I don't know how to calm down.

My stomach is doing backflips, screaming again and again *What did she see? Where? In front of the Christian Science building? Please, please God, not there.* "You saw him, huh?"

"I did."

"Oh," I say. "He's just—a friend, that's all," then, in what strikes me as a brilliant afterthought, "An old family friend."

"I see," she says, and the half-smile is back.

"Anyway," I say, hand on knob again. "Maybe we should get out there, huh?"

"Oh, Eric, come off it," she says, so full of impatience that I slam back shut the door I've half-opened. Then I just stare at her, trapped, and she pulls off her knit cap.

"What is it?" I ask, point-blank, too frayed to play it cool anymore. "What'd you wanna ask me?"

"Eric," she says, sighing, smiling, sitting down. Then, in a very bored, very just-the-two-of-us voice, she says, "Now, Eric, what is this tom-foolery of a meeting about tonight, anyway?"

"It's about the riot," I say. "And what to do about it."

"And what do you think the gentlefolk of West Mendhem are going to do about it?"

I don't say anything for a minute. I can hear them out there, Phoebe's mother's voice, shrill and earnest, over the microphone, then a loud up-rising of applause, a scattering of hollers. In the minister's office, just above our heads, there's the buzz of the fluorescent lights. "Nothing," I say.

Mrs. Bradstreet nods, slowly, about eight times. Then she says, "Now, Eric, this meeting has been called because the people in this town don't know what they can do to get along better with people whose skin color is different from their own. Am I correct?" She's talking to me now very slowly, very pedantically, the way my cousin Bethie Lynn talks to Joani.

"I guess so. Sort of." I want to say that it's more complicated than that, that it's about crime and safety and so on, but more than that, I just want to leave, get home, so I decide to go along.

"Now, Eric. When I was just a few years older than you, many, many eons ago . . ." She pauses, waiting for me to laugh, or protest, so I smile dimly. "When I was just a few years older than you, I boarded a bus in Boston filled with many other people, some whose skin color was the same as my own, some whose pigmentation was—not the same. And we took that bus down to Mississippi, because, at that time in our lives, at that moment in the history of this country, we thought our single most pressing duty was to find a way to better the relations between people of divergent flesh tones. Okay?"

I nod obediently. *She's crazy,* I'm thinking.

"And do you know what happened?"

"The Civil Rights Act," I say.

The loony smile again. "The Civil Rights Act, yes. Praise be to God. Free at last, free at last. And do you know what happened to me on that trip?"

"No," I say, fervently not wanting to know.

"I met a young man, a lawyer, the color of whose skin was not my own. And then I fell in love with that man. And then, after I had made up my mind to stay in Mississippi and make a life with that man, I found out I was going to bear his child."

She's speaking so slowly, so calmly now, looking at me so intensely, it's almost as though she expects me to whip out a notebook and take notes. I swallow. I don't know what to say.

She lights another cigarette. "And do you know what I proceeded to do then?"

I swallow again. "No."

"I was so . . . startled"—and there's a catch in her voice, but she seems to recover, and go on—"at the thought—not the thought, but the *reality*—of having that child, that I took the necessary steps. You know what I mean, don't you?"

"Uh-huh."

"And, Eric, do you know something?"

"What?"

"That act—and the consequent act of leaving him and coming back north and getting on with what is conventionally described as the rest of one's life—I have come to regret more than any other decision I've ever made. And that includes marrying Nathan Bradstreet, to answer a question I'm sure you and many others have always wanted to ask."

I want to tell her that I never wanted to ask, but I don't. "I'm sorry" is all I say.

"So am I. But 1987 isn't the time for sorry. Now, my point is, I wish

I could go out there and get up on that podium and tell *them*—"she says, disdainfully, indicating with her cigarette the room beyond the office where the congregation sits—"what I just told you. But I can't. Why? Because. Because I made my choice. And I also made a choice to live with it." She pauses to exhale. "You, on the other hand, can get up on that podium and use the voice with which this community has invested you, and tell them that you have a friendship at stake."

"With *who?*" I burst out.

"With your African-American friend," she says again in that baby-talk voice, diagramming the sentence in the air for me with her hands.

I'm so confused I laugh out loud. "But Mrs. Bradstreet, you don't *get* it."

"What I get is that what's happening in this community is a crisis of faith. And what I get is that you are in the very special position of having a choice to make: you can exacerbate it with your silence, or you can use the persuasive power of your age, and start the healing in this town."

"But Mrs. Bradstreet—"

"It's your choice to make, Eric."

"But Mrs. *Bradstreet*—"

"But *what*, if you know your choice and you feel—"

"He's not my *friend!* That guy isn't my friend! *Do you get it?*"

I'm jarred back into silence by the sound of my own voice reverberating against the walls of the office. She looks at me, frozen, over her cigarette, the ash of which threatens to fall onto the desktop, and she says nothing, but I watch as her eyebrow arches, slowly, to the top of her forehead, and I'm actually dizzy, and a weird, sweaty, bitter, hateful kind of triumph rushes over me, and it only seems to sink in deeper, deeper, as she says nothing. Outside, I can hear the ridiculous treacly chords of godjangle, and then Phoebe's voice, overemoting, grotesquely distorted by the bad sound system, on top of them.

She ashes her cigarette just before it collapses under its own weight. Putting it out, looking down into the ashtray, she says softly: "I guess there are some other issues here, aren't there?"

"Can we just forget we had this conversation?" I say, my hand on the doorknob again.

She looks up at me, looks away, nods vigorously. "Of course. Eric, please. I'm sorry."

"It's okay," I say. "Let's just forget it, okay?" And before she can answer, I'm out the door, leaving her sitting there in her big Nepalese coat.

For a second, delirious, I stand in the doorway in the back of the church and look in. Now godjangle has launched into "Turn, Turn, Turn," with Phoebe singing and playing the tambourine, that revolting song—"a time that you may embrace, a time to re-e-frai-yun fro-om um-bray-sing"—and Mrs. Shapiro-Signorelli is sitting in her moderator's chair in her Liz Claiborne coordinates playing a woodblock, and half the place is clapping and swaying along, and there are kids on the shoulders of their parents: whole families, whole pews, and people don't look so anxious anymore; some of them even have that wintry Sunday night glow.

I just stand there. I want to scream "Fuck you!" so fucking loud that I blow the roof off the whole place. But I don't. I don't. I just screw up my face and stand there and throw the whole place the finger—but no one sees, anyway; their backs are turned to me—and then I run outside and drop down on the steps and pound them again and again with my fists until I'm out of breath, and when I'm done, I just sit there for the longest time, with my head in my hands.

"Hey, Fitzy, why aren't you inside bonding with the natives?" someone calls to me from across the street, and I look up, bewildered. It's Mr. Fazzi's two thuggy sons, Joey and Mitch, the ones who regularly give me wedgies in gym class; they're walking toward me, bouncing a basketball back and forth on the icy street, and laughing.

I'm trying to think of something to say to them, to excuse my solitude, but before I can think of anything, someone else calls out to me, in a hoarse, drunk-sounding voice, from the middle of the common. I squint, and I make out the silhouette of a figure reeling its way across the frozen common, toward the church. At first I think it's Charlie, but then I realize the figure is calling out *"Mon vieux! Mon cher!"* and the bottom falls out of my stomach when I realize it's him.

Oh shit, I whisper to myself, but it's too late. Joey and Mitch have already turned in the direction of the voice, and when they make him out, Joey shouts, "Get that fucking spic!" and they drop the basketball and start running toward Brooks. "Gentlemen, *please!*" I hear him protest, freezing in place, but Joey and Mitch don't stop. Joey runs headlong toward him and pounces, knocking him to the ground as he lets out an excruciating, "Lord!" In a minute, they're shouting again and again, "Get the fuck out of this town, you fucking spic!" and hitting him in every conceivable place.

For a split second, I stand there on the steps of the church, frozen, wanting to run to the car and drive home, lock the doors, wrap the pillow around my head, and never emerge again. But I don't. I don't know what seizes me, but I run out into the street, heedless of cars, and across the common, where I try to pull Joey and Mitch off him. They've closed in on him so completely I can't even see his face. "Leave him alone! Guy, guys, leave him alone. He's not a spic!" I'm screaming, and I can't even believe what I'm saying.

"Leave us the fuck alone, you fucking pussy," Mitch spits at me, and pushes me away, onto my ass on the frigid ground. For a moment I'm stunned, but in a minute I'm staggering toward them on my knees. I'm absolutely hysterical now. "Get the fuck off him! *Get the fuck off him!*" I'm hollering louder and louder. With every punch, he lets out a groaning gag that goes straight to the pit of my stomach.

By this point, the music inside the church has stopped and people are flooding out, across the street and into the common, men first, women and children behind him. "Stop them!" I yell. "They're beating him, and he's innocent, and they're gonna kill him!"

About six guys run over and pull Joey and Mitch off Brooks, holding their hands behind their backs while they try to break free and keep saying, "Fucking spic," over and over again. Now, for the first time, I see him. His face is all fucked up; there's blood running out of his nose and his mouth; he's on his side, groaning, in a fetal position, his hands clutched around his stomach. I notice that a silver flask and something in a white envelope have fallen out of his coat pocket. I'm still kneeling, only a few feet away from him; slowly, I stand up and move back half a dozen paces until I'm halfway between him and the crowd. Everyone's crowding around us now, staring, stricken, chalk-white. Out of the corner of my eye, I see Phoebe and godjangle run across the common and come around the far side of the crowd; Phoebe, her hair flying, still holding her tambourine, gives me a look that says, "What the fuck are you doing?"

"What the hell is going on here?" Mr. Fazzi bellows; Joey has been passed on to him and he's restraining him now, both their faces red and swollen.

"This fuckin' spic was—"

"Watch your goddamned mouth, Joey," Mr. Fazzi splutters, mortified.

"This—*guy* was running into the church, probably with a knife or something! He was probably gonna fuck it all up!"

Mr. Fazzi shoves Joey aside and stands over Brooks. "Son, can you talk? Who the hell are you, anyway? What're you doing here?"

But Brooks doesn't answer, just groans and rolls over, then on to his belly, where he's facing away from everyone, looking like he's trying to crawl away.

"Somebody call an ambulance. He's in bad shape," Mr. Fazzi says, and about nineteen people run back toward the church. "Son, what the hell are you doing here?" Mr. Fazzi persists.

"He's not doing anything," I hear myself saying, my voice a tiny thing in the midst of a roaring ocean. "He's not a criminal. Your two sons starting beating him up for nothing."

"Well, who is he?" Mr. Fazzi asks me, defensive.

"He's *not* a criminal" is all I can say.

"Well, do you *know* him?" Mr. Fazzi's eyes look like they're going to pop out of his head and into my face. Just at that moment, I glance in Brooks's direction. He's turned back somewhat, and he's staring straight at me, his right eye beginning to swell. *Go ahead and say it,* I want to holler at him, but he doesn't say a word. He keeps looking at me, but his fucked-up eyes don't say anything, either. I turn back to the crowd, and they're all looking at me, too.

"No," I say, and he looks away. "But he's not doing anything wrong. He was just walking across the common."

"Well, he picked a bad night to leave Leicester," Mr. Fazzi says.

Does he look like he's from Leicester, you fucking idiot? I want to shout, but I don't. I just stand there, ready to puke. Suddenly, Officer DeMarco and another cop come running over and stand over him. "Oh, Jesus Christ,"

DeMarco says, sounding more annoyed than upset. "This is that S.B.A. kid we picked up on Great Lake last fall, remember, Mel? He's from the South or something."

"He goes to S.B.A.?" some woman cries out, and suddenly there's this general cry of dismay and regret, and about five women rush forward and pull out handkerchiefs and try to sit him up and start swabbing at his face and saying, "It's okay, honey. It was a misunderstanding. It's gonna be okay." He can't answer; he just sits there, like a corpse, and lets these women wipe him up.

"Smart move, guys," Mr. Fazzi says, and slaps both his sons upside the head.

"Well, I don't know why this guy likes sneaking away from school so much and walking around in the dead of night," DeMarco says, pointing at Brooks. "All right, everyone," he says, turning to the crowd. "Let's get back inside the church. That's enough excitement for tonight."

"Come on, West Mendhem," Mrs. Shapiro-Signorelli calls out. "We have some serious reckoning to do tonight." There's a general murmur of assent, and the crowd starts splintering off, walking back across the ice toward the deserted church with its lighted front doors wide open. But I can't leave; I can't say a word, but I can't leave.

The ambulance siren has been gaining on us. It pulls up now and two medics come running over with a stretcher. "That's it, buddy. You're gonna be fine," one says, as they move him onto the stretcher and strap him in.

Suddenly, he manages to lift up his head. What he says is obscured by his fat lip, but we can all still make it out. "I have some unfinished business" is what he says.

The medics and DeMarco stand there a minute, perplexed; then they laugh. "You can finish your business later, buddy," the medic says. "Right now, you should probably get some stitches."

As they carry him away, I move toward the stretcher to say something to him, but as I do, I notice that they've left his flask and the envelope behind. I look around once, then stoop, all in a flash, and just before I stuff it in my pocket, I notice exactly what I had expected: it has my name on it: "The Hon. Eric Fitzpatrick." By this point, they're putting the stretcher into the ambulance, and in a moment the siren starts up again, and it careens around the corner and out of sight.

"What the fuck was that all about?" Phoebe steps up to me.

"Didn't you hear?" I snap, distracted. "They were beating the shit out of him for no good reason."

"And you tried to pull the Fazzi brothers off him?" she asks, incredulous.

"Well, I saw them do it! What was I supposed to do?"

"All right, all right," she says. I'm shouting at her and I don't even know it. "Come back inside and get warm." She takes my hand.

"Hunh?" I don't hear her.

"I said come back inside—"

"All right!" I shout at her. "Would you just give me a fucking second!"

"Jesus Christ!" she shouts back at me. "Go to fucking hell, Eric! Go to hell!" And she runs across the common, back toward the church.

I'm alone here now. I can't believe it. Right there is the spot where he lay; we were seen by everyone moments ago, and now he, everyone, is gone. The cold was too much to bear; the last people are filing back into the church and the doors are closing behind them.

I pull the envelope out of my coat and open it up. In old-fashioned semi-blotted ink, on a piece of pale, formal stationery, is written:

17 January 1987

I'll either speak to you tonight or leave this in the hands of some trustworthy soul. I can't bear this wretched place another day, and I also can't bear to see you in this tortured equivocating state. I'm leaving Mendhem in twenty-four hours, so if you are to join me this summer, you must call me at Goolsbee and let me know within that time. Then I'll give you numbers where you can reach me and we can work out the details in the months to come.

I don't know if you can fathom just how unhappy I've been (I don't suppose you've been terribly happy either)—or, conversely, how very, very content I was with you in that ghastly motor inn last night. It just seems prudent that in a generally unhappy world, if you find some small reprieve from unhappiness, you should do all you can to sustain it. Don't you think? I do. Even though I don't let on. Even though we probably seem like the most egregiously mismatched pair ever to walk Job's earth. We're so wrong for each other in so many ways, we must be doomed to each other. Isn't that terribly historic and exciting?

Please don't let us just drift away. We've said it before, but I'll say it now in English. Eric, my angel, I love you.

B.J.T.

For a long time, I just stand there, in the middle of the freezing common, and stare at the last line of the letter. For one moment, the faint faraway sound of an ambulance siren heading toward Leicester crests, between the hills to the south, then falls away again. I look up at the church, then once more at the letter before I fold it up, put it back into the envelope, and stuff it in my pocket. *I am going in that church to get my coat,* I say to myself, *and then I am getting in the car and driving far away.*

I'm halfway up the church steps when Mrs. Bradstreet steps out from behind a column, smoking again. "They're waiting for you inside," she says.

I can't even begin to think of what to say, so I just sidestep her and go inside. Everyone is seated again, and Mrs. Shapiro-Signorelli is addressing the congregation, but when she sees me standing, shivering, at the back of the church, she stops short, gestures to me, and says into the microphone, "And here he is!"

Everyone turns, and before I can run, the entire church breaks into applause. Phoebe comes running up the aisle and starts leading me back down, pushing me from behind. The applause keeps going, ringing in my ears, and Phoebe leads me up to the altar, or whatever it is that Unitarians call it, where Mrs. Shapiro-Signorelli puts her arm around me and says into the microphone: "Eric, you intervened tonight and saved a life. We need the sensitivity and the foresight and the *heart* of young people like you if we're ever going to get over this craziness that's tearing our community apart. Will you talk to us? I mean, will you really *talk* to us?"

With that, she pushes me up to the podium and the applause starts up again. There are hundreds of faces out there, but I'm not seeing any of them; I just stare out blankly. The applause finally dies down, and I keep staring.

"What happened tonight—" I hear myself say. I can't make out anybody's individual face; I just see a bobbing pink sea of hollow smudges.

Eric, my angel—there it is, black ink on pale paper.

"I think what happened tonight—"

Eric, my angel, I love you.

The last thing I can actually really hear, will remember hearing, amplified monstrously through the sound system, is my voice cracking, the way his did when they jumped him and he fell to the ground. After that, all I'm doing is bawling and bawling and bawling, right there on the podium, even as they start applauding again. I'm bawling in front of hundreds of people, and I am absolutely alone.

April 1987

Eleven

Goody Farnham called this winter the winter of our discontent (it figures she would), but it has passed, and I am now on a train bound for New Haven, Connecticut, to visit Yale University, where I have been accepted as part of the class of 1991.

That's a lie. Not the being accepted part, because I *was* accepted, with a sizeable scholarship to boot, which of course made everyone very happy. The lie is that I'm going to New Haven this weekend, because I'm not (even though there is some kind of welcome program going on there, and that's where everyone *thinks* I'm going, of course, and this train *does* seem to be full of St. Banner types who are probably on their way.) Instead, I have an address on a slip of paper in my pocket, courtesy of the afternoon receptionist in the admissions department at St. Banner. She gave me a phone number, too, but it's disconnected. I'm not sure what I'm going to, or why, but they're letting off in New Haven right now—there go the preppies, and out go the lights in the train as they switch engines or something—and for a moment, I go stand out on the platform and drink a Coke, watching my probable classmates tramp away with their duffels and sleeping bags, and I'm wondering which direction Yale is from here, but not following them. Instead, I'm stepping back on the train, and in a minute the lights come back on, it rolls out of New Haven, and now it's just me and all the other people with un-finished business points south of here.

All the insanity between West Mendhem and Leicester is basically over. Believe it or not, even during the riots, in the end it was only Jesús Antonio de la Costa who died, when they finally unplugged his life support two nights after the beating. There was what I guess you could call a full investigation for his aggressors—of course, after Beating Number 2, a lot of people thought it might have been the Fazzi boys, until about thirty kids vowed to the police that the brothers had been with them at a party at the exact time of Beating Number 1. In the end, the investi-gation never came to much—it's still open, presumably, as is the Kerrie Lanouette case, but the last tip on that, though, was that someone matching the suspect's description was spotted near San Diego, so all the action has shifted across the country. At any rate, the *Leicester Tribune* ran a story last month called "Kerrie: Half a Year Later," in which the Lanouette family said that they still cried for Kerrie every night—they hadn't touched one of the Cabbage Patch Dolls in her room since the day she left it and never came back—but that basically they couldn't stand any more publicity, any more rallies, any more stress. They just wanted to get on with their lives. They wanted peace back.

After Beating Number 2, it was Mrs. Shapiro-Signorelli herself who implored the parish priests in Leicester to extend an open invitation to the mothers of Leicester to come to *her* church for a "meeting of neigh-bors." Surprisingly, they did come, the following Sunday night, droves of mothers, in secondhand cars and bargain-basement coats, entering at first distrustfully, then warming to Mrs. Shapiro-Signorelli and her legions, then finally letting it all out, crying, "We don't want to bury any more of our children! Do you? Do you?" "No," cried the mothers of West Mendhem, "no more than you! We are all mothers!" And then they were all laughing and hugging. "See how much we have in common?" they said, and "Why didn't we ever do this before?" That meeting, slated to be the first in a series, was the last—but the important thing, according to Mrs. Shapiro-Signorelli, was that the two communities *shared*. It didn't mean that mothers in West Mendhem started shopping in Leicester (it had nothing to do with the people there, they maintained; it was just that the produce was better at the grocery in West Mendhem), or that people from Leicester started moving into West Mendhem (the real estate and the taxes obviously priced them out); it just meant, they said, that no one wanted to go through the senseless grief and nonsense that had gripped everyone in January. The *Leicester Tribune* published several articles and editorials about the joys of finding common ground, about a renewed sense of security, about what they called "the healing." Buried in one of these pieces was a quote from a sociology professor at Tufts saying that what had happened between Leicester and West Mendhem was part of a growing pattern, was attributable to white flight and the ever-widening gap between haves and have-nots, and that it was just a matter of time before something similar, or worse, happened again—something that would really shake West Mendhem to its very foundation—but nobody really dwelt on that.

Everybody wanted peace back, and it's important for me to explain: *I* was the one who made them want it. They would all say, shortly thereafter, they never realized how bad things were getting—not from Kerrie, not from Jesús—until that poor boy, who intervened to save the life of some crazy kid he didn't even know, just stood up on that podium and broke down crying, so broken was he by the senseless acts of hatred taking place before his very eyes. I can't forget that night: Mrs. Shapiro-Signorelli and Phoebe helping me from the podium and escorting me back up the center aisle of the church, not being able to make out individual faces for my blurred vision, wanting to run out into the night and stop the ambulance, abduct him, take him away, nurse him back to the unbattered Brooks, stay with him forever, and never come home. But they wouldn't let me. I wasn't halfway up the aisle, the grave, uncomprehending applause had hardly died away, when it seems like the entire congregation closed ranks around me, hugging me, kissing me—"Don't you worry, honey, this is never gonna happen again, you'll never have to do that again"—hugging and kissing each other, virtually hugging themselves.

"I wish my son could be so brave, taking on those punks," some woman said to me, strangling me in her arms. "I hope that boy gets to thank you someday."

"You don't understand," I whispered, looking crazily into her eyes. It was virtually the only thing I had said since stepping back into the church.

"No, honey, I don't understand," she said back to me, squeezing twice as hard. "No one understands this insanity. Only God understands."

"Let this kid get through and let him get some rest," Mrs. Shapiro-Signorelli called out. In the lobby, I waited while Phoebe fetched our coats from downstairs. I sat down on a bench, felt the letter in my pocket, and started crying all over again. When Phoebe came back up, she sat down and put her arm around me.

"Eric, baby, it's okay. He's gonna be all right. They only roughed him up a little."

"But he was *gagging!* Did you hear him gagging?"

"At least they didn't kick in his head, like they did to the kid last night. Man! Why the fuck do we live in such a barbaric society? It's like the Crusades or something. Or the Huns!"

I hardly heard Phoebe's inanities. "I could have stopped that from happening."

"What the fuck are you talking about? You *did* stop it. Maybe they *would* have kicked in his head if you hadn't intervened."

"Oh, Feeb. I hate myself. I wanna die."

"Oh, for God's sake, Eric. You're suffering witness guilt now. Go home and get some sleep. I'll see you in school tomorrow." She gave me a long hug good-bye, then sent me out into the night, the church behind me bright and warm, the common before me deserted now, haunted with him.

Over the next week, things happened. The *Leicester Tribune* published a story on me, "Teen Essayist Lives by His Words," in which I was quoted as saying about the intervention, "It just seemed like the natural thing to do." I became a sort of town hero, with freshmen passing me in the halls saying, *"You're* the guy who saved that black kid's life," and teachers joking, "Where's your white hat and trusty steed, Fitzpatrick?" Mr. McGregor asked if I would give the keynote address at graduation. Unbeknownst to me, Mrs. Farnham sent a second letter to Yale telling them about the incident and my "extraordinary heroism," and someone from Admissions called me to say that although they couldn't suggest how the act would bear on my application, I had demonstrated the kind of character they looked for in a student, and that I had their hearty congratulations. My mother hugged me (even while screaming that I could have gotten myself killed), my father's eyes leaked with pride,

Brenda (who's still living in Billerica, avoiding Frank, and, I presume, getting bigger every day) called to tell me that what I did "took balls," and Joani started sewing me a Superman cape. By this point, Grandma was too disoriented to understand; when my mother showed her the article in the *Tribune*, she spat, "Leave it to a Polack!" which threw us all for a loop.

All along, I was making myself sicker and sicker. It culminated one night when I went to speak to a troop of West Mendhem Boy Scouts about heroism. There were about twenty of them, assembled in the cafeteria of my old junior high school, squirming and farting in their little chairs, the two troop-leader dads hushing them up. I sat on a table, lording over all of them, unable to look into any of their combative, porcine faces.

"Let me start by asking what heroism means to you—" I began, but my voice cracked wildly on *you,* sending them into their own chorus of falsetto hysterics.

"Hey! Hey! Show some respect," the troop leaders called out.

"I'm just going to get a drink of water from the bubbler," I said, excusing myself and heading around the corner. But when I got there, the distorted image of my own face in the stainless steel fountain was too much for me to take. I slipped out a side door, drove out on Great Lake Drive and parked along the stone wall that holds back Lake Chickering, a clear view across the water, through the dark trees, and toward the lighted yellow window squares of St. Banner.

Of course he's out of there, now; whether he had been serious or not in that letter about leaving of his own will, I knew it was the end of his tenure at St. Banner the minute they carried him away in the stretcher— off campus after curfew, stinking drunk and beaten from a brawl with village thugs. For the first three days after the beating, I was too stunned to call S.B.A.; instead, I just walked around at school, at home, like a zombie, going through the motions, fighting off a creepy numb fear that at any solitary moment, someone was going to tap me on the shoulder and when I turned around, it would be him, lacerated from head to foot, his mouth hanging open in a mute scream, and that I would answer him with an all-too audible scream of my own. Finally, when I felt like I was getting my wits about me, when three days passed and there was no news about him in the paper other than the obligatory short piece accounting for the interruption of the Sunday night meeting, I crept upstairs to the phone in my parents' bedroom one afternoon when nobody was home.

"St. Banner, Admissions, can I help you?" This time, it wasn't the champagne voice of Susannah Bailey, but the cigarette-wasted rasp of a receptionist, a local.

"Yes. Could you please tell me what dorm Francis Tremont is in?" I asked, lowering my voice and carefully effacing the remains of my own North Shore accent.

"Oh, I'm sorry, honey, he don't go here anymore."

"He doesn't?" I asked, faking surprise, even though she was confirming exactly what I had expected. "He did just a few weeks ago."

"Yeah, well—" She sounded uncomfortable now. "Who's this, anyway?"

"I'm a good friend of his, from Virginia."

"You don't sound like you're from Virginia."

I laugh. She doesn't. "Um, that's 'cause I've gone to school up here for the past three years. And Virginia's not so Deep South, anyway."

"Yeah, I guess that's so," she says, and I hear her lighting up a cigarette, probably menthol. "Anyway, I guess you're outta touch with Francis Tremont, 'cause he don't go here no more, honey."

"What happened?"

"Aw, jeez. You really wanna know?"

"Well—yes, if it's all right."

"*It's* all right, I guess, but *he's* not. Honey, they had to expel him for a whole buncha things. Sneakin' off campus, and drinkin', and gettin' in a fight, and God knows what else. I mean, I know that a lotta stuff goes on here. I know a lotta stuff goes on with kids—I got three of my own, at the high school here in town, but *that* kid—your friend. He's another story. He's got troubles, you can tell. My heart kinda went out to him, actually. He's just about the only, you know, the only black here, except for one other, I think, a pretty little girl from the Bronx or somethin'."

"Yeah," I said tentatively. "He mentioned that to me."

"Anyway, Headmaster here gave him a lot of chances in the past—but this time he said your friend Francis needed help beyond anything he could get at St. Banner. It's funny, though. Headmaster wasn't mad at him, really. More *confused* by him than anything else, if you know what I mean."

"I do. I definitely do. He's a character, all right."

"Yunh," she grunted in agreement, exhaling smoke.

"Anyway, did he go back to Virginia?"

"Hmmmm. You know, I'm not really sure, honey. I'm just the afternoon receptionist here. But it's a small school, so everyone knows everyone's business."

"Sure," I said. "Well, would you have his phone number and address in Virginia? I want to try him down there, but I've lost it myself."

"What'd you say your name was again?" she asked me, the original hint of suspicion creeping back into her voice.

"Fitz!" I spat, before anything else came to mind. "Jeff"—his middle name, Jefferson, suddenly popped into my head—"Jeff Fitz."

"Fitz?" she asked, her voice cracking in surprise. "Just Fitz? Not Fitzwilliam, or Fitzgibbons, or Fitzsomething?"

"No," I said, calm by now. "Just Fitz."

"Oh," she said, accepting it. "Is that Irish?"

"No, Jewish."

"Oh." She sounded suspicious again. Then, after a pause: "I'm Irish myself. One hundred percent. Wouldn't want to be anything else."

"That's nice."

"Well, I like it!" she exploded, then started laughing hysterically. Finally, when she subsided, she said, "Hold onna minute. I've got the face book right here. Lemme getcha his number and address." I heard a bit of rustling, then she was back on the line. "Here we go. Francis Jefferson Tremont." Then she recited the address and phone number back to me in a labored, slow voice—it was the city he'd mentioned before, and his entire background seemed so mythological to me that I was almost surprised the place she named matched up with what he'd said— and I scrawled it down on the back of a school notebook.

"Thanks so much," I said.

"Don't worry about it. And if you do catch up with your friend, tell him Mrs. Lacey says she hopes he's feelin' better. I always liked the kid. I don't care how weird he seemed."

"I will," I said. (It occurred to me that I *did* know her kids, and they were all alcoholics.)

I hadn't planned to call the number right away, but no sooner was I off the phone with the receptionist than I was dialing, furiously, my heart pounding. It rang three times—*What the hell am I supposed to say? Why am I calling? Why am I even calling?* I was thinking, then, the even colder fear: *I betrayed him, to his face. He's not going to want to talk to me*—but before I had mustered enough fear to hang up, the ringing stopped.

A burst of static, then in a saccharine southern accent: "We're sorry. The number you have dialed has been disconnected. No further information can be provided about—"

It finally hit me, then. He was lost to me. He could be at his dead aunt's house in Virginia, or he could be in Paris, or on the French Riviera with his mother, or fallen clean off the face of the earth, for all I knew. The only place I saw him now was in my dreams: his lips curling in the hysterical scorn for mankind I was already beginning to ache for, or bubbling with blood and unintelligible protestations as they had on that final night, or surfacing back up through leagues of my unconsciousness, bowing for a kiss, just above me in the bed. Some part of me—the practical boy, the safe boy, the boy who had bullshitted his way through life, onto newspaper pages, into Yale—said this was the time to let it go, said *You've come out of this by the skin of your teeth*, said, *Consider yourself lucky.* But some dimmer part of me—not *me*, maybe, but something colonized in me—said the contrary: that it wasn't supposed to have ended where it ended, that there was something to be seen through.

No one knows, of course, except for Mrs. Bradstreet. She was out of school, mysteriously, on the Monday and Tuesday following the church meeting, but on Wednesday she was back, ashen and distracted. I stared down into my book through her entire class while she droned on tonelessly about the New Deal, terrified of making eye contact with her. At the end of the class, I slammed shut my book and readied to make a beeline out of her teaching pod, but she hastened to me and put her hand on mine, making the hairs on the back of my neck stand on end.

"Will you stay a minute?" she asked me. I could see, horrifyingly, that her lower lip was trembling.

"I can't—I can't," I stuttered, gathering my books, looking away.

"I just want to know how your friend is doing," she says, low, leaning in to me, before I can get away.

I looked up into her eyes and saw something there that stayed me for a moment; she was, after all, the only one who knew the whole story (or at least *half* of the whole story), and she didn't seem to be judging me, or threatening me with blackmail, which I had had some wild paranoid feeling she was planning to do.

"I don't know," I whispered back, looking down again.

"Will you let me know when you find out?" she asked me.

"Um—"

"I'm just thinking of you, you know. We odd birds have to watch out for each other."

For some reason that made me laugh a little, sadly, and she smiled along with me. "I will," I said.

"Thank you," she said, businesslike, before she hustled back to her desk and began arranging her papers, as though the conversation had never happened.

I've had that address in Virginia now for three months, balled up in the top drawer of my desk. Life has gone on. Things are fine, really—and they're not. And that is why this train is pulling into Union Station in Washington, D.C., right now, at eight o'clock on a Saturday night, and I am stepping off it, my own duffel bag in tow, stepping into the vaulted heights of the train station here, where I've never been before, standing in place as a million people crisscross before me, looking for the arrow, the sign, the clue that will bring me to a certain Virginia bus line, which will bring me to anything, anyone, or nothing at all, but maybe something—maybe just something.

The station here is so crowded. It's in the midst of the crowd that I pass and see it: two guys, maybe in their thirties, in business suits and with briefcases resting by their calves, kissing each other hello or goodbye. I don't even know I'm doing it, but I just stop and watch them, like they're a statue in a museum and there's nobody in the gallery but me.

Finally, one of them catches me out of the corner of his eye, pulls away from the other, and stares back at me. The other one joins him, and in a moment they both start laughing.

"Well?" one calls to me. "Aren't you going to throw change at us?"

I don't answer; I don't know what to say. I just stand there and smile stupidly.

"Are you okay?" the other one asks me.

I hold out the crumpled paper on which I've written directions to myself. "Do you know how to find this bus line?"

"Why, are you running away from home?" the first one asks me.

"Uh-huh," I say, surprising myself.

They both laugh again and say, virtually in unison, "Oh *really?*"

"Well. Just for a little while."

They nod, and the first one points me in the direction of the bus line. They both have crew cuts, I notice, and wing tips.

" 'Bye," number one says to me. "Don't run away for *too* long, like me."

"I won't," I say back. "Maybe." Number one arches his eyebrows, and I smile, even though I'm becoming a little afraid now, as I venture on, leaving them behind.

I'm on a strange bus now, full of strangers, staring out the window into the night at a strange highway, passing signs for towns I've never heard of. It occurs to me that I've never even been this far away from home alone before; in fact, the farthest I've been absolutely all by myself is maybe to Boston on a few occasions when Phoebe couldn't come, and even that felt faintly illicit. Now, I'm getting that half-creepy, half-exhilarated feeling I had that night with him in the motor lodge, coming back from Boston, that feeling that you've taken yourself off the grid, that you've wiped yourself off the face of the earth: no one back there knows where you are and no one here knows who you are. What if those two guys in the train station called it? I wonder. What if I never came back? And then I think, *What the fuck are you thinking? You don't even know where you're going.*

My heart jumps when the driver calls the name of the stop I've written down. I pull my duffel off the rack and file off with the others, some weary-looking working types, some white, some black. I look around: it's a random street corner, nine-thirty at night, faintly chilly, in what could be any town in the United States, I guess. I can smell ocean vaguely from here, and I remember what he said about coming from a coastal city. I see a woman who looks a little like Charlie's mother, Mrs. Metengarten, heading toward her car, and ask her if she knows how I can get to the address in my hand: 1400 Boulevard Aubergine, in a part of town called New Calvary.

"You wanna get to New Calvary, sweetie?" she says to me, laughing, in a thicker southern accent than I thought people had around here. "That's all the way across the city. You see that hill up there?" She points westward to what looks like a small black mountain that looms over the rest of the city, an enormous crucifix lighted up at the very top. "That's why they call it New Calvary, 'cause of that giant cross at the top," the woman tells me. "It's been there virtually since electricity came to the city, I hear. Of course, the residents of New Calvary pay the electric bill on it. Lord knows they can afford to."

"Is there a bus line up there?" I ask the woman. It's definitely too far away and too steep to walk.

She laughs again. "Oh Lord, sweetie, no! New Calvary is like a city unto itself. I'm surprised there aren't gates up there or something—or guards—to keep poor white trash like us from comin' up there and tainting the race."

"What do you mean?" I laugh.

"Are the folks you're going to see up there black folk?" she asks me with startling directness.

"Um—yeah," I answer. "As a matter of fact, they are—I mean, *he* is. He's a friend from high school."

"Well, that figures," she says, cheerily enough. "Virtually everybody up there's black. But there's no way you can make it up there on your own two feet," she says, reading my mind. "It's too steep. With that big old bag you got there, you'd topple over and roll all the way down." Then, apparently amused by that picture, she starts laughing. "Come on, sweetie," she says. "I'm not in any special hurry to get back to my old man. I'll give you a ride up."

"Thanks." I pick up my bag and follow her to her car.

"As a matter of fact, I'm a little excited to see things up there myself. I haven't been cruising up on New Calvary since I was in high school, when we'd get real plastered and speed race up and down Boulevard Abberginny"—that's how she pronounces it—"and the old spade dad-

dies would come out of their homes in their robes and slippers screaming they were gonna get their shotguns and chase us back down the hill.
But by that point, we *were* well enough outta there! You gotta excuse my
language, too, sweetie. You're from up North, aren't you?"

"Yeah, how'd you guess?"

"I could just sense it in your voice," she tells me, airily, starting the
car. "And in your demeanor. But you folks from up North gotta understand somethin', which is that we down here might still say words like
'spade daddy' or 'coon's eyes' or just plain old 'nigger' from time to time,
but we don't mean nothin' *racist* by it. It's just the way our mamas and
daddies talked, it's in the blood. And the other thing, you know, this part
of Virginia isn't even really the South—it's too close to Washington for
that. You gotta go much deeper than this, boy, if you wanna hear some
real southern fried fuck-all!" Now she starts laughing harder than ever—
an oddly good-natured laugh—and it seems wise to laugh along with
her just a little bit.

"Why are all the people who live in New Calvary black?" I ask her
as we cruise down what seems to be the main commercial street of the
town, the dark mountain looming ahead of us.

"I don't know exactly, sweets. You don't mind if I light up, do
you?" she asks me, shaking a long slender cigarette (it reminds me of
Brenda, who seems as far away as another planet right now) out of a
golden box.

"Of course not. It's your car."

"I suppose it is," she laughs, cracking the window and lighting the
cigarette. "Now, why is that so, you ask. I think it's 'cause—say, back in
the twenties or thirties or so, when black folk starting moving into the
city from the country, some from West Virginia—I mean, I was just a
little thing, then—well, *obviously* white folk in town didn't want them
comin' into their neighborhoods. I mean, this is back when the Klan was
still ridin' high, you know."

"Uh-huh."

"So, what happened was, all the poor black folk moved into the
slummy part of town on the west bank of the river"—I have no idea
what river she's talking about—"but . . ." She exhales grandly. "But, well,
there also happened to be some of 'em with money—doctors and
lawyers and morticians and such, there's bound to be a handful, you

know. And no way were these uppity black folk living in those slums. So they settled the mountain"—she points ahead—"and named it New Calvary and built that big electrified cross. Until then, the mountain was kind of unpopulated except for a little bit of trash livin' in caves or somethin', and these uppity Negroes come on in and—well, kinda *colonized* it, like Pilgrims or something."

"Hm" is all I can think to say. It sounds fantastic, but reasonably in keeping with everything he's told me about his aunt, and I'm surprised again that he presumably wasn't overstating himself.

"And built some mighty fine homes, as you're about to see. Now I hope my goddamned four-wheel-drive comes through for us," she says. Pretty soon, she's pulling off the main road and onto a narrow dark street virtually hidden in the overhanging boughs of trees lush with spring. Through the crack of her window, despite the cigarette smoke, I can still make out the overpowering scent of lilacs mingling with sea air. Pretty soon, we're just crawling up the steepest of inclines—she's right; there's no way I would have been able to walk this with my bag—and through the screen of trees I begin to make out the suggestion of grand houses set back from the street, swathed in darkness—a pitched roof here, what I guess would be called a veranda there, the glint of expensive cars in driveways, mailboxes nestled in shrubbery.

"This *is* steep," I say, my head flat back against the seat of the car.

"That's how they like it, I suppose," she says. "Keeps fools like me from making a habit of this."

We keep climbing, climbing, the car straining against the incline, until finally we level off and the street splits in two and wraps around a dark, velvety village green upon which sits the electrified cross of Calvary, bathing the entire lawn in an eerie white light, and absolutely monstrous, stadium-sized, from where we idle just a hundred yards away.

"Oh my God," I gasp when I see it.

"I expect that's what they want you to say when you see it. Keeps us all in our place, huh? Look back behind you."

I twist around in the seat. We're at the very top of the mount, and the view is staggering, what seems like miles of inky, undulating treetops giving way to the thousands of lights of the town, leagues below, and beyond that the sea, a glittering plane of jet and diamond, wrapping around the mainland in a jagged crescent.

"That's amazing."

"I'll say," the woman says. "I'd forgotten how pretty it is. Some people live well, huh?" I nod absently, still caught between the twin spectacles. "What number Abberginny did you say your friend was?"

I tell her, and she drives around the left flank of the village green until we're on a wide avenue with a flower-drenched divider in the middle and houses on either side that seem to grow grander and grander as we pass. They're like no houses I've ever seen, certainly not the staid black-and-white Federal-style boxes that pass for estates in West Mendhem; instead, each one seems to have come out of its own separate fable, each one a different configuration of sprawling, candy-colored turrets, porches, widow's walks, and gables set against wide cool lawns broken up by histrionically arched willows or tiny, gnarled dwarf trees that look like they were grown in Japan, uprooted, and replanted here, to effects no more fantastic than the houses they stand before.

"Well, here you go, sir," the woman says. "What's your name, anyway?"

"Eric," I say. I'm staring at a little blue-and-white cottage of a home that reminds me faintly of a Swiss chalet.

"I'm Charlotte," she says, offering her hand. "Nice to meet you. This is your stop. Fourteen hundred."

"This?" I say, pointing to the blue-and-white chalet.

She laughs. "Hardly, sweetie. That!" And she points to the house at the very end of the boulevard, and I have to catch my breath. Set back on what seems a half-mile of lawn from the street sits, ponderous and dark except for one faint pinkly lighted window on an upper floor, a mausoleum—a massive square of spectral white granite, broken by nothing but a rotunda at the top, five rows of dark curtained windows and an immense portico, at the base of which is a flagstone walk that scrolls its way down to the street. There are trees towering behind the house, but none in the front, suggesting a boxy white ship anchored in the middle of a placid black pool. At the end of the walkway, there is a bronze mailbox on a marble pedestal, and as Charlotte pulls up directly in front of the house, I can make out the inscription:

Florentina Jefferson
1400 Boulevard Aubergine

Florentina is Fleurie, I think, *and she's dead now*. And then all I can think is, *This is* his *now?* And it occurs to me that when he told me he was filthy rich, he really wasn't kidding.

"So your friend lives here, huh?" Charlotte asks, glancing first at the house, then me, then back at the house. I can't tell if she's impressed or suspicious.

"I guess so," I say, not wanting to compound her suspicion about my right to be here, even though my own is growing by the second.

"Don't really look like anybody's home," she says, "except for that itty-bitty light way up in that window."

"Oh, my friend said he'd definitely be here," I lie quickly. "He also told me where to find the key if he stepped out for a minute. I'll be all right. Thanks a lot for driving me up here. It's a long haul."

"That's okay," she says, distracted, still staring up at the house. "Say, what do your friend's folks do for a living, anyhow? Are they entertainers or something?"

"Real estate, I think," I say, remembering what he told me once about Fleurie's big land coup.

"A helluva lot of it too, I suppose," she says, looking back to the house one more time before turning to me and smiling. "All right, Eric, I wish you the very best up here among the gods. You have a lovely stay in our little town. You'll find we Rebels ain't so bad."

"You don't seem so bad at all," I say, taking my duffel bag, smiling but thinking, *What the hell am I supposed to do now?* One thing is certain: after coming this far, I'm not turning back.

"Take care, sweetie," Charlotte says, before gunning the car and pulling a U-turn around the divider, back down Boulevard Aubergine. In a moment, the car is out of sight and the silence, not to mention the smell of lilacs, is overpowering. I think about what she said about the spade daddies running out of their fancy homes with shotguns—oh, dear—and look back up at the glowing white monster of a house. My watch says it's ten o'clock now. There is only one place for me to go.

My bag over my shoulder, I start the long walk up the pathway toward the house, my sneakers maddeningly noisy on the flagstones in the middle of the otherwise silent neighborhood. Worse yet, underneath the portico, my footfalls echo as if I'm at the bottom of a cavern. My heart jumps when I see two relatively unweathered cigarette butts on the black welcome mat, then jumps twice when I bend down, pick one up, and see that it's actually his brand, Camel filters. I press the bell and hear it echo through the rooms of what seems to be an abandoned house. If an old black woman who fits Fleurie's description answers the door, I tell myself, I'll scream and run away—this seems just like the sort of house to be haunted. If a stranger answers it, I'll just say I'm a friend of Brooks from St. Banner and he once said I could drop by anytime, so I happened to be in Virginia, and so on. And if it's him—if it's him, well, I don't know what I'll say.

But no one does answer the door. I wait a full minute, then ring again—twice, those chimes flying around a darkened house—then wait another full minute. Nothing. Finally, feeling like this whole scenario is so Gothic it couldn't actually be happening to me, I reach up for the enormous brass knocker—and it happens. Without a hitch, with hardly an ounce of pressure from me, the front door gives way, opens up. It could hardly have been closed, let alone locked, at all.

For the longest time, I just stand in the doorway and stare inside into the dark hallway. It could be the front hall on *Dynasty* or some such show—a colossal oak staircase that seems to go up and up and up, landing after landing; polished marble floors; arched entryways that open seductively on room after vaulted room—except that everything, *everything*, is packed and ready to leave. There are pale white squares on the walls where I suppose pictures once hung; furniture is covered in dropcloths; and besides that, it's just a chaos of trunks, crates, and cartons. It looks like an entire house, dismantled, packed up, anonymous, readied for evacuation—and it fills me with creepy panic.

"Hello?" I call out feebly into the hallway, and hear nothing but the echo of my own voice, which doesn't sound like me at all. Then, louder, more boldly: *"Brooks?"* I wait. Again, nothing.

I step inside, close the front door silently behind me, leaving it just slightly unlatched, the way I found it, and walk across the marble floor to the foot of the stairs. For what must be another minute, I just stand there, immobile, frozen by the silence and the shadows; then I start climbing, each scuff of my sneakers on the marble giving me a little chill. At the first landing, I call his name again, but the sound of my own voice rattling up the flights alarms me too much, so I keep climbing in silence—to the second landing, then the third, feeling like I've gone completely insane, like I don't know the meaning anymore of the idea of limits.

It's at the top of the fourth that I rediscover the light I saw from outside, falling in a loose pale shaft from an open doorway at the end of an empty hallway. I brace myself, call out his name one more time, then, when I get no response, proceed down the otherwise darkened hallway to the shaft of light at its end. Finally, when I get there, I swallow hard, readying myself for anything—a dead body, a pool of blood, a vampire, God knows what—and poke my head inside.

No one is there, but I notice immediately that someone *has* been, only a short while ago. It's a mess: there's a half-eaten pizza lying in an open box on the bed next to a dented pack of Camel filters, an uncapped bottle of gin upright on the floor, a dirty water-filled two-foot bong beside it, and a frenzied array of books, newspapers, magazines, tapes, soiled socks and underwear, shirts and trousers absolutely everywhere. It's unmistakably his room; not only do the gin and the bong give it away, not only do I recognize some of the twisted clothes, their Brooks Brothers tags plainly in view, but it *smells* just like him—that confused mix of cigarettes, pot and cedar chips, that odd combination of dissolution and gentility that threw me into a wonderful panic every time I inhaled it. All of a sudden, I'm just so *happy*—happy that's he still obviously alive and in the same country, happy that I've tracked him down of my own will, happy that in probably no time we'll be together, regardless of what I'm going to say to him, together in this room, his *real* room in his *real* house, just the two of us, about a thousand thoughts away from anybody else. I'm so happy that I just throw down my bag and pick up one of his smelly Brooks Brothers shirts and wrap it around my neck and sit down on his bed next to the congealing remains of the pizza. And I sit there and start thinking about all the things I'm going to tell him—how I wanted to run back to the medics and claim him as mine but they took him away too quickly, and about how I've been thinking of nothing but him for three months now. I think about how he'll be so happy to see me that he'll forgive me for betraying him, and how we'll start making plans right now for meeting this summer, in Paris or anywhere else, whatever it takes. And I get so caught up in my thoughts that I lose all track of time, and I feel completely at home in this strange house that I've virtually broken into on this strange mountain with the strange, God-sized electric crucifix glowing at the top of it.

I don't know how long I just sit there, drinking him in, until the sound of an engine gunning, then coming to a full stop far down below on the street, snaps me back to life. I run to the window—the lone lighted window I saw from the front yard—duck down, then peek out: I can see it now, a sorry-looking gold Maverick that's pulled up clear in front of the house. It just sits there, silent, until the passenger door opens. I squint hard, but I don't have to squint for that long: it's him, not even a shadow of doubt, taking one final drag on a cigarette, then stubbing it out by the curb. Then the driver's side opens, and who the hell is this? It's some tall, skinny white boy with a white-blond crew cut, lanky and slack-looking in a ratty T-shirt, cutoffs, and sandals, with his own cigarette. Hardly a moment goes by before Brooks virtually sprints up the flagstone walkway, the skinny white boy tailing him indifferently, at his own pace. In a moment, the boom of the great oak door closing behind them hurtles up four flights of stairs, straight through the stairwell, along with what sounds like his laughter.

My heart is trampolining out of my mouth. There is no way out of this house, and I'm too paralyzed to rally enough to take flight in one of the other, undiscovered rooms. *I could just present myself,* I think wildly. *After all, he is my friend.* But something about the presence of this unknown lanky white boy completely disconcerts me. Of course, I do exactly what they'd do in a Restoration comedy or an episode of *Three's Company:* I dive underneath the bed, dragging my body over a litter of socks and magazines. I'm not in there a moment, their twin footfalls growing closer, when I realize I've left my duffel out, within view. Frantically, I reach out for it and drag it into the dark with me.

I can hear them now at the top of the landing, first a boy's thick-as-molasses southern drawl (so much for Charlotte's claim that this isn't the Deep South), treble and gravelly: "Francie, didja really come all the way back here just to make me into a big ole faggot?"

First a razor-sharp laugh, then his voice—*his* voice—and when I hear it, my insides go sick, it's been so long: "Oh, *please,* don't let's start on that again, Brickhouse. You know this is a story that began many, many years ago. In the flush of youth."

They're in the room now, their voices so near I'm tempted to call out just to break this tension; as it is, I'm trying so hard not to so much as rustle that my whole body is shaking. I can see their feet now: Brooks sockless in his old loafers, which haven't been polished in some time, and this Brickhouse, whoever he is, doughy in his sandals, white-blond hairs sprouting from the bridges of his feet and his alien, slender toes.

A soft, guilty fraction of a laugh from Brickhouse, then: "Mr. Jefferson Tremont, I don't know what you're talkin' about." Then the sound of someone wetly smacking someone else's lips. My whole body goes rigid with horror, revulsion, and rage: is that what *we* sounded like? I can't believe he's subjecting me to this. Shouldn't he, with his keen intuitive powers, know that I have arrived?

The sound of a zipper unzipping, then Brooks again, gurgling with laughter (and it occurs to me he's probably drunk), "No, Mr. Brickhouse, I rather think you *do*. A certain boy, say, thirteen years old, whose poor honky mama came up here to clean windows for a certain poor little rich nigger boy's maiden aunt—"

"Mmm, God rest her soul. . . . I loved your auntie," this Brickhouse says, all grave now.

"Yes, I loved her, too." Then more smacking. "Anyway. A certain boy who came up here every Wednesday in the summer to cut hedges and knew that when he was done a certain poor little rich nigger boy would be waiting for him in the garage with his allowance and a bottle of Wesson oil?" His voice seems to be getting more drawlish as he goes along, and I don't know if it's a put-on or not. "And then a very, very sad following summer when a certain nigger boy was sent away to camp, but a certain fourteen-year-old piece of poor white trash still had to keep trucking up to Calvary Hill every Wednesday because his poor mama needed the extra eight dollars a week?"

There's a long pause, before this Brickhouse says, with fake giggly thoughtfulness: "Hmmmm, I don't seem to be recallin' no such thing."

"Like hell you don't!" Brooks lets out heartily, and then they're both laughing and they're at it all over again. A pair of filthy cutoffs falls down around the doughy sandal feet and is hastily kicked away, followed by khaki camp shorts landing in a clump on top of scuffed loafers. There's more smack-smack-smacking, before Brickhouse sighs.

"I sure miss your Auntie Fleurie, though. That was a sweet kick-ass lady with more class than any white girl I ever knew."

"She's flattered in heaven right now, I'm sure."

"Every Wednesday when I was through, she'd give me my eight dollars, then you know what she'd do? *Every* Wednesday?"

"Pray tell."

"She'd give me some old *book!* She'd have it set aside for me. Then the next week, she'd ask me if I'd finished it—and I'd always lie and say, 'Yes, ma'am, I sure have and it's mighty good!'—and she'd give me a big old smile, and give me another, hand-picked. Always boys' stuff. Probably *your* old stuff. Like Hardy Boys and shit. I wonder if she ever caught on to your game, Francie."

"Hm" is all he says, ruefully, then, "Yes, giving away books seems to be just one of the damnable traits I inherited from Fleurie."

"You talking about that little pussy Catholic boy up North again?" Brickhouse says, infinitely bored, and I want to come bounding out with an Apache scream.

"Hm?" he asks again, distracted, then, in that old weary drawl, "Yeah. I suppose I am. Now I'm sorry I ever told you about that if you're going to rub salt in my wounds every fifteen minutes by bringing it up." I hear the crack of a match, then inhale the familiar smell of his cigarettes.

"All the books in the world wasn't enough to get him to save your ass when he coulda," Brickhouse says, like old sage, then, so tenderly I want to puke, "Lemme see that head scar again, sugar?"

"You've gotten awfully affectionate in your old age, Brickhouse. What happened to the little no-necked monster who used to let me suck him off, then call me Fudgie Fudgepacker before he took my money and headed off to shoot dogs with his BB gun?"

"Well," Brickhouse says philosophically, dragging from the cigarette, "the little monster grew up. Lost his mama, like you."

"Fleurie wasn't my mama," he says sternly. "You know that."

"Yeah, but she raised you, so she may as well a been your mama. And *you* know that."

"I suppose," he says indifferently. "Proceed."

"Like I said." Brickhouse drags again. "Grew up. Lost his mama."

"Never left town," Brooks says—a little meanly, I think.

"Couldn't leave town," Brickhouse says, unperturbed. "Had two baby sisters and a baby brother." Then, as though he's having a delayed response to Brooks's slur, "At least I finished high school, you snotty-ass little cocksucker."

"I know," he says. "Cum laude in woodworking."

"Go fuck yourself!" Brickhouse virtually shrieks, and I hear the sound of a slap. Good for Brickhouse, I laugh to myself; even though the sight of him (or the sound of him, and the sight of his pasty feet) repulses me, I feel a peculiar laborer's allegiance with him—right here, from underneath the bed.

"Good Lord!" from Brooks. "I'm just kidding, for God's sake. Come here"—and as he crashes down on the bed, the mattress drops so perilously low that I'm sure it will completely smother me, forcing me to cry out, announcing myself, as soon as Brickhouse joins him on the bed.

But Brickhouse doesn't. "I want some more of that gin," he sulks.

"It's right here."

"Well." Brickhouse pauses. "I want more tonic to go with it. I'm goin' downstairs."

"There's no more tonic. The house is empty."

"I saw one lyin' in the wet bar when we were packing up earlier today. And I left it there."

"How sly for you. Well, hurry back."

I watch Brickhouse's sandals scuff out of the room, until there's silence. It's just the two of us in here now. His loafered left foot, dangling off the bed, is so close to me it's virtually in my face. Infinitesimally, I creep my right hand along my side and reach out until I'm an inch away from plucking one of the hairs out of the knob that is his anklebone. I want to scare the living hell out of him. But then he sighs dramatically and pulls his leg up onto the bed. Then, aloud, in a private voice that's either the saddest or maddest I've ever heard him, he says into thin air: "Oh, fuck fuck fuck. *Fuck!*" and he pounds his fist four times on the mattress. Then he makes an odd little whimper—it vaguely recalls the horrible sounds he was making that night on the common—and then he's silent. And all of a sudden, I want to call out his name—I want so badly to let him know I'm here, I want to crawl out from under him, tell him not to make a sound, say a word, and just curl up with him on his own bed, Brickhouse be damned. And I swear I'm so close to saying it—

"Brooks"—that my heart is throbbing in my trachea; I've got my hands on the underside of the mattress, separated from him only by a matter of layers, when he leaps off the bed, crosses the room, and picks up the phone. I hear him dialing—four digits, a pause, then another seven—and I see his feet shuffling in place as he waits. Then I hear him slam it down and say it one more time—"Fuck!"—before he throws himself back down on the bed, and the mattress closes in on me again. Now I've lost my nerve.

Brickhouse comes back. "See, I told you so," he says coyly, and I hear the hiss of an uncapped bottle.

"Would you put that down and come here?"

"Oh, all *right.* Lord, you're horny!"

Brickhouse gets on the bed, and the mattress drops to within three inches of my upturned face. They're at it all over again now, the bulge in the mattress shifting from side to side.

"Why do you hafta leave so soon?" Brickhouse whines out of nowhere. "Couldn't you just keep this house and live here for a little while? You ain't got nothin' else to do with your life now."

"Impossible."

"What the fuck does that mean?"

"Impossible, you idiot," I want to say, but Brooks says it for me. "What am I supposed to do all alone in this big house on Calvary Hill? Start a Fleurie Jefferson Memorial Museum? Anyway, Godfrey's already put it on the market."

"I hate that old bastard," Brickhouse says. "He never tipped me more than a dollar."

"He's tight," Brooks says. "But he's giving me my freedom two years short of twenty-one, so I'm not cussing him."

"Where you gonna go anyway?" This seems to be the eternal question with him, I'm thinking. "You sure ain't goin' back to that school. They won't have you no more!"

"No, mercifully," he says. "I think I'll go to New York for a little while. Then—well, the world is my home."

"Oh, Lord," Brickhouse groans. "Well. Just don't forget where you came from."

"How could I? I'm in bed with it right now."

Brickhouse laughs triumphantly. Then they're *really* at it, and I'm convinced that any minute I'm going to bolt from this bed, terrifying the shit out of both of them, and run right out of this house, down Calvary Hill, and all the way back to Washington. But of course I don't. I just lie here, rigid, my face screwed up, listening to them: Brickhouse's little moaning declarations—"Oh, sugar," and "Oh, yeah, like that"—and Brooks's deeper sounds of mild discovery and surprise, as if he's on a particularly fruitful archaeological dig. I have to lie here and listen to the whole thing as it builds and builds, shifting around uncomfortably to avoid the moving mattress, and the worst thing is that even in the middle of my distaste and acute, acute jealousy, I'm getting unbearably stiff, like I'm the invisible third party in a very odd little ménage à trois.

Then, finally, they're done. Brooks reaches his hand down and pats around on the floor—I cringe away in fright—until he locates a dirty shirt.

"You're really leavin' tomorrow, baby?" Brickhouse says, still whiny but sounding half asleep now.

"Why shouldn't I?" Brooks says, as unsentimental as ever. "Everything's packed, and you'll be here when they come to put everything in storage. Wouldn't I just be prolonging the inevitable if I stayed?"

"You could stay on my account," Brickhouse persists.

He laughs. "Don't you think we're a little mismatched?"

"We don't sound any more mismatched than you and your little buddy in Connecticut."

"Massachusetts."

"Whatever. Wasn't I better than him just now? I bet I was."

Another laugh. "Not necessarily. When you scratched the surface of his Catholic guilt, he had a certain frisky quality. It was endearing." I feel myself blush furiously in the dark.

"I'll bet," Brickhouse drawls skeptically. There's a pause, then, "You know, I think you're a bit of a freak, Francie Tremont. A mean, lonely, out-of-place little freak. You got too much money and too little love."

"Speak for yourself," he says, unfazed. "The fairheaded concubine-for-hire of Calvary Hill." He explodes laughing, and Brickhouse joins in, sounding oddly melancholy. "You're an asshole, sugar," Brickhouse says.

"Oh, be easy on me, darling."

His last words linger in the air, because they're silent now, and I guess they're falling asleep. (By the glow of my watch in the dark, it's now after midnight.) At least, Brickhouse is falling asleep, because in a matter of minutes, I hear ungainly, ragged snores, and I know they're not Brooks's. I want to make a getaway now, but I can't—he could still be awake, and even if he is asleep, I don't know how I'd slip out through this mess, duffel bag intact, without rousing them. So for what seems like an eternity, I just lie there, trapped, every muscle in my body cramped, including my stomach, which is screaming for food, and I'm afraid it's going to start protesting aloud pretty soon. I'm starting to get the paranoid feeling that he knows I'm down here after all and he's doing this just to spite me, to see how long I can last.

But I guess it's just paranoia, because, thankfully, after about half an hour, I hear a rustling, then his voice: "Brickhouse. Are you asleep?"

From Brickhouse, groggily, "Hmph?"

"Wake up. Let's go spend the night at your house."

"What the fuck're you talkin' about, Francie?" He sounds functionally awake now.

"You heard me. I can't spend my last night in this house. It's giving me the creeps. I feel like Fleurie's creaking around downstairs."

"You're just sad to be goin'. Can't you go to sleep an' forget about it? It'll be morning soon."

"I can't *make it* until morning! Did you fucking hear me? Now, are you going with me or not? Because if you're not, I'm taking your junkheap of a car and checking into a hotel downtown and I'll come fetch you in the morning."

"Jesus, Francie, you're a crazy man," Brickhouse says, as awake as Brooks now. "All right, all right. You can spend the night at my house. But you're spooked, sugar. Fleurie's a peaceful soul. She's fast asleep in heaven. She's not walkin' around haunting the earth."

"It's not just Fleurie," Brooks says. "It's this whole damned house. It's *ma vie incompréhensible.*"

"What's that?"

"Just skip it and get dressed."

"All right already. But I'm gonna have to kick you outta my bed before morning and put you on the floor. There's little kids in the house."

"Fine," Brooks grumbles, rolling off the bed, Brickhouse following. "Far be it for me to bring the stench of Sodom into La Casa Brickhouse."

Now I can see his slender hand rummaging around on the floor for his doffed clothes; for a moment I'm terrified he's going to conduct a full-scale search for something clean and get down on the floor, eye to eye with me. As soundlessly as I can, I slide my fetal body toward the far, linty depths of the underneath. Then, from him, "Oh, *je m'en fiche.* I'm fine like this. So are you." I watch his feet, reloafered now, proceed out the door. Then Brickhouse's sandals advance on them, stopping him in his tracks.

"Why you scarin' me, boy?" he asks, low, not coyly at all. I can see their four feet shuffling around in an uneasy little dance, then Brickhouse's sandal crawling up the length of Brooks's leg. "What's wrong with right here, huh?"

A pause, then, sternly: "Brickhouse. For all the allowance money I forked over to you, would you please just humor me my last night in Virginia? This fucking house is haunted."

"Ain't!" Brickhouse laughs.

"*Is!*" Brooks yells, so harshly he gives me a start under the bed. Then, his voice breaking that same terrible way it did the night up in the loft when I found him with his shoebox of pictures, "*Please,* Brickhouse. Just please let's get out of here."

"All right, sugar, all right," Brickhouse says, softly, and I'm ripped that it's him giving the comfort here, while I cower under the bed. "Don't go cryin' on me. You go cryin' and I'll start cryin' with you."

There's a dignified little sniffle from Brooks, then, in a small voice, "We certainly couldn't have that."

"Let's go," Brickhouse says, flipping off the light, and I hear them rustling out the door. *Fuck!* inside my head, and I pound my fist on the floor under the bed.

"What the fuck was that?" from Brooks, farther away, in the hall now.

"What?"

"That bang?"

"I didn't hear no bang. Guess that's your Fleurie sayin', 'Clean that room!' Guess you're right after all about the haunted."

His final words float back to me: "You're droll, Brickhouse." Two sets of footfalls recede down the staircase. In a moment, I hear the great boom of the front door again; then the house is silent. I wait five seconds, then scramble out from under the bed, my whole body aching, and over to the window. They approach the car—I can faintly make out a second of flame as one of them lights another cigarette—then they're in the thing, there's an explosion of engine in the still night, and they're off. I'm alone in this house again, as though they'd never come.

I don't turn the light back on. I stand in the middle of the dark room, in the middle of his debris, and I stretch in every possible direction to take the cramps out of my arms, neck, and legs. I feel my way down the dark hallway until I find a bathroom—a gleaming porcelain chamber, stripped bare like the rest of the house—and the sound of myself hitting the bowl, the subsequent flush of the toilet, seems to fill up the entire house, rattling its way down to the lowest depths. Then I go back to the room, get my hands on the last, congealed slice of pizza in the box, sink down on the floor, and devour it in the dark even though it tastes like a triangle of plywood. Brickhouse never touched the tonic, but he did uncap it; I pick it up, pour half a dirty glass of it, fill it up with the gin, stir it with my index finger (a habit of my father's), pop my finger in my mouth, gag, recover, and sit there, cross-legged, drinking the rest in tiny, mincing sips.

I don't know how long I sit drinking, trying to sort out thoughts and feeling nothing but a block, like a lump that's passed from my throat to my brain, but when I finally look at my digital watch, it reads one-thirty in the morning and it occurs to me that I'm not going anywhere, at least not until light comes. It also occurs to me that I'm rather drunk now, in a pleasant, fuzzy way that makes any hysteria impossible. I set my watch alarm for five-thirty in the morning, stand up, pull off all my clothes in about three gestures, and throw them in a heap on the floor along with his. I climb in the bed and press my nose into the dirty pillow until I locate his smell—cedar, cigarettes, some kind of hair jelly? Then I press my whole face into it, wrap my arms around it, clasp the opposite end of it with my pulled-up knees. I'm dropping off now, conjugating thickly: *Frottage, frottage. Je frotte, tu frottes, il frotte, ils frottent, nous frottons.* Now I'm seeing those old monster cartoon tombstones in my head: *Florentina Jefferson was here. Kerrie Lanouette was here. Jesús Antonio de la Costa was here. B.J.T. was here. Brickhouse was here. Fudgie Fudgepacker was here. E.F. was here.*

You were here. We were here. I was here. I swear to God, I was here.

Four hours later, there's a digital trill in my ear. At first I think it's the familiar whine of my radio clock, in my bedroom in West Mendhem, summoning me to school, to a bathroom competition with my father or Joani. Then sight clicks in—books, smoked butts, boxer shorts—and memory—"You're droll, Brickhouse"—and I'm scared shitless, wondering how I'm going to get the hell out of this house, flooded with white morning light, and to the bottom of Calvary Hill before they return. I give myself thirty seconds to think. Then I pick up the phone, call the operator, ask her to dial me a cab company, get one, submit the address, hold my breath for a refusal. None comes, and, emboldened, I ask them to come quickly. I dress, picking my clothes out of the salad of his own, throw my bag over my shoulder, piss in the porcelain bathroom, whiter now for Saturday morning sun, race down the four flights of stairs, and perch at the window in the cavernous abandoned foyer. If they come, I tell myself, I'll find a back door and head into the woods. But they don't; the cab comes first, honking at the foot of the flagstone walk, the engine a trembling valedictory report. I open the front door, signal "Five minutes" to the cabbie, then, like a madman, run back up the four flights of stairs and into the bedroom.

I want to leave something, but I don't know what. My eyes seize upon the empty pizza box, the cardboard flapping open like a huge panting mouth, the inside dark with old grease stains. I find it on the desk: a blue Flair marker holding a page of Racine in place. I prop the pizza box on the bed, uncap the pen, and kneel over it—poised, stumped.

The pen strokes immediately bleed over the stained parts, but I leave my headstone for him: "I was here. Where were you? *Je t'aime encore.* EF."

"What were you doing up on the Hill?" the cabbie asks me as we drive away. I'm seeing them now, the groomed, prosperous folk of Calvary Hill on this fine Saturday morning, walking dogs, walking strollers, watering incandescent green lawns. They stare right into the cab at me as we pass, and I stare back, wondering if they would have descended upon *me* if I had been found on their village green on a midnight Friday, a lone white boy with a duffel bag, revealed in the light of the cross—a looming black T-bar of bulbs and wires as we pass it now, in the stark God-given light of day—with a connection to one of their own I couldn't dare utter in my defense?

"Visiting a friend. A guy from school," I say to the back of the cabbie's head.

"Oh, yeah?" He laughs, a knowing little laugh. "Rich friend, right?"

"I guess."

"Rich nigger friend, right?"

I stare at the back of the head, picturing the eyes on the other side of the outgrown sandy blond crewcut.

"Yeah," I say slowly. "A rich nigger friend."

"Yep," the back of the head says, vindicated. "Had to be."

Blessedly, the bus is waiting at the stop when the cabbie pulls up. "That's fifteen bucks," he says affably, "but take ten off. Make it five, okay?"

"Thanks," I say, standing at his window, handing him bills. I look into his face now; his eyes are slack, following the trajectory of three high school girls in shorts as they walk down the sidewalk and into the Arby's on the corner.

I stare off with him, then look back into his eyes and say, "You know my friend I mentioned?"

His eyes turn back to me, pleased. "Yeah?"

"We—" I choke on myself, then recover. "We fucked each other once. It was so great. I wish you could know."

His face turns red, and mine does too. "Get the fuck away from me," he says, and starts the cab.

"I just wanted you to know," I say again, but he's already off. I shrug my bag up high on my shoulder and step up into the dry heat of the bus. After I pay the driver, I walk the aisle for a seat, and faces look up sleepily and smile.

Twelve

❖

On a Sunday morning in May, I wake up to a finger jabbing me in the back. Phoebe, Charlie, and I spent last night getting stoned on the docks at Lake Chickering; it was still too cold to swim, so instead we sat there playing Either Or, as in "You either have to give Goody Farnham an erotic sponge bath or wrestle naked with Mr. McGregor in front of Honors Math." Charlie grimaced a lot, Phoebe found everything kinkily exciting, and my mind kept wandering away from the faces I knew toward other scenarios, and I kept yanking it back into place. My first thought this morning is that I'm going to have a fuzzy head all day.

The jabbing persists until I roll over. "Joani, baby, what is it?" I mumble, making room for her on one half of the bed, an invitation she immediately seizes.

"Today's the day," she says gravely.

"What day?"

"What *day?* What do you think? My Confirmation! I'm gonna wear the dress."

"The dress I took you to buy the stuff for?" She nods at me: *Duh.* "I thought it wasn't ready yet."

"I finished it early. Erky?"

"Yeah?" I'm focusing now. Joani has her hair in an approximation of braids, with some white ribbon woven through them unevenly.

"What's Confirmation, anyway?"

"It means you're now an adult in the eyes of the Lord," I say, repeating the same old thing everyone always said to me.

"That's what Grandma says. But what is it?"

"Joani, I don't know," I say, exasperated, because I honestly don't. "Think of it as a chance to wear your new dress. And everyone comes, just to see you. And after, you get to have your picture taken in front of the church with Eddie, and you guys can smooch."

"You're gross, Erky," and she pushes my face away with a scowl. Then, brightening: "Everybody's comin', aren't they? Even Grandma."

"Yep. All for you, babe. You're a legend."

"You think Brenda's comin'?" she asks, frowning.

I feel like I know the answer to that right away: if Brenda hasn't come home since Christmas, not even for Easter, not even now, in what are supposed to be the last weeks of her pregnancy, it's unlikely she's coming home for Joani's Confirmation today, when she would have to see not just us, but *everybody*. "We'll see" is all I say to Joani, as brightly as possible. "She's *really* big now, Joani. She might not fit in the church."

"Shut up!" Joani explodes laughing. "She's not that big!"

"How do you know? You haven't seen her. Maybe her baby is as big as this house. Maybe it's a monster."

"Erky, I'm not stupid," she says, sensibly.

I look at her. She's been getting bigger in the past year, and she scared us this past February when she caught a cold that lingered for two weeks. I'm glad that her dress is ready—it's been her all-consuming project for months—and I'm glad that today is going to be all about her, a Joani-fest, and that I'm here to see it.

"I never said you were," I say, kissing her on the forehead and getting out of bed. "How could you be? You're *my* sister, after all."

"I know." She groans sarcastically. "Lucky me."

"Lucky you," I parrot, throwing on clothes. "Lucky Joan Erin Fitzpatrick. Are you coming downstairs to have some doughnuts?"

"In a sec. I gotta finish my braids."

"Why don't you just let Ma help you with them later? It's too early in the day to do them now, anyway."

"I'm *practicing!*" she enunciates.

"All right, all right. Excuse me, ma'am!"

Downstairs, my parents are sitting around the kitchen table, drinking coffee and reading the *Sunday Leicester Tribune*. Grandma is sitting there, too, with an untouched glass of grapefruit juice and a slice of toast in front of her. She's permanently settled in with us now—it just worked out that way—and even though she seems to be slipping fast, the fact that her mind is going has made her more subdued than ever before (with the exception of a rare outburst, à propos of nothing, usually delivered in Italian, which in her lifetime she only spoke to her husband, because she always felt that Americans should speak American.) Her quiet, though eerie, is sort of a blessing to all of us, although no one, least of all my mother, would dare admit it.

"Hi, honey," my mother says, leaning back for a kiss. "You sleep good?"

"Okay. Morning, Grandma." I step over to plant a kiss on her cheek, which makes her smile and mumble approvingly at her toast.

"Hey, look at this." My father waves some of the paper at me. "There's a little notice about graduation with your name in it."

Sure enough, there's a sidebar with the rundown for the forthcoming West Mendhem High graduation, including "Keynote Speaker: Eric Fitzpatrick."

"That's nice," I say, handing back the paper. The reminder of the speech leaves me feeling slightly queasy, because I haven't given it any thought at all. I don't want to make any more speeches, and I don't want to stand up in front of any more crowds. I just want to graduate and slip out of town, as quietly and inconspicuously as possible. To those ends, everything is going as planned. I have no reason to complain, but West Mendhem has started feeling sort of haunted to me.

"Big, big year," my father says. "When you get to Yale, how you gonna stand being a little fish in a big sea?"

"I'm actually looking forward to it."

"He'll be big soon enough," my mother says matter-of-factly, ripping out a coupon for chicken breasts at the supermarket. Grandma declares something in Italian—I think something about a little bird learning to use its wings, but I'm not sure, since my knowledge of Italian is scattered and secondhand; then she trails off.

"Okay, Mama," my mother says soothingly. My father squirms a bit in his seat, clears his throat, and glances my way.

"Is Bren coming to Joani's Confirmation thing today?" I ask of no one in particular, as casually as possible.

There's an awkward pause, as there always is whenever someone brings up Brenda. By this point, she's brought my mother and father such grief that they can hardly bear to say her name. My mother is also going into a panic that Brenda is due within the next week or two and she hasn't even been in touch. On top of it all, whenever Brenda's name comes up, Grandma doesn't make a sound: she just mashes her lips together and her eyes bulge out of her head like they're going to explode.

"I don't know," my mother says, tight-voiced, shrugging too vigorously and not looking up from her clipping. "I left two messages with her roommate—that good-for-nothin' airhead little thing—"

"Hey, Terry, *easy*—" my father interjects.

"—but she didn't return 'em, so who knows? Maybe she'll come, maybe she won't. It's no skin off my back."

"Hm" is all I say, sipping coffee.

"Why don't you call her yourself? I don't think she hates you as much as she hates me."

"Hate's a bad word," Grandma splutters, leaning toward my mother.

"I'm sorry, Ma," my mother says wearily. "I didn't mean it. I meant, Eric, maybe she'll listen to you."

"Actually," I say, thinking of Joani and the white ribbons falling out of her faulty braids, "I think I'll drive over there and see if I can get her to go."

My mother shifts around in her seat. My father looks up, arching an eyebrow over his bifocals. "You mean you're gonna go all the way to Billerica?" My mother sounds scandalized.

"It's not that far, Ma," I say, gulping down the rest of my coffee. If I'm going to do this, I think, it's going to be now or never.

"Here," my father says, handing me his keys. "Take my car. It's better on the highway."

"There's nothing wrong with my car on the highway!" my mother pipes up now, offended. "I take excellent care of that car."

"Terry, you need to get your brakes tightened."

"I do not! I just got them tightened six months ago!"

"Fine, don't listen to me." My father shrugs and turns back to the paper.

"My brakes are fine!" my mother persists, her pitch cresting.

Grandma, who's been taking all this in with her eyes bugging out, finally slams her palm down on the table and sputters, "Listen to your husband! He knows these things!"

My father and I burst out laughing. "Thanks, Ma," my father says, patting her on the hand. Then, triumphant, he turns to my mother and says sweetly, "See? Listen to your mother, Terry. She knows best."

Her eyes narrow. "I'm gonna get you later," she says to him, under her voice. Then she turns to me, as though nothing had happened at all. "Eric, we don't expect you to perform miracles," she says, smoothing down my hair and kissing me good-bye. "But if you can't bring her back, would you at least get her to promise that she'll call me when she's ready to go in the hospital? And tell her we'll come get her?"

"Okay, Ma."

"And tell her she's breaking her mother's heart?" She hugs me, her voice breaking. Then she abruptly unlaces me. "No, don't tell her that. Just tell her we're here for her. Okay?"

"Okay."

It's a glorious day outside when I pull onto the highway in my father's car. I know that all over the Merrimack Valley, all over Massachusetts, people are celebrating confirmations and weddings and other rites of spring, and it's only when I notice that my father has taken the picture of Brenda, Joani, and me at Disney World, the one of the three of us sticking out our tongues at the camera and pretending we have boobs, that he's taken the picture out of my parents' bedroom and mounted it on the dashboard of his car, it's only then that I concede I'm going to see Brenda as much for myself as for Joani. She hasn't been in the house for months, but then again, in a way, neither have I.

Her friend Lori's apartment complex is a sorry-looking collection of two-story fake Colonial buildings set amid winding driveways, marked on the road by a battered scroll-like sign that says "Billerica Arms" in chipped Olde English–style letters. After wandering around the driveways, I finally spot the number Brenda gave me, for emergency purposes only, months ago. Her car is parked outside.

I park on the street and walk up to the building. There are eight entryways; each screen door leads into a living room that faces out on the parking lot through cheesy little bay windows. I walk up to Lori's apartment, then decide it might be smarter to peek inside before I ring the bell. I pick my way around the grim little bushes below the bay window and press my nose against the window screen.

The living room is a disaster: clothes, tote bags, women's magazines, dirty plates strewn everywhere—on the floor, on tabletops, over the tacky-looking furniture, including the unmade foldout sofa. The only adornment on the walls is a giant poster of the faceless Soloflex man taking off his shirt, from which I immediately avert my eyes. The back of an armchair is facing me, the front of it facing the TV, which is blaring Home Shopping Club loud enough for the whole apartment complex to hear. Some southern woman with big hair is pitching an E.T. commemorative Hummel figurine. I'm not sure if anyone is sitting in the chair until I see it rock a bit.

"Bren," I call through the screen.

The chair lets out a scream, and I know immediately it's Brenda. "Who the hell is it?" she lets out, angry. I make out someone trying to struggle out of the chair, then giving up and wheeling it around. It's Brenda, with neon apricot masque on her face, her hair pulled back grotesquely with a rubber band, barefoot, splayed there in a tent-sized nightshirt that reads "Contents Undisclosed Until ???" in big pink bubble letters. She looks frightening, frightened, and, sure enough, as big as a house. I couldn't have imagined her that big if I had tried; she must be carrying quintuplets.

She just sits there, glued to the chair, her face a frieze of shock and fury. "What the fuck are you doing here?"

"Bren, you're huge!" I cry out in spite of myself.

"Eric, what the *fuck* are you doing here? How did you know where to find me?"

"You gave me the address once, remember?"

"I did not!" She's struggling out of the chair now, pulling the nightshirt down around her mountainous middle. The sight of her propping her hand behind her back and groaning just to stand up stabs into my chest.

"Yes you did! Way back. In case of emergencies."

"Well, is this an emergency?" she asks, more rhetorically than earnestly, and I realize now, acutely, how much I miss her, my battle-ax, bad-ass, foul-mouthed, knocked-up older sister.

"Not really," I venture. "I just came to say hi."

"Well, why didn't you ring the bell? You scared the living shit out of me."

"I wanted to see if anyone was home," I answer, innocently.

"Bullshit," she says, hobbling toward the door. "You saw the car. You just wanted to see what a fuckin' sty this place is so you can go back and report it to Ma."

I pick my way out of the bushes and up the steps, where she unlocks and opens the door, scowling at me.

"Hi!" I say, wanting to charm her, hugging her gently under the arms. "You're humongous."

"Don't kiss me," she says, patting me cursorily on the back. "I've got this stuff on my face. And you don't have to tell me I'm humongous. It's not like I haven't noticed."

"All right," I say, stepping in. "I won't do either."

"Good." She closes the door behind her. The two of us stand there, in the derelict living room, and stare at each other, me smiling dopily, completely at a loss for what to do or say next, her still frowning.

"I'm sorry the place is such a mess. It's not usually like this. It's just that I can't bend down much, and Lori's had to work the past four days in a row, double shift. She took over my shifts for me until this is over," she says, gesturing lamely at her belly.

"That's okay," I say, picking up a dirty plate off the floor and putting it on the coffee table. "I didn't come over to do a cleaning inspection."

"Then why'd you come?" She's still got one hand on her back, looking fierce and put-upon.

"To see how you're doing. Why else?"

"I don't know," she mumbles, waddling into the equally disheveled kitchen, and I trail her. "To get me to go to Joani's Confirmation. It's not like I don't know it's today. I *got* the messages," she says, significantly. "Shouldn't you be getting ready for it?"

"It's not till three," I say.

"Is Joani all excited? You wanna cup of coffee or somethin'?" she asks, washing out two mugs in the sink. She's still not outright warm and welcoming, but at least she doesn't seem angry that I'm here anymore. I notice a paperback book with a pen stuck in it lying on the dining island: *What to Expect When You're Expecting.*

"Yeah—I mean, I'll have some coffee. And yeah, she's excited. She's wearing this dress for the first time that she's been working on for months now."

"That's cute. She's really into all that sewing stuff now, isn't she?" Brenda sets down my coffee.

"Yeah. Bren, should you be drinking coffee?"

"It's decaf," she says. "Hazelnut. Lori got it for me."

"Oh. Okay."

"But thanks for your concern," she says, flashing me a mock-sweet smile.

I laugh. "Don't mention it." Then neither of us says anything. I sip my coffee, which is stale and awful. Brenda's eyes wander to the book. She reaches over, pulls out the pen, caps it, and puts it back in place.

"Doing your homework, huh?"

"Yeah." She laughs grimly. "It's the first time in a while."

"How you doing, Bren? It's any day now, right?"

"That's what the doctor says," she says, singsong. Then she shrugs. "I'm fine, I guess. I'm just hanging around like a hausfrau, watching HSC and waiting for the big ka-boom. I can hear it thumpin' and kickin' all the time now. Here, feel."

She puts my hand on the middle of her belly; it feels strange, hard and taut, like a huge basketball, but silent nonetheless. "I can't feel anything right now," I say.

"You can't?" she asks, putting her own hand there. I shake my head. "Oh, well," she says, picking up her coffee. "Maybe later."

"Who's gonna take you to the hospital?"

She shrugs again. "I don't know. Lori, I guess."

"What if Lori's at work?"

"I don't know. I guess I'll call an ambulance or something."

"Brenda!" I protest.

"Well, who the fuck am I *supposed* to ask. Ma and Dad? Frank?"

"Have you called Frank recently?" I don't tell her that Frank calls our house virtually every night, looking for an update, and usually ends up crying on the phone with my mother, both of them wondering aloud why Brenda is making their lives miserable.

"No," she scoffs. "Why should I? Just so he can call me a fucking bitch and an unfit mother and say he's gonna come get me? He'd probably try to trace the call!"

"Oh, Brenda, come on! Somebody's gotta go to the hospital with you. And what if I'm in school when it happens? You gotta call Ma."

"Eric, *why?* So *she* can call me an ingrate and all that shit? No, thanks. I can get through this myself. It's not like I'm the first or anything."

"Jesus, Brenda, you've gone off the deep end."

She glares at me through the apricot masque. "Do you wanna just *leave*, buddy?"

"All right, all right, I'm sorry," I say hastily. "I just don't know why you're making things so hard on yourself."

"No, I guess you don't," she sulks, and then we're both silent again. That goddamned southern belle is screeching on about some do-it-yourself sequin stapler on the TV in the other room. "So, you got into Yale, huh?" she finally proposes.

"Uh-huh," I answer warily.

"You psyched, or what?" She sounds like she's trying to be nice now, and I would be touched if she already hadn't gotten me so down.

"I guess so," I say, assuming her fuck-all tone. "I'm not really think-ing about it right now. I have to give another stupid speech for gradua-tion next month."

"Oh, poor baby!" she bursts out, then with unmasked rue, "Jeez, Eric, you got it fuckin' made."

"That's not true!" I say, wounded. "I hate it when you say that."

"Okay, sue me"—broadly sarcastic. Then, gesturing first at herself, then around the apartment, "I guess I mean *relatively* speaking." I just stare down into my coffee, a little pissed that I even decided to come now, and I guess she senses it, because she says, mimicking Joani, "Hey, Erky. Hey! Just kidding, okay?"

"Whatever." I look up, smiling weakly.

"But Eric, listen. If you came out here to get me for Joani's Confir-mation, you know I can't go to that."

"Why not?" I whine. "It was the first thing out of Joani's mouth this morning when she woke me up: 'Is Brenda gonna come?' She misses you so much, Bren. She doesn't understand why you're doing this."

"She's too young to think one way or the other about it."

"You're so wrong!" I say. "She misses you a lot. We all do. You don't believe it, but I swear to God we do. Ma hasn't been the same since you left. She's a nervous wreck, she lashes out at everyone, she can hardly say your name without bursting into tears. And Dad's not any better. I mean, living in that house has been like—"

But I stop then. She's been frowning down into her coffee, and all of a sudden I realize that she's crying, shaking infinitesimally, tears running down her face, cutting jagged lines into her dried-up apricot masque. The sight of her, crying so softly, scares me. Awkwardly, I take her hand in mine on the dining island. "Bren," I say quietly. "Bren, it's okay."

"Oh, God, Eric," she says in a tiny, tight voice. "It's not okay. It's not. I mean, I miss you guys, too—even Ma. I hate it here, I swear. But, Eric"—and she looks up at me, her face filled with clayey anguish— "look what I've done to my life! Look at the fuckin' mess I've made! I'm not even twenty-one and I'm gonna have a *baby* in a few days—" She stops and coughs, like the very thought overwhelms her. "—And I don't know what the fuck I'm doing with my life, and I *don't* want to get married, not yet, and—and so what have I done? I've disgraced the whole family! It's bad enough with Ma, but I can't even *think* about Dad, let alone talk to him. Do you think I don't know how humiliated he is when he's walking around town thinking that people are sayin', 'Oh, there's the guy whose daughter's a fuckin' slut!' Eric, I know that's what he's thinking!"

"Brenda—"

"And then there's Grandma—Doris!—and her wrath of God on my back."

"Bren, forget about Grandma. She's an old woman from the old country. She doesn't even know what's going on anymore."

"And then there's *you*, this walking picture of perfection. I mean, you're three years younger than me, and you're outta here! You're gonna have a life, and I'm trapped here—with *this!*" She gestures at her belly. "Eric, what's gonna happen to me?"

I take a deep breath, and brace myself. Then I say, "Bren, I gotta tell you a few things. First of all, nobody's judging you—nobody that matters. You're wrong about Dad, I swear. He's not hanging his head in shame. He'd gladly walk down Main Street with you right now, just as you are, carrying a big sign with an arrow that says 'My Pregnant Daughter,' if only you'd stop shutting him out of your life and let him be your father. And as for all the rest—all the aunts and cousins, and all the philistines—"

"What?"

"—and all the assholes in West Mendhem, then you just have to tell them to go fuck themselves. Because the people who really matter—your family, and your real friends, and Frank—we're all behind you. And you just have to be able to smile at all the other losers who have nothing better to do than cast judgment on you, and tell 'em to fuck off."

"Easy for you to say."

"Second, you're gonna have a life. You're gonna have a beautiful baby, and Ma's gonna help you bring it up for as long as you want, and you're gonna figure out what you want to do with your life—whether that's going to computer school, or just being a mother, or whatever—and you're gonna do it. And you're gonna have to work it out with Frank that you don't commit to anything you don't want until you're ready. He's gonna have to understand. But he will, if you finally sit down and talk to him."

"Easy for you to say," she repeats, implacable.

"There's one more thing I have to tell you," I push on, and this is where my hands start to shake around the coffee mug, and I feel that horrible tremor come into my voice. "And that's please don't ever tell me that I'm the picture of perfection again, or that I don't have any problems. Because you're wrong in a big way."

"Oh, really?" she scoffs, pushing me further. I can feel it. I'm not going back this time.

"Yeah, Bren, really!" I come back, harder than her. "Really. 'Cause you don't know this, but I fell really hard for somebody this year."

She looks at me, quiet for a second. Then she goes, "So? It's about time."

"Yeah, but it's not that simple."

"Why, who is it—Phoebe? What's the problem? 'Cause she's half Jewish? Who cares?"

"It's not Phoebe. It's nobody like Phoebe."

"So?" she keeps pushing. "Who, for God's sake? Some *black* girl?" She laughs.

"No, some black—" I retort, then stop, my heart racing.

Then she suddenly stops, too. "Some black what?"

I don't say anything. I just stare at her defiantly, shaking like crazy.

"Are you saying what I think you're saying?" she asks me in a tiny little voice.

"I think so," I say.

"Like, what everybody at school always said about you?"

"Yeah." Now I *know* she knows what I'm talking about.

"Oh," she says, then, oddly, "And I always told them they were wrong."

"Well, thanks for defending me," I say, for lack of anything else. I feel like I've pushed a boulder off the side of the cliff and I'm waiting for it to crash. But it doesn't seem to crash. Southern Belle keeps carrying on in the other room.

"But I guess *I* was wrong. Right?" She looks up cautiously at me, and I feel like she's looking at me for the first time, like she feels like she's looking at a total stranger. "Is that what you're tellin' me?"

"I guess so," I say, shrugging. For the longest time, she just stares down into her coffee mug, perplexed, and I begin to wonder if it was such a good idea to tell her, but for the fact that I wanted her to know that, like her, I wasn't without dilemmas. Finally she looks up at me and goes, "Are you *sure?*" She sounds more annoyed than anything else, like I've just asked her to work out on paper some mathematical brain-teaser.

"About what?"

"About—*you* know. I mean, what about Phoebe?"

"What *about* Phoebe?"

"Well, I mean, you spend all your time with her. Aren't you attracted to her?"

"No! Not that way! Would *you* be?"

Brenda throws her hands in the air. "Oh, fuckin' A, Eric, don't make this any more confusing than it is! I mean, you're not attracted to girls *at all?*"

"Bren, *I* don't know!" Now I'm getting exasperated because I hadn't expected the conversation would go this far. "I really haven't given it that much thought. It's not like it's forever, or anything. Or—I don't know. I just wanted you to know, that's all."

But I can't seem to pull her out of her distraction. "Because if it's forever"—and she actually lowers her voice—"do you know what kind of a fuckin' *life* you're gonna have? People are gonna be beating on you for the rest of your life!"

"Not necessarily. Not at Yale. Anyway, Bren, this is all beside the point. I just wanted you to know that I'm not perfect, and I'm sick of hearing it from you. It's presumptuous."

"Huh?"

"You heard me," I say, feeling stern and authoritative.

She gets up and pours more coffee for herself. "You want some?" she asks, waving the pot at me.

"No thanks."

She sits down again, pats at the remaining apricot masque on her face, looks uneasily at me, sips, looks away, then looks back again. Finally, she puts down her mug. "*Who* did you say this—this *person* is? Some *black*—some black person?"

"Yes, Brenda, some *black person*," I say, rolling my eyes. "Who happened to go to St. Banner. Who's really smart and really rich and really fucked up, okay? And who doesn't happen to go there anymore, okay?"

"Oh my God," she says, going blank. "Is he that kid who, you, like— the one, you know, who you saved his life? The kid getting beaten up on the common? And all that publicity and everything?"

"Yep." I nod gravely.

"Oh my God, Eric, this is too much for me to take in all at once. Do Ma and Dad know about this?"

"No!" I say. "And you're not gonna tell them. You gotta promise me that, Bren. The time's not right to tell them. Maybe it'll never be."

"All right, all right." She sounds faintly offended. "I wasn't gonna say anything. Does *anybody* know?"

"No."

"Not even little Phoebe?"

"Not even Phoebe," I say. "Well, actually, no one except this creepy teacher at school who saw us in Boston once."

"This really gets weirder and weirder. Which teacher?"

"Mrs. Bradstreet."

"I always hated her."

"She's weird," I concede.

"Yeah," Brenda says blankly. She's silent then, absently running her hand over her belly, and I fall silent, too. It's May outside—so warm and guileless—and it's pressing in unbearably upon the kitchen windows, summoning us out of this squalid double helix of secrets and into the sun.

"Are you mad I told you?" I finally ask her.

"What?" she says, looking up. "Mad? No!" She seems offended again. "I'm just taking it all in, that's all."

"You promise?"

"Yeah! Eric, for God's sake, you're my little brother. The last thing I'm gonna be here is *mad*. I'm not some bigot or something."

"I know," I say indulgently.

There's another long, funny pause. I wonder if, my primary mission failed and my secondary, spontaneous one eliciting such an ambivalent response, I should cut my losses and leave now. I'm about to propose as much when she slides herself off the barstool and puts her hand over my arm. "Look, honey," she says, "do me a favor. I'm gonna go in Lori's room and do my breathing exercises and put myself together, and think this through, and make a phone call I have to make. And when I come out, we can talk some more, okay? Why don't you hang out in the den and watch some TV or something? Or did you bring a book?"

"No."

"Well, just watch the TV for a half-hour or so. You'll be okay."

Brenda suddenly seems oddly businesslike to me. "You sure you don't just want me to go?"

"No, no," she says. "Definitely not. Just give me a little time, hunh?"

"I can't stay too late. I gotta get back for the Confirmation."

"I know. Just—just bear with me, okay?" And she looks so funny, standing there pleading with apricot flaking off her face, and she sounds so much like our mother, that I shrug—confused, still feeling half-freakish for my confession—and plant myself in front of Home Shopping Club while she waddles off down the hall.

I don't know how long I sit there watching Southern Belle, who sounds all pumped up on helium, hawk cubic zirconia earrings and home blood pressure kits, but it's coming up on one-thirty and I'm anxious about getting back to West Mendhem in time for the Confirmation. Brenda is in Lori's room, on Lori's phone, having some sort of animated conversation—I can hear her voice rise and fall in exasperation and entreaty from time to time—but I have no idea whom she's talking to. Finally, fed up with Southern Belle, I decide to flout Brenda's wishes and make myself useful. I gather up all the dirty plates, glasses, and cutlery lying around the apartment and start scraping them off in the kitchen sink.

It's when I'm loading everything into the dishwasher that she returns. "I told you not to do that," she says behind me.

"I'm sorry, but this place was filthy and—" I turn around and gasp. She's not in her nightgown anymore. Instead, she's standing there in a cream linen maternity dress, balancing herself precariously on heels, a straw boater on her head with a black ribbon around it. The apricot masque is gone; she's smiling sheepishly from under her hat, and she is radiant.

"Come on," she says, her smile mingling oddly with her usual sourpuss voice. "I just talked to Frank. We're picking him up and the three of us are going to Joani's Confirmation."

I'm flabbergasted, and amused, and so happy I want to cry, but I don't. Instead, I just say the first thing that came to mind. "Bren, you look fabulous."

"It's wicked cool, huh?" she responds, fidgeting. "I bought it all a few weeks ago at Bun in the Oven in the mall, thinkin', you know, just in case—"

"Right," I say, nodding.

"Anyway," she says, taking the dish towel away from me. "You don't have time for that. We gotta make tracks if you're gonna get ready and we're gonna get there on time."

"All right, I'm coming."

On the highway, she touches up her makeup while I drive. Hit radio is playing "Sympathy for the Devil," one of her favorite songs when she was twelve (hence, one of mine when I was nine), the windows are down, and we both sing to ourselves as the wind rushes in.

Otherwise, we're quiet until she finally says, over the wind, "You know this person—what's his name?"

"It's Brooks."

"Oh." More touching up. "Are you ever gonna see him again?"

"I don't know. It doesn't look like it." There's a lot I could tell her, I think—so much I could tell her—but I don't.

"Oh," she says again, not looking away from her makeup. "Well, maybe next year, when you're safe and sound at Yale with all the other bohemians of the world." This rather shocks me, and I glance in her direction. She's got a smug little smile on her face because she thinks she's thrown me on two counts: she knows I didn't expect she'd be that open-minded, and she knows I didn't expect she'd know what *bohemian* meant. The thing is, on both counts, she's right.

"Maybe so." I smirk to myself.

"You never know what life's gonna bring you," she says, snapping shut her compact and throwing it in her purse, smacking her lips together.

The house is empty when we get there; everybody's already off at St. Matthew's because the confirmees (I guess that's what they're called) and their parents have to get there early, for a little talk with old Father Horrigan, probably the same little talk he's been giving for the past twenty-three years. Brenda waits for me while I hurry to shower and put on a coat and tie, but she won't wait in her room; instead, she waits uncomfortably in the kitchen, sipping ginger ale and fiddling with her hat.

Twenty minutes later, we pull up in front of Frank's parents' house, the second story of a peeling brown-painted triple-decker in the part of West Mendhem that just borders Leicester. Brenda's suddenly nervous, twisting the strap of her purse in her hand and looking straight out the car window.

"Why don't you go up and ring the bell?" she says to me sharply.

"You sure?"

"Yeah, I'm sure!" she snaps. "If I wasn't sure, why would I've asked you in the first place?"

"All right!" I say, and walk around the side of the house to ring the bell. Inside five seconds, I hear Frank's heavy footsteps pounding down the stairs, until he's standing there, his short hair spiky and gelled up in the front, long and plastered down in the back. He's wearing a brown three-piece suit with a little enameled Italian-flag clip on his tie, and he's smiling nervously.

"Hey, Eric," he says, crushing my hand in his and pumping it interminably. "Long time no see."

"Yeah. Not since Christmas, I think."

"Oh, yeah." He laughs feebly. "We can just forget about that, right?"

"Sure, Frank."

He laughs nervously again. "Thanks. Uh, where's Brenda?"

"Out front, in the car. She's waiting for us."

I round the corner of the house first. Brenda's stepped out of the car and she's standing at the end of the walkway, bag in hand, scuffing at the ground with her heels. When Frank sees her, he stops dead in his tracks. "Oh, man," he says, fiddling with his tie clip. "Oh, *man.*" I have to turn away—it's too much for me to take today.

Brenda half-grimaces, half-smiles down at her feet as Frank approaches, and I hang back about six feet. They face off about a yard away from each other.

"Hey," he says, shuffling in place along with her. He offers her his hand.

"Hey," she says, accepting it.

"You're—" And he stops.

"I'm *what?*" she says, laughing. "Go ahead and say it."

"You're—*big.*"

"No! *Really?*" she lets out, burlesque-style, looking from him to me and back. "I'm so glad I've got you guys to let me know. Otherwise I really wouldn't notice."

"No!" he protests. "No, I mean—I mean, you look great."

"Oh, yeah?" she says, laughing again. I'm remembering them in high school now, Frank at our house for Thanksgiving dinner after West Mendhem won the big holiday game against Mendhem for the first time in seven years; Brenda, in his football sweatshirt, sitting on his lap, running her hands through his crew cut and calling him a big goofball—and Frank, lapping it up, unintelligibly in love with my older sister.

"Yeah," he insists. "Seriously."

"Well. Thanks. You look good yourself."

They keep on just staring at each other, sizing each other up, until finally Brenda says, "We better go or we're gonna be late." I walk around the car, and Frank reaches for the door to the backseat, but I'm not halfway around when Brenda, in a strange cracking voice, goes, "Wait a minute, just—hang on a second." And she totters around in her heels and puts her arms around him, and he goes, "Oh, man," and does the same to her, and the two of them just stay that way for I don't know how long, separated by nothing but the big basketball of their baby, until Brenda finally takes a big breath, says, "All right, Eric, let's motor," and they get in the car, and we're off, and she's reapplying her eye makeup in the passenger seat mirror.

At St. Matthew's, the entire parking lot is filled and we have to drive around the block until we find a place on the street. When we get to the front of the church, and the steps are empty and we hear organ music coming from inside, it's clear that we're late. The three of us hasten up the long sweep of stairs leading to the entrance, Frank and I on either side of Brenda, but just as we come to the last landing before the doors, Brenda freezes, a hand dug deep into each of our arms, her hat slightly askew on her head.

"Oh my God," she says aloud. "What the fuck am I doing? *Look* at me! What the fuck do I think I'm doing?"

"Brenda, come on," I say. "You can't go back now. Remember what we talked about."

"Eric," she says absurdly, gesturing up at the stucco St. Matthew's steeple, "this is a house of God!"

"Fuck that," Frank says. "It's our house, too. It better be, for all the money they make you put in that friggin' basket every week." He lets go of her grip and walks ahead of us three steps, then holds out his hand. "Now you comin', babe, or not? 'Cause I'm not goin' in there if you're not comin' with me. I got better places to be on a beautiful day like this."

"You guys are insane," she says, looking heavenward. Then she refastens her grip on me and takes Frank's arm again, and the three of us proceed up the steps to the entryway.

It takes a moment to adjust to the cool darkness of the church; they've started the ceremony, the organ is whining, the choir is singing some hymn about little lambs, and the confirmees are lined up boy-girl, procession style, down the length of the main aisle, boys in navy blazers and girls in white dresses, approaching the priest. Joani and Eddie are at the back of the line (for a moment I wonder if this isn't some sort of Down's syndrome discrimination thing) with their backs to us, but I spot Joani's white self-fashioned dress and the beribboned braids, finally in place. There's a camera flash as they pass, among many other flashes, and I spot the two pews where my entire family is sitting—parents, aunties, uncles, cousins, Grandma leaning slightly to the left on the far end, everyone probably itchy to leave the church and come back to the house for meatball-and-sausage subs.

Frank heaves forward to join them in their pew. Brenda, who's moved slightly ahead of the two of us in her panic, totters backward to wait out the rest of the ceremony in the wings; that's when Frank stubs his right foot on the back of Brenda's left heel and she lets out a cry that shoots down the length of the church and straight up into the rafters.

"Ah, *mengia*, Frankie!" In a moment, her face turns scarlet; she stands there, frozen in place, facing the congregation, which turns around in its entirety to behold the mortified tableau of the three of us.

"Brenda!" Joani screams.

"Brenda!" exclaims my mother, forgetting herself.

Brenda waves weakly in a dozen different directions and mouths a dazed "Hi" to Joani, who is beaming. The Ianellis are making noisy room for us in their pew, and to the achy buzz of whispers over the organ, we squeeze our way down the aisle and into seats. As we sit down, Brenda squeezes my hand, smiles thinly, and stares into the middle distance, poised grandly to vomit.

June 1987

Thirteen

I don't want this dream to end. Some consciousness is creeping in now; it must be the hottest morning of the year so far. Slippery warmth is filling up this entire room, and lying here, I'm glistening in a film of salty sweat, my T-shirt flung on the floor out of arm's reach from this burning bed, my whole skinny body red and translucent except where my briefs lie. I'm thinking that if I can just sustain this a second longer, then something really extraordinary is going to happen, some densely packed bomb in the depths of me is going to detonate, and I'll be loosed from this reedy, high-pitched eighteen-year-old prison house forever. And someone's coming with me, another time-bomb ready to self-uncork, and they'll be picking up the brilliant, steaming shards of us for years and years.

My mother, from below: "Eric! Get up! What are you gonna do, sleep through your own graduation?"

It's over—the dream, and the year. High school and West Mendhem. It ends this morning at eleven in the field house. Then I'll have two months of working on the loading docks of my father's company's warehouse by day and making pizzas at Sal's at night—but after *that,* my life commences, in a blaze of spires, gargoyles, and ivy. And the first thing I think as the dream evaporates, as I squint against the scalding light filling this room, is *You made it. You got out alive, off clean, over easy.* No less than that, and, really, no more. In a few hours, I'll give my valedictory address to the good people of West Mendhem, all the right sentiments and flourishes on one typed piece of paper that Goody Farnham has proofed and approved, and after that, diploma in hand, we'll part ways. Phoebe has been saying all week she can't believe it's over because she never truly believed it would end. What I didn't tell her was that I felt just the opposite: I never could have gotten through it if I hadn't known it wasn't forever, that the palpable promise of this very day on the calendar has been the only thing that's seen me through.

"I'm getting ready!" I yell down the stairs. I'm in the shower. I'm shaving. I'm putting on a coat and tie, loafers and chinos, readying myself to stand before the polity for the last time.

"Smile!" I blink as a camera flash pops in my face when I'm halfway down the stairs, and they all laugh, the reunified lot of my family: my mother wielding the archival camera, my father, his right eye unabashedly leaking, Brenda and Frank, Brenda cradling in her arms my six-week-old nephew and godson, Arthur Terrence Fitzpatrick Mellucci, a big, swarthy, serene infant with a lot of hair on his head, who sleeps upstairs with Brenda in the Black Sabbath bedroom they've turned into a nursery while Brenda prepares to go to computer programming school and courts Frank again as though they were both seventeen. Joani's there, healthy and flushed, in her confirmation dress but with different braids this time, and Eddie's parents have let him serve as her date this Saturday morning, to accompany her to the high school graduation of her only brother, at whom she's beaming right now in a state of awe and wonderment. Grandma's there, too, on her walker, and when I descend, she reaches up to my forehead, brings it down, kisses it, and says, lucidly, "Bless you, *bambino.*" They're all there, my family, happy and under one roof again, and there they shall remain for some time; it's only me who's leaving now.

"You look so handsome," my mother says, hugging me. "I can't wait for your big speech today."

"Don't go crying on us, again," my father jokes. I won't, I say, and even though the remark bothers me more than he meant it to, I dismiss it and embrace him too.

"Erky, whatchoo gonna talk about in your speech?" Joani shrieks.

"Yeah, Erky, whatchoo gonna talk about?" Eddie mimics, tickling

Joani. She wheels around, pushes him into the wall, then turns back to me, still beaming.

"It's all about you, Joani," I tease. "What else *could* it be about?"

She doesn't laugh or protest. Instead, she just walks up to me, smiles—her smile is so placid and mature that it startles me—and gives me a hug. "I love you, Erky," she says, matter-of-fact.

"I love you, too, Joani," I say, guiltily. "I was kind of kidding, though. It's not just about you. It's about all of us—you know, people in general."

"That's okay," she says, unperturbed, squeezing tighter. "I still love you."

I pull her away from me and look hard into her face. It's the same face it's always been, doughy and pink with the wandering, even-natured hazel eyes, but I'm detecting traces of a woman inside it now, some woman growing inside her who's never going to fully come out, who's never going to emerge with woman's instincts and grown-up shrewdness fairly matched. I wonder how long I'll have to see that face again—how many times I'll even get to see it before I lay eyes upon it last.

"Thank you," I whisper to her. Everyone else is chattering around us, leaving the two of us in this funny pocket of confidence. "You know I love you, too, right?"

She rolls her eyes, squeezes me back. "Eric! You *know* I know!"

I look at her again. "Do you know what you just called me?" I want to ask her, stunned. I want to tell everybody. But for some reason, I decide not to; Joani herself doesn't even seem to have noticed. "I know you know" is all I say.

"Good."

The phone rings. "That's probably Phoebe," I say, stepping into the kitchen to answer it. I'm right.

"Are you having a *cow?*" she asks. Cows have been on her mind a lot ever since she got accepted at this alternative college in Vermont where the students can tend livestock for credit.

"Sort of. We're just about getting ready to go. My mother's camera-happy all over the place."

"So's mine. Anyway," Phoebe says, brightening, "you know my mother made lunch reservations for us and your family and Charlie's family afterward at this seafood restaurant in Newburyport, so we all have to meet up after the ceremony."

"That's cool," I say. "I'll see you in a little bit."

"All right, darling. This is it! Home free!"

"Yep. See you soon." I hang up.

"Eric, honey, come on!" my mother calls from the din in the hallway. "That field house is gonna be as hot as an oven, and I wanna get seats not too high up."

"I'm coming." I check for my speech in the pocket of my jacket, but the phone rings again. "Dammit, Phoebe!" I say to myself, then into the hallway, "I'll get it. Hello?"

There's nothing on the other line but someone's jagged breath.

"Hello?"

"Thank the Lord it's you." At first I can't place the voice—deep, velvety, edged with sarcasm—but as soon as I do, I freeze in place and the hair stands up on the back of my neck.

I glance back into the hallway—they're oohing and aahing over Arthur Terrence—then pull the phone cord around to the other side of the refrigerator. "Is this *you?*" I ask, low.

He laughs. "My good Mr. Fitzpatrick, who else would have the audacity to call and scare the living wits out of you on the morning of your high school graduation?" He laughs again, sounding faintly manic.

My heart ratchets up higher in my throat. "How'd you know it was today?" I ask in a hysterical whisper.

"Did you actually come *all* the way to Virginia just to leave a cryptic message for me on a pizza box?" He laughs heartily. "I *thought* somebody else was in that house with Brickhouse and me!"

"I did," I admit feverishly. "I did. But I can't talk now. Can't we talk some other time, because—'cause I have to go graduate. Give me your number," and I reach dumbly for pad and pencil on the countertop. "Where are you?"

"I'm right here."

"But *where are you?*" I plead, breaking out into a cold sweat.

"I told you. I'm right here. I'm outside the Cumberland Farms in West Mendhem!"

"Shut up."

"I *am*. I'm passing through on my way from New York to Montreal, and I'm coming to your graduation!" He's absolutely, viciously gleeful. "I want to hear your speech, seeing as I missed the first one. The one on racial harmony, remember?"

"Brooks, please don't do this to me," I fairly beg him. "I want to see you, I swear I do, but please not at my graduation. Everybody's gonna be there."

"The same fun crowd that gathered on the village green that night to watch you betray me? I loved them! Those local *frauen* were so sweet to me the minute they found out I wasn't your average street nigger, but a real boy-made-good from St. Banner Academy."

"Brooks, please."

"Eric, come on! You'll see Phoebe there!" my mother calls from the hallway.

He laughs softly. "Oh, please, Eric. I'm not going to force you into a repeat performance. I just want to watch you graduate before I leave the country. You won't even know I'm there."

"Brooks—" My voice has faded away to a little rasp by this point.

"Eric, don't worry about it. We're eternally devoted to each other, remember? Now go knock 'em dead!"

And with that, he hangs up, leaving me shaking with the dead receiver in my hand. "Let's go," I say, chalky, in the hallway, zipping up my crimson gown and pulling on my mortarboard; then we file out the door.

"He's nervous about his speech," I hear my mother tell my father under her breath as I stalk ahead of them to the cars.

When we get to the high school, they all see me off with hugs and good luck wishes, then file away to find seats in the bleachers of the adjoining field house. I wait until they're well away, then stand there, shielding my eyes with my hand, looking for a patch of black in the gathering congregation of flushed high-noon faces. I look and look, expecting at every moment to light upon his Cheshire grin glowing back at me, damning me to hell, but I don't see it anywhere, even as the field house grows hotter, more crowded, so I walk outside, twisting my tie under my gown, until I come to the spot where the graduating class of 1987 is milling about in a sweaty tangle of crimson and red, soap bubbles and tacky neon sunglasses. All of a sudden, kids who only used to sneer at me or ignore me completely are coming up to me, shaking my hand, giving me hugs, asking me if I'm all excited about Yale and everything. And even though my first impulse is to say, "Why are you treating me like a human being *now?*," I don't. I just hug them back, shake their hands back, and wonder if I'm exuding so much paranoia that it actually looks like self-possession.

Phoebe wends her way through the crowd of crimson, smirking at the spectacle of herself swallowed up in gown and mortarboard.

"Can you believe this?" she says, giving me a hug. "It's like, I know I'm supposed to sneer at this, and be all cynical and everything, but I keep going up to people I've always hated and hugging them and saying, 'Oh, let's keep in touch!' and I feel like any minute I'm gonna start crying."

"It's just because you're secretly ecstatic you're never gonna have to see them again," I say, adjusting her mortarboard distractedly. I can't keep my eyes fixed on her; my eyes are darting all over the place, and I'm wondering if he'd ever just walk right up to me in the middle of this crowd.

"Oh, c'mon, Eric," she says. "This is the last hurrah. Can't you just get *into* it a little? You *are* giving the big send-off, after all."

"All right!" I protest. "I'm into it, okay?"

"Good. You're going to Wendy Lemieux's party with us after, right? Charlie got some really good weed."

"Of course I'm going. We're going together. I told you I'd go, right?"

"Okay, chill out. I was just checking."

Charlie comes over to us, hairy legs and Converse high-tops sticking out under his gown. His mortarboard is pushed way back on his head and he's wearing little round mirrored sunglasses. "My children," he greets us, and starts to sing: "Na na na na, na na na na, hey hey hey—good-bye!"

"I can't believe you're wearing those things," I say, staring at my twin reflection in his glasses. I decide I look like an idiot in my mortarboard.

"I'm going incognito to my own graduation," he says.

"So am I." Phoebe pulls out her matching pair. They bought them together on a trip to Boston, back when they were still giving each other the vibe.

"You two look like John and Yoko," I say.

"That's 'cause we are," Charlie says, and they both crack up laughing.

In a few minutes, the teachers come outside to line us up. I'm already in my place, standing next to some track star girl who got an athletic scholarship to Holy Cross, when I feel someone tug on the sleeve on my gown, and turn around. It's Mrs. Bradstreet.

"I'll look for you in the future, in the pages of the better periodicals," she says gravely.

"Thanks," I say, laughing. I'm still uneasy around her.

"I also wish you the best of luck next year. Maybe at some point you'll find a moment to drop by here, or to write me a little note, and tell me about your studies and what you're reading, and keep me abreast of all the new scholarship. And what exciting new friends you've made."

"I'll try," I say.

"Then again, maybe you won't have the time after all."

I look at her. She's smiling, the same old spooky smile, but for the first time, I'm not freaked out by her. I think of her when she was seventeen, graduating from Emma Willard, or wherever she went, and where she thought she might be at the age she is now, whether she thought she'd be married to a man who would make her the heiress to half a town she never expected to live in, let alone inherit.

"Don't worry," I say. "I'll have the time. You can tell me how you're doing, too."

She nods. "Fair enough." Then she hands me a little box wrapped in ethnic-looking paper, along with a card. "Here's a talisman for you," she says. "You can decide whether you need it or not. And by the way, Mr. McGregor says that after you've received your diploma, you can slip outside for some air if you want to look over your speech one last time."

"Okay. Thanks."

And she nods again, and walks off, listing slightly to one side.

I unwrap the box and open it. Inside there's a little carved-wood, Third World–looking mask thing on a piece of rope. It's smiling and it's got sunlike rays emanating out of its head. I open the card: "June 1987. Think clear. Do much. Love hard. Virginia Brace Bradstreet."

"What's that?" the track star girl asks me.

"It's a talisman," I say.

"She's a weird one," Track Star Girl says, nodding toward Mrs. Bradstreet.

"She is." I shrug and put the charm over my head and around my neck, then under my gown.

The marching band starts in with "Pomp and Circumstance"—they play it at a dirgelike tempo, filled with clinkers—and we file into the field house, through the chain-link fence and into rows and rows of folding chairs in a ragged rendition of the two-step march we learned at rehearsal the day before. The selectmen are seated on their guests-of-honor riser, alongside Mr. McGregor and Mr. Fazzi. The faculty and staff sit behind them, and the bleachers opposite us are full of the gleaming faces of family and friends, what seems like the entire population of West Mendhem herded into one sweltering room. And even though the moment I've taken my seat, my eyes are weeding through every bleacher, I can't, for my life, see him anywhere. I ease up on the tie underneath my robe: maybe it was all a joke, I tell myself; it certainly wouldn't be the first time he'd threatened something he didn't carry out. Yet under that half relief, I'm thinking: *If he's not here, but if he's in West Mendhem, then where is he? Will I see him? And what if I don't?* Now we're all seated, and the band completes what must be the twenty-seventh round of "Pomp and Circumstance," and I realize for the first time that my hair is drenched with sweat under my mortarboard, that sweat is running in rivulets down my neck and into my shirt collar, that I've never been so hot in all my life.

The proceedings begin: an invocation by the pastor of St. Matthew's Church; a short, hugely well received send-off from Mr. McGregor ("Let's have a big round of applause for a class that knows how to work hard, knows how to come together in a crisis, and, for better or worse, knows how to *party!*"); the first annual Kerrie Lanouette Memorial Scholarship, presented amidst protracted applause by Kerrie's steely-voiced mother to a girl who hobbled through her entire senior year on crutches after a soccer team casualty; a pitch from the head of the Booster Club for more donations if West Mendhem expects to keep its stellar football record alive in '87–'88; a few remarks from one of the selectmen on the need to conserve the town water supply; and three unplanned warnings from Mr. Fazzi that if people don't stop blowing bubbles and tossing around beach balls in the graduates' section, they'll cut the ceremony short and mail everyone their diploma. (The beach balls stop, the bubbles don't, and the ceremony goes on.) Then Doreen Prose, the chairwoman of the School Committee, steps up to the podium to hand out the diplomas, alphabetically, accompanied by the band's turgid rendition of the recessional from *Star Wars*. Hours seem to pass as we shuffle along, but she finally slouches her way into the F's, calling out my name over the microphone. I finally locate my family when I hear a concentrated burst of applause rise up from the lower left end of the bleachers. Doreen Prose and I smile and shake each other's sweaty hands, then, remembering my special dispensation from Mr. McGregor, I step down off the platform and slip quietly out of the field house into the hallway.

It's blessedly cool, dark, and quiet here after the bright, noisy heat of the field house, and for the first time since arriving at the ceremony, my body slackens, my head stops spinning and I begin to feel the sweat soaking my entire body dry up, cold and prickly, underneath my clothes. I rub my eyes, adjusting to the gloom, and pad down to the water fountain at the far end of the empty hallway, Doreen Prose's amplified, monotone litany of names and the colossal murmur of hundreds of voices fading off behind me. I bend over the fountain, draw a dozen gulps of water from it, catch some water in my hands and run it over my face, dry my hands as well as I can on my nylon robe, then pull my speech out of my coat pocket and begin scanning it in the half-light.

"Four score and seven years ago, the world was not yet blessed with *moi*," comes a voice from the opposite end of the hallway.

I turn on my heels, looking helplessly down the dark passage. At the end of it, silhouetted against the afternoon light shining in from the far glass doors, is a figure: standing erect in the middle of the corridor, arms crossed over chest, loafered feet planted apart, leading up to skinny dark legs in shorts, ramrod-straight back in a luminous white tank top, and a face, head fully shaven, a more wickedly clean profile than ever before, obscured all but for the smile—wide and vicious and full of glee—and eyes masked behind the twin glints of horn-rimmed glasses.

I don't say anything. I don't move—but he does, in slow, measured, inevitable steps, the metrical clack of loafers on freshly waxed floor coming closer and closer, the ceramic smile unmoved, until he stops, not six feet away, face to face with me.

From within the fieldhouse, Doreen Prose's affectless nomenclature: "*Jeanni Gregorian. Patrick Grogan.*"

I just stare and stare. I can't speak, but I can't look away. The last time we stood or lay close to each other, the last time we so much as re-garded each other, unmediated by public appraisal or personal con-cealment, was in an earth-toned, anonymous hotel room in the seized-up middle of January. Here it is, months later, heat crowding the distance between us, and the torched fever rush of a lost autumn is flooding back upon me now—all the things he said, all the things we did, recapitu-lated in this moment. I'm so dizzy I can't talk; the earth is breaking away in huge, ungainly plates just beyond the realm of us, and I'm wonder-ing how I've gone so long without the earthly matter of him within my grasp—the face and limbs, the cedar smell and contemptuous tone, all the brittle, glittering atoms of him that encircled me in my terror and confusion and helpless, covetous rage. Did I encircle him? I wonder. Did I ever engulf him? Even now, in this moment, I don't know.

"Heather Ianucci. Dick Inskeep."

"You really did come," I finally manage to say, and my voice sounds small and faraway.

"I told you I'd come." The smile falls away. His voice sounds deeper, graver, than it did before—or is it that I've heard it hardly at all in so many months, that the voice of his I've taken to bed every night has transmuted in my head into something not what it ever was, the voice I wanted to hear? "What did you think, that I called just to fuck with you?"

"I don't know," I say, honestly. "It wouldn't be the first time."

He laughs, conceding. "Well, I'm through fucking with you, Eric."

My speech, which I've been clutching in my hand, has become drenched and smudged in sweat. I stuff it in my pocket. "So, then, why'd you come?"

"What did I tell you on the phone?" He's speaking so softly now, with-out his familiar sardonic mania, that it sends a chill creeping up my back under my robe. "I wanted to see you graduate. It's your big day, your grand culmination. And I thought I might get to say good-bye. It looks like I'm having my chance, *n'est-ce pas?*"

"To say good-bye? Why? Where are you going?"

"To Montreal, briefly, for a party some friends from New York in-vited me to. Then, next week, to Barcelona, to join my mother for the summer. She finally had the good sense to dump that little gnome René and now she's taken her hostessing gig on the road. She wants me to join her as her sidekick."

"To do what?"

"To play the washboard in a jug band or something." He laughs, dismissing himself. "I honestly don't know. Just to keep her company, I guess. To get reacquainted. The good people of St. Banner dispatched me to her when they finally decided I was beyond their sphere of influence. She took one look at me and said she wanted me out of America. For the rest of my reckless youth, if not for good."

"Where have you been since you left?" I ask.

"Phil Kozinski. Wendy Lemieux." Doreen Prose's recitation proceeds dimly, but the rest of the world seems to have broken off from us. It's as though we're floating away on a piece of ground all our own, and for once, I don't really care if I ever come back.

"Mostly in New York. New York is really quite extraordinary these days. It's sort of like Berlin during Weimar. There's nothing that money can't buy." He unfolds his arms and slips his hands into his pockets.

"What are you doing there?"

"Oh, you know," he says airily. "Just running around. Staying with friends."

"I didn't know you had any."

He rolls his eyes. "That's because, Miz Laura, you never axed."

I stare blankly.

"Haven't you ever seen *Imitation of Life?*"

"No." I say. "Why?"

"Oh, skip it. Anyway, I've made some," he replies. "They're really a wonderful bunch. All shapes. All sizes. All colors. All sexes. I wonder how you'd find them." Then he laughs. "Oh, Lord! Maybe I don't want to know!"

"Maybe you don't," I say, hurt.

"So that's where I've been," he continues brightly. "There, and Virginia for a while, settling Fleurie's house—but of course you know as much, anyway, don't you, you little housebreaker?" He's smiling now, amused.

"I came down to find you," I say, point-blank. Everything now seems rather absurdly beyond the point of saving face.

He shakes his head. "I absolutely can't believe that! How in hell did you ever find Calvary Hill? It's the most out-of-the-way place in the world."

"Some woman gave me a ride up. A white woman."

"Pray tell, the natives didn't take potshots at you, did they? They're known to do that, you know."

"That's what she said. But no. We came up at night."

"Well, that's certainly no protection around *here*," he says breezily. "Even if you blend in with the night."

I wince—I don't even know how to bring up the matter of that night on the common—but he rushes past it. "Tell me. You weren't in the house when I was there with a friend, were you?"

"With Brickhouse?" I ask. "Yeah. I was there. I was under the bed."

"My good man!" He looks fairly stunned, which pleases me. "I didn't know you were quite so fearless"—which makes me look away. Then, "Well, Brickhouse is no intrigue. He's just an old boyhood friend. Southern comfort, that's all. I'll probably never see that poor boy again."

"That's a shame," I say sourly.

"No, not really. Did you hear us say anything incriminating?"

"I don't really remember," I lie.

"Oh. Well, that's good, I suppose."

"Margie McCannell. Amanda McCarthy. James McCarthy. William Mc-Carthy. Debbie Messina."

"So you're leaving?" I say helplessly. I can't think of anything else to say, or do, for that matter. It's like water, or blood, running between my fingers, and I can't contain it, and in seconds, it will be gone and there will be nothing left but the wet, or the stain, on my hands.

"On y va," he says, shrugging. "And off to Yale University for you, young man, if I presume correctly."

I nod blankly.

"Well, good for you," he says. "You deserve it."

"I have to go make this speech," I say dully.

"Indeed, you do."

It's at that moment I see it: the faint trace of a scar on his forehead, a jagged line of pink just below his shorn hairline. "That's from that night," I say, and I reach out to touch it.

"Get the fuck away from me!" he screams, and he slaps back my hand with a crack that pinballs off the walls of the empty hallway.

That's it—that's the living end. I lurch toward him, throwing my arms around his neck, holding on to him like a madman. "Brooks. I'm sorry. I'm sorry. I hate myself. You gotta know that. I hate myself. Oh my God, Brooks, I'm so sorry."

"You *should* be sorry! You *should* hate yourself!" he screams at me, hoarse, with his hands wrapped around my head.

He's bawling now, too, and the two of us are locked here, clutching each other, pushing each other away. "Fucking monsters beat the living shit out of me, like I was some fucking *animal*, and you said you didn't *know* me! In front of all those people. Oh my God. Oh my fucking God. You *fucked* me—and you said you didn't *know* me! You fucking, *fucking* coward!"

I can't let go of him. The entire hallway, the rest of the world, has melted into nothingness around us, and he's the only piece of matter, the only *thing* that matters, left in the whole world. I pull his shirt out of his shorts and dig my nails into his back, up his back, while he hitches up my gown and seizes me by the hips underneath, his scarred forehead against mine, my mortarboard fallen away from us, off the earth.

"Sophie Rybold. Mark Salois. Phoebe Margarita Signorelli."

"I know. I know. I'm sorry," I say to him through clenched jaws. "But don't go. I'm gonna go away with you. I'll go now. Let's go now. Come on—*come on*. I love you, Brooks. I swear to God I do."

He pushes the two of us against the wall, holds my head against it with one hand, shoves his other down inside my pants, then comes up close until his bared teeth are an inch away from me, and he's spitting in my face. "You say you love me, but you *can't*. You're not supposed to. No one should because I'm a *freak*, I'm a *monster*. I don't belong *anywhere*, there's *nowhere*—Oh, God!"—and he gasps—"there's nowhere on this *earth* that I'm ever going to fit, so don't even fucking try—you stupid, *stupid* white boy with your *stupid* family and your *stupid* ambitions and your *stupid* Yale! Go to your fucking Yale! Go and have a life for yourself, don't fuck it up, don't fuck it up, no, no way, not with *me*, not with the crazy *nigger* who talks like a white boy, dresses like a white boy, with *no* home, *no* fucking father, not even a fucking *stupid motherfucking mother* on this continent. Look at me!"

"I'm looking at you!" I'm sobbing, clutching at him, fuck-flat against the wall.

"But *look at me!* Look at this face! Whose is it? Do *you* know? Because *I* don't. I *think* it's mine. But I can't even go walking at night without getting the crap and the shit and the *piss* kicked out of me by a bunch of fucking stupid, stupid devils! You'll *never* know that! How could you know? Eric—Eric"—and he's suddenly quiet, and we're still holding onto each other, not bawling, just weeping—"Eric, baby, tell me. Where do I go? I'm nineteen years old today. I bought myself a black 1966 Karmann-Ghia. It's outside. Where do I go in it?"

"James Tetley. Lisa Marie Torricelli. Ashley Tucker."

We're perfectly still now, entangled, up against the wall. "Wherever you go, I'll go with you. Let's go right now. Let's just walk out the door and go. Fuck this," I say, looking eastward, westward. "You fit in with me. I swear, you do. Fuck everyone else." And I put my hand up to his face and smooth the wetness into his hard, trembling cheekbones.

"How in the name of the Lord did we ever happen?" he says, hoarse and expended, and suddenly we're sucking face like we never have before, we're molesting each other through our trousers against the gleaming dark wall of this hallway inside West Mendhem High School, and it's feeling better and better, and I'm envisioning a lifetime of this, and I'm feeling more fully a man than ever before in my life, more deeply an adult, a dark, visceral being freighted with meaning who can see clearly and bravely through the haze of children's inchoate caprices, straight through to the pure, grave commandments of the heart, the incontrovertible imperatives that men and women design whole lives around, and I'm wanting to go there, full of astringent resolve, with him.

Applause and hollers, just for the two of us, huddled here, exhausted and sticky inside. Shoes and rice, shoes and rice. I smile at him. "Let's go."

He takes a step back, smiling. "Okay," he says, docile, and then I see it in his right hand: a long jackknife, retracted, glinting wanly in the shadows of the hallway. I gasp; he steps in again toward me, smile crooked, and the knife lies now just between our two thighs, the blunt edge to his, the sharpened to mine, until he flicks it the opposite way, then back again, dully curious with his own toy.

"What the fuck is that?" I say, low, standing stock still.

"Eric, come on," he says quietly, reasonably. "I told you way back that I carried knives. Remember?"

I don't say anything. Our faces are inches away from each other, his still luminous with drying tears, but smug now—smug, and oddly serene. He keeps rotating the knife loosely in his palm, its either sides announcing themselves in silent flashes of white, whispering faintly against his shorts, drily against the nylon of my crimson robe, in an interminable, steady tattoo, like a clock of palm leaves, an unhurried swish.

"Kristina Uttley. Randolph Scott Vallone. Elizabeth Vance."

He lifts his free hand up, places it gently over my forehead, and props me back against the cold cinderblock wall. He inches in closer; we're up against each other now, an infinitesimal, edgy chorus of rustlings and breath. The knife is rising up our sides, closer to our hearts, until he holds it, propped, like a birthday candle, hovering between our cheeks.

"Come on," he says, grazing his lips against mine, blowing his words into my mouth. "You wanna go with me?"

"Uh-huh," I say, blowing back, my hands pressed against the wall, not moving.

"Go with me right now."

"Just like this?"

"Uh-huh," he says, and his lips widen in a smile—so dreamy, so content, so restful that I'm nearly swooning. I want to dissolve into him, gracefully and without a fight, I want him to completely swallow me up until there's no more me left, just a quivering imprint on the wall.

"Brooks." I expel air, sleepy. "Are you sure, Brooks?"

"Eric, I'm so sure," he answers, low and reassuring. "It'll be so much better for me there." Breath. "In that place. Fleurie's there. She'll like you so much, I know it." More breath. "It's easier there, I tell you."

He's running the end of the knife now in the tiny cavity between our lips—no action, just a fuzzy rumination. It tastes cool and precise there, like an engraved invitation.

"I always want to be with you," I say.

"Not here," he says, understanding, a grown-up's regretful tsk-tsk. "We're doomed here. I told you that before."

I'm caught somewhere in the network of the veins running through his brown eyes; they've become huge, like a map of roads to a place growing larger and larger under a microscope, through a dilating lens. "I know," I say petulantly.

"So." He dials the end of the knife into the soft flesh of his lower lip. "You ready?"

"Uh-huh."

"I love you."

"I love you, too."

He smiles again, leans his head back, and I'm breathing hard down in the depths of his glistening tonsils, struggling to come up for air. The entire hallway darkens; somebody turns out the lights and the sound and the circuits, and I watch the flat lip of the knife coast in a shallow arc, across his distended neck, leaving in its wake one shimmering, prefatory ribbon of crimson, then tiny bubbles of blood that murmur seductively over the surface of the line.

"There, that's a decent start," he gargles, smiling. "You go now, Eric."

"John Xavier. Patricia Young. Mary Ann Zinno. Ladies and gentlemen, presenting the West Mendhem High School graduating class of 1987."

I kick him, hard, in the stomach; he staggers back, groaning, and hits the opposite wall of the corridor with an offended smack; the knife, veined in blood at the tip, falls from his hands and clatters to the polished floor. He looks up at me, shocked and indignant, then reaches for the knife, but I kick it out of his reach, send it skidding down the hallway, then begin pummeling him on the back, dragging him to his feet, pushing him across the light-soaked foyer toward the glass doors.

"Get out!" I'm screaming under my breath, in counterpoint to his aggrieved groans. "Get the fuck out of here! You were gonna kill yourself!"

"So were you," he chokes.

"I know," I gasp, and for the first time, lucidly, out from under a narcotic fugue, the thought strikes me—*I was. I was.* I push open the doors and haul us both out into the open air, where his black 1966 Karmann-Ghia sits, lustrous in the sun. "Get in that car," I say, dragging him to it, hauling him whole-body over the driver's door and into the seat. He just sits there, splayed out, stunned, the one line of crimson drying, ineffectual, on his neck, staring straight ahead.

"Drive!" I scream at him. "Go away, go away, go away. Go clean off your neck. Go help yourself. Brooks, please!"

But he doesn't drive, doesn't say a word, just turns to me with a dead look that says, *"So?"* And stays that way.

"Drive!"

Nothing.

"Fuck!" I stare at him, horrified, that ghost of a face, then run back inside the school, stand in the middle of the foyer, in the center of the light, shaking, my fist in my mouth, a crazy man. Right now, I feel like there are about a million things I want to do, and each one with the pyrotechnic rage of a million wild horses.

Applause and hollers are subsiding inside. Doreen Prose back at the helm: *"The keynote speaker for the graduation ceremonies for the class of 1987 will be Eric Arthur Fitzpatrick, with a speech entitled 'Reflections.' "* Then the low roar of restive murmurs from within.

"Eric Fitzpatrick, you can come in now."

I grab my mortarboard, jack down my robe, slip and slide my way to the end of the hallway, grab the knife, shove it into my pocket, then push open the doors to the field house and stalk toward the platform, laughter and murmured gossip cresting around my ears in waves. Passing the faculty seating area, I notice out of the corner of one eye the stricken, bewildered faces of those who have guided me—Goody Farnham, Mrs. Bradstreet, Mr. McGregor, who whispers to me "Fix your hat!"—but I disregard him and all the rest, and succeed Doreen Prose at the podium. A bloated, luminous sea of grinning, gaping faces greets me, and my mad haze clears, only to be replaced by something harder, and calmer.

I pull the speech out of my pocket, fold it open on the podium before me, swallow hard, blink, and begin, my voice an insane, swooping chaos of pitch and inflection. "Superintendent Riley, Principal McGregor, honored guests, faculty, staff, family, and friends. Today we, the graduating class of 1987, gather not only to gird ourselves for the achievements of years to come, but to reflect on the events of the past year, both within these walls and in the broader community of West Mendhem. I think everyone would agree that it was not the easiest year in the history of this community, and for many, certainly not the happiest. However—"

I stop, suddenly, take the speech, refold it, and put it in my pocket. There's silence, and the murmuring starts up again.

"I just decided I don't want to give that speech. There's something else I want to say. It won't take long."

The murmuring and titters recommence, in earnest this time. Inadvertently, my eyes fall on the faces of my parents—confused, concerned, and wary. I swallow again, and force myself to look away.

Mr. McGregor half stands in his chair. "That speech was *approved*, Mr. Fitzpatrick. I advise you not waste time, and deliver it."

"This'll be even shorter," I say.

"Don't do it," he says.

"There was a beating this year," I say, rushing ahead. "Right after the beating of Jesús Antonio de la Costa, a student from St. Banner Academy was beaten up on a Sunday night on the town common."

Now it's Mrs. Bradstreet who half stands. "Eric," she says over the rising din, "you don't have to do this."

"I guess I sort of stopped that beating from going too far, even though it went pretty far. But when people asked me if I knew the student personally, I said no."

The din seems to be getting more indignant. "Why are you wrecking the graduation, Fitzpatrick?" some guy from the graduating class seated behind me calls out.

"Well, I lied," I continue. "I did know him. I knew him really well. His name was Brooks Jefferson Tremont. He was my good friend."

I pause. Somebody else might have hijacked my voice for all I feel that this is coming from me. "A lot of you, over the years, have called me certain things—a certain kind of person, and I think I don't need to say what it is. Well, you might as well know. That's the kind of good friends we were."

If there was murmuring before, there's suddenly virtual silence. "I wasn't supposed to tell you that," I say, and then I scare the living shit out of myself by laughing into the microphone. "But I honestly don't care anymore. So now you know."

Silence but for the buzzing of the fans, the buzzing of a thousand overhead fans, roaring into a vortex that must surely lead to an end to this day.

"Now you know," I say again.

More silence. Then a rising murmur. Then, from somewhere in the dumbstruck crowd: "Faggot!"

"Uh-huh," I say into the microphone.

Then another: "Fuckin' faggot!"

Then, a girl's voice, from off to the left. "Shut the fuck up! Shut the fuck up, or I'll fuckin' kill you!" It's Brenda, standing up in the bleachers, everyone pulling at the hem of her dress to make her sit down, but she won't.

The murmur is cresting, cresting, breaking out into full-throated voices—confusion, outrage, grief, hilarity—in a hundred different places now. I just stand there, wooden, as the pitch rises.

The fracas continues—it's become a free-for-all: Brenda fighting with my parents, half my graduating class mimicking me, the other half laughing or bawling; faculty and staff blah-blah-blahing amongst themselves. *I don't wanna be here*, I think to myself. *I have to say good-bye.*

So I just walk away, off the platform, across the floor, toward the doors.

"Fitzpatrick, get back here," Mr. McGregor bellows, but Mr. Fazzi, of all people, bellows back: "Just let him go."

"Thank you," I call back to him, and I do go. I step off the podium, in the opposite direction, through the door, back into the cool hallway—out the door, into the sun, the first one out of the building, a whole flailing congregation just at my back.

The black Karmann-Ghia is still there, idling, and so is he, cigarette steadily in hand. When he sees me, he turns and smiles—a perfect smile, wicked and poised, the summary of all the smiles that came before and the prologue, we know, of all that will follow.

"I just told them everything," I say, approaching the car.

He unfurls in laughter. "The greatest story ever told, I'm sure."

I smile back, sheepishly.

I dreamed last night of a wild party, ecstatic and glittering, that was born at the foot of a hill—it was Calvary Hill, briefly, and then it wasn't—and manically, on a thousand drugged legs, it wended its way to the top, such a convention of gaiety that faces and voices merged into a horrible, dazzling whole, and for your life you couldn't distinguish friend or foe, brother or viper, so keenly hungry you were to celebrate, or mourn, or just plain old fuck to death the first living creature you could secure squarely between your two burning hands. I can't remember the name of one single creature in the throng, but I assure you everyone was there, and I was swollen with honor and pride to be leading this naked, black-tie legion up this steepest and most treacherous of hills, and when we reached the top, he was waiting there, naked and black-tied from head to toe, bearing torches for all, with a million drugged limbs clambering up behind me, and when he saw me and my great work, he laughed a laugh that shook the lighted wooded crown of the hill, and he said, low, "Baby, we've arrived," and then the great mad revel commenced.

"Where are you going?" I ask him now.

"To Montreal. I'd invite you along, but it looks like you've got some unfinished business here." He turns the key in the ignition.

I smirk. "Happy birthday. I'll pray for you," I say.

"Girl, don't pray for me. Pray for *yourself*, that the Lord might hear ye!"

"I'll still pray for you," I say.

He drops the smile, extends his hand, all business now. "And I'll pray for *you*, harder, and may the best fool win."

"Good luck, Brooks," I say, offering my hand. He draws it forward and presses it briefly into his lips.

"Good luck, Fitzy. *Ciao*, then."

I watch as the car pulls away from the curb, up the driveway, and around the bend. When it's out of my sight, I turn back to the building. The first dizzy ranks are emerging, my own family among them, dazed and wounded around the eyes.

I straighten my mortarboard, pray for myself, and retrace my steps, knife in pocket, to meet the oncoming crowd.